the last dunes girl

The Logan Wells Mysteries Book Two

M.D. CARROLL

coffeetownpress

Kenmore, WA

coffeetownpress

A Coffeetown Press book published by Epicenter Press

Epicenter Press
6524 NE 181st St.
Suite 2
Kenmore, WA 98028

For more information go to:
www.Camelpress.com
www.Coffeetownpress.com
www.Epicenterpress.com
www.mcarrollauthor.com

This book is work of fiction, but its genesis is an actual event: the disappearance of three women from the Indiana Dunes in 1966. Some real locations and events are used in a fictitious manner in the novel to provide context; otherwise, all other locations, events, and characters, are fictitious, and solely a product of the author's imagination.

Cover photo of Lake Michigan by M.D. Carroll
Cover design by Scott Book
Design by Melissa Vail Coffman

The Last Dunes Girl
Copyright © 2024 by M.D. Carroll

Library of Congress Control Number: 2024933675

ISBN: 978-1-68492-306-9 (Trade Paper)
ISBN: 978-1-68492-307-6 (eBook)

To my nephew, Michael, a truly amazing young man.

acknowledgments

To my wife Carol, and my friend Barbara Moody, for their insightful comments, remarks, and suggestions for improvement on the work in progress. Barb was especially helpful with suggestions for early edits to the book.

chapter 1

IT WAS A GREY AND CHILLY EARLY SATURDAY MORNING in late May. I stood in the street in front of the Prairie County, Indiana courthouse, at close quarters with five hundred or so other hearty souls. From the fidgeting going on, there was anticipation and some anxiety in the crowd, and plenty of pent-up energy awaiting release. At 7:30 a.m., about ten minutes from now, there would be the blare of an airhorn, a device invented, if not to cause outright hearing loss, then at least serious aural distress. Given our go signal, we would move forward in a human wave toward to the start\finish banner, about fifteen yards and a few hundred people in front of me. Then we were off to run five miles, to the best of our ability, at least on this particular morning.

The courthouse stood amidst the commotion, as it had for nearly one hundred years. The building's opening ceremony had been held on Memorial Day in 1890, and in two days, on Memorial Day 1990, it would reach its centennial of service, and not without a few bumps along the road, either. The four-story structure had survived a major fire back in 1935. Although its Indiana limestone proved mostly impervious to the flames, the blaze had gutted the interior of the building. The fire also destroyed the large ornate clock tower which rose another one hundred fifty feet above the roof. There was speculation that faulty electrical wiring caused the fire, but, in one account of the disaster, the county sheriff at the time suspected "socialist agitators" of arson. It later came out that the sheriff's brother had been the electrical contractor on some updates to the building. My late father would have cynically described the sheriff's remarks as those made by a 'quick thinker,' but he was part Native American and didn't trust white people, especially ones in authority. Since the fire occurred during the Great Depression, it took a while before the building was repaired. The clock tower was a victim of the economic times and not rebuilt. About ten years ago, a few tall unsightly radio antennas had been mounted on the roof, technology trumping aesthetics. I glanced up at the antennas, hoping to see a break in the clouds, but no such luck.

I would have thought the courthouse's centennial was reason enough for today's run, but that wasn't mentioned on the race entry form. The Indy 500 was, along with the Memorial Day holiday, even though we were two days away from the holiday and the auto spectacular wasn't until tomorrow. I thought the Saturday of a holiday weekend was a good day to have a race, had the organizers caught some good weather. Not sure what the temperature was 150 miles south in Speedway, Indiana, but it was unseasonably cool here in Prairie Stop. The weather in Northwest Indiana was unpredictable in May. On Memorial Day you could either be swatting mosquitos the size of quarters in eighty-degree heat or shivering around a barbecue grill from the chilly breezes off Lake Michigan, a little over ten miles to the north.

Previously the biggest running event in Prairie Stop took place in the fall. A five-mile 'Pumpkin Panic' kicked off the city's annual Pumpkin Festival, held the weekend after Labor Day. A lengthy parade followed. Then the town square was closed off, street vendors would set up booths to sell crafts and novelties, and the downtown restaurants would sell food outside. Later in the day, musical acts would perform on a stage near the courthouse. In nice weather, the festival attracted over 50,000 to the town, almost twice Prairie Stop's population, and the run usually had over a thousand entrants. The city fathers were so pleased by the prosperity thus generated that they decided to try today's inaugural Indy 5 Run\ Memorial Day Festival. Lacking some originality, the race organizers were using the same five-mile course used for the Panic, except, to change it up, they had the loop part of the course, miles two through four, go in the opposite direction from September. Either way was ok by me. Due to circumstances, I was not able to run last fall, but the year before I had somewhat surprisingly finished fifth in my age division. I had now moved up another age bracket. I had hopes that with the smaller crowd in today's run I might be able to place in my age group.

The all-night showers had stopped just before dawn, but chilly breezes still blew cold rain remnants off the trees and buildings onto the horde below. Most in the crowd seemed focused on their preparation for the run and didn't seem to notice. I was immersed in my own pre-race reverie, wishing I had used the john one more time, when I felt a tap on my shoulder—not a delicate one either. If someone was trying to get me to move out of the way, I wasn't so inclined, and irritated, turned around.

"How's it going, Logan?"

The voice asking that question was familiar, but the face was covered by a bushy salt-and-pepper beard, sunglasses, and a battered Chicago Cubs ballcap, so I did a double take. There was no mistaking the giant of a man now facing me.

"Chief?" I asked, recognizing William "Big Bill" Hanlen, until recently the long-time sheriff of Prairie County. "It's not Halloween is it?"

"No," he replied. "Just don't want to shake hands a dozen times every time I turn around."

I could understand that, although I doubted that the beard, cap and shades were an adequate disguise. Standing near 6'5" and solidly build, Hanlen would stand out in a crowd anytime, but he had been county sheriff for almost three decades and was well-known, and by most, well-liked and respected. Although the population of the county had increased exponentially during that time, Hanlen somehow managed to keep his persona of a folksy, unsophisticated, small-town sheriff remarkably intact. It was a pretense. Anyone who knew him more than casually recognized he had an acute understanding of both modern law enforcement practices, and the political process that went along with the job.

I noticed he had also lost some weight. He had never been overweight, but he appeared leaner and more muscular than I could recall. I knew he was in his early sixties but could easily pass for ten years younger. Along with the Cubs hat, he was wearing baggy grey sweatpants, and a black and gold hooded sweatshirt, with "Purdue Football" emblazoned on it. He had a white gym towel wrapped around his neck and tucked into the sweatshirt. If it hadn't been for the beard and sunglasses, he could have just stepped out of one of those 1950s phys-ed films.

"Looks like you've been working out," I said. "Get a tryout with the Bears?"

I knew Hanlen had been an offensive lineman at Purdue University, doubled as the punter, and had been named to a couple all Big Ten teams.

"Did that forty years ago," he replied. "Might have made it, too, except the Marines had other ideas. Figured since I don't got a regular job anymore, I should get in shape."

"You sure succeeded. Try not to run into me. It would be like getting mugged by a train."

"Don't worry," he replied. "I run like a three-legged tortoise. I shouldn't be up here, but I saw you and figured I'd say hello."

It might be said that Hanlen was no longer sheriff due to a series of events that I was part of, or instigated, about six months ago, shortly before Christmas. The events also led to me getting shot, and my best friend since childhood, Buzz Wildrick, being killed. Buzz had been tight with Hanlen too, and consequently it would be fair to say that events had not ended well for any of us. Still, on the occasions I'd bumped into him since, he didn't seem to blame me for what happened. He even seemed glad to see me sometimes. In fact, we got along better now than when I first met him, years ago, when I was an investigator for the Prairie County Prosecutor's Office. I didn't take the enmity he displayed back then personally. I think he viewed the prosecutor's office as an impediment to his enforcement of law and order in Prairie County.

"I see you out running a lot," he said. "Must take a lot of dedication."

"More of an obsessive personality," I said, truthfully.

"How fast you figure you're going to run today?" He seemed genuinely interested.

"I'm hoping I can duck under 36 minutes. That might be good enough for me to place in my age group. Not as many people here as in the fall." Although as I said that I noticed more and more people sifting into the crowd. In my imagination, they were all my age.

"That's quick," he said.

Despite what I told him, I was hoping to go well under 36 minutes, maybe close to 35. I thought the latter time doable today, as I had been putting some extra miles in, and I usually ran well in damp conditions. A coach I had in college claimed when there was light rain you could run faster, his reason being there was more oxygen in the air. I'm not sure what science he had to back that up, but it sounded good to me.

Hanlen glanced at his watch. "I'm moving to the back of the pack."

He turned to go, then stopped. "Hey, this is my first race," he said. "Got any suggestions?"

"Go home. Get back in bed."

"I considered that." He paused, seemed to be making up his mind about something.

"Glad I bumped into you," he added. "Saved me a phone call. I've been wanting to talk to you about something. It's sort of important. How about meeting me over at the VFW for a beer after the run?"

The Prairie Stop VFW was just south of the town square. I knew first-hand that they opened early during the fall festival, hoping to entice thirsty runners with a post-race beer. Still, the idea of a cold beer on a wet chilly morning didn't do much for me. I was also wary when he said had been wanting to talk to me, given the events of six months ago.

"What's the something important?" I asked.

"A case I worked a long time ago. There's been a new development, but it'll take some time to explain. I'll see you at the VFW."

"Think they'll be open this early?" I asked.

"Oh, yeah. It's Memorial Day weekend. If it's not, I'll open it." Hanlen was a decorated Korean war veteran, and active in the local posts of both the VFW and American Legion.

"All right," I said. "I'll see you later."

He gave me a nod and turned to make his way through the crowd.

"Hey, chief," I called out, and he turned back.

"Don't go out too fast," I said. "Go slow and pace yourself. Five miles is a long way."

He touched his cap in acknowledgment. "Will do. See you later."

chapter 2

H EEDING YOUR OWN ADVICE ISN'T ALWAYS a good decision. In my case, it seldom was. Most of the first mile in this race was up a long gradual hill. My observation was that casual runners, doing an infrequent race, were keyed up at the start and went out too fast. That's why I told Hanlen to go out slow. Expending too much energy early on was problematic in any run but going fast uphill at the start could be perilous. There wasn't much worse than being gassed out at the one-mile mark of a five-mile run. The last mile here was mainly downhill, obviously, since you can't start uphill and finish uphill on a loop course, but at that point there was limited ground you could make up.

My problem was I went out too slow. I was too far in the middle of pack at the start and had to work my way through the crowd before I could generate a rhythmic pace. I was weaving and zigzagging around people like Gale Sayers returning a punt, except I wasn't near as agile as the Kansas Comet. When I finally got some daylight and began to pick up the pace, I began straining, my breathing labored and my stride tight. I chided myself for not warming up more, but I had never been one to like stretching exercises.

They were calling out times at the mile marks, and when I heard 7:45 at the first mile, I knew I was already well behind my target pace, even allowing for the uphill and the crowd. I settled in after that and made up some time, but when I heard 29 minutes plus at the four-mile, I knew 35 minutes was out of reach. I had the brief optimistic thought that if I ran the last mile downhill in seven minutes flat, I would get close to 36. That was immediately superseded by the more likely thought that I would be fortunate to go under 37.

They had one water station on the course, logically situated at the one mile and four-mile marks. I didn't want water, but at the four-mile, a guy who grabbed a cup came careening back into the middle of the street towards me. I broke stride and reached out to nudge the back of his shoulder to let him know someone was there. Maybe it was a little too firm of a nudge, but the guy turned his head and gave me an angry glare. I glared back.

He said loudly, to no one in particular, "guy thinks this is the Chicago Marathon!"

"Just watch what you're doing," I replied, irritated.

He came right back with a "watch yourself!"

"Clever," I muttered.

I turned the final corner and headed up the straightaway to the finish. This was downtown's main street and cheering spectators lined both sides. Being a small town, many were calling out the names of family and friends as they ran by. I recalled how one year I puked about a hundred yards from the finish, and I slowed in an anxious reaction to that memory. Several people passed me. I watched in fatigued frustration as I crossed under the finish banner while the race clock ticked to 36:30.

To make matters worse, the guy who told me off at the water stop sprinted by me just before I finished. I was both surprised and pissed-off. In what can only be described as an odd act of sportsmanship considering our recent exchange, he turned, stuck his hand out, and said, "good job." The words were sincere but sounded condescending. Taken aback, I could only shake his hand limply and reply "nice race." I regretted then that I didn't tackle him back at the water stop, but that would have probably gotten me a lifetime ban from area running events. The only consolation I had was he looked at least five years younger than I, so I doubt if he displaced me from an award.

I chalked up my effort to a nice try that fell short and walked back to my car for a dry shirt and sweats. I jogged around a while in a likely futile attempt to avoid tightening up. While I was cooling down, the clouds started to break, and by the time I was done, the sun was starting to peek through. The breeze had also subsided. With the early morning chill and clouds disappearing it was beginning to warm up quickly. Despite the gray start it looked like we were going to have a nice day. A beer or two with Hanlen didn't seem like a bad idea.

The Prairie Stop VFW was a two-story white brick building located two blocks south of the courthouse. The small yard in front of the structure was trimmed short and they had miniature American flags lining the walkways. Hanlen was standing by a World War II era howitzer which was permanently moored in front of the place, and talking to a couple of portly white-haired gentlemen. When I was a boy, I remember asking my dad when we drove by the VFW, if he thought the cannon still worked. That was during the Cold War, when we were doing missile drills in elementary school, and I wondered if the weapon could be used to repel Russian hordes. My dad laughed and remarked that if there was a nuclear war, an old cannon wouldn't be of much use.

The men Hanlen were talking to were both wearing khaki shorts and long sleeve olive sweatshirts with the Marine Corps emblem emblazoned on the front. Each had on garrison or forage caps, decorated with various campaign ribbons. When Hanlen saw me, he motioned me over. He didn't look like he had just run five miles.

"Nice going, Logan," he said, reaching out to shake my hand.

"What for?" I asked, puzzled.

"I was just talking with one of the race guys. He says you were third in your group. Billy Mills would be proud of you."

When Hanlen referenced Mills, the Oglala Sioux who scored a stunning upset by winning the 10,000 meters at the 1964 Tokyo Olympics, I figured he was pulling my leg.

"You're kidding me," I said, then, "And how do you know who Mills was?" Other than track aficionados and Native Americans, I doubt that there were many people who had ever heard of him.

"He was a jarhead, that's how," Hanlen said, reminding me that Mills served as a Marine. He shook his head. "If I told you I finished dead last, would that make you happy?"

"I could use a beer," I said, now feeling pleased with myself.

Hanlen turned to one of the elderly gentlemen.

"Colonel, this man just took third place and needs a beer. Might as well bring me one too. Put it on my tab."

The colonel gave Hanlen a mock salute and quick timed it over to the beer tent.

"He was a corporal, really. But we don't stand on ceremony here." Hanlen said. "Have a seat."

"How about you?" I asked, sitting down on one of the folding chairs that had been placed by some card tables covered by red, white, and blue vinyl tablecloths. Hanlen did the same, but tentatively, probably wondering, as I did, if the small chair would handle his bulk.

He gave me an odd look.

"Oh, better than I thought. Just under fifty minutes. If I could always shoot under fifty for nine holes of golf, I would be in hog heaven." Hanlen was an avid golfer, although from what I'd heard, he wouldn't be getting his Senior PGA card anytime soon.

The colonel, or corporal, brought two beers back and put them in front of us. He put his hand lightly on my shoulder and said, "nice going, son" and walked away.

"How's retirement going?" I asked, after we each took a sip of beer. It looked flat and tasted a little skunky.

"I stay busy. I'm up early. After forty years, that's a hard habit to break. Usually at the Y to work out. I'm benching within 60 pounds of what I could do in college."

"Guessing the Y will need some more weights soon," I said.

"If the weather is good, I might get in some golf," he continued. "Not much improvement there, sorry to say. Most afternoons I've been helping my oldest out. He's got a construction business. Not sure you noticed, but new homes are going up like weeds in Prairie County. Big and expensive ones."

"Yeah," I said. "Wonder where all the money is coming from."

"Chicago, I imagine. The steel business is in the crapper."

"Is that your son who worked at Burns Harbor?" I asked, vaguely recalling his son was an engineer and worked at Bethlehem's Steel's massive Burns Harbor plant.

"Yeah. He saw the handwriting on the wall and went into business for himself."

"How's that going?"

"Ok," Hanlen said. "Construction can be feast or famine, but right now he's got more jobs than he can handle."

We each took a pull on our beer.

"Memorial Day is one of my favorite holidays," Hanlen said, contentedly. "It's the start of summer, and it's low key. Usually you get a nice day, and if not, there are plenty of war movies on TV."

"I watched some of *The Longest Day* last night," I said.

"That's a good one. Course I'll watch just about any movie with Robert Mitchum in it."

"Don't forget Richard Burton," I said. They didn't have any scenes together in *The Longest Day*, but I thought Mitchum and Burton would have made an odd pair hanging around the set. I would have liked to hear a conversation between those two.

"Last night I was watching *Battleground* with Van Johnson," Hanlen said. "I like the black and white ones. They seem more realistic for some reason. Ever serve your country, Logan?"

"Sort of, I guess," I said.

"I would have thought that would have been a simple yes or no."

"It's a long story, but the short one is I needed money for college, so I signed up for the ROTC. But they didn't have it where I went, so I had to drive up to Purdue for the classes and meetings. I did it for a couple years, then Uncle Sam and I parted ways."

"When you signed up, you weren't worried about Vietnam?"

"No," I said. "The war was winding down then."

"Did you have to go through basic training?"

"Sort of a mini version," I said. "We had to attend camp two weeks in the summer."

"How was that?" Hanlen asked.

"Well, I was in decent shape, and my dad used to yell at me a lot."

Hanlen smiled. "So, an obstacle course and someone in your face didn't rattle you much."

"It was easier for me than some."

"I'm of the mind that all young people be required to do military service," Hanlen said. "No long commitment, just basic training, and time in the reserves. Other countries have that."

"How about if you got a problem with killing people?"

"Well, they could do non-combat stuff. It would be a common bond if everyone has served their country. God knows we could use one today. You know I was in Korea, right?"

"The Forgotten War," I said.

"Yeah, well, I didn't forget it," Hanlen said, "and neither did anybody who was there. Especially the ones at the Chosin Reservoir."

"You were at Chosin?"

"I was. Matter of fact, parts of my toes are still over there. Frostbite. It got to thirty below that winter. Course having a hundred-thousand Chinese trying to kill us kept us moving. They would have if it hadn't been for General O.P. Smith."

"We aren't retreating, we're just advancing in a different direction," I said, recalling the celebrated Marine general's assertion during the Chosin fighting.

Hanlen raised his beer in salute. "I didn't know you were a student of military history. Most Marines today haven't even heard of the Professor," he said, using Smith's nickname.

"Used to be," I said. "Not so much anymore. I started feeling uncomfortable reading about wars and battles. The violence and killing and all."

"You don't have to look at a book on war for that," Hanlen said. "Pick up the paper and read about how many people got shot or stabbed in Gary and Chicago the night before."

"True," I agreed, "but I think most of that is done on impulse by criminals, drug addicts or hotheads. War is institutionalized killing, done just because some guy in charge says so. That seems worse."

"Sounds like you're a pacifist," Hanlen said. "How come you were watching a war movie last night?"

"You got me there. From now on, no more war movies," I said. "Although most war movies don't show violence in the same casual way a lot of the stuff out today does."

"Yeah. Senseless violence passes for your high-quality family entertainment these days," Hanlen said. "The folks making those movies might have a different viewpoint if they'd seen frozen bodies stacked up like cordwood, like I did in Korea. And people wonder why the homicide rate has doubled since the fifties."

A far-away look came over his face. "What I remember the most is the smell when the bodies thawed out."

"What did you want to talk to me about?" I said, thinking it best to change the subject.

He leaned forward and looked directly at me.

"You ever hear of the Dunes Girls?"

I knew immediately what he was referring to.

"Not sure there is anyone in law enforcement in Northwest Indiana who hasn't," I replied. "I take that back. At least anyone who has been on the job over 20 years."

"Tell me what you know, then."

I took a pull of beer as I collected my thoughts.

"It was summer, 1966," I began. "Three young women, friends from the Chicago area, decide to take in a day at the beach. They drive over in one car to the Indiana Dunes State Park. It's a nice Saturday afternoon on a holiday weekend, Fourth of July, and thousands of other people are doing the same thing. The girls are seen by people on the beach and then getting on a boat. Then maybe back on the beach again. There is some question about that, I think. Anyhow, at the end of the day, when everyone is getting ready to leave, a couple sitting near the girls sees their stuff is still there. Towels, sandals, even purses. They mention this to a park ranger. He picks the stuff up, figuring the girls will eventually be back for it. But they don't come back that day or the next. The ranger later checks the purses and finds ID, money, and keys, all inside, which he notes as peculiar." I paused.

"What woman leaves her purse with personal stuff in it behind on a crowded beach?" Hanlen said.

"Right," I continued. "Meanwhile, the girls' families get worried, and file a missing person's report. Eventually someone contacts the ranger's office, and they begin a search. But it doesn't turn up anything, except the car of the girl who drove, which they find in the parking lot. The girls, on the other hand, were never seen again. A lot of theories have been proposed over the years as to what happened to them, but since the girls were never seen or heard from again, I'd say none of them have been proved correct."

I paused, and then added, "how'd I do?" I knew quite a bit more of the details of the case but kept to the main facts. From my years working in law enforcement as a detective, I took great pride in being able to provide concise summaries.

"You got a good memory," Hanlen said.

"My firsthand knowledge isn't much." In truth, I was a self-absorbed teenager back then, and only vaguely remember my mom talking about the incident with one of the neighbors. I remember her using the word "appalling," which wasn't a word she used a lot.

"I looked at the case a few times when I was in the PA's office," I added. "If there was a gold standard for cold cases, that's it."

"What was your take on it?" Hanlen asked.

"Not sure I had one." I replied.

"I hadn't been sheriff long when it happened," he said. "Plus, even though it was in the county, it wasn't my jurisdiction. The state police and park rangers were in charge and did most of the initial stuff. That wouldn't be how it is today. Command and control, communications, is light years ahead of where it was. There would have been a multi-jurisdictional task force set up immediately. You know better than me that the first 24-48 hours is critical for finding a missing person. Nobody here knew those girls were gone until almost three days later."

"I don't think there was much in the way of leads," I said.

"You're right," Hanlen said. "There were all kinds of theories, from they staged their own disappearance, for whatever reason, to white slavers took them."

I suppressed a grin when Hanlen said 'white slavers.' I hadn't heard that expression in a while but did remember someone using it in the case file.

"Or maybe they got on a boat and it was in an accident," Hanlen said. "At first, the thought was maybe they drowned. They had divers out in the lake a couple days later."

"I remember," I said. "But they found out one of the girls could swim like a fish."

"I don't think they drowned," Hanlen replied, "but not just cause one, or all of them, were good swimmers. More than a few good swimmers have drowned up at the Dunes over the years. People think of the lake as always calm. Then they'll be standing on a sandbar up to their waist, a sudden breeze picks up, and a rip current is pulling them 300 feet into the lake. Or five-foot waves will kick up, which doesn't sound like much, except they're coming at you every 30 seconds. And there are plenty of people who drown trying to save a friend from drowning."

He was right. The lake could change from placid to turbulent in minutes. It was rare that a summer season passed without several people drowning at the Indiana Lake Michigan beaches. I also knew that in an average year, more people drowned in Lake Michigan than in all the other Great Lakes combined. Of course, the area around Lake Michigan was more populated than the other lakes, but as Hanlen said, people underestimated its potential for danger.

"There are problems with the drowning theory," Hanlen continued. "By all accounts, it was nice weather that day and the lake was calm. Plus, there were a lot of people on the beach. You would think someone would have seen someone in trouble in the water."

"I don't know about that," I said. "I bet a lifeguard would tell you their job is hardest when the beach is the most crowded."

"Maybe. The problem is that no bodies were ever found. Like I said, they had divers off the beach shortly after we knew the girls were missing. But even if they didn't find them then, why didn't the bodies surface later? Kind of the same logic for a boat wreck."

Hanlen was referring to the principal that a drowned body would initially sink, as water in the lungs displaced oxygen. The body would eventually decompose in the water, depending on water temperature, depth, and other factors. As it decomposed, gases were created which would make the body buoyant again and it eventually would float to the surface. Back in the Roaring Twenties, when gangs battled for control of bootlegging in Chicago, a macabre rite of spring occurred after the first big thaw when the bodies that were deposited in Lake Michigan over the winter surfaced and drifted onto the beaches.

Thinking of that, I said, "Cement overshoes?"

He frowned. "Ok, so somebody kills them and disposes of the bodies, in the lake or otherwise, and in such a way that they are never found. That raises a bunch of other questions, the big one being motive."

"I got to ask, Chief, why the interest in this, after twenty some years?"

He raised his cup and slowly drank the last of his beer. "I was wondering when you were going to get around to asking me that. Let's grab another beer, and I'll tell you."

chapter 3

A FEW OTHER RUNNERS HAD WANDERED OVER from the finish area to quench their thirst. One of them, a tall young guy in good shape, recognized Hanlen, and came over to greet him. Hanlen introduced him as his nephew. The young man was holding a surprisingly large plaque that proclaimed a second-place age group finish. I congratulated him and asked where he got it. He pointed back to the courthouse.

After we got refills, Hanlen guided us to a different table, furthest removed from everyone else. He obviously didn't want anyone overhearing him.

"I've not told anyone else what I'm going to tell you." Hanlen said. "And it may be hard to swallow."

"Hope it's not as hard as this," I said, raising my beer cup slightly and frowning. "This tastes like the keg sat out in the sun too long."

"I'll pass that on to the refreshment committee," Hanlen said. "Now pay attention. After I announced my recent, and somewhat unexpected, retirement, I got plenty of calls, and letters, cards, what have you, from folks wishing me well. Most from people who I had worked with, others from folks who I had done something for over the years. I'm still surprised when someone who I did a small favor for comes up to me years later and tells me how much it meant."

"That's not surprising," I said. "You helped out a lot of people over the years." Despite Hanlen's gruff exterior and blunt manner, I didn't know him to be a hardliner, which was rare in the law enforcement community. The profession tended to attract the authoritarian type.

"I always tried to do what was right," Hanlen replied. "And I've found you can't always go just by the rule book. And maybe I did help some folks out from time to time."

He paused and glanced out over the crowd.

"But let's say there were a few salutations from those that didn't hold me in such a high regard. I'm guessing from those unwilling guests of the county detention facility. 'Course most of those were anonymous."

He gave a grin. "Seems to me if I felt strongly enough about someone that I took the trouble to send them a fuck you letter, I would want them to know who it was from."

"Were any of those in the form of threats?" I asked.

"No, at least none I took seriously," he said. "There was one I recall that said, 'we hope your retirement ends soon . . . in a train wreck.' But that's not what I want to talk about."

"The Dunes Girls," I said. "What could you stepping down have to do with a twenty-year-old disappearance?"

"Well, for one thing, it's the biggest unsolved crime during my time as sheriff," Hanlen replied. "Hell, it's the biggest unsolved crime in Prairie County, maybe even state of Indiana history."

"Technically, not sure you can really call it a crime," I said. "Nobody has ever proven the girls aren't still alive. There's claims they've been sighted over the years, right?"

"Yeah, there were." Hanlen agreed. "But most of those were made in the first six months after the girls vanished. As you would expect, they weren't too credible, the kind you get any time somebody disappears and its front-page news. Be like if you and I claimed we saw Jimmy Hoffa stroll by while we were sitting here chatting."

I gave a small smile when he mentioned Hoffa's name. The combative Teamster leader and Indiana native had gone missing fifteen years ago near Detroit, yet the other day I had seen a bumper sticker that read 'JIMMY HOFFA, CALL YOUR OFFICE.'

Hanlen shook his head slowly. "I think sometimes if we hadn't spun our wheels at the start there, with the delay in realizing they were gone, and then being fixated on they were in the lake, maybe we would have found them," he said.

"I don't like clichés," I said, "but hindsight is twenty-twenty. And like you said, you weren't in charge."

"Plus, about a week after the girls went missing Richard Speck went on a rampage in south Chicago," Hanlen said. "That kind of took the attention away from the girls."

He was right about that. The brutal killing of eight student nurses in Chicago by Speck on the night of July 13, 1966, had the entire nation riveted in horror. Media coverage which might have gone to the disappearance at the Dunes was focused on the horrendous murders in Chicago. You had to wonder if even a few of the thousands who saw something at the beach that day didn't come forward because of ignorance.

"A whole lot of attention, I'd say," I agreed.

"I've kept in touch with a sister of one of the girls over the years," Hanlen said. "She lives about an hour southwest of here, just across the state line. Name is Ellen Musick. Her older sister, the girl who disappeared, was Deborah Jean Musick. In case you don't remember, the names of the other two girls were Janet Blair and Betsy Collins."

"The sister never married?" I said to let Hanlen know I was paying attention. I rarely knew him to be other than direct, and I was wondering where this was going.

"No, she's married, or at least was. She kept her maiden name. Thought it would be easier for her sister to find her that way, if she is still alive. She used to call me once or twice a year, usually around the anniversary of the disappearance, or maybe at Christmas. Started about ten years after the girls vanished. Wants to know if there are any developments in the case. She must think I'm the only law that still cares."

"Got to be hard for the family to let it go," I said. "How old was she when her sister disappeared?

"Early teens, I think. I always try and talk to her for a bit," Hanlen said. "Even though I have nothing new to tell her. Except recently that is."

"What happened?"

"Well, I told you. I got a lot of mail when I left the county. After a bit, I got tired of looking through it. Made me kind of melancholy, truth be told. Lot of water under the bridge since I took the job. I piled the unopened stuff in a file box and took it home. A couple weeks ago, the wife is straightening up and finds the box. She gives me holy hell. You are going to open every one of these, and write a thank you letter, she says. So, I start to go through them. Probably good I did it. Folks put in gift certificates, for restaurants, car washes, and such."

"Chief, what does you getting a free car wash or hotdog have to do with the missing girls?"

"Hang on, I'm getting to that. Anyhow, I'm near the bottom of the pile and there is an envelope that kind of gets my attention. Feels like there is something in it. I open it and a piece of jewelry falls out . . . a gold locket on a gold chain. I open the locket and engraved on the inside are the initials DJM. I thought, now whose initials would those be?"

"Ok. I'll bite," I said, figuring out where he was going. "Deborah Jean Musick."

"Well, I didn't know that right away," Hanlen said. "Until I looked at the note."

"Was there a postmark on this envelope?"

"Chicago," Hanlen replied.

"Where the girls were from," I said, immediately realizing that wasn't a particularly bright thing to say.

"That doesn't mean much," Hanlen said. "Somebody could have driven to Chicago to mail it."

"Right, dumb question," I said. "Must be the stale beer."

"But like I said, there was also a note."

"Typed or handwritten?" I asked. "And was there a date on it?"

"Handwritten. Dated February, 1990, when I stepped down."

"Don't tell me. It said, 'I heard some people were looking for me. I went to Ferdinand and joined the convent there. Love, Debbie.'"

He shook his head in annoyance. "Enough with the wisecracks," he said.

"Sorry," I said. "What did it say?"

"I brought a copy with me." He reached in the kangaroo pocket of his sweatshirt.

Before looking at it, I said what I had been thinking for the last fifteen minutes. "Tell me, Chief, you didn't really run five miles this morning, did you?"

"I couldn't do five miles if you spotted me four and a set of roller skates. Like I said, I'm not much for running. Did I mention my toes? Came down to watch my nephew mainly. Then I saw you. I did walk part of the first mile and back. Read the note."

I unfolded the piece of paper. In longhand, a distinctive style with large letters leaning slightly backwards, was written "Chief Hanlen: You can't leave until you find out what happened. (Signed) The Last Dunes Girl."

I looked up at Hanlen and hoped 'you got to be kidding me' wasn't written all over my face.

"Well? What do you think," Hanlen asked, after a pause.

"I could start by saying what I don't think," I said. "I don't think this is from one of the girls. Or the only surviving one, if I understand the implication of 'last,' and the locket, which would mean it was the Musick girl."

"All right. Why not?"

"Where do I begin? Too obvious and connected to you, to start. If it was from Debbie Musick, why would she wait until you were retiring?"

"Maybe that's just a coincidence. Maybe something else happened. Something related to the circumstances of why they originally disappeared."

"What would that be?"

"That I don't know. All I got is a locket and a letter," he said. "Ok, it isn't from the Musick girl. Then who?"

"That one I got answers for," I said. "One, someone familiar with the disappearance who likes playing macabre practical jokes. Better yet, somebody who likes macabre practical jokes who has an ax to grind with you. You said you got some nasty notes when you stepped down."

"Well, I did consider that, but someone would have to be real disturbed to play a joke like that," he said.

"In case you hadn't noticed, there are some real disturbed folks out there," I replied. "Two, how about the sister? You said, she still has an active interest in this case. You also said she thought you were the only law who still cares. Maybe she was worried you were her last chance of finding what happened. She sends you something, like a locket with her sister's initials, hoping you stay interested."

"That thought also crossed my mind," Hanlen said, "even though that doesn't seem like her, little I know her. Still, it seems peculiar."

"I agree," I said. "She's got a continuing interest in the case and it's apparently her sister's locket you got."

"Yeah," he said.

"What do you figure on doing about it?" I asked.

"Well, I've been giving it some thought and it's worth checking out. That's where you come in."

"Me? How?"

"Thought you and me could take a drive down there and have a talk with her. Like I said, she's only an hour away."

"Chief, I'm not sure about that," I said. "Even if it's ancient history, this is still an open case. If you even have an inkling that this woman is interfering, it's best you turn it over to Ivan."

Ivan Rich was the former county detective who to my, and many others' astonishment, won the recent special election to replace Hanlen as sheriff of Prairie County. There were three candidates running, and Ivan had shrewdly managed to position himself as the most qualified, as well as the most conservative one of the group. The latter being more significant, since Prairie County, despite its rapid growth over the last thirty years, and an influx of outsiders, remained politically a conservative place. Ivan had surprised me both with his political savvy as well as a new-found talent for not putting his foot in his mouth. He had worked on the case six months ago that brought grief to me and Hanlen, but he emerged from the events unscathed and with blooming political prospects. I had a tough time picturing him as county sheriff, but he won the job, so you had to at least give him the opportunity to see if he could do it.

"I don't want to go official just yet," Hanlen said. "Ivan would think I was crazier than a loon, and rightly so. Plus, since it's likely this is a hoax, and in the unlikely event this woman had something to do with it, she's been through enough. She doesn't need getting charged with tampering."

"Yeah, but that would be Ivan's call, not yours."

"She sent me the letter, not Ivan."

"Ok. What exactly do you plan on doing?" I asked.

"Like I said, we'll go have a talk with her. I'll tell her you are taking a fresh look at the case. We won't mention the letter or locket right away. Or maybe at all. You ask her about her sister, and what she remembers happening before she disappeared."

"How old did you say the sister was when Debbie went missing?" I asked.

"Early teens. Twelve maybe. Debbie was nineteen."

"You remember much from when you were twelve?"

"No," Hanlen replied, "but I played football for ten years. I got hit on the head a lot."

"Ok, we ask her some questions," I said. "Then what?"

"Then depending on the answers, we'll decide what to do. Maybe bring up the letter. Or not. Most likely we'll just go home and forget the whole thing."

"How do you know I'll ask her the right questions?" I asked.

Hanlen didn't say anything and took an unhurried sip of his beer.

"I was a county sheriff," he said. "Some might argue the point with me, but I like to think a good one. I know my limitations though. I'm not much of a detective. I'm going to run out of questions right after I ask her if I can have a glass of water. You're a detective, a good one."

"Let's not overdo it," I said.

"I'm not, but I think if someone is making up a story, you'll see right through it."

"What if I say I'm not too keen on going to talk to this woman?"

He frowned. "What else you got to do? Sit around and wait for your disability money to show up?"

I was receiving a small disability pension from the county, after being seriously injured in a bad car accident almost a year and a half ago, before the stuff happened related to Buzz. I had been returning to Prairie Stop and a sudden blizzard had whipped in off Lake Michigan, bringing a lot of lake effect snow with it. I stopped to help a woman whose vehicle had slid off the road. As I was standing by her car, an old man driving an old Buick didn't see me and ran into me. It was bad. My injuries were severe enough that I couldn't return to my job in the prosecutor's office. The county pension board, being the decider in these matters, ruled that technically the accident was not a line of duty one, and accordingly reduced the disability pension I was to receive. They cited some rules and a formula, which I never understood. When I asked some questions, they gave me the impression that if I kept asking, maybe there wouldn't be any pension at all. I was still irked about that, and while physically I had recovered to the point where I could have applied for reinstatement, I chose not to in view of how I was treated.

"Don't get me started on that," I said.

"I had nothing to do with it. Truth be told, I think you got screwed and let some people know I thought that."

He was right on both counts. Because of his position, Hanlen was on the pension board, but I knew he had argued against the reduced amount. I'm not sure he did it for me so much as on general principle, but I figured I owed him for that, plus, I admit, I was curious as to why the long-dormant mystery of the three girls had suddenly surfaced.

I looked at him for at least twenty seconds without saying anything. He stared impassively back at me.

"All right. I suppose it can't hurt any to go talk to her. Like you said, probably won't amount to much." I had an uneasy feeling I might regret making that decision.

chapter 4

HANLEN HAD SOMETHING HE WANTED TO GIVE ME on the missing girls, so we walked over to his car. He was close because he had parked his black Ford Bronco in front of a fire hydrant. There was a ticket on the windshield which Hanlen picked up, didn't look at, tore to pieces and tossed into the back seat. He handed me a brown accordion file.

"There isn't much in there and sounds like you already know most of it," he said, "but if you get a chance, glance through it before we go and talk to Ms. Musick."

He told me he would call her as soon as he got home and arrange a time to meet. He was hoping as early as Memorial Day, figuring if she worked, she would have the day off. As he was getting into the car, he turned to look at me.

"You think about Buzz much?"

"I try not to," I replied. "It can turn a good day into a bad one. Sometimes a really bad one." Then I added, truthfully, "but all the time."

Hanlen nodded. "Yeah, me too. Guys like him don't come along very often. I'll be in touch."

I watched him drive off and then circled back by the courthouse. The sun was now out in full force and a lot of people were milling around the square. The streets were closed off, but only around the courthouse block itself, unlike the fall festival, when most downtown streets were closed. There were vendor booths set up but not as many as in the fall. I noticed with interest a booth selling items handcrafted by Native Americans. I stopped to look. Some of the 'handcrafted' items appeared mass produced, but I was the cynical type. I picked up a small painted wooden turtle.

"Do you know what that is?"

A woman near my age was next to me, asking the question. She was about five foot three, with a rounded, but not heavy, figure, and a brown oval face with dark brown eyes. Her long black hair was pulled back and braided. She was wearing blue jeans, cowboy boots, and a denim shirt with beadwork on the shoulders and sleeves. She also wore a variety of turquoise jewelry: earrings, bracelets, and a necklace.

I looked at the figurine thoughtfully.

"I'm going out on a limb here, but it appears to be a wooden turtle," I replied.

That got a bemused look.

"Many tribes associated the turtle with creation and fertility," she said. "If a young woman wanted to become pregnant, she would put a turtle carving near her bed. Some refer to it as a fetish. Maybe your wife would like it."

"My wife, maybe. Unfortunately, I'm shopping for my girlfriend."

She laughed. "Buy one for each and see what happens."

I smiled. "I think I will take it. It's growing on me. Slowly, though."

"You're funny. You get a discount because you made me laugh. That will be $17."

I dug a crumpled twenty from my sweatpants pocket. She moved to her cashbox at the rear of the stall. I handed her the turtle and the twenty.

"If you don't mind me asking, what tribe are you?" I asked.

She glanced up curiously from the box.

"I don't mind. I'm Chippewa," she said.

"I thought you would have said Ojibway."

"I could have. Most people in the States refer to us as Chippewa; that is why I said it that way. You know something of the People?"

"My grandfather was a Mohawk, of the Six Nations," I said. "He worked in New York City, building the skyscrapers, and married a white woman. Their son, my father, also married a white, so I guess that makes me one-eighth Mohawk by blood."

"I believe the Ojibway and the Iroquois were once enemies," she said.

"There goes my discount," I replied.

She laughed, then handed me my change, and put the turtle in a small paper bag.

"Again, if you don't mind me asking, where are you from?"

"Mt. Pleasant, Michigan. It's about four hours from here."

"Do you live on Isabella?" I knew that the Isabella Chippewa Reservation was in Isabella County, Michigan, of which Mt. Pleasant was the county seat.

"Part of Mt. Pleasant is considered in the reservation, part isn't. My husband and I live in the part not within the reservation boundary. Are you familiar with the area?"

"My father was proud of his bloodline," I said. "Isabella is the closest large reservation to us, so we went there a couple times for the annual Powwow."

"That's a big event for us," she replied.

"We always liked going," I said, remembering the event fondly. "Guess it will take a back seat to gambling once that gets going." Almost two years ago, President Reagan had signed the Indian Gaming Act, which was supposed to open the door to casino gambling run by Native Americans. I was unsure of the morality of legalized gambling, but I was all for anything that would allow the red man to fleece the white. My opinion was that Native Americans were entitled to some payback after their abysmal treatment by the white man.

"We already have bingo," she said, smiling.

A couple had entered the booth, so I thanked her, wished her luck, and made my way back into the street. When I got over to where I had picked up my race packet, nobody was there except a young man throwing piles of t-shirts into boxes. I asked him about the awards.

He looked up at me with a slight frown.

"You're about ten minutes too late. They took the unclaimed ones back to the parks building. You know where that is?"

"Still by the golf course?" I asked.

"No, it's off Calumet, by Glenbrook Park. But they're closed today, and Monday is a holiday. You can pick it up Tuesday morning."

"When did they move over there?"

"Been a while. Little over a couple years."

"Nobody told me," I said, with a feigned tone of hurt feelings. I was a little giddy on account of the beer.

He stopped throwing shirts in the box and the frown changed to a look of amusement.

"We weren't keeping it a secret," he said. "It was in the newsletter."

"There's a newsletter?"

"The Parks Department sends out a quarterly newsletter to all households. At least to all the residents we know about," he said, the implication being since I didn't get the newsletter, I couldn't be an official resident.

"I could get your name on the list, if you like," he added.

I contemplated that. "Nah. I get on a list, and I'll start getting all kinds of junk mail."

"We don't share our mailing lists," he said.

"Well, still shouldn't do it. The authorities in three states are looking for me."

The kid laughed.

"Then getting our newsletter is probably the least of your problems," he said. He shook his head, then resumed throwing the shirts into a box.

I headed for my car.

chapter 5

W HEN I GOT TO MY STREET, I SAW AN OLDER MODEL Olds Ninety-
Eight parked in from of my house. It was the car Kathy Plemmons,
my once and now current girlfriend, drove. It belonged to her dad. He
always bought the flagship model of Oldsmobile, and this one was from
1976. It was the last year before GM, in a belated attempt to compete
with the surge in small, fuel-efficient import vehicles, began to radically
downsize its big land cruisers. According to Kathy, her dad, a World War
II veteran, refused to buy a new one, even though the interior space in
the new downsized cars was slightly larger than the previous model. He
told her 'if I wanted to drive a Volkswagen, I would have surrendered to
the Krauts.'

Kathy had moved back to Prairie Stop, temporarily, from Southern
California, a little under a year ago to help care for her terminally ill
father. He had been diagnosed with cancer and given only a few months
to live. Being the contrary, and stubborn, man I knew him to be, he had
already outlasted even the most optimistic prediction given him by the
medical doyens. About the only advice his doctors had given him that
he followed was giving up smoking, and that was mainly due to Kathy
confiscating his cigarettes.

I liked Kathy's dad, and the thought of him dying was sad enough, but
I had selfish reasons for hoping he would be around a while longer. Kathy
had a job and a condo in Southern California. She ran her own small

marketing company. Although born and raised in Prairie Stop, she left to attend an Ivy League school and had never looked back. I think some part of her liked being back home, and she could run her company via fax, computer, and phone, but I didn't see her hanging around Prairie Stop forever. It caused me considerable distress when I thought of her leaving. Our relationship was fun, spontaneous, and not complicated, and my perception was that Kathy liked it too. That should have been good enough for me too, but the more time we spent together, the more I thought about how much I would miss her if she left. My fear of abandonment had increased after Buzz's (my best friend) death last year.

I walked in and heard her in the kitchen. She evidently heard me too, since she loudly called out, "I got sandwiches for lunch!"

I was surprised and pleased to see she was wearing only one of my t-shirts, and her hair was wet. She had obviously just showered.

She came over to me and we hugged. I noticed she wasn't wearing anything under the shirt and felt immediate desire. She noticed my reaction and pressed close.

"How was the race?" she asked, then added, "Exciting, apparently?"

"Only a fanatic would consider running exciting," I said, "but the race was good. Not quite as expected, but otherwise good."

"What wasn't expected?"

"I was hoping for a faster time," I answered, breaking our embrace.

"Don't be such a Gloomy Gus," she said. "After what you've been through, it's amazing you can even walk around."

"Perhaps, but twenty years ago, I would have run ten minutes faster."

She gave that some thought.

"That's only 30 seconds a year," she observed. "That doesn't sound too bad."

"Nice math," I said. "Now you're getting all upbeat on me."

"What was good?" she asked. I told her I took third in my age group.

"Wow! That's great! Congratulations." She looked at the small bag I was holding. "Did you get a medal or something?"

"A plaque."

"A plaque? That looks too small."

"I missed the awards ceremony," I said. "I bumped into Chief Hanlen and we had a beer and got to talking. I'll get the plaque next week."

"What did you and the Chief talk about?"

"I'll tell you later," I replied. "They got craft booths set up downtown, like for the Pumpkin Festival. I got this for you. The woman who sold it to me was an Ojibway."

I handed her the bag with the turtle.

"How beautiful!" She exclaimed.

"She said the turtle was a fertility symbol."

She giggled. "Your timing is perfect, or maybe I should say lucky."

"I would rather be lucky than perfect any day, but what are you talking about?"

"Well, I said I got sandwiches for lunch. But they'll keep. There was something I was hoping to do with you. In the bedroom."

"Change the sheets?" I asked.

"I'll say this for you, Logan. You aren't one to pick up on subtle hints."

chapter 6

WE WERE IN BED, KATHY'S HEAD ON MY CHEST, my arm around her. "I don't know how you do it," she said, languidly.

"Don't sell yourself short," I replied.

She laughed. "I didn't mean that. I was referring to running five miles."

"You'll get there," I said. Not long after she returned home, and we resumed our relationship, Kathy complained she was overweight due to, as she put it, "a lack of exercise and a lack of sex." We started to work on the latter shortly afterwards, and the former when spring finally showed up a couple months ago. We would try and walk and jog a few miles together, two or three days a week. Either the sex or running or both aided her effort to lose weight, and a week ago she announced she had dropped fifteen pounds.

"What did you and Hanlen talk about?" she asked.

I briefly described our conversation about the missing girls from twenty years ago. I decided not to mention the locket or note. I just told her that Hanlen had expressed interest in the long dormant case.

"The Dunes Girls," she said. "I remember. Years ago, I saw something about them on TV. They were featured on one of those shows about missing persons. How could they just disappear like that?"

"Doubt if anyone will ever know," I said. "Unless one of the girls reappears or someone decides to make a deathbed confession. Either would be unlikely."

"You must have some thoughts about what happened, if only out of professional curiosity," Kathy said.

"Matter of fact I do. During our slack time in the Prosecutor's Office, which wasn't a lot, by the way, we would come up with theories of what happened to the girls."

"And what did you come up with?"

"Are you really interested?"

"Of course, I love mysteries."

"Ok, I'll tell you. Just don't fall asleep."

"You have my complete attention," Kathy replied, then made a snoring noise.

"Funny," I said. "In any investigation, what you try and do is eliminate what is impossible or unlikely. Then you take what's left and see if it fits the facts you have. An analysis by elimination, if you will." I paused. "Hey, I think I may have just invented a new buzzword."

"Sorry to disappoint," Kathy said. "But I don't think so. I was a math minor in college, and there is an elimination method for solving equations. But go on."

"Figures. In this case, it's not likely the girls drowned. It just doesn't make sense." I repeated some of what Hanlen and I had discussed.

"Ok, they didn't drown. What's next?"

"In general terms, there are two possibilities. More precisely, two categories of possibilities," I said. "One, they disappeared on their own, for reasons unknown, and managed to stay disappeared. Or, two, as the newspaper would say, they met with foul play."

"And of the two, what do you think happened?"

"The first is unlikely," I said. "These girls were nineteen and twenty. When you were nineteen, and assuming you had a good reason, do you think you could have run away, got yourself a new identity, and never had contact with your family or friends again?"

"Probably not," she said. She paused, thinking. "But then again, you hear of those college kids in the sixties who disappeared. You know, the anti-war protestors. They lived under the radar for years and didn't get caught."

"You're referring to members of the student militant group, the Weather Underground, or the Weathermen?" I asked. "By the way, that group was started four hours from here, up in Ann Arbor, Michigan." I found it interesting that the group was founded at the University of Michigan, rather than one of the purportedly more liberal colleges located in the Northeast or California.

"You're right," I continued, "the ones you hear about get tired of living on the lam and turn themselves in. I don't think it's the same for these girls. The Weathermen who disappeared had to, otherwise they were going to get tossed in jail for blowing stuff up, including themselves. The girls had no known motive for taking off, which makes it hard to believe they left on their own. And even if they did, would you put your family through the worry and agony of wondering what happened to you?"

"Maybe the girls had a motive," she said. "Just one that nobody knew about."

"What do you think you could have done at age nineteen that would make you want to disappear?" I asked.

"A medical reason, perhaps," she said after a pause.

"What medical reason?"

"Being pregnant and unwed. It's not a big deal now, but as you may recall, it was at one time. Do you remember Wanda Klepsky from high school?"

"She didn't come back from Christmas vacation one year. I heard she had a bad case of the mumps."

Ellen laughed. "You don't miss a year of school for the mumps. I can't remember the father's name, but he also left school. He joined the Navy, I think."

"Brad Miller. He's got his own plumbing business now."

"Plumbing. Figures."

"It may be relevant that you mention this because there was talk that one of the girls might have been pregnant."

"What do you mean, 'talk'? Either you are or you aren't pregnant."

"Agreed, but remember that there were no bodies found, so no autopsy, and therefore no proof she was pregnant. Maybe she was, maybe she wasn't. She apparently told at least one of her other friends she was, though."

Kathy thought about that. "She wouldn't have been the first woman to think she was pregnant when she wasn't. And I can understand her needing to talk to somebody about it."

"Incidentally, that's part of another theory of what happened to the girls."

"Which is?"

"The girl who is pregnant doesn't want to be. Let me get back to that one."

"Ok," Kathy said. "If they didn't disappear on their own, that leaves foul play."

"Correct, which presents its own challenges," I said.

"Like what?" she asked.

"Well, if you assume someone abducted the girls, and did away with them, was it a stranger, and a crime of opportunity, or someone they knew?"

"A stranger? You mean like a sociopath who just happened to be at the lake that day?"

"Yes," I said. "Although, personally, I never cared much for the big bad wolf wandering down out of the forest theory."

Kathy turned her head to look at me.

"I thought the authorities always rounded up suspicious strangers and drifters after a horrible crime," she said.

"There are always the usual suspects," I agreed, "and I'm not saying that the menacing strangers don't exist. But there is kind of a self-serving tendency to think that the real shocking crime is committed by outsiders and strangers. I know from experience that isn't the case. It's just easier to accept if the villain is an outsider."

"Why?"

"Think about it," I said. "If a stranger abducts my neighbors' daughter, it's shocking. I'm terrified and worry it will happen to my own daughter. I tell her to run away screaming whenever someone unfamiliar approaches her. But what if instead of a drifter, the guy doing the abducting is the dentist who lives three doors down?"

"A dentist?" Kathy asked, puzzled.

"Or the plumber," I said. "For my hypothetical villains, I like to use the guys who charge the highest hourly rates."

"Fair enough," she said. "And if the villain is the dentist?"

"My point is now I can't trust anybody. Not my neighbors, not the school bus driver, not the pastor of the local church. That prospect is far more disturbing to me than the drifter. In a way, it's easier for me to accept if a stranger is responsible."

"Got it, but where does this leave us with the missing girls?" Kathy asked.

"According to witness statements, the girls were seen going into the lake, then getting on a white and blue motorboat. A man described as having black hair and wearing a red beach jacket was operating the boat. Age indeterminate, anywhere from mid-twenties to mid-thirties. That's not surprising. People are usually inconsistent when judging age."

"Did the girls go with this guy willingly?"

"Good question. None of the witnesses said anything to the effect that the girls appeared to be coerced onto the boat. Which leads me to think this guy must have been someone one or more of the girls knew. I figure at least two of them, maybe all three, knew him."

"Why not just one of them?"

"Again, I pose the question to you," I said. "Even if you were with a couple friends, safety in numbers, that sort of thing, would you get on a boat with a stranger?"

"I don't think I would," Kathy said.

"Me neither. But if your two friends knew this guy, maybe you would. Here is another interesting piece of information. The girls had been to the Dunes the prior weekend."

"How do you know that?"

"The source was a family member," I said. "It came out later and for some reason was not widely reported in the papers."

"That is interesting. Maybe that's when they met this guy on the boat."

"Yes, that would be a logical conclusion," I said. "But if they did meet him then, they apparently never mentioned that particular detail to anyone."

"Maybe they didn't want anyone to know about this guy."

"Another good one," I agreed. "But it was only a week, after all. It may just not have come up."

"I just thought of something," Kathy said. "Maybe there was an accident or storm and the boat sunk."

"Possible, but unlikely," I said. "Lake Michigan can be unpredictable, if not downright dangerous at times, but on that particular July day, the weather was perfect. No storms, big waves, or high winds. Nothing more than minor boating accidents reported."

"Couldn't there have been an accident that didn't get reported?"

"Definitely," I said. "But the harbors near the Dunes were checked. No boats matching the description were found or reported missing either. Of course, it was a while before they got them all checked. Since it was a beautiful day on a holiday weekend, there could have been over five thousand boats out on the lake. And that's just from Chicago to Michigan City."

"Five thousand. That doesn't exactly narrow things down." Kathy said.

"Right. Here's the clincher," I said. "All the personal items belonging to the girls, purses with IDs and money in them, were left on the beach. Would you leave your purse on a crowded beach?"

"Not unless I was sure I would be right back," she said. "Probably not even then."

"Exactly. Which means they didn't think they would be gone long. And returning to the man on the boat, they apparently trusted him enough to think he would bring them right back."

"Which goes to your point that they knew him," she said.

"Yes," I said. "But it seems he didn't bring them back. If we knew who he was, we might know why."

"And how do you find out who he was?"

"That's a tough question. It wasn't answered at the time, which makes it doubtful it will be answered twenty years later. But the girls knowing the guy on the boat is just one possibility. That doesn't rule out that someone, a stranger to the girls, brought a boat to the lake that day, lured the girls onto it, did away with them, then got rid of the boat and the bodies."

"Wait a second," Kathy said, confused. "You said before you didn't think it happened that way."

"Right. I stated what was the most likely to me, which I thought is what you asked. I'm not saying there aren't other theories."

"Such as?"

"Here is one. I mentioned one of the girls might have been pregnant. Maybe she didn't want to be and met someone at the lake who was going to help her with her problem. Illegally, of course, since this was before Roe vs. Wade."

"What about the other two girls?"

"They went along for support," I replied. "Then, according to this theory, something went wrong with the procedure, and the girl who was pregnant didn't make it. Whoever did the procedure then decided he needed to silence the other two, permanently."

"I don't know," Kathy said. "That could be implausible."

"Yes," I agreed. "For one, would you go off to have an abortion in a bathing suit? With none of your personal effects? On a motorboat?"

"That's creepy."

"I agree, but that's not the main issue."

"What is?" Kathy asked.

"Let's say I'm the guy who performs, for a fee, this service. I'm not exactly going to be putting my name and address in the phone book. If something goes wrong, I vanish. And let's say the authorities do manage to track me down. If I get a good lawyer, probably the worst I'm looking at is manslaughter and a few years in prison. Maybe not even that. But if he does away with the other two girls, that's first-degree murder, and good for a trip to the electric chair."

"That sounds logical to me, but I would think you are more pragmatic than most criminals," Kathy said.

"I certainly hope so," I replied.

"Where does this leave us with a possible theory?"

"I got one more for you," I said.

"My head is spinning now, but ok."

"Two of these girls share a hobby, more of a passion, really," I said. "They both love horses. One of the girls even owns a horse. She boards it and the girls ride together at a place called Twilight Stables. The stable is owned by a man named Luther Brame. Ever hear of him?"

"No, should I have?"

"He was a somewhat notorious character in Chicago back in the fifties and sixties," I said. "He spent most of the seventies in prison."

"For what?"

"He had a business partner he did away with," I said. "The guy also happened to be Brame's cousin. But that was only the end of a long list of bad stuff."

"What kind of bad stuff?"

"He started out with rape and assault when he was in his teens. Did some time, then moved on to larceny, arson, conspiracy to commit murder, etc. A lot of it not proved, by the way, due to witnesses gone missing or changing their testimony."

"He sounds charming," Kathy said.

"When he wasn't doing that, he was a horseman. Owned a couple stables and a lot of horses. One story about him is that he arranged a fire at a stable of one of his rivals. The horses were inside when the place went up in flames."

"How horrible!" Kathy exclaimed, sitting up.

"Yeah," I said. "And you gotta figure since he was a horseman, he probably liked horses. Imagine what he would do to someone he didn't like. The theory is one or both of the girls who used his stable may have witnessed or heard something there that incriminated him."

"For what?"

"Who knows? Something serious," I said. "Something which, if the authorities found out about, could get him sent away for a long time. So Brame arranges the permanent disappearance of the girls, just in case they were thinking of going to the police."

"Doesn't sound like he would have any qualms about murder," Kathy said.

"Oh, there's no doubt he could have done it, either personally or arranging it. I just don't think he did."

"Why?"

"Pretty sure he had an alibi for that weekend," I replied.

"Couldn't he have arranged their disappearance?"

"Sure, but if he arranged it, we get back to the 'why' on a packed beach at a state park on the Fourth of July? Why not some place where there was nobody around?"

"Maybe that was the whole idea of getting them on the boat," Kathy said, "so they could be taken somewhere where nobody was around."

"Another good point," I said, "and if so, that would explain why the guy in the boat was never found."

"What do you mean?"

"I don't think Brame would leave someone alive who could finger him for murder. Especially someone who witnesses could identify. Which again makes it difficult to believe he chose a crowded state park to get rid of the girls. In any case, if Brame had something to do with it, we're never going to hear about it from him."

"You don't think he'll confess?"

"Here's the thing. He couldn't, even if he wanted to," I said. "He died a couple years ago of cancer."

There was a pause, then Kathy said, "You've listed a bunch of theories, Logan, but pointed out issues with every one of them."

"Yeah, I know. The fact that this case has been unsolved for twenty years doesn't do much for the credibility of any of them."

Kathy thought for a second. "If you were involved with this investigation from the beginning, what would you have focused on?"

"That's easy," I replied. "I keep going back to this guy in the boat. I don't think he was a stranger. I believe the girls had some type of connection with him. If you could figure out that connection, and who he was, even now, you might get somewhere. It's puzzling to me that they didn't focus more on him at the time. Who knows? Maybe they did but couldn't track him down. In which case, like I said, it won't be any easier twenty years later."

We were silent for a couple minutes.

"I think you and Hanlen should try and figure out what happened to those girls," Kathy said, at last. "You both have some time on your hands, and it sounds like you already have some ideas about what happened."

"Right," I said. "All I need to do now is find the mystery man who knew the girls twenty years ago. Said individual had a mystery boat, got the girls on to it, and decided to make off with them, reasons unknown. Then he makes the boat and the girls vanish. I might as well find a haystack and start looking for a needle."

"No need to get sarcastic," Kathy said. "But I see what you mean."

"And maybe it's a mystery that should remain one."

"Why do you say that?"

"After twenty years, I think it impossible that these girls are going to be found alive, so what good is going to come of finding out what happened to them?"

"How about closure for the families and justice for the girls?" Kathy asked.

"Maybe. But that might be an unfair trade-off."

"Trade-off for what?"

"Whatever happened to these girls, there was bad karma involved, a lot of it. Unleashing that after all these years might cause more grief than good."

"That's a mystical thing to say," Kathy said. "I didn't know you were that way."

"You should know by now that I'm a very mystical person." I paused. "I'm beginning to think you are interested in me in only a shallow, physical way."

"That's not true," Kathy laughed. "But since you mentioned it . . ." She reached over to the nightstand and picked up the turtle I bought for her. "Let's see if this thing works."

chapter 7

HANLEN CALLED ME THE NEXT DAY, ABOUT AN HOUR into the Indianapolis 500. I was watching the race with interest. I thought it more of a technological spectacle and a duel of nerves than a sport. Yet I still found it absorbing that someone could drive a car at 200 miles per hour while other vehicles inches away were going just as fast. Me, I got stressed out negotiating the occasional trip on the expressway into Chicago.

"Watching the race?" Hanlen asked.

"Yep, What did the sister say?" I asked.

"She wanted to talk. Was eager to, as a matter of fact. Said we could come down this afternoon if we wanted."

"What about the 500?" I didn't think Hanlen would want to miss out on Indiana's foremost sports extravaganza.

"We'll leave right after it's over, or at least when we know who's going to win." he said. "Be ready."

I stopped watching the race to shave and shower. It had been a nice morning, and I had jogged a little with Kathy. I then ran a couple more miles by myself after she went home.

When I went back to the race, a Formula 1 driver from Europe took the lead with about 30 laps to go, and it didn't appear anyone was going to catch him. It was then when Hanlen's Bronco pulled in my driveway. I had thrown on some khakis and an old, but reasonably decent dark blue dress shirt. Hanlen nodded approvingly when I got in the car. He wore a blue polo shirt and lightweight dark green pants. It looked like clothes a guy might play golf in.

"Hit the links this morning?" I asked, as we pulled out of the driveway.

He nodded. "Yep, bright and early. See, I said you were a good detective. Too nice a morning not to. Got in nine before the race started. Only bad thing was I had to skip church to do it."

"I'm guessing God will understand. I'm sure He plays golf. Probably to a three handicap."

"Why not par?"

"Even God has to have something to strive for. What do you figure He says when He misses a short putt?"

Hanlen looked over at me. "I'm not worried about God. If I don't get home in time for the evening service, my wife will crucify me."

"Perhaps she'll just wash her hands of you," I said.

We went through downtown and got on Route 2 heading southwest. We drove in silence, except for the country station Hanlen had on the radio. I couldn't help but tap my foot to Stonewall Jackson singing "Waterloo," his biggest hit and one of my dad's favorite songs. My father wasn't much for music, but when that one came on, he would belt out the song's catchy chorus along with old Stonewall. The lyrics probably appealed to his fatalistic view of life, which I attributed to his Native American ancestry. We would all meet our designated fate and there wasn't a whole lot to be done to change it.

Then, after Stonewall, to my surprise, Emmy Lou Harris came on singing Townes Van Zandt's "Pancho and Lefty." The version you usually heard on the radio was the hit version done by Merle Haggard and Willie Nelson. Me, I thought Emmy Lou's plaintive voice better matched the melancholy character of Van Zandt's song. Years ago, I drove a couple hours into Michigan to see him perform with Sammi Smith at Kalamazoo College. I was a fan of Van Zandt's, and also interested in Smith, because I heard she was part Apache, yet I wondered about their appeal to kids attending a small liberal arts college in Michigan. The lack of same became evident when the show started with the school gymnasium about half-empty. Smith was the headliner, having had several chart hits and a Grammy win, but, somewhat surprisingly, she went on first. Me and about fifty other die-hard Van Zandt fans stayed until he stumbled out 45 minutes later, obviously under the influence. Some left in exasperation or embarrassment for him when he couldn't remember all the words to his first few songs. Then Sammi Smith calmly walked back on the stage. She and Van Zandt proceeded to do flawless versions of "Tecumseh Valley" and "Pancho and Lefty." There was not a dry eye in the place. Even remembering it now, I thought I was going to tear up. I sniffed and coughed a couple times.

"What's the matter with you?" Hanlen asked.

"Hay fever," I mumbled.

The music was interrupted with a news bulletin about the winner of the 500.

"God bless America," Hanlen said, upon hearing the news. "That's the second year in a row a foreign driver has won at Indy. Doesn't seem quite right."

"I didn't know you were a xenophobe, chief," I said.

"If I knew what that was, I think I might be mad," he replied.

"At least nobody got killed," I said.

"I was at Indy a few years ago when a loose tire went over the screen and killed a man from Wisconsin," Hanlen said. "My home state. I used to like to go to the race, but after that happened, I didn't much care for it."

More silence as we crossed under I-65. I thought maybe Hanlen was going to get on the interstate, but he stayed on 2.

"Where did you say the sister lived?" I asked.

"Just across the state line. Outside of Kentland," Hanlen replied.

"Kentland? Jeez, that's got to be two hours from here. I thought you said it was an hour."

I had a mild phobia about being in a car driven by someone else. It started after I had been hit and almost killed, and became much worse after another car accident last year. I had been trying to get away from a couple guys who seemed intent on doing me grievous harm and totaled my car when it went off the road. My fear was usually manageable for short trips, but my heart raced a bit when Hanlen said Kentland.

"It's not two hours," Hanlen said, dismissively. "Anyhow, we'll make better time once we get on 41."

U.S. 41 ran from Chicago all the way to Evansville, roughly parallel-ing the Illinois-Indiana state border. At one time, not only was it the main north-south thoroughfare in the state, but you could continue on 41 all the way to Florida. When the interstate system, particularly I-65 in Indiana, was completed, use of 41 declined. If you were headed southeast to Indy or Louisville, the interstate was more direct, but I preferred 41 otherwise. It was two lanes both directions, most of the way, but saw much less traffic than the interstate. Sometimes you could drive for miles without seeing another vehicle—nothing but farm fields, and the occasional abandoned gas station, diner, or small roadside motel at a formerly busy crossroads.

"Did you look at the file?" Hanlen asked.

"Yes, although there wasn't anything in there I hadn't seen before. No offense, but not sure anyone would consider that a textbook missing persons investigation."

"I said as much yesterday," he replied.

"Is Jacobi still around?" I asked. Art Jacobi was the state police detective lieutenant who handled the case of the missing girls.

"If you mean alive, I believe so. I heard he retired to Florida a while back. Tampa area, I think."

"How about Lanz?" Ken Lanz was the park superintendent at the Dunes back in the summer of 1966. That was when it was still a state park, and not designated as a National Lakeshore.

"You may know Ken drew some unwelcome attention for some things he said and did when it was first realized the girls were missing," Hanlen said. "That came back to haunt him when the girls didn't turn up. He excused himself from the superintendent's job a year later."

I knew Lanz had made an ill-advised remark to the parents of one of the missing girls, to the effect that "she's just off having a good time." He may have said it in a manner meant to be reassuring, but unfortunately, valuable time was lost before a search for the girls began. The remark was later seen as indicating his blasé attitude toward the situation.

"I remember that," I said. "Any idea where he is now?"

"May have heard he had gone out west somewhere, but not sure where."

"And Banks?" I asked, then added, remembering, "he died in an accident not too long after that, right?"

Mason Banks was the police chief of Glenbrook, the then small, now large, Chicago suburb where two of the girls lived. He performed a lot of the background work on the girls. Jacobi, Lanz and Banks were the principals in charge of the investigation into the girls' disappearance. Three men, each representing a separate authority. From what I had read about the case, I had the impression they didn't interact much. That would not have been all that unusual back then. As Hanlen had alluded to yesterday, the investigation would be handled much differently today.

"Ah, Mason Banks," Hanlen said. "Him, I know for sure about. You're right. He's dead. And it was a farm accident. Supposedly."

"Supposedly? What, his tractor turn over on him?"

"No, if his tractor turned over on him, I would have said that was an accident. Banks lived in Glenbrook, but also had a small working farm down in Kankakee County. No, he blew himself up. Accidentally, of course."

"How did he manage that?" I asked.

"You know what ammonium nitrate is?"

"Fertilizer?" I replied.

Hanlen looked over at me and nodded. "I would have bet you didn't know that. Yep, it's a common fertilizer. I even got a couple bags in my shed. Did you also know it can be used as an explosive?"

"That I didn't know," I said.

"It's not explosive, or even particularly flammable by itself, but you combine it with fuel oil, in the right ratio, get a detonating source, and you got yourself a pretty good explosion. The combination of stuff is known as ANFO, which in case you can't figure it out, stands for Ammonium Nitrate Fuel Oil. Even if you don't have a detonation source, a fire and the right type of conditions in a confined space will make ammonium nitrate explode. That's why once in a blue moon you'll hear about a warehouse with the stuff in it exploding."

"What was Banks doing with ANFO?"

"I didn't say he had ANFO." Hanlen said. "He had some ammonium nitrate in his barn, stored in some big fiber drums. Hence the confined space. He apparently made the unwise decision to place it near an old rusty tank in which he stored diesel fuel."

"What happened?" I asked.

"No one really knows, but they think the tank leaked. Either Banks didn't notice the tank leaked, or if he did, he wasn't too concerned about it being near the fertilizer drum. Over time, they think enough fuel soaked into the bottom of the drums to create an accidental ANFO."

"You said the stuff had to be mixed in the right ratio. How does that happen by accident?"

"You're paying attention," Hanlen said, glancing over at me. "Way I understand it, once you get the minimum ratio, the stuff is ready to blow. Too much is ok. You don't get a bigger explosion, but it will still explode. Whatever leaked into the drum was enough. They think Banks comes into the barn on his tractor, dragging his plow, whatever, and generated a spark off the concrete floor."

"I didn't think you could ignite diesel with a spark," I said, remembering something from a basic arson training course I once took.

"You can't," he agreed. "In fact, one time I saw a guy douse a match in diesel. It's got what you call your high flash point. Much higher than gas. Diesel will burn, but it won't ignite easy. They think some was out on the floor mixed with straw and smoldered for a while. Once the drums started to burn, it was a matter of minutes until there was an explosion."

I thought about that. "Wouldn't Banks have noticed a fire and tried to put it out before the stuff exploded?"

"Good question. They assume he didn't notice the fire at first, then saw smoke, went back into the barn to investigate, which is when he got blown to kingdom come." Hanlen said.

"And wouldn't a law enforcement officer have known about ANFO?"

"You didn't," Hanlen observed.

"Yeah, but Banks was a farmer and a cop," I said. "By the way, if there was an explosion and fire, how did they identify the body?"

"His wife identified his wedding ring."

"That was it?" I asked.

"I'm not sure how much of him was left to identify, and they didn't consider it could have been anybody else. That was another odd thing, by the way. His wife usually went down to the farm with him. That weekend he apparently told her to stay home."

"Anybody think maybe it wasn't an accident?"

"If anyone did, they kept it to themselves," Hanlen said.

"What did his death do to the girls' investigation?" I asked.

"Another good question," Hanlen said. "Glenbrook is, or was, a small town, not much in the way of a police force, so Banks was handling most of the background investigation on the girls by himself. Interviewing the girls' families and friends, things like that. He had a case file, of course, but it has gone missing right around the time he died."

"Missing? Maybe he took it out to the farm with him."

"That possibility was considered," Hanlen replied. "His wife let some officers look around, there and his home, but they didn't find it. We're pretty sure he passed most of the information on, but with him dead and the file gone, how would anyone really know?"

I thought about that. "You ever meet Banks?"

"Yeah. A month or so after the girls disappeared. That was the only face to face. I might have talked to him a few times on the phone after that."

"Well?" I asked, when he didn't add anything about the conversations.

"For one thing," Hanlen said, "we learned we were both in Korea together."

"At Chosin?"

"Matter of fact, he was there," Hanlen answered.

"Did you know him?"

"I don't remember him, but he claimed to have met me."

"But you don't remember him?"

"It was almost forty years ago and there were 30,000 men there. And it's not like it's a real fond memory for me."

"What did he have on the girls, background wise?" I asked.

"Not a whole lot, and you probably know most of it. The girls led tame lives. Two were single, one was married. Neither of the single girls had a steady boyfriend. They all did secretarial or clerical work. One was going to college-part time. Two of them liked horses. Debbie Musick even owned a horse."

"Which she kept at a stable owned by Luther Brame."

Hanlen glanced over at me. "You don't like Brame for this do you?"

"It's an odd coincidence, don't you think, that two of the girls rode at his stable."

"I agree, but what's his motive? Aside from that, Brame died a couple years ago. Natural causes. If he did it, we aren't going to hear it from him."

"Just because we don't know his motive doesn't mean he didn't have one," I said. "What if he arranged it? The killer could still be alive. Did Banks talk to Brame?"

"Yes. Brame apparently laughed and told him he had girls buried under his house. Then he told Banks he had nothing to do with it and to get the hell off his property."

"Guess Banks didn't take the buried under the house remark seriously," I said.

"Would you?"

"Might be interesting to talk to Banks' wife," I said. "Maybe he told her something that didn't go into the file."

"Maybe, but that was twenty years ago. Even if we track her down, what do you think she'll remember?"

"Banks dies under strange circumstances and his case file vanishes," I reflected. "When I was in the PA's office, we used a technical expression for stuff like that."

"What was that?" Hanlen asked.

"A mighty funny coincidence."

chapter 8

Tʀᴜᴇ ᴛᴏ ʜɪs ᴡᴏʀᴅ, Hᴀɴʟᴇɴ sᴛᴇᴘᴘᴇᴅ on the accelerator once we got on 41 south. I didn't have a good view of the speedometer but figured we were doing well over 80. Despite the highway being straight and flat with few other cars in sight, my anxiety increased the faster we went.

"The 500 is over, Chief," I said, trying to keep the rising discomfort out of my voice.

He glanced over at me but didn't say anything.

"Not worried about the state police, are you?" I asked.

Not even a glance this time. He probably found it ludicrous that any law enforcement officer in this part of the state would even think about citing him for speeding.

"I got it!" I exclaimed, slapping the dashboard.

He looked over at me, annoyed.

"Are you having some kind of fit?"

"You're trying to get us up to the speed of light," I said.

"What the hell are you babbling about?"

"Einstein's Theory of Special Relativity. It implies that if we could travel faster than the speed of light, we could conceivably go back in time. Then we can figure out what happened to the missing girls. Or maybe even keep them from going missing."

"Now that's an idea," Hanlen said. "How fast do I need to get this rust-bucket up to?"

"Only about 186,000," I said.

"Miles per hour?"

"No, miles per second, I said. "I'd stop trying, if I were you. I think the theory also implies nothing can go faster than the speed of light. The problem is mass. It increases as you go faster."

"Am I going too fast for you?" Hanlen eased off the gas, but only slightly. "Just relax and enjoy the ride. I'll worry about the state police."

Road signs announced we were going by the small town of Morocco, Indiana, named after the African country. I wondered who thought a few, flat as a pancake acres in Indiana reminded them of a distant coastal kingdom teeming with mountains and deserts.

"Know what happened near here?" Hanlen asked.

"A fatal one car accident?"

Hanlen snorted.

"A few years ago," he said, "a farmer found the Spilotro brothers in a shallow grave in his cornfield a few miles from here. They were beaten so bad they had to be identified from dental records."

"That was here? I thought that happened in Chicago," I said.

For many years, Anthony "the Ant" Spilotro was allegedly in charge of the Chicago mob's activities in Las Vegas. He got the nickname the Ant from an FBI agent, who referred to him as "that little pissant," which for reasons of civility the newspapers shortened to Ant. Spilotro's main duty was collecting and distributing the "skim," the off-the-books cut the mob took from legal gambling profits. Apparently, this wasn't enough to keep the Ant busy. He and his brother Michael ran a sizable burglary operation in Vegas. Their gang eventually had as many as ten henchmen and operated a large pawn shop where they fenced the stolen goods. They weren't exactly subtle in their activities, and drew the undesirable attention of the authorities, who eventually arrested most of the gang, except for, surprisingly, the Spilotro brothers. It was assumed that his bosses in Chicago got tired of the Ant's flamboyant ways and had him and his brother executed; assumed, because nobody was ever charged with the murders.

"Well, wherever it happened," Hanlen said, "their bodies wound up under a few feet of dirt just east of town here. There was even talk at the time that they were buried alive."

I winced at that. "Irrefutable proof that crime doesn't pay."

"I need to make a pit stop," he said, and we exited 41 and headed east.

We drove for a few miles until I saw a sign announcing we were entering Brook, Indiana, population 926.

"Ever been to Brook before?" he asked.

"Close," I said. "I went to college in Dyersville. I drove by here on the way home, once in a while. For a change of scenery." There wasn't a whole lot of variety to the terrain in western rural Indiana.

"Wallace College?

"The one and only," I replied.

"That's a good school. They used to play Houghton Tech, where my son went."

"The construction son?"

"Yeah."

"That's a pretty good school too," I said.

"Some would say it's the best undergrad engineering school in the country," Hanlen replied. "Wallace used to kick Houghton's ass in football, though. Wallace was always undefeated, at least at the time they played Tech. You guys were a regular small college powerhouse."

"We had some good teams," I agreed. "Even had a couple guys go to the pros. But they ought to be good. It's an all-male school out in the middle of nowhere."

"No distractions, way I look at it," he replied.

We drove through Brook, a small, sleepy, pleasant looking town. Hanlen went by at least two gas stations without stopping. I wondered why as I thought he got off the highway for fuel.

A short distance outside of Brook a golf course appeared on our right.

"That's Hazeldon Country Club. I've played there a few times," Hanlen remarked. "Nice course. I almost broke par there once."

"You only played ten holes?"

He gave me a dirty look.

We crossed a small river, which a sign identified as the Iroquois River.

"The Iroquois didn't live out this way," I said. "The tribes in this area were mainly the Miami, Kickapoo and Potawatomi."

"I didn't name the river," Hanlen said, then added, "Although there used to be a roadhouse down this way called the Potawatomie Tavern. The

Newton County sheriff once told me there were more fights in that place on Saturday night than Madison Square Garden."

"What happened to it?"

"Burned down, years ago."

"Figures," I said.

"Why's that?"

"A river named after the wrong tribe, and a burned down dive. Nice memorials to the indigenous people who lived here."

"I wouldn't take it personal, Logan," Hanlen said.

"Easy for you to say."

A grove of mature oaks lined the river. As we approached the entranceway to the country club, a large, two-story, Tudor-style home appeared on our left. The walls of the first level were brick, the second level was wood, with large windows and a distinctive Tudor style steeply pitched roof. A one story, more modern structure that looked like a small school or office building was on the other side of the parking lot. Hanlen made a left into the lot.

"This here is the George Ade House." Hanlen said pointing to the house. "Why don't we take a quick walk around? I've never taken a close look at it."

Behind the house and to the side were a couple much smaller brick buildings, of a similar style, one of which I guessed might have been a caretaker's quarters. There was a lot of land behind the house and buildings, and I wondered if part of it had once been farmed. Oddly enough, the substantial manor home and grounds seemed to fit right into the bucolic scene presented by the golf course and river.

"Ever hear of George Ade?" Hanlen asked.

"Sure," I replied. "He was a famous writer from these parts, back in the early part of this century. He was pals with Booth Tarkington."

"Booth who?"

"Don't tell me you never heard of Booth Tarkington."

"Any relation to Fran Tarkenton?"

"Not spelled the same. No, Ade, Tarkington and the poet James Whitcomb Riley were nationally known writers. Together they constituted what is referred to as Indiana's golden age of literature."

"I didn't know Indiana had a golden age of anything, except maybe basketball," Hanlen said. "Only reason I heard of Ade was 'cause he gave a lot of money to Purdue. The football stadium is named after him. What books did he write?"

"I can't give you a specific title," I answered, "but I believe he was known for writing about the little man."

"Midgets?"

"I don't think they like being referred to as midgets," I said. "No, 'little' meaning the common, ordinary folk. Humorous stories about their struggles to adapt to rapidly changing times. Guess the stuff he wrote didn't hold up too well. Not many people have heard of him."

"Yeah, well, he must have done well for himself to build this place," Hanlen observed, as we strolled near the house. "Guessing he built the golf club too."

"Ade was a millionaire. Friend of a few U.S. Presidents. And his sister was married to the governor of Indiana. Of course, he might not have been too proud of that. His brother-in-law was the only Indiana governor to serve time in prison. I think our neighbors in Illinois got us beat on that, two to one."

"Yeah, Walker was a disappointment," Hanlen said. "He was a Korean vet."

"I understand Ade liked to throw lavish parties for his friends. Maybe that's why he built this place," I said. "One other thing. You know who Orson Welles was?"

"The fat guy who said we will sell no wine before its time." Hanlen replied.

I smiled at his description of Welles.

"Poor Welles," I said. "Painful to see the man who made *Citizen Kane* reduced to uttering lines like that. By the way, his full name was George Orson Welles. Ade claimed that Welles was named after him and a friend of his named Orson. Apparently, they met Welles' parents on a ship somewhere in the Caribbean. Welles' pregnant mother was so taken with them she decided to name her son George Orson."

Hanlen shook his head. "I'll give you this, Logan," he said. "You're a fountain of useless information."

"Thanks, I appreciate that," I said. "Oh, circling back, Welles later made a movie out of Booth Tarkington's novel *The Magnificent Ambersons*, about an Indianapolis family. The studio execs cut the hell out of it, which didn't make Welles so happy. You should watch it sometime. Cut or not, it's considered a classic. You said you like black and white movies."

"War movies. By the way, where was Ade's wife?"

"When?"

"On the ship, when he met the parents of Orson Welles. You said he was with a friend."

"I don't think he was ever married," I said.

"Huh," Hanlen responded.

"Huh, what?"

"A bachelor who writes Broadway musicals, goes on cruises with a male friend, and likes to throw fancy parties," Hanlen said. "What do you make of that?"

"Not sure. Why?"

"Do the math, and you might think Ade was light in his loafers," Hanlen said.

"So?"

"Nothing, except it supports another theory of mine."

"I can't wait to hear this one," I said.

"You might agree with me that there are those in this country who think that the folks who live in these small rural towns are all ignorant, intolerant hicks."

"That's the theory?" I asked.

"No, it supports my theory."

"Which is?"

"Well, here's George, maybe a little different, maybe not. Brook is a small town, and I'm guessing if he is different, people are aware of it. Yet he feels comfortable enough that he builds his dream home here."

"I'm not with you," I said. "He was from Brook. He liked it and wanted to live here."

"My theory is that the only thing people out here are intolerant of is people from some big city telling them how intolerant they are."

"Got it," I said. "Is imparting that bit of wisdom the reason we drove over here?"

"No, I want you to meet someone. She's in this nursing home here," Hanlen said, pointing at the more modern structure on the other side of the parking lot.

"This used to be the Newton County Hospital. Ade gave the county a lot of the money to build it. It closed a while back, and now it's a nursing home."

"It must have been a small hospital," I observed.

"It's a small county."

"Who are we here to see?" I asked.

"The grandmother of the Musick girl. Her name is Virginia Musick."

"How'd you know she was here?"

"Ellen mentioned it once," he said. "I hope she's still alive."

"And why do we want to talk to her"

"It came out in Bank's investigation that Debbie was very fond of her grandmother. Visited her a couple times a month. Sometimes stayed with her. That was the reason the family first got worried. The grandmother called and asked why she hadn't come by. Apparently, Debbie had called her and said she was going to stop by over the weekend, but never did."

I thought about that.

"When did the grandmother get the call?" I asked.

"Friday evening, I think." He paused. "Come to think of it, I seem to recall Debbie's parents were out Friday night, and then out with Ellen Saturday morning, so the grandmother might have been the last family to talk to Debbie."

"Do we know if Ellen gave the grandmother a specific time when she was coming by?"

"That I don't know," Hanlen replied. "Banks interviewed the grandmother. Other than that, she talked to Debbie on Friday, not sure he noted any other information about the conversation. Why?"

"If Debbie told the grandmother Saturday, as opposed to Sunday, or Monday, since Monday was a holiday, that might mean something," I said.

"Like what?"

"That Debbie was expecting to be returning from the lake Saturday."

Hanlen frowned. "We already know the girls were expecting to be back the same day."

"We do? How about if they were staging their own disappearance?"

"Not sure I ever bought into that one," Hanlen said, "but I can't see a young girl lying to her grandmother."

"I agree. That's exactly my point," I said. "And how about this guy with the boat that the girls got on? If you assume that they wouldn't jump on a boat with a stranger, it may mean the girls knew him. Maybe even met him at the lake before."

"How you figure that?"

"I tell my grandmother I'll be by Saturday evening. I tell her this because I've done it before. Met this guy at the lake, taken a boat ride, then headed back in time to go see grandma."

"I'm not sure what you're getting at," Hanlen said.

"Who knows, maybe for some reason I'm not too keen about my folks knowing about the boat guy, so I tell them I'm going to the lake and then to grandma's. That way they don't ask any questions. Where was the grandmother living back then?"

"Somewhere east of Kankakee, I think. Near the state line," Hanlen said.

I figured it was a little over an hour from the Dunes to Kankakee. Debbie could have easily spent most of day at the beach and made it to the grandmothers by evening.

"Do you think the grandmother will remember something from twenty years ago?" I asked. "If she's alive, that is."

Hanlen thought about it. "No, probably not. In fact, since she's got to be pushing 90, she may not remember anything at all. But since she was the last family to talk to Debbie, I thought it might be worth talking to her. We were heading down this way anyhow."

chapter 9

MY FATHER SPENT THE LAST FEW MONTHS OF HIS LIFE in a nursing home. When we visited there was always the smell of bleach or disinfectant, which concealed --but not completely—an odor of human waste. The place was always clean, yet there was always that smell. That sad familiar odor greeted me when we entered the Ade Facility.

Hanlen had the same thought. "These places all smell the same," he said.

We walked into a lobby, where a thin woman who looked to be in her mid-fifties was sitting behind a desk on the far side. Two hard plastic chairs were in front of the desk. A couple worn upholstered chairs, a wooden end table, and a large potted artificial tree were on the other side of the room. The woman watched us impassively as we approached. She wore round wire rimmed glasses which gave her an owlish appearance, and when I got close, I saw her handwritten name tag, 'Joan K.'

"May I help you?" Joan asked, in a cautious voice. We were in a small facility in the middle of nowhere. She probably saw mostly the same people coming and going. Yet here we were, two strange men, one of whom could be described as hulking. I would have been wary too.

"Good afternoon, Joan," Hanlen said, cheerfully, as if greeting an old friend. "We're here to see Virginia Musick."

Joan considered that. "Are you family members?"

"Not exactly," Hanlen answered. "But we are friends of the family."

"May I ask which family member?" Joan said, curiosity now with the caution.

"I'm a friend of Ellen Musick, Betty's granddaughter," Hanlen replied, confidently.

"I see," Joan replied. She hesitated a second, then pushed a clipboard over the desk and asked us to sign in. While we did, she picked up the phone. Whoever she tried to call didn't answer. She frowned, told us to have a seat and said she would be right back with the nursing supervisor. Joan disappeared behind a double set of doors to the side of the desk.

"Do you think Joan volunteers here, or they pay her?" Hanlen asked after she was gone.

"I hope they pay her something," I said. "Can't be a whole lot of fun sitting here all day. Wonder if you ever get used to the smell."

"I was thinking that myself."

About five minutes went by before Joan returned. She was with a short rotund woman who was wearing turquoise green scrubs. She looked to be in the vicinity of 40 years old but could have been five years either way. I noticed some streaks of grey in her ginger hair, and she had some pronounced worry lines on her forehead, yet she bounced into the room with some noticeable energy. She came along with a strong cigarette smell and a harried yet bemused look on her face. The kind of look someone might have who saw a lot of woe on a daily basis but managed to keep a sense of humor. Her printed badge identified her as "Rhonda H. RN."

"Rhonda, these men are here to see Ginny," Joan said.

Rhonda gave us a half nod and smile of greeting.

"Do I know you?" she asked Hanlen, squinting up at him, brow wrinkled. "You look familiar."

"I'm not sure we've met," Hanlen said, smiling. "I usually don't forget pretty faces."

She smiled back. "Ah, a charmer."

Then a look of recognition.

"Now I know you. The beard threw me. You're the Prairie County sheriff or used to be. Bill Hanlen, isn't it? My husband worked for you for a while."

"One of my deputies? What was his name?"

"Roy Hubbard. I'm his wife Rhonda."

I vaguely remembered Hubbard, and that there was something about him that I didn't like.

"Sure, I remember Roy," Hanlen said. "He was a good man . . . hated to lose him. Does he still work for Newton County?"

"No, Roy got on with the police department in Rensselaer a while back. He's deputy chief there."

"Well, good for him," Hanlen said. "Please tell him I said hello."

"I will when I see him. We're separated right now," she said, matter-of-factly.

"Sorry to hear that," Hanlen replied.

"Thanks, but not needed. We'll work it out. We've been down the road before."

Hanlen glanced over at me.

"This is my associate, Logan Wells." He looked at his watch. "Rhonda, we know you're busy. We would like to have a word with Virginia Musick."

Rhonda's brow wrinkled again. "May I ask what this is about? Joan said you mentioned Ellen, Ginny's granddaughter. Does this have something to do with Ellen? Is she all right?"

"No," Hanlen replied. "Sorry if there was any confusion. Not sure if you were aware, Rhonda, but, twenty years ago, Ginny's other granddaughter disappeared, along with two other young women, from the Dunes State Park."

"I did know that. How awful." Rhonda said. "Those poor girls. Her name was Debbie, wasn't it?"

"That's right," Hanlen said.

"And how sad for the families," Rhonda added.

"Yeah," agreed Hanlen. "Not sure how I would keep it together if one of my kids just vanished." He shook his head.

"To answer your question, we are reviewing some of our unsolved cases," he continued. "We aren't naïve enough to think we are going to solve this one, but we owe it to the families to take another look at the information we have. Make sure nothing was missed."

"I thought I read you retired," Rhonda said, with a slight note of suspicion.

"We're looking into the case on a semi-formal basis," Hanlen said quickly and confidently. "Unfortunately, the sheriff's department has their hands full with today's mayhem. They don't have much time to devote to something that happened over twenty years ago."

"I see," she said, not sounding entirely convinced. "But what does this have to do with Ginny?"

"She may have been one of the last family members Debbie talked to," Hanlen replied. "Ellen mentioned she was here. We just wanted to see if she remembers any of the conversation. Maybe there was something Debbie said to her that would help us. I know, it was twenty years ago, but it's worth a shot."

Rhonda frowned. "Not sure I would remember what I was doing twenty years ago. And I'm not eighty-five, either."

Hanlen's brow furrowed. "Is there a problem with us talking to her?" he asked.

"Not necessarily," Rhonda said, "but as you might expect, many of our residents suffer from varying degrees of dementia. Most of them love to have visitors, especially family, yet sometimes strangers provoke agitation and fear." She smiled, then added, "and that is something we do our best to discourage."

"Understood," Hanlen said. "Do you think we would upset Ginny?"

"Hard to say," Rhonda replied. "She's still sharp, but like most here, has her moments. I'm concerned about what might happen if someone shows up out of nowhere and asks her about her missing granddaughter. I really wish you had called first."

The chief's face conveyed that he didn't quite understand. I wasn't sure talking to an eighty-five year old woman about something that happened over twenty years ago was going to accomplish much, but I piped in.

"How about this, Rhonda," I said. "You talk with Ginny. Let her know who we are and that we would like her help with something related to Debbie. Maybe that will get her more curious than upset. The chief here is good with people. He can handle a little agitation. If she gets distraught, we'll be on our way."

Rhonda looked at me and then slightly nodded. "Ok. I think we can try it like that."

"Great," I said. "By the way, you said Ginny is still sharp. Can I ask why she is in here?"

"She fell and broke her hip two years ago. She underwent a couple surgeries, but the first one didn't take. She has bad osteoporosis. The second one was a replacement but there were complications. Ginny wasn't able to do much in the way of rehab, so here she is."

"Sorry to hear that," I said. "Will she ever be able to go home?"

Rhonda paused before she answered. "Not likely. She requires a level of care that would be difficult to provide in a home setting. Not to be depressing, but I think you would be surprised by how many people over seventy with hip fractures pass away within a couple years. Losing your mobility is not a good thing."

She added, "I guess the moral is, don't get old, and if you do, don't fall and break your hip. I'll go and speak with Ginny. Be right back."

The phone rang at Joan's desk. We moved over to the other side of the room.

"Once Rhonda told me who her husband was, I thought maybe she would give me a hard time," Hanlen said.

"How's that?"

"I said her husband was a good man. I lied. I was either going to fire Hubbard or he was going to resign. He resigned. Maybe him losing his job didn't put him in wife's good graces."

"I knew there was something about the guy I didn't like. He seemed kind of sleazy."

"He had a wandering eye and a dirty mouth. A couple of my female dispatchers complained about him."

"Maybe that explains why they're separated," I said.

"Yeah, she doesn't look like the type that would put up with that sort of thing. Course, he added reflectively, "it looks like Rhonda might have put on some weight. Maybe Roy wasn't too enthusiastic about performing his marital duties."

I smiled when he said that. "I remember Hubbard, Chief. He wasn't exactly Burt Reynolds either."

After about fifteen minutes, Rhonda was back.

"Sorry it took so long, but when Ginny found out she was having visitors, she insisted on putting on makeup," she said, smiling. "Since it's a nice day, we are going to bring her out to the patio. She loves being outside. Right this way."

We went through the double doors and into a short hallway with offices on both sides. The hallway dead-ended into another longer one which ran perpendicular to the first and seemed to be where the patient rooms were. There were half a dozen people out in the hall, all elderly women in wheelchairs, except for an older gentleman who was leaning on a walker. Despite it being late May, he was wearing a red plaid flannel shirt. When we passed through, Rhonda stopped to have a word with another woman wearing scrubs. As we paused, the man on the walker made a beeline for me, covering the twenty feet that separated us faster than I would have thought possible. He grabbed my sleeve.

"Buddy, can you get me out of this place?" He said, then lowered his voice. "The people here are trying to kill me."

I looked down at his hand on my arm, then down the hall.

"You mean them?" I asked, nodding toward the old women in wheelchairs.

At that, he looked over at Rhonda and her associate, who were both looking at us. I had the feeling the old guy wanted to say "no, you idiot, them!" but since they were looking at him, he just rolled his eyes and nodded his head in their direction. I laughed.

Rhonda stepped over and gently disengaged the man's hand from my sleeve. She put her arm around him.

"Nobody here wants to kill you, Red," she said, in a practiced tranquil tone. "We only want to help you. Why don't we go back to your room and get ready for snack-time. I heard the cook has made some cupcakes for Memorial Day."

"My ass," Red muttered, but when Rhonda passed him off to the other woman in scrubs, he went with her without further complaint.

Rhonda shrugged, and we continued to an alcove at the end of the first hallway, on the other side of which was a glass door. She punched a number into a reader on the wall, there was a click, and she pushed the door open to a small brick patio outside with several white wicker chairs. The patio overlooked the surprisingly substantial, well-landscaped grounds behind the facility. An asphalt path led from the patio about thirty feet down a small slope, where the path split to go around a large four-tier stone fountain, with a pool at the base. The pool was surrounded by colorful flowers in large terra-cotta pots, and a couple benches. Somebody had put a lot of effort into making the place tranquil and peaceful.

"I wish my back yard looked like this," Hanlen said, admiring the view.

"Some of the Ade estate went into a trust to preserve both properties, the house and the hospital," Rhonda said. "We have volunteers who maintain the grounds. Unfortunately, everyone is getting old. Not sure what will happen when they're gone."

There was another click and the same woman in scrubs was pushing a wheelchair out onto the patio. The woman in it looked just like the women I had seen in the hallway: thinning white hair, glasses, hunched over. She wore lipstick and rouge, which had been overdone a bit, giving her face a slightly comical appearance. Even though the temperature was in the seventies she had a blanket around her.

"You aren't the man I spoke to before." She said, confused, looking up at both of us, then locking in on Hanlen.

"Mrs. Musick, my name's Bill Hanlen," he said. "I was the sheriff of Prairie County for many years. This is my associate Logan Wells," gesturing toward me. Then he stooped to one knee, so he was eye to eye with her.

"Years ago, you may have spoken to the police chief of Glenwood, Illinois, a fella by the name of Mason Banks, about your granddaughter, Debbie."

She thought about that.

"Yes, that was him," she said, nodding, pleased that she had recalled. "I used to work in a bank, so I remember his name. Banks." Then she frowned. "But it wasn't years ago. It was just a couple months ago. I think something happened to him after I talked with him."

Hanlen glanced up at Rhonda, who shrugged.

"Chief Banks was in an accident," Hanlen said. "There was a fire, and Chief Banks was . . ."

"Injured, but now he's ok." I said, interrupting Hanlen. He gave me a confused look.

"I'm glad to hear that. He seemed like a nice man," Ginny said.

Hanlen continued, "Yes ma'am. We were wondering if we might talk to you a little about Debbie. Probably ask some of the things Chief Banks asked you. Would that be all right?"

"Of course," she replied. "But poor Debbie was lost a long time ago. I'm not sure what I can remember."

"Call me Bill, please. I'm sure you will do fine." He stood up and pulled one of the wicker chairs over by Ginny's wheelchair and motioned for me to do the same. The aide went back into the building. Rhonda said she would be down in the garden.

"May I call you Ginny?" Hanlen asked after we were settled.

"Of course," she replied.

"I understand you and Debbie were close," Hanlen said.

"Very close," she said. "The first grandchild is always special. She was such a sweet girl. I still can't believe she's gone. It was all so horrible." She started to tear up.

"I'm sorry," she said, pulling a Kleenex from her blouse sleeve, and dabbing her eyes.

Uh-oh, I thought. Thirty seconds into this and we already have her in tears.

"I'm sorry for having to bring back bad memories," Hanlen said, reaching over and touching her lightly on the arm.

"Ginny, how often did Debbie come and visit you?" I asked, glancing down at Rhonda, relieved that she wasn't looking our way.

"She was such a sweet girl," Ginny repeated. "Of course, when she was small, she would always come along when our daughter and son-in-law came to see us. That was when my husband and I had a place in Kankakee. The town hadn't started going downhill. I have some friends that still live there that visit me. They say it's terrible what happened."

Kankakee was a city about the same size as Prairie Stop located an hour south of downtown Chicago on I-57. It had been named after the river which bisected it, which in turn was the English pronunciation of the Native American name for the river. Like Prairie Stop, Kankakee was the county seat. It had once been a vibrant community, distinguished by having not one, but two homes designed by Frank Lloyd Wright. Unlike Prairie Stop, Kankakee had seen a decline in its fortunes over the last twenty years. Several large factories had shut during economic downturns in the seventies and eighties. As jobs were lost, property values declined, and homes were taken over by less stable elements. Considering it wasn't that large of a town, the city had even developed a gang problem.

"They got a lot of nice golf courses there," Hanlen mentioned.

I gave him a look. He shrugged.

"You were saying about Debbie visiting you?" I asked.

"Yes," Ginny continued, "later when she started driving, she came by herself. I didn't care for her to be out on the highway by herself, but she said it didn't bother her. She would visit a couple times a month. She kept doing that, even when we decided to move to the country. We got a place a few miles northeast of Kankakee. That was my husband's idea, not mine. I wouldn't have moved, even if there was trouble in Kankakee." She added, "I'm a city girl."

"Did you ever have occasion to meet any of Debbie's friends?" I asked.

"A few of them. The place we bought in the country had property and a barn. The people who sold it to us had an older horse, a mare, that they couldn't take with them. My husband wanted to keep it. I didn't, but I changed my mind when he said Debbie would ride it. Debbie loved horses. Sometimes she would bring a friend."

"Was one of her friends named Janet?" I asked.

She thought about that. "That sounds right. She loved horses like Debbie did."

"Debbie had her own horse later, right?"

"Yes. I wasn't happy about that," Ginny said, frowning. "She was going to high school and had no business taking care of a horse. Her father said he would buy it for her if she made straight A's for a semester, and of course she did. They kept it here for a while, but it was too far away, so they took it to a stable near Glenwood. That's where they lived."

"Did Debbie ever have occasion to talk about the stable in Glenwood?" I asked.

Ginny gave me a curious look. "In what way?"

"Whether she liked the place, the people that worked there, any problems with them taking care of her horse, that sort of thing," I said.

Ginny hesitated before answering. "She enjoyed going to the stable, but I don't think she cared for the owner. I don't remember his name. I might if you said it. I think he made her uncomfortable. George, my husband, thought the man had been in trouble with the law."

"Does the name Luther Brame ring a bell?"

"That sounds familiar," Ginny said, "but I can't say for sure."

"What about him made her uncomfortable?

"I know he was an older man," she said. "From the way Debbie talked about him, I got the feeling he liked the young girls who boarded horses at his stable. But I don't think it was in a fatherly way," she paused and lowered her voice.

"We used to call his type a lecher."

"But she didn't say anything specifically he did that made her uncomfortable?"

"No," Ginny replied. "I have a feeling she was afraid I might tell her parents if she did."

"Did they ever express concern to you about Debbie being at the stable?"

"No," Ginny said. "George said something once to our son-in-law about the man who ran the place, about his trouble with the law, but nothing came of it. Debbie's parents were busy people. They both worked. I think they were happy she had something to do with her free time, instead of running around after boys."

I was glad she mentioned boys. "Did Debbie have a boyfriend?" I asked.

"She dated, but I don't know that there was anyone special. Debbie was on the shy side. She spent a lot of time at the stable, I think." Ginny said, then paused. "I just remembered something about the man who owned the stables."

"What's that?" Hanlen asked.

"I know he took them places that they had no business going. When she was here with her friend once, I overheard them talking about being out at a nightclub with him. I should have said something but kept my mouth shut."

"Anything else you can think of about him?" I asked.

Ginny's brow furrowed. "I remember Debbie was here once and she was wearing a gold locket. It had her initials on it. It didn't look to be the inexpensive type a young girl might wear. It was right after her birthday, so I assume it was a birthday present. I asked who gave it to her, and she said it was a present from her parents. I was talking to her mother later and complimented her on the locket. She didn't know what I was talking about."

"You thought maybe she got it from the owner of the stable," I said.

"Yes."

"Do you know if she wore the locket all the time?" I asked.

She thought about that. "I'm not sure."

"Ok." I said. "I want to talk to you about the day before Debbie went missing. You told Chief Banks that Debbie called you Friday night before she went to Lake Michigan. It's been a long time, but can you recall exactly what she said to you?"

"Her exact words? No," she said. "As you said, it's been a long time. I know she told me that she and two of her friends were going to the lake on Saturday, and that she hoped to see me Saturday evening and would stay the night. She had done that before. I asked her about dinner, but she said not to worry about it."

Her answer made me pause. "You just said 'before,'" I said. "Did you mean go to the Dunes or come by in the evening and stay overnight with you?"

"Why, both. She had gone to the Dunes the weekend before and then come by to visit us in the evening. She stayed the night. I remember because she was a little sunburned. But, of course, she never came by the week after. That's why I called her parents."

"Were Debbie's parents concerned?"

"I didn't call them Saturday night," Ginny said. "I thought Debbie had just changed her mind about visiting. But they got very upset when I talked to them on Sunday afternoon and told them Debbie wasn't with me. That's when they started calling around to try and find her."

"And they eventually called the police?"

"Yes," she replied.

"Just a few more questions, Ginny," I said. "You've been a great help. Do you remember about what time Debbie called Friday evening?"

"Well, I know it was after dinner sometime," she said.

"When you talked to her, did she sound pre-occupied or anxious about anything?"

"Not that I remember," she said. "We didn't talk long."

"Did she happen to mention anything about meeting someone at the park?"

"No, but I guess she could have been going boating again."

"Boating?"

"Yes. She said they met a nice young man with a boat at the lake the week before."

Hanlen and I looked at each other.

"She say anything about this young man with the boat, like his name, what he looked like, anything like that?" Hanlen asked.

"No, she didn't say much about him," Ginny replied. "She said they met him on the beach and took a short ride on his motorboat. He apparently told them he might be back next week if they wanted to do it again."

"Ginny," I said, "when you talked to Chief Banks, you told him about this young man, right?"

"Of course," she said, a tone of indignation in her voice.

"I'm sorry," I said. "I didn't mean to infer anything. It's just that the girls were apparently seen, by at least a couple witnesses, on the day they went missing, getting on a boat with a man, or men."

"Well of course I know that. It was in the newspapers at the time. But when I told Chief Banks about this young man with the boat, he said they didn't think this had anything to do with Debbie's disappearance."

chapter 10

"WHAT DO YOU MAKE OF THAT?" I asked Hanlen, as we headed back toward 41.

"I hope I'm as sharp as Ginny when I'm eighty-five," Hanlen said. "Course, I don't think I could take being cooped up in a place like that, in a wheelchair."

"Right. I mean why do you figure Banks told Ginny the guy in the boat had nothing to do with the girls' disappearance? And why did he apparently not let anyone else know about this guy from the week before?"

"To the first," he said, "at the time there was nothing to prove that the guy in the boat had anything to do with the girls vanishing. I mean, it seems obvious now, but there were a few who claimed they saw the girls on the beach *after* the guy on the boat picked them up."

"Ok, but why didn't Banks mention that the girls may have seen this guy the week before?"

Hanlen scratched his beard. "That is mighty peculiar. He could have just forgot. Or maybe it was in his file that went missing. One thing I know for sure is we aren't going to be able to ask Banks about it."

"Maybe," I said.

"Maybe what? You going to arrange a séance with Banks?"

"Ginny said she spoke with Banks a couple months ago."

Hanlen glanced over at me. "I said she was sharp for eighty-five," he said. "But even sharp old folks get confused with dates and time. My grandfather, in the last year of his life, which was 1965, thought Herbert Hoover was still president. Hoover wasn't even alive then."

"Just seems funny that you got the mysterious note with the locket a few months ago, and that Ginny says she talked to Banks a couple months ago."

"Keep it up, and I'm going to take back what I said about you being a good detective," Hanlen said. "Banks has been dead for twenty years. The old lady just got confused. By the way, how about the locket?"

"Doesn't mean it's the same one you got," I said.

"Well, the odds are better on that than Banks still being alive."

We got back on 41 south and drove about twenty miles when we came upon a short caravan of National Guard vehicles heading the opposite way. The military vehicles seemed incongruous amid the serene Indiana farm fields.

"Probably heading from the armory in Terre Haute," Hanlen observed. "Too bad they caught duty on a holiday. Wonder where they're going."

"Maybe Governor Bayh is trying to intimidate Michigan," I said. "Probably trying to muscle in on the tart cherry crop."

"I'm still scratching my head over how his dad could have lost to Quayle," Hanlen said, "He was a great man. I knew him in college."

Birch Bayh was a Purdue graduate and popular Indian senator for three terms, until he surprisingly lost to future Vice President Dan Quayle.

"It was a Republican landslide that year with Reagan," I said. "Besides, Quayle wasn't that bad. I saw him walking in the Pumpkin Parade once."

The Pumpkin Festival in September was a big deal in Prairie Stop, and in an election year just about every politician looking for votes in Prairie County walked in the festival's parade. It wasn't as easy as it might sound. The route was over two miles long and if you caught a warm morning in early September, you could be sweating when done. Ask any of the kids who marched in their heavy band uniforms.

"I remember that," Hanlen said. "It was the year Larry Csonka was the grand marshal. He sat in the back of a Cadillac convertible, and I swear the front end of that thing was tilted a foot off the ground. What a tank that guy was."

We were a couple minutes past the military convoy, and Hanlen glanced over at me.

"You never told me why you dropped out of the ROTC."

"I didn't say I dropped out," I said. "I said the army and I parted ways."

"Same difference."

"If I tell you, will you slow down?"

He eased off the gas. I breathed a small sigh of relief.

"I don't know how they do it now," I said, "but back when I was in the ROTC, you weren't really committed to anything until your junior year. Then they asked you to sign a commitment letter and pass a fitness test. I had a problem with the latter."

"Mental deficiency of some kind, I'm guessing," Hanlen said.

"I would have thought that too, but no, it was just physical fitness. And it was my knee. Ever tell you I used to play football?"

"You continue to astound, Logan," Hanlen said. "How long?"

"Three years in high school. I didn't play my senior year. My folks thought I needed to focus more on my grades. 'Course that was the year Prairie Stop won the state championship."

"That was a damn good team. What position?"

"Defensive back, safety, mainly. I also returned punts and kickoffs," I said. "Which brings me to my knee story. I told you I went to Wallace College."

"You played ball at Wallace?"

"Not exactly. I decided my football days were over when I got there and took a stroll over by football practice. There wasn't anything small college about the size of the guys I saw. I decided to try cross-country instead. Since it was an all-male school, you had to do something, or you'd go nuts. I did that for a couple years, then, in my junior year, and over a period of a few weeks, the Wallace football team lost most of its defensive backs. Injuries and such."

"And you got drafted to help out?"

"Yeah," I replied. "It's a small school, and it's not like they got a cache of football players. There was a guy from my high school who told the football coach about me. I was assured he'd only use me if he is really desperate, so I'm now on the team."

"How'd that go?" said Hanlen.

"Well, the last game of the year is coming up. The rivalry game against DeFord College. It's a big deal."

"Yeah," Hanlen said. "I went once with a friend whose kid went to DeFord. Must have been ten thousand people there. They brought in portable stands to hold them all."

"Some years they've even shown the game on TV," I said. "That year, due to all the injuries, Wallace had lost four times. DeFord is undefeated. We're at home and everybody is pumped. Me, I'm looking for a place to hide. I was watching DeFord during warmups. They had a receiver who was a small college All-American. He was twice my size and fast. There was no way I could cover him if I got put in the game."

"Always the optimist," Hanlen said. "What happened?"

"For reasons unknown," I continued, "since I hadn't been on the team that long, and had never practiced with the special teams, the coach sticks me in for the opening kickoff. I go running down the field, and out of nowhere a DeFord player nails me with a cut block."

"Ouch," Hanlen said.

"Ouch is right. My left knee felt like it exploded. Next thing I know I'm being carried off the field. The trainer takes one look at my knee and says I need to go to the hospital. I get there in an ambulance, they do an x-ray, ice my leg up and give me something for pain while they wait for the doctor. I fell asleep. When I come to, there's a guy yanking on my leg. I let out a yell, he stops what he's doing, and introduces himself as Dr. Peterson."

"Hopefully an orthopedic surgeon," Hanlen said.

"I found out later he was actually a well-known one, plus a Wallace graduate. First thing he tells me is that 'we' won the game. He must have thought I was George Gipp."

"What about the knee?"

"My kneecap was dislocated, but he says he was able to manipulate it back in place. Then he explains in an injury like mine there is usually cartilage damage, but you can't see that on an x-ray. It may get better on its own, or not. He says if he operates, no matter how good a job he does, there is going to be arthritis later."

"I've heard that," Hanlen said. "What did you do?"

"I did what the doctor suggested, which was give it six weeks to see if it improved. I left the hospital on crutches with a knee brace and some pain pills."

"I take it the knee got better," Hanlen said.

"Slowly and not in six weeks. I'm up at Purdue for ROTC early next year and the guy in charge notices me on crutches and asks what happened. When I tell him, he frowns and says, "that's a problem." He tells me I got training camp in the summer, and wonders if I'll be ready. He strongly suggests I have the surgery. I would have except there was an issue with my dad's insurance paying for it. They said the school should foot the bill."

"Figures."

"Yeah. In any case, I didn't have the surgery. That's when Uncle Sam and I parted ways. My military career, over before it started. Who knows? I could have been a general by now."

"I doubt that. I've known a couple generals, and trust me, you aren't general material. What about the knee?"

"It eventually got better by itself. I could even run, if I didn't need to turn quickly. After I got hit by the car, the first one that is, they had to operate on it and its basically ok. For now."

"The wonders of modern medicine."

I suddenly remembered what Kathy had said yesterday, about medical reasons for the girls' disappearance.

"One of the girls might have been pregnant," I said. "Was it the one who was married?"

"No, Betsy Collins was the only one who was married," Hanlen said. "She was also the oldest, by a year. She was twenty, the other two were nineteen. And it wasn't her, in fact, she may even have been having some marital trouble, according to some friends. Janet Blair was the one who may have been pregnant. The source again being some friends."

"What kind of marital troubles was the Collins girl having?"

"She complained her husband was spending too much time with his friends, and not her."

"Sounds like both husband and wife were spending a lot of time with their friends. Any idea where her husband is now?"

"Nope. We could ask the sister. Maybe she knows."

chapter 11

ROAD SIGNS ANNOUNCED WE WERE APPROACHING Kentland, at the intersection of 41 and U.S. 24. Highway 24 went east to Fort Wayne and Ohio, and west a short distance to the Illinois border, and then on to Peoria. A fast-food place and a gas station stood at the intersection, just past a small one-story motel. The motel was dilapidated, weeds sprouting in the parking lot and the siding chipped and rusting. A hand-written sign in front of the place advertised "HOURLY, DAILY, WEEKLY AND MONTHLY RATES AVAILABLE." A few of the letters had faded, noticeably the 'e' on the 'rates,' and at quick glance, the last words read 'MONTHLY RAT S AVAILABLE. The only activity appeared to be at the fast-food place, where half a dozen teenagers stood in the parking lot, drink cups in hand. I thought, due to a combination of paranoia and pretentiousness, we might get sullen stares as we drove by, but the teens took no notice of us, talking and laughing with each other. Guess their small-town life wasn't as boring, or we weren't as noteworthy as I thought.

An old man in a wheelchair sat a few feet away from the intersection. He had two small American flags attached to the back of the chair, and he was holding a piece of cardboard reading 'Vet Needs Help.' Hanlen barely slowed as he made the right onto 24, and the big rear wheels of the Bronco spun, throwing some gravel and a dust cloud up in the old man's direction. I glanced in the outside mirror and saw the old guy shake his fist angrily at our receding vehicle. I looked at Hanlen but he was oblivious to the distress he had caused his fellow vet. He gestured toward a few larger buildings about a quarter mile down a side street.

"That's downtown," he said. "The Newton County Courthouse is over there in case you were ever looking for it."

"I've been there a couple times," I said. "There used to be a good place to have lunch across the street."

"You're talking about Patsy's. Been closed for years now. Patsy hit the lottery and moved to Florida," he said.

"She hit the big prize?" I asked, mildly curious.

"Patsy's a he. Used to be a cook in the Navy," he said. "Nah, it was just a hundred grand. Still, probably the biggest news here for 20 years."

"Bigger than the Spilotro Brothers?"

"I should have said 'good' news," Hanlen replied.

"Guess they don't get much of that here."

"Yeah, other than the courthouse, there isn't too much to Kentland, or even Newton County. I bet they got the same number of people living here now as forty years ago. The population of Prairie County has tripled in that time."

"Yet some folks stayed," I observed.

"A lot of the people down this way are German. They're stubborn."

"Not to worry," I said. "The Chicago sprawl will eventually catch up to them."

We drove west on 24. Unlike 41, 24 was one lane in each direction. Like 41, it was flat and straight. Once out of Kentland, Hanlen accelerated. Soon we were back doing over eighty, and I cringed each time we approached the slower moving vehicles in our path. Hanlen passed them at his first, if not most prudent, opportunity. A couple miles outside of Kentland we came up quickly behind an elderly woman driving an Olds Cutlass. Hanlen passed her, but then had to cut quickly back into the right lane in front of her to avoid a pick-up coming fast in the other direction. He glanced in the rear-view mirror and grinned.

"What's so funny?" I asked.

"The old lady driving the Cutlass just flipped me off," he replied.

"You're making friends fast in Newton County, Chief."

"Just keep an eye out for County Road 12. We make a left there."

"These side roads all look the same to me," I replied.

"She said there will be a sign for the First Baptist Church. Reformed."

"Glad to hear they got reformed," I said. "Hey, you'll like this one. How come Baptists don't have sex standing up?"

"Watch it, Logan," Hanlen warned. "I got good friends who are Baptists."

"'Cause people will think they're dancing."

I didn't see the turn, but Hanlen did, at the last second. We made another hard turn and I thought we might wind up skidding off into a field. The Bronco held, but just barely and I banged into the passenger door.

"Sorry about that," Hanlen said.

County Road 12 was narrow, the asphalt worn and cracked. The farm fields on either side stretched for as far as the eye could see, and the houses we passed were few and far between. We were entering the heart of corn country. If you drew a line straight west to Nebraska and tacked on the three hundred miles both north and south of that line, that area would be where most of the corn in the world was grown. Not much was visible now in the fields other than some small green shoots. I knew nothing about farming but thought making a living off the land had to be arduous and subject to all sorts of vagaries, both natural and man-made. I couldn't see myself lasting long as a farmer.

As if sharing my thoughts, Hanlen said, "Can you see yourself living out here, off the land?"

"No," I replied. "But thank God there's some that can. Hard to believe we're only a couple hours from downtown Chicago. How about you?"

"I grew up on a dairy farm. It's a hard life. But you never have any trouble getting to sleep at night."

"Looks like this is it," he added, slowing down.

I didn't see a house, but a white wooden fence appeared on the left side of the road.

"She said she's got a white fence and a brick mailbox with a white horse on top," Hanlen explained.

The fence went on for a bit until we saw the mailbox, with a white horse figurine on top. As we turned into the asphalt drive, I saw the house, well shaded by a couple mature oaks and a large weeping willow. It was a large brick Victorian home. Two three story turrets flanked the main part of the house. The bricks were a pale yellow, with the wood trim, shutters and door painted a dark purple, giving the home a striking, almost fairy tale look. A wrap around porch, painted in darker yellow than the brick, with colorful flower baskets attached to the front of each support post, added to the effect. A woman was sitting on the porch.

"Nice place," Hanlen said, then as we got closer, added "she's got horses." He was looking at the small bright red barn about thirty yards to the right of the house, further back on the property. The area around the barn was enclosed, with more white wood fencing, and two horses grazed in the paddock. Both the barn and the house seemed in immaculate condition. The horses stared impassively at us as he pulled off onto a gravel area in front of the corral and we got out. I turned to him.

"Did you intend to mention our visit with the grandmother?" I asked.

"Hadn't thought about it. Is there a reason I shouldn't?"

"Probably not," I replied. "But if it's ok, let me bring that up."

Hanlen shrugged. "Whatever you say."

It was warmer here than in Prairie Stop, and a light breeze stirred the slender branches of the willow tree. The woman on the porch stood and stepped down into the yard as we approached. She was a slim five six and wore jeans and a blue button-down shirt untucked. She had light brown hair, medium length, pulled back behind her head. Large oval sunglasses covered her eyes, and if she had makeup on, it was minimal. I figured she was in her mid-thirties. The way she wore her hair, the lack of makeup, and her casual dress indicated she was more about function than appearance. I also noticed her resemblance to the pictures I had seen of her sister.

"Sheriff Hanlen," she said, smiling, as she approached. "Thanks for driving down on such short notice. It's good to finally meet you in person." She extended her hand, and Hanlen engulfed it gently with his massive one. I noticed a plain gold wedding band on her other hand.

"It's not Sheriff, anymore, Ellen. Call me Bill. This is the fellow I told you about, Logan Wells. He used to be an investigator with the Prairie County Prosecutor's Office," he said, adding, "and a pretty good one, too."

She turned toward me, at the same time removing her sunglasses. Her eyes were light grey, and even though she was smiling, I thought I could pick up a guarded sadness in them.

"I'm Ellen," she said. "It's a pleasure to meet you, Logan."

"Likewise." I gestured at the house. "Quite the place you have here."

"Thank you. Since it's nice out, I thought we could talk out on the porch," she suggested.

"Good idea," Hanlen replied. As we walked up the porch steps, he asked how many horses she had.

"Just the two," she replied. "It's not good to have just one. They are herd animals and don't do well without company. It might even be considered cruel to just have one."

"I've heard that sometimes a solo horse may bond with a dog or cat in lieu of another horse," said Hanlen.

"Yes, I think that happens. You know my sister loved horses. Debbie owned a horse, as a matter of fact."

"I remember that," Hanlen said. "I have a daughter who loves horses. We came close to buying one when she was young, but decided it was either that or save for college. We opted for college."

Ellen laughed. "A wise choice. Horses are expensive and high mainte-nance. Not like having a cat or dog."

"You probably have a dog or cat around here too," I said.

"Yes, to both, and plural to cats. My dog's inside. She loves company, but sometimes gets wound up around strangers. I didn't want her jumping all over you. The cats are likely in the barn, stalking something. Probably be a mouse on the doormat later."

There were four cushioned wicker chairs on the porch to the right of the front door, circled around a small wicker table with a pitcher of lem-onade and three glasses.

"Is this a working farm, Ellen?" I asked, as we sat down.

"Yes, but not by me. We rent most of our fields out to our neighbor, who does the actual farming. He's done ok some years, but farming is unpredictable. We also pay him to do some maintenance around the place. When you add everything up, most years we don't even break even."

That she said 'we' and 'our' after using the singular pronoun, along with the wedding band, made me curious.

"Will your husband be joining us, Ellen?" I asked, as we sat down.

"I hope not," she said, giving a wry smile, then a pause. "But there's that possibility."

Hanlen and I glanced at each other.

"My husband and I currently don't live together," Ellen said, pausing as if deciding to continue. "You could say we have a commuter relationship. It's relatively cordial. My husband is a commodities trader on the Chicago Mercantile Exchange. He's good at it and makes a nice living, but it's very stressful. He's been doing it since he got out of college. He had a physical some time back, and Steven's doctor told him if he kept up his lifestyle, he was looking at an early coronary. Shortly after that we decided to move here, although we kept our place in the city. This was my grandmother's home and, unfortunately, she had to go into a nursing facility. Did I mention that to you?" She said, questioning Hanlen. He nodded.

"Matter of fact, we stopped and talked to your grandmother on the way down here," I said. "The chief thought it might be useful."

Ellen seemed surprised by that, but then said, "And was it?"

"Some," I said. "By the way, she's seems to be doing good."

"I hope I'm doing that good when I'm her age," Hanlen said.

Ellen looked like she wanted to ask another question but instead said, "Well, I'm glad to hear that."

"You were saying, about your husband?" I asked.

"We were thinking we would transition to a life of gentleman farming, maybe start a family. It took Steven about six weekends down here before he decided the country life wasn't for him. He said the sound of the crickets at night was driving him nuts. He went back to Chicago, and I stayed here." She smiled, and added, "he shows up occasionally to harangue me about various things."

"Like what?" I asked.

"Logan," Hanlen interjected. He was going to add something, but Ellen interrupted him.

"Not to worry . . . my life is an open book," she said. "Mainly Steven harangues about when we are going to sell this place and I move back to the city. I don't know if that's going to happen. As I said, this was my grandmother's house and I have a lot of fond memories here. He also doesn't care for what he refers to as my unproductive obsession with finding out what happened to my sister."

She looked at her watch. "I thought he might be here today, since it's a holiday weekend, but I don't imagine he will be showing up now. I told him you were going to be here. Maybe he decided to stay away for that reason."

"Sorry I brought him up," I said.

"I hope I didn't give you the wrong impression," she said. "Steven isn't a bad guy. He's just under a lot of stress."

Back when I was in uniform, I wish I had a dollar for every time I heard that line or something like it from a woman who was mistreated by a husband or boyfriend yet chose not to leave him.

"Do you work, Ellen?" I asked.

"Yes, I'm a psychologist," she said, smiling. "And therefore, Steven is probably correct about my obsession with my sister. I should know, right?"

I thought about that for a second, wondering how thriving that particular occupation could be out in the middle of the rural area we were in.

As if reading my mind, she laughed and said, "I have a very specialized practice. I treat only depressed farmers."

"I grew up on a farm," Hanlen said. "I wouldn't imagine most farmers have time to be depressed."

"You're right," Ellen agreed. "Certainly not the ones who live around me. But on the other hand, farming is a stressful life. Maybe some of them could use counseling." Just then one of the horses snorted and she looked over at the paddock.

"No, I drive into Chicago a couple days a week and see clients there," she continued. "Occasionally I may stay with Steven if he is in a good mood. I also do some consulting work."

"Sounds like you keep busy," I said. "Why did you refer to yourself as obsessed with your sister? I wouldn't think calling the Chief up once or twice a year qualifies as an obsession."

Of course, sending him a locket and a note purporting to be from a girl missing for over twenty years would be different. My first read on Ellen Musick was that she wasn't the type to to send the locket to Hanlan.

"You're quite right, Logan," she said. "Still, I do think a lot about her."

"Why don't we talk about Debbie?" Hanlen interjected.

"Poor Debbie," Ellen said, her voice breaking slightly. "She's been gone for over twenty years, yet I think one day there will be a knock on the door and there she'll be."

"How much older was Debbie?" I asked.

"She was nineteen when she vanished. I was twelve."

"No other brothers and sisters?"

"No," Ellen replied. "My parents weren't exactly young when they got married, but they got married in a hurry, if you know what I mean."

"Debbie was unexpected?" I asked.

"I think so. I suppose it's odd that I never discussed it with my parents, at least my mother, but their anniversary and Debbie's birthday are only five months apart."

"What did your parents do?"

"My father was a pipefitter. My mother was a clerk at Marshall Fields. She wanted to make more of herself, so when Debbie went to kindergarten, she went back to school to become a nurse. She only went part-time, and it took her a while, but eventually she got her degree."

That might explain the gap of seven years between the children.

"She went to the nursing school at Michael Reese Hospital in Chicago," she added, "which is where she got her first job."

"That's off Lake Shore Drive, isn't it?"

"Yes," she replied, "although the nursing school closed about ten years ago. You know it?"

"My ex-wife worked there for a while, when she was first starting out, like your mom," I said. "Are your parents still living?"

"My mother is," Ellen replied. "As you might expect, my parents went into shock after Debbie vanished. After a few months went by, with no progress in finding her, the shock turned to grief and depression. What an awful time that was. My father couldn't handle it. He began drinking heavily. It got worse as the years went by. Coming back from a tavern one evening, about fifteen years ago, he ran into the back of a semi on I-80. He was killed instantly. Probably could be better described as suicide by vehicle."

"I'm sorry," I said.

"It sounds harsh, but it could have been worse. He could have hurt or killed someone else. For all purposes, he died a long time ago. Whoever took Debbie also took him."

"And your mother?" I asked.

"My mother is a very pragmatic woman. She eventually concluded there was nothing she could do to bring Debbie back, so she threw herself into her work. She is still at it, even though she's in her sixties. She even re-married after my father died. She and her husband live in southeast Wisconsin. Near Fort Atkinson, if you are familiar with that area."

"Does she work at the Memorial Hospital there?" Hanlen asked.

"Why, yes. You know it?"

"I used to live in Wisconsin and have family there," Hanlen said. "Fort Atkinson isn't far from where we lived. It reminds me some of Prairie Stop."

"Do you see your mother much?" I asked.

"Once in a while, she'll drive down here," Ellen said. "Usually on one of the lesser holidays. After she got married again, I guess you could say we drifted apart. Not sure if our experience with grief is a common one, but for my mother and me, it's an associative thing. When we are together, we are reminded about Debbie and my father, and we get sad. I don't like to think we avoid each other, but we avoid the sadness."

"I know," she added, with another wry smile, "avoidance isn't something a psychologist would recommend, so I'm not following my own advice. She does call me once a week. She started doing that after Steven and I started living apart. I think she worries about me being out here all alone."

"Tell us what Debbie was like," I said.

She paused. "It's amusing to me, that in the stories in the papers about Debbie's disappearance, she was almost always described as a 'quiet girl.' In fact, all three of them were described as quiet girls. It's almost as if being quiet somehow explains what happened to them."

"Newspaper reporters, for that matter, people in general, don't go for complexity or nuance," I said. "They prefer simple characterizations and explanations. I venture to say any young person who wasn't the prom queen or football star would be described as quiet. Doesn't mean it's true, just easier to absorb."

"I believe you're right," Ellen said. "And how about you, Logan?"

"I like simple explanations as much as anyone," I said. "But I've found that things aren't always how they seem. In fact, frequently just the opposite."

"Really," Ellen said, then surprised me by adding "give me an example."

"Sure," I said, "here's a mundane one. If you polled some pizza delivery guys as to where they got their largest tips, what would they say? The big homes in the rich part of town, as you might expect, or the smaller homes in the middle-class part of town?"

I looked over at Hanlen and he was frowning, obviously not caring for my rhetorical aside.

"That sounds like a trick question, but I will say the big homes," Ellen said.

"I think the majority would say the smaller homes, where working class people live. In fact, I bet most of them would say they seldom got a large tip from the owner of a fancy house."

"Why's that?"

"That's easy," I answered. "People of modest means who work hard for a living appreciate other people of modest means working hard. It's a value judgment."

"Are you saying rich and successful people don't work hard?" Ellen said. "My husband would be very offended by that."

"Not at all. I'm saying that the rich person's value judgment is that the effort of delivering a pizza isn't worth much," I said.

"We're getting off track here," Hanlen said.

"Right," I said. "I'm guessing if your sister was described as quiet in the newspaper, she was probably like a lot of young people, shy in the presence of strangers, but outgoing and sociable with her friends and family."

"That's an interesting theory you have," Ellen said. "And if my sister was the mousy type, it was certainly not around me. She was clever and funny and could always make me laugh."

"Did Debbie have a boyfriend?" I asked.

"She dated, but not a lot, and I don't remember anyone she was serious with. She spent a lot of time with Janet and Betsy. They all loved horses, especially Janet and Debbie."

"When did she get her horse?" I asked.

"Her sixteenth birthday. My mother had just started a new job and got a raise, as well as a bonus. That was how they were able to afford it."

"Where did she and her friends ride?"

Ellen looked at Hanlen. "He doesn't know?"

"He knows, but he still likes to ask the questions," Hanlen said. "Most detectives do that."

"They rode at different places, but their horses were kept at the Twilight Stable," she said. "It was not too far from where we lived. By the way, it's no longer in existence. It got turned into part of a subdivision years ago." She paused. "I'm sure you know who the owner of the stable was."

"Luther Brame," I said. "The Al Capone of the Chicago horse set, except maybe not as nice."

"From what I've heard about him, that's an apt description," Ellen said. Then, leaning forward in her seat, she added, earnestly, "I'm convinced he had something to do with Debbie's disappearance."

I returned her gaze for a couple seconds, then broke it off and poured myself some lemonade.

"I'll be candid with you, Ellen," I said. "I'm aware of the facts, such as they are, regarding the disappearance, and the various theories regarding same. Including the one that Brame was somehow involved. From what I know about him, he was capable of anything, but I'm not sure I see him involved in this. Why do you think he was?"

"I think something bad happened at the stable in the weeks before Debbie disappeared," she said. "I don't know what it was, but I'm sure it must have involved Brame. I think Debbie knew about it and was scared."

"But you don't have any idea what it was?" I asked.

"No, but I think someone hurt her. Probably as a warning to keep her quiet. Maybe she ignored the warning and Brame decided he needed to do something more drastic."

Hanlen and I looked at each other.

"Hurt her how?" Hanlen asked.

"One day she came home with a black eye and a red mark on her face. When my mother asked her what happened, she laughed and said Cherokee, that was her horse, got spooked in his stall and pushed her into the wall. I didn't think anything of it at the time, but now I wonder."

"Ok," I said. "Maybe she ran into the horse, maybe she ran into something else. But why do you think she was scared?"

"A few days before the Saturday they went to the lake, I was in bed, and she came in to say goodnight. She was upset. We had talked before about me going to the Dunes with her and her friends that weekend, but now she told me I couldn't go. I asked her why and she said it just wasn't a good idea, but that I could go another time. Again, in hindsight I think she knew something was going to happen and was scared, scared enough to tell me I couldn't go."

"No offense," I said, "but if my older brother was going somewhere with his friends, the last person he would want along, next to my dad, would be his little brother."

Ellen frowned.

"You said you knew the facts about Ellen's disappearance," she said, sharply. "If Brame wasn't involved, then what do you think happened?"

"I'm sorry, Ellen," I said. "If what I said sounded flip, it wasn't meant to be. I agree that nothing can be ruled out. It just doesn't seem plausible that Brame was involved."

"Him being dead doesn't help matters much," added Hanlen.

"Maybe he hired someone to do it," Ellen said, "and that person is still around."

"Could be," I said. "But as to what I think, even if Luther Brame was involved in some way, finding out how hinges on figuring out who this guy in the boat was. The boat your sister and the other girls were seen getting onto. It's curious that they couldn't find him at the time."

"We had investigators talk to every harbormaster from Chicago to Michigan City," Hanlen said. "They got reports from the Coast Guard on all accidents in Lake Michigan for the day in question, plus two weeks afterwards. There were even Civilian Air Patrol flights over the lake for a week or so. No boat matching the one the witness described was found."

"Did they talk to the area boat dealers?" Ellen asked.

Hanlen and I looked at each other.

"That's a good question," I said.

"I don't think so," Hanlen said. "Maybe if they had all the computer stuff they got now, it would have been easy to find it that way. But this was back in the sixties, remember."

"There might be an issue with the Coast Guard too," I said. "At least as far as the accident reporting goes."

"How so?" Ellen asked.

"The chief can correct me if I'm wrong," I said, "but unless the Coast Guard is actually involved in a rescue related to an accident, or they find out about it another way, it may go unreported."

"Logan is right," Hanlen agreed. "Boat owners are required to report any accident where there is a fatality or injury. The Coast Guard investigates those automatically. Boat operators are also required to self-report accidents where there is over a certain dollar amount of damage. But if no one reports it, and the Coast Guard wasn't called to the scene, who would know?"

"I can attest to that," Ellen said. "For years Steven had a cabin cruiser on Lake Michigan. He used it to entertain clients. Basically, the boat was for beer bacchanalias disguised as fishing outings. He wrote it all off as business expense. Once, Steven ran it up on jetty, causing considerable damage to the boat. Nobody got hurt, but I'm quite sure he didn't report it to the Coast Guard, but he did report it to his insurance company." She shook her head. "I made him get rid of the boat shortly after that."

"Interesting," I said. "I didn't think of that."

"Think of what?" Hanlen said.

"This guy with the boat at the lake that day. He knows everybody is looking for him and his boat. And if they find the boat, there probably is going to be some evidence on it as to what happened to the girls. So, what does he do?"

"He hides it?" Ellen said.

"He could hide it, paint it. Move it out of state. But, given the circumstances, I think he would want a permanent solution."

"He destroys it," Ellen said.

"That's what I would do, given the circumstances," I said, nodding. "And maybe to really cover his tracks, he files a claim with his insurance company that says the boat was destroyed *before* the day the girls disappeared. Plus, that way there is the added advantage of getting some money for it."

"Did anyone check on insurance claims made for boating accidents around that time?" Ellen asked.

"I can't say," Hanlen said. "But it seems to me checking with the harbor-masters and Coast Guard was thought sufficient. Not sure we are going to be able to track an accident from twenty years ago."

"Right," I said, "even on the chance the boat was destroyed, and an insurance claim filed, that leaves trying to track down a claim that's over twenty years old."

"I would think insurance companies keep records forever," Ellen said.

"I would think so to," I said. "But that doesn't mean they are going to drop everything and go rooting through old files just because two retired cops ask them to. They may even say their records aren't public."

We pondered that. Hanlen looked like he was about to say something when Ellen spoke.

"I may be able to help you," she said.

"How so?"

"One of my clients is an insurance broker in Chicago," she replied. "She's been doing it a long time. She is very successful, and I imagine has a lot of contacts. I bet she would know the right way to approach this. The inquiry to be made and the right people to ask."

"Wouldn't it be considered inappropriate to ask a client to do something like that?" I asked.

Ellen smiled. "Probably, but I helped her through a difficult divorce. She would be more than happy to help me if she could. In any case, let me worry about the ethical side of it."

"All right," I said. "Ask her to dig up what she can. It's a long shot, but if we could track down the boat and the owner, that would definitely be something useful."

"Then I'll call her. First thing tomorrow. She should be home." Ellen seemed excited to be doing something to find her sister.

"I just thought of something else," I said. "Ask her not to limit her search to boating accidents just on Lake Michigan."

"You want to include the other Great Lakes?" Ellen said, puzzled.

"No," I replied. "Northwest Indiana has a lot of small lakes. It would be good if she could include those in her search."

"That could be a lot of work," Hanlen said, doubtfully. I could tell he thought trying to find the boat or owner was a waste of time.

"I don't think so," I said. "We don't need a list of every boating accident that happened in Northwest Indiana in 1966. We are looking for a specific boat, a 20-foot runabout with a blue hull. That's how the witnesses described it. And the insurance claim would have been for something like a fire, explosion, or other accident where the boat in question was destroyed. She could limit the time period from June to August 1966."

"Got it. We'll see what she can find."

"Ellen, do you remember your parents talking to the police chief of Glenwood, a fellow by the name of Mason Banks?" I said.

"I remember him. He came to the house a couple times to talk to them," Ellen said.

"Were you in the room when he was there?"

"No," she replied. "My parents thought the conversation might upset me. In fact, I recall the last time he came to the house, they were the ones who were upset. They may have even told him not to come back. At least I didn't see him again."

"Have any idea why they were upset?"

"From some remarks I overheard them make later," she said, "I think he may have insinuated that Debbie and the others decided to run away due to their own personal problems and staged their disappearance."

"By the way, that's another theory I don't subscribe to." I said, "But do you have any idea what personal problems would cause Debbie or the other girls to run away? Other than possibly being afraid of Luther Brame?"

"None that I know of. Other than being quiet girls, of course," she said and smiled. "Debbie and Janet both seemed happy with their lives. I did read later that Betsy Collins was having marital troubles. I don't know if that's true or not."

"Ever have occasion to meet Betsy's husband?" Hanlen asked.

"No," Ellen replied. "Janet and Debbie were friends for a long time. Betsy was more Janet's friend. I'm not sure how they met, and I never met her husband."

There was a pause.

"Something happened to him," Ellen said. "Banks, I mean. Sometime after he came and talked to my parents."

"He died," Hanlen said. "In a farm accident."

"Now I remember. It happened not long after he interviewed Luther Brame," Ellen said. "Did anyone find that suspicious?"

"It wasn't right after," Hanlen corrected. "At least a few weeks later, as I recall."

"What kind of accident?" Ellen asked. "Was there an investigation?"

"An explosion," I said. "One of those accidentally on purpose ones."

Hanlen scowled. "There was an investigation, which concluded that it was an accident, and due to carelessness on Bank's part. That's how most accidents happen."

"Maybe Brame had something to do with it," Ellen said.

"Well, that's another question we won't be able to ask him about," Hanlen said.

"One other thing, Ellen," I said. "Did Debbie have any piece of jewelry she wore a lot? Maybe very fond of?"

"I don't remember anything in particular," she said. "Debbie wasn't much for wearing jewelry. Why do you ask?"

"Your grandmother mentioned a locket that Debbie wore," I said. "Maybe she didn't wear it around the house."

"I don't remember a locket."

"Ok, probably not important."

In the distance, we heard the noise of an engine. Due to the loud revving, I thought maybe it was a souped-up pickup truck. I was surprised when a Porsche convertible turned briskly into the front entrance, sped up the drive and skidded to an abrupt stop by Hanlen's Bronco, almost clipping both the Bronco and the corral fence. A big cloud of dust went into the air and the horses, startled, galloped to the other side of the paddock.

"You gentleman are in for a treat," Ellen said, after the Porsche came to a stop. "My husband has decided to pay us a visit."

chapter 12

"HE KNOWS HOW TO MAKE AN ENTRANCE," Hanlen said. "Wish he had hit my Bronco. I've been itching to get a new one."

"Steven thinks having an expensive sports car automatically makes him a good driver," Ellen said.

"He wouldn't be the first," I said. "What's Steve's last name?"

"Reinking. Just so you know, it's Steven; he doesn't care for being called Steve."

Steven Reinking was a big man. He wasn't as tall as Hanlen, by a few inches, but he wasn't as lean either and had a bit of a paunch. He looked to be over two hundred pounds easy. He had to peel himself out of the tight cockpit of the Porsche. Kathy always scoffed, 'mid-life crisis,' when we saw a man over a certain age in a small expensive sports car, especially if he was a big guy, and I guessed Reinking fit the mold.

Reinking was wearing tan khakis and a bright green polo shirt with a designer logo on the chest pocket. The green contrasted with his rather florid complexion, which might have been due to driving with the top down on a sunny day, or maybe a pre-drive beer or two. He wore a Cubs hat, and curly light brown hair tinged with gray was visible beneath the cap. Gold-rimmed aviator sunglasses completed the look. As he walked over to the porch, I decided he had the confident stride of a successful man. Of course, I knew what he did for a living and saw the type of car he was driving. I also would have said he looked a lot older than Ellen, and even older than me.

"Hope I'm not interrupting a group therapy session," he said, smiling, as he stepped up onto the porch. He had taken a brown bag out of the car with him, which looked like it contained a six pack. He removed his sunglasses, revealing dark brown eyes.

'I've asked you before not to scare the horses," Ellen said, reproachingly.

"Oh, they're fine. Probably could use the excitement," her husband replied.

"I'm surprised you're here. I wasn't expecting you." Ellen said, but got up and gave her husband a brief and perfunctory hug and kiss.

"I surprised myself," he replied. "I did some work on the car yesterday and wanted to see how it was running. Hope you don't mind me barging in on you." He set the bag down on the table. There was the clink of bottles.

"I'm guessing you are the celebrated Sheriff Hanlen of Prairie County, Indiana" he said, nodding to Hanlen. "I'm Ellen's husband, Steven Reinking."

"Former sheriff, now retired," Hanlen said, rising, and they shook hands. I imagine that was a real bone cruncher. "Glad to meet you, Steven, but I think the only time I was celebrated was when I stepped down."

He glanced over at me.

"This here's my associate, Logan Wells."

I did a quick rise and shake, careful not to let his big paw get a good grip on mine, and we all sat down.

"Is that a 930 you're driving?" I asked.

"Yep."

"1980 model?"

"No, it's a '79," he replied. "They didn't sell the 930 in the U.S. in the early eighties due to emissions regs. You know something about cars, Logan?"

"Only how to wreck them," Hanlen said.

Reinking laughed. "That's probably cheaper than trying to maintain them."

"You work on it yourself?" Hanlen asked.

"If and when I can. My father was old school. He used to say, 'how can you drive something if you don't know how it works.'"

"Sounds like something my dad would say," Hanlen commented.

"To be honest, I leave the complicated stuff to the mechanics at the dealer, but I like to tinker. Unfortunately, I still have to buy the parts. Just about everything on a Porsche is expensive."

There was a pause.

"Like I said, I hope I'm not interrupting anything," Reinking said.

"I think we were about wrapping it up," I said, looking at Hanlen

"Good. In that case, who wants a beer?" Reinking reached for the bag and pulled out a six pack of brown bottles. Hanlen looked at the bottles with curiosity, Ellen with some distaste.

"What's a Honkers?" Hanlen asked. "Never heard of it."

"It's made by Goose Island," Reinking said, "a small brewery that opened in town last year."

"Never heard of it," Hanlen said.

"Try one. I'd be interested to know what you think." Reinking handed him and me a bottle.

"I think these small breweries are onto something," he added. "Might be a good investment opportunity down the road. Remember I said that."

He reached back into the bag and pulled out another bottle.

"I brought you a wine cooler," he said, extending it to Ellen.

She didn't reach for it. "Thanks, Steven, but I think I'll pass for now."

"Don't be a killjoy, Ellen," he said. He had a smile on his face, but I thought I detected a testy note to his voice.

"I'm going to check on the dog. I'll be back in a bit," Ellen said. We watched her walk in the house.

After she was gone, Reinking frowned. "You guys married?"

"Coming on 40 years," Hanlen said.

"Divorced," I said.

"I might be joining you soon," he said, sighing. "You'd think a psychologist would let me know what is on her mind, and what I was doing that ticked her off," he said.

"Don't take this the wrong way," Hanlen said, "but she's still a woman. They don't always say what's on their mind."

"That's a little chauvinistic, don't you think Chief?" I said.

"Even if it is, doesn't mean it's not true," Reinking said, and took a pull of his beer.

"I've heard a lot about you," Reinking said to Hanlen. "You played ball at Purdue, right?"

"Yep," Hanlen replied. "Guard, mainly. I was the punter for a while too."

"I heard you were an All-American," Reinking said.

"No, not true," Hanlen said, smiling. "That was a rumor started by a reporter. He liked to refer to me as a former All-America. He never checked his source, and I didn't bother to correct him. I was on a couple All-Big Ten teams, though."

"Did you think about going pro?"

"I went into the Marines when I graduated," Hanlen replied.

"Think I heard that too. I understand you were a war hero," Reinking said. For someone just dropping by, he seemed to know a lot about Hanlen.

"I got a few medals in Korea. Not sure that qualifies me as a hero. The way I look at it, the real heroes never made it back."

There was an awkward pause, and then Reinking changed the subject.

"How do you like the beer?" he asked.

"It's different," said Hanlen, tilting the bottle and looking at. "I usually drink Hamm's."

"Ah, from the land of sky-blue waters."

"I don't think they make Hamm's in Minnesota anymore. It's Stroh's now," I had read something about the Hamm's brewery in St. Paul being traded between the two beer companies.

"I believe you're right," Reinking said. "Hamm's should be charged with phony advertising. How do you like it, Logan?"

"It's good," I said, even though it was a little heavy for my taste. "Give me a call when the IPO comes out."

Reinking grinned. "You know what an initial public offering is?"

"I meant to say IPA. I get my acronyms easily confused."

"Good one. Ok, when either one comes out, I'll let you know."

He looked back at Hanlen.

"I played linebacker at Northwestern. Early sixties," Reinking said. "Second string, not a star like you. You probably know Ara Parseghian coached there before Notre Dame."

That would have made him at least 45, so I was right about his age. Not exactly a winter-spring romance between him and Ellen, but a sizable age difference.

"I've met Ara," Hanlen said. "He was a great coach, but he's an even better man."

"You guys were ranked number one for a while in 1962, weren't you?" I asked.

Reinking saluted me with his beer.

"It was 1962. My sophomore year. We were undefeated and ranked number one in the country for two weeks. Pretty heady stuff. Then we had a bunch of injuries. Ara could coach everything except how not to get hurt. Our team didn't have a lot of spare parts. How about you, Logan? You play football?"

"A few years in high school," I replied. "About fifteen seconds in college."

Reinking laughed. "A short college career. Guessing maybe you got injured."

"It was a small college. And it was a knee."

"Ah, the football knee," Reinking said. "I got one of them myself. Makes getting in and out of the Porsche tricky sometimes. Where did you go to school?"

"A small college in Indiana. Doubt if you ever heard of it."

"Try me."

"Wallace College."

"No kidding. A couple guys I work with went to Wallace. They're pretty sharp."

"I was associated more with the dull crowd," I said.

Reinking laughed. "You're a real Renaissance Man, Logan," he said. "You know something about cars, finance, beer and Northwestern football. A Wallace graduate to boot."

"It was Wallace or the service, like the chief," I said. "Or the steel mill like my dad."

"And, since I see you here now," Reinking said, "you apparently know something about the disappearance of three young women, including Ellen's sister, from the Indiana Dunes twenty years ago."

"In a former life, I was an investigator with the Prairie County Prosecutor's Office. That's when the chief and I first became acquainted. I've looked through the case file on the missing girls many times."

"And what did you think?" Reinking said. "Anybody ever going to figure out what happened to them?"

"Nothing is impossible, I guess," I replied. "But as you noted, it happened over twenty years ago. As more time goes by, the odds of figuring it out get more remote."

There was a pause, and we drank our beer.

"Before Ellen gets back," Reinking said. "I'd like to ask you something, Chief."

"Ask away," Hanlen replied. "I can't guarantee I'll answer but ask."

"Got it. I know Ellen has talked with you before on the phone about her sister. But now you're here in person with somebody else who knows about the case. Something happen? As Logan here just implied, I find it hard to believe there are any new developments in the case."

"You're right," Hanlen said. "Ellen and I have talked on the phone about her sister. She always asks if there is anything new. Unfortunately, I always tell her no. I have more free time now that I'm retired and thought I'd like to meet her in person. Nothing more than that."

Reinking glanced over at me.

"I brought Logan along for the ride," Hanlen added. "He knows something about the case, and he's good company. As you said, he knows a little something about everything. Makes for an interesting traveling companion."

"Ellen mention anything about me?" Reinking said.

"She said you were a commodities trader in Chicago," I said.

"That's true. She say anything about our marital status?"

"Not really," I replied. "Just that she was living out here and you were in the city."

"It's really none of our business," Hanlen added.

"Well, as long as the present living relationship exists, I think we're heading for divorce," Reinking said. "Not that I want one."

"Sorry to hear that," Hanlen said.

"Yeah. Along those lines, I was hoping maybe you could help me out, Chief. It's something to do with Ellen."

Hanlen looked puzzled. "I always like to help when I can, but not sure what I can do for you, Steven. Until now, all I've done is talk to your wife on the phone."

Reinking leaned forward in his chair.

"Did you know this place was her grandmother's?" he asked.

"She mentioned it," Hanlen replied. "By the way, we stopped and visited with her grandmother on the way down."

Reinking looked surprised. "Really? How's Ginny doing?"

"Seems to be doing just fine," Hanlen said.

"You know, Ellen is obsessed with her sister," Reinking said. "This place has a lot of happy memories for her. Of when her sister was alive. But it's not good for her to live in the past, including living on her grandmother's farm. I'm surprised she can't see that for herself."

"Somebody once said it can be difficult to see when you have something in your eye," I said.

"I think that comes from the Bible," Reinking said, "and it's applicable to this situation."

"How did you two happen to end up owning the farm?" I asked.

"Good question. That's part of the issue I have. As you know, Ellen's grandmother is in a nursing home. We, or should I say, I, bought this place from her. The idea was the money would be put into a trust to pay for her care. The place she's in isn't cheap, but even if she lives to be two hundred, there is more than enough in the trust to provide for her care. I should know, I invested the money."

"And you would like to sell the farm and get some of your money back?" I asked.

Reinking nodded. "You got a quick mind, Logan. I respect that. Let's just say I'm now looking at a business opportunity that requires more capital than I can get my hands on. But I can't sell the farm or even borrow on it without Ellen agreeing. I can't even get money out of the trust without her signing off on it. Ellen wanted it that way, and I went along with her." He shook his head. "That's what happens when you do things from emotion and not logic."

"I'm not with you, Steven," I said. "How can the chief help you?"

"I'm sure you've seen situations like this before, Chief. Ellen obviously trusts you. She needs some plain speaking to from someone she respects. Remind her that it's been over twenty years and her sister is not coming back. Sad but true. This obsession with finding out what happened to her isn't healthy. She needs to give it up."

"And the farm," I said.

Reinking gave me a quick look and nod. "Especially the farm."

We both looked at Hanlen. He didn't say anything right away.

"I can't do that, Steven. For one, it goes against my grain to butt into people's private affairs," he said, shaking his head.

"And two, I'm not sure she trusts me as you seem to think. Like I said, we barely know each other."

"You know I'm right, though," Reinking said.

"If you are asking if I agree with you, I might say yes. I've seen people lose a family member tragically and never get over it. Especially if there is no closure in finding out what happened. Some spend the rest of their own life trying to make some sense of something that doesn't make sense. After I got back from Korea, I spent a lot of time wondering why I made it through when so many others didn't. Then I finally figured out I couldn't change what happened and needed to move on with my life. You ever read any Stephen King, Steven?"

"Sure, who hasn't?"

"He wrote a short story that I liked a lot," Hanlen said, then smiled. "Now I can't even come up with the title. There was a line from that story that really stuck with me. Something like, life is a simple choice, either get busy living or get busy dying."

"Then you know what I'm talking about," Reinking said.

"But that's still a long way from me making personal suggestions to someone I don't know well."

Frustration if not anger came over Reinking's face but quickly changed into a tight smile.

"Well, I tried," he said.

The door creaked and Ellen stepped out onto the porch.

"How's it going out here?" she asked, smiling.

"Just fine, honey," Reinking said. "We were telling old football stories."

"In that case, I'm glad I went inside," she said.

Reinking took his last gulp of his beer and stood.

"I think I better be on my way. Meeting some friends for dinner," he said. "Glad I got to meet you guys. Finish the beer for me."

"We were about ready to head out too, right, Chief?" I said.

Hanlen looked at me questioningly, and then at his watch. "Yeah, we should get on the road. Hope to see you again sometime, Steve," he said. They shook hands.

"It's Steven, my dad was Steve," Reinking said.

"Hey, I got a customer in Prairie Stop. He's a dentist. Maybe I'll visit him some day and take you guys out to lunch."

He didn't seem like he was going to his car until we did the same.

"Sure. Ellen's got my number," Hanlen said.

"You sure you won't stay?" Ellen said, clearly wanting us to.

"Some other time, maybe. We need to get going," I said.

"We'll be in touch, Ellen," Hanlen said.

I wondered what Reinking thought when he said that.

chapter 13

"I THOUGHT WE WERE GOING TO TALK WITH ELLEN again before we left," Hanlen said, as we were pulling out of the driveway.

"Not sure I wanted to," I replied.

"Why not?"

"I think she knew we weren't talking to Steven about football. I didn't care to get into with her what it was," I replied. "Plus, based on the conversations, I think one or the other of them, or both, was shading the truth. I'm trying to figure out why."

"Does it matter?" Hanlen asked.

"How do you mean?"

"Well, one, or both, maybe wasn't straight about their marital situation or finances. What does that have to do with the disappearance of three girls twenty years ago?"

"Probably nothing," I said. "But I'd like to mull it over. From my days at the Acme Detective School, I learned you don't show all your cards right away."

"You think one of them had something to do with the note I got?"

"Pretty sure it wasn't Ellen. She didn't blink an eye when I mentioned the locket."

"I noticed that too," Hanlen said. "Why didn't we just tell her about the note?"

"I might have got to that point, but then her husband showed up."

"You don't think Steve had something to do with it, do you?"

"He prefers Steven," I replied. "Think about it for a second. Steve needs money, and he says he's got a lot tied up in the farm. But his wife has control over whether the property can be sold. She has strong emotional reasons for not wanting to sell it. He needs to make her accept reality. He sends you the note, hoping maybe you will think it came from her, and that you do exactly what you did. Pay her a visit. Maybe tell her to move on with her life, like Steven asked you to. Or maybe she gets in some trouble for interfering in an investigation. Either way, it might work out to his advantage. He's got nothing working for him right now."

Hanlen shook his head. "I don't know. Reinking doesn't strike me as the devious type."

"Again, I agree," I said. "All of this is speculation and possibilities. The sky's the limit as far as those go."

"Maybe we do find out he wrote the phony note," Hanlen said. "Then he might be looking at some trouble."

"Doubtful," I said. "Say we tell Ivan about this. If he doesn't break out laughing, he is going to ask how come we didn't go to him with the note in the first place. Plus, I'm not sure how excited he's going to be about charging a rich guy like Reinking with obstruction in an old, unsolved case. Ever see the way he toadies up to someone with money?"

"Yeah. So, what do we do?"

"Nothing has changed from the other day. We went and talked to Ellen. And the grandmother. And now the soon to be ex-husband. I met some people I didn't know and learned a couple things. Maybe Ellen's client comes up with something on the boat. In the very unlikely event she does, we figure out what to do next. Otherwise, we do like you said, which is nothing. And maybe nothing is best."

chapter 14

W HEN WE GOT BACK TO 24, HANLEN TURNED WEST. I figured he was heading over to I-57, taking it north to I-80 at Joliet, and then east to Chicago and back to Indiana. We hadn't gone very far when Hanlen made another right onto Illinois One, which ran north-south along the Indiana border.

"Not taking the interstate back?" I asked. I was fine with missing the Chicago traffic.

"I'm getting hungry. I know a good place to eat near St. Anne. An old friend of mine owns it."

"I thought you said you needed to get back for the evening service," I said.

"Yeah, I did say that," Hanlen said, glancing at his watch. "I'm already going to miss it. I'll have to come up with a good excuse for the wife."

"What about God?"

"Who's to say we aren't doing His work right now?" Hanlen said.

"Driving aimlessly around the backroads of Illinois?"

"The Lord works in mysterious ways."

"It's s going to be dark soon," I said. I had told Kathy I would be home by evening and was hoping I would get a chance to see her.

"What are you, an old man? Hanlen asked. "Have to be home by dark?"

"I just don't want you to get us lost out here in the middle of the sticks."

"Don't worry about that. I know these roads like the back of my hand. I used to hunt and fish over this way."

Shortly after the turn, I saw a sign proclaiming the road part of the old Dixie Highway.

"Know anything about the Dixie Highway, Logan?" Hanlen said.

"Not much," I replied

"Before the interstates, they were the state highways that were the main north south route for travel in this part of the country. My dad took us from Wisconsin to Florida a few winters on the Dixie Highway. That was a heckuva drive."

"I bet."

"I wouldn't care to make it today, but it didn't seem that bad at the time," Hanlen added. "My dad was a Civil War buff, and we must have visited every fort and battlefield between here and Tallahassee."

"My dad was into history too, but Native American," I said. "One summer we drove out to the Little Bighorn in Montana. Now that was a drive."

"Poor ole Custer," Hanlen said. "Shoulda been runnin' away when he was attacking."

"My dad hated Custer. As much as you can hate anyone who isn't alive, I suppose."

"Was he the one who said the only good Indian is a dead Indian?"

"I don't think so, but he probably shared the sentiment. No, his boss, Phil Sheridan said that. Custer said, 'where did all these damn Indians come from?'"

"No kidding? That's a good one."

"Yeah, I bet his men were laughing their asses off when they heard that. What's the name of this place in St. Anne?"

"The Red Cedar Inn. Ever hear of it? It was popular place back in the day."

"Doesn't ring a bell."

"My friend knows a lot about the goings-on in Kankakee County," Hanlen said. "He might remember something about Banks."

"Who is this guy?"

"His name is Mitchell Bryce. His son Bill and I played at Purdue together one year. He was a senior when I was a sophomore."

I did a quick calculation. "Mitchell Bryce must be around the same age as Ginny Musick."

"Mitch? That sounds about right. Bill was in Korea too; except he never came back."

"Was he a jarhead like you?"

"No," Hanlen said. "He was in the Air Force ROTC at Purdue. Wanted to be a pilot."

"What happened to him?"

"He made it to flight school," Hanlen said. "He wound up in an F-86 Sabre squadron."

"I take it an F-86 is a plane."

"The first jet fighter the U.S. built that was a match for the Russian MIG. Here's one for you. Know who flew the first F-86? I'll give you a hint. He also went to Purdue."

"Chuck Yeager," I answered.

"Good guess. No, it was, a guy by the name of George Welch."

"Wasn't he one of the few U.S. pilots to get in the air at Pearl Harbor?"

"Give that man a cigar. He shot down two jap planes that day, and some more later on in the war. Afterwards, he became a test pilot. Some think he might have been the first pilot to break the speed of sound."

"Now I thought that was Chuck Yeager," I said.

"Most think so and likely it's true. Yeager broke it in the X-1 in October 1947. There's a story that Welch cracked the sound barrier two weeks earlier in the F-86 prototype. A few who were there claimed they heard sonic booms over the desert that day. Welch never said yay or nay. Years later, he crashed and died in another test plane, so if he planned to write a tell-all memoir later, he didn't get a chance."

"How do you know so much about flying?" I asked.

"My son the engineer had a keen interest in all things flying when he was young. He wanted to be a pilot. Turned out he didn't have the eyes for it. He got his mother's eyes."

"What happened to Bill Bryce?" I asked.

"He got shot down over North Korea. A place known as MIG Alley. There were reports he bailed out, but if so, nobody saw him again. At least on our side. Some think that a number of F-86 pilots who were shot down and captured were handed over to the Russians."

"They didn't let him go at the end of the war?"

"No," Hanlen replied. "It was referred to as a 'conflict' at the time, by the way. Like calling an orgy a sock hop. The Russians wanted to grill the captured pilots on the technology in the new F-86. Then afterwards they were given an all-expenses paid trip to Siberia."

"Nice," I said. "How many of them were there?"

"Mitchell Bryce seems to think there could have been as many as thirty, including his son. Maybe more," Halen said.

"That's a lot of pilots to go missing."

"Yeah. How would you like to get shot down, tortured, then spend the rest of your life in a God-forsaken frozen hellhole, wondering if anyone back home was doing anything to find you."

"Real nice," I said. "Why didn't somebody raise hell about it?"

"Like who? Everybody was sick of the war and just wanted it to be over with. POWs weren't on anyone's priority list, most of all North Korea's. They never released thousands of South Koreans. And maybe as many as five hundred Americans, including the pilots."

"I can't believe Eisenhower would have let that go," I said.

"Mitch Bryce claims that Ike knew about the prisoners still there but wasn't going to start a nuclear war with Russia over it."

"How did Mitch handle that?" I asked.

"About as good as you might expect. After forty years you'd think he'd give up hope, but not Mitch. He still sends letters to congressmen, generals, and military bureaucrats. He must have written thousands of them by now. He gets the usual, 'we're checking into your claims.' Oh sure, there were inquiries made to the Russians and Chinese, but they stonewalled them."

"And maybe there's nobody in Russia now who knows what happened to them," I said.

"Yeah, from what I understand, one day you're the torturer, the next day it's your turn."

"How does Mitch know so much about Kankakee County?" I asked.

"Well, he eventually figured out that letters from somebody who owned a roadhouse out in the sticks weren't going to get much attention. He decided to go into politics. He ran for the county board of supervisors. He served on the board for years and then ran for sheriff, and did a couple terms. He even ran for state rep but lost."

"Did anybody take him seriously then?" I asked.

"What do you think?"

"I think not."

"You're right. Maybe the responses he got were more polite, but not any more helpful."

We drove in silence along empty roads through farm fields until a few buildings appeared in view. A water tower in the distance displayed 'St. Anne,' as we went by a town welcome sign. Below the welcome was another sign announcing one of St. Anne's most famous native sons. Hanlen noticed it too.

"Jack Sikma played high school ball at St. Anne High School," he said, "but he was from Wichert. It's a little bit east of here. He was known as the Wichert Wonder."

"Wish I had a nickname like that."

"Move to Wichert, maybe they'll let you rent it," Hanlen replied. "I saw him play against BHU when he was in college. He lit them up pretty good."

"I know zilch about basketball, but he doesn't seem to get the credit he deserves, in the pros, at least," I said.

"Agreed. His game isn't flashy. Just pivot and shoot. Plus, he came along right before Larry Bird. Bird cornered the market in pretty good big white basketball players."

There wasn't a whole lot to St. Anne, and we were through it in minutes. We went by the St. Anne Church and Shrine on the north side of town. The church was a large limestone building with a copper steeple. For reasons that escape me now, I took a course in architecture when I was in college. Based on the little I remembered from that, I would say the church was built early in the century, in the neo-Gothic style. It was an impressive structure for a small town in Illinois. I noticed Hanlen glancing over at it too.

"They don't build churches like that anymore," I observed.

"They couldn't afford to even if they wanted to," Hanlen replied. "Only about a thousand people live here. Mitch was telling me the priest who founded St. Anne was a bit of a character. Got himself tossed out of the Catholic church and then sued for libel."

"Who did he sue? The Pope?"

"Not sure but guess who was his lawyer."

"F. Lee Bailey?"

"Nope, it was Honest Abe himself."

"Yeah, from what I know about old Abe, it sounded like he represented everyone in central Illinois at one time or another," I said.

A mile or so outside of St. Anne, Hanlen made a right turn. On the right side of the road was a decrepit Texaco gas station, on the other, well off the road, a large one-story wood building. Large white script letters on the side of the building proclaimed, 'The Red Cedar Inn." The wood looked to be red cedar, and then somewhere along the line, probably after the owner got tired of refinishing the cedar, painted a blood red. I guessed it was built in the late thirties, shortly after the Dixie Highway was completed. There was a wood porch in front with a dark red awning. Although it was a nice day and there were a couple tables and chairs on the porch, no one was sitting outside. There were only a few cars in the large parking lot, but about a dozen motorcycles were right in front of the place. A neon sign over the door flashed "Welcome!"

"Haven't been here in a little while," Hanlen said, as we pulled up. "Looks like the place could use some work."

The building was in better condition than the gas station across the street, but it needed some repair. A coat of paint would have been a cheap start, but the roof looked in sad shape. I deduced that the Red Cedar Inn may have been a popular spot before the interstate highways were built with fast food places every twenty miles. Might have even been a destination spot for folks from Chicago wanting a pleasant Sunday afternoon drive followed by a tasty meal. Times had changed and the inn locked like it had seen better days.

Even though Hanlen parked well away from the building, we could hear the music coming from within. I was surprised when I recognized an Aerosmith song. I would have figured Merle Haggard or George Jones to be the music of choice out this way.

We walked by the motorcycles, and I said to Hanlen, "Gang?"

He looked at the bikes. "No. A club maybe, but no gang. Those are bikes made in Japan. Any self-respecting gang member rides a Harley."

"I didn't work much traffic," I said.

"Everybody knows that," Hanlen said.

We entered a dark anteroom which smelled of tobacco smoke. A couple benches lined the wall by the door, while a hostess podium was on the other side. After my eyes adjusted to the dark, I saw a 'please seat yourself' sign on it. We continued into the large bar area of the restaurant. The long wooden bar was to our right. Some high-top tables sat in the middle of the room, with booths on the other side of the tables. It appeared like the main dining area was in the back of the place, but it looked empty—probably closed off unless there was a crowd. There was another smaller room to the left of us, where I saw a pool table. That seemed a little out of character with the rest of the place. Maybe the owner had added it to attract more business as the restaurant business declined.

It didn't take me long to figure out who the motorcycle owners were. There was half a dozen or so guys sitting or standing near the bar, and a few more at one of the high-top tables. They were all dressed in a similar fashion: ankle motorcycle boots, jeans, and t-shirts of various styles and colors. Some had on thin black or brown leather riding jackets. I'm not a fashion follower, but the boots and jackets looked new and expensive. I would have guessed most of them were in their early or mid-thirties. They were clean-shaven for the most part, hair neatly cut, no earrings or visible tattoos, which led me to agree with Hanlen's assertion that they weren't part of a gang. One of them at the high-top looked out of place. He looked older, and unlike the others, he had long grey hair, pulled back in a ponytail, and a thick white Fu Man Chu. He was not a large man but wore a tank top displaying an impressive pair of biceps. On one of them was a tattoo of a skeleton on a motorcycle. When I was in uniform, if there was a call for a disturbance at a bar, I would have picked him out as one of the likely instigators. Prejudicial, yes, but something about the way he looked said trouble. The others looked more like friends out having a good time. I pegged them as well-paid young professionals from Chicago: bankers, or brokers, marketing reps, accountants, and tech salesmen.

It looked like they were having an enjoyable time, laughing, and talking loudly over the heavy metal music. As we walked by, a couple of them glanced over at us, including the guy with the biceps. It was hard not to take note of a man Hanlen's size. It looked like biceps might have been judging how tough Hanlen was.

We walked into the back part of the bar area and took the last booth. I saw now that the main dining room was open, with a couple families and elderly couples sitting on one side, probably to be away from the noisy bar.

A pretty waitress saw us from the dining room and came over to the booth. She had short auburn hair and looked to be in her mid-twenties.

"You guys can sit in the dining room if it's too noisy for you out here," she said, glancing over at the bikers.

"We're ok here," Hanlen said. "Is Mitch around?"

"You know Mitch?" the waitress said, smiling. "I'm his granddaughter, Penny."

"I've heard of you," Hanlen said. "I'm an old friend of his. Bill Hanlen is the name."

"Oh, sure, Sheriff Hanlen. He's mentioned you. How are you?"

"Fair to middlin'. I'm retired now, so call me Bill. And this here is Logan."

She looked at me and nodded hello.

"Ok, Bill. Grandad is in back. I'll tell him you're here. In the meantime, can I get you guys something to drink?"

"What do you have on draft?"

"Old Style and Michelob," Penny replied.

"Michelob on tap? Must be my lucky day," Hanlen said. "I'll take a Mick. Bring Logan one too."

"Be right back," she said and turned toward the bar. A few of the bikers gave her a good look-over as she walked by. One of them said something to her and smiled. She shook her head slightly and frowned in response.

When she returned with the beers, Hanlen asked if the guys in the bar were in the place a lot.

"Guys, or guys like them. If the weather is nice, they ride down from Chicago on the weekends." She glanced over her shoulder.

"Personally, I would just as soon they stayed in the city."

"They bother you?" I asked.

She shrugged.

"In the way wannabe macho guys do who drink too much. Loud and rude," she said. "Nothing I can't handle. I'll go get Mitch."

A family emerged from the dining room. Parents and three kids, the oldest a teenage girl. Sixteen maybe, cute. She was wearing short shorts and sleeveless top. It seemed a little on the cool side for that attire, but I guess with young people fashion trumped function. As they went by the high-top the bikers gave her the once over. Biceps said something to her.

She gave kind of a confused smile, but her dad frowned. I thought he might say something, but his wife got a nervous look on her face and touched his arm, and he didn't. Probably a good idea.

Hanlen had noticed the exchange too.

"You got kids, Logan?"

"You know I'm divorced."

"Right. Got any kids?"

"Not that I know of."

"Huh. You got a sister, don't you?"

"One sister, one brother," I answered.

"See much of them?" he asked.

"Only when absolutely necessary."

"What's that supposed to mean?"

"My dad died about ten years ago, and then my mother relocated to Florida. After that happened, there didn't seem much reason for us to get together, or even talk to each other."

It was more complicated than that. My dad's exit from this life wasn't a peaceful or quick one, and there was a divergence of opinion regarding the situation, with my brother and sister apparently of the mind that it didn't need to concern them much. I suppose a death in the family can be a bonding experience for some families, but it sure wasn't in ours.

"I only got brothers and sons," Hanlen said. "But if I had a sister or daughter and someone made a crude remark to them, I'd shove his head three feet up his ass."

"Chief, I don't think defending a woman's honor is an acceptable defense for assault anymore. Especially if the assault is in the form of cranial-anal inversion."

"What a shame."

Somebody at the bar loudly yelled out 'bartender!' I guessed it was directed at the middle-aged woman behind the bar at the end closer to us. She was wiping the bar off while talking with a woman across from her. She startled at the yell, then angrily slapped her bar rag down and headed to where the yell came from. The guys at the bar thought it was hilarious and burst into more raucous laughter.

Just then on the jukebox, Lynyrd Skynyrd's 'Free Bird' came on, which caused high fives and more raucous noise.

"Boy, you hardly ever hear this one in a bar," I remarked.

"I took my wife to see Tom Jones at the Star Theatre in Merrillville for our anniversary a while back," Hanlen replied. "He did a few songs and was talking with the audience when some ass yelled out 'Free Bird.' Ole Tom was ready for him though."

"What did he do?"

"He said 'my pussycat ate your bird.' Get it? He had a hit song called 'What's New Pussycat.'"

"I bet that got a big laugh," I replied.

"I almost pissed my pants."

I was sipping my beer when a large, square built man using a walker emerged from the dining room and approached our booth. He was a couple inches over six feet and well over 250 pounds. The walker almost seemed to bend when he leaned on it. He wore a light yellow short-sleeve dress shirt, dark brown pants, and cowboy boots. His thick white hair was trimmed in a crew-cut, and he wore gold wire-rimmed glasses.

"I'll be damned! Wild Bill Hanlen!" He exclaimed, in a booming voice. "How the heck are you?"

I'd never heard anybody call Hanlen 'Wild Bill" before.

Hanlen stood up and extended his hand. "I'm good, Mitch. How about you?"

"As good as a one-legged man in an ass-kicking contest," was the response, only slightly less booming.

Other than the walker, and some extra pounds, Mitchell Bryce looked like he had aged well. His face was weathered and lined, but his large blue eyes were clear and vibrant.

"Can you sit for a minute?" Hanlen asked, after introducing me to Mitch.

"Sure. We aren't too busy right now, sad to say," he said, glancing over at the bar, "except for those knuckleheads."

I pushed over and Mitch carefully lowered himself into the booth. My end of the seat tilted up a bit when he sat down.

"Damn arthritis," he said when he got settled. He smelled like Old Spice and meat being cooked.

"Did you make ribs today?" Hanlen asked, anticipation in voice.

"Yeah, but they're all gone already," was Mitch's reply.

At Hanlen's crestfallen look, Mitch laughed.

"Give me some credit, would you?" he said. "I knew you were coming, so I saved some for you. They'll be out here in a minute."

More loud laughter came from the bikers. Penny had picked up another couple beers and was weaving her way through the bikers. One of the bikers got off his stool and made a stumbling attempt to dance with her as she went by. She easily dodged him, but some of the beer in her hand slopped out of the mug and onto the jeans of the would-be Fred Astaire. His friends laughed. Penny gave them a dirty look.

Hanlen looked over at them.

"You get much trouble from Hell's Angels over there?" he asked Mitch.

He snorted. "I wish they were Hell's Angels. They're at least predictable assholes. These guys act all polite until they get liquored up, then they start behaving like the meatheads they really are."

"Have you seen these particular guys before?" I asked.

Mitch gave me a quizzical look, and then glanced over at the bar.

"Them guys? Maybe. My memory and eyes aren't what they used to be. If not them, guys like them."

"How do you mean . . . them?" I asked, curious.

"Guys from Chicago. Guess they are what you call Yuppies. They got too much money and time on their hands. They buy expensive Japanese bikes and for kicks ride out of the city on weekends. For some reason they've taken a shine to this place."

"Well, the food's good," Hanlen said.

"This is the kind of roadhouse that Marlon Brando might have stopped at," I said.

"Marlon Brando? What has he got to do with anything?" Mitch said.

"You know, like in that big biker movie he was in from the fifties. The Wild One."

Mitch looked at Hanlen, who shrugged.

"Yeah, whatever," Mitch said. "Guess they come down here to show how tough they are. Shit. In my day, I'd scrape guys like that off the bottom of my shoes."

"They ever cause any real trouble, other than being annoying?" Hanlen asked.

"About a month ago, a bunch of them were in here, got drunk and tore up the men's room, including ripping the sink off the wall. A big mess.

They threw a few bills on the floor like that made it ok. I told them to stay away and to let all their buddies know to do the same."

"That didn't deter them, I take it," I said.

"Nope. A few of them were back in a couple weeks. I told them they weren't welcome. I got a half-assed apology and they said they wouldn't cause any more trouble. I said I didn't want an apology, just wanted them to stay away."

"What did they say to that?" I asked.

"Well, one of them said that was discrimination and they might just have to sue me. From the way he talked, I guess he was a lawyer. I talked to the county sheriff about it. That useless wuss told me to let it go. When I was sheriff, I would have headed out with six of my biggest deputies and cracked some skulls faster than you can say 'police brutality.'"

Hanlen laughed. "You wouldn't have done that, Mitch."

Mitch gave a small grin. "I guess not, but I wouldn't have ignored it, either."

"So, these guys drink a lot of beer and get loud," Hanlen said. "They pay for everything right?"

"Yeah," Mitch said.

"What can your sheriff do, then? It's still Slawinski, isn't it?" Hanlen said.

"Yeah, Easy Ed Slawinski. Guy's got an apt nickname. I'm supposed to just take it?"

"I didn't say that," Hanlen replied. "I've seen guys like this before. I bet in a few weeks, a few months, tops, these guys are going to get bored with heading down this way. They're going to find another direction to go, another hangout, and then they'll be someone else's problem. Just let it go."

"You and Ed must have attended the same law enforcement seminars," Mitch said, shaking his head. "Looks like your ribs are here."

Penny placed two large platters in front of us: ribs, coleslaw and cornbread. Hanlen's plate looked like it had twice as much stuff on it than mine. I wasn't really a big fan of ribs or cornbread so was glad for the smaller portions.

"Logan, you don't look like a chowhound like the chief here," Mitch said, reading my mind.

"You're right," I said. "I'll be lucky to make a dent in this."

"Keep your hands away from his mouth, Logan," Mitch said, "and watch out for flying bone fragments. We'll talk later."

"We were going to talk about Mason Banks. Remember him?" Hanlen asked.

"Sure. Like I said, we'll talk later. I got some things to do in back."

Mitch painstakingly got up and shuffled off into the dining room on the walker. Hanlen had already started working on his first rib while I was still deciding where to start. My need to do so was eliminated by what happened next.

chapter 15

As I looked down at my plate, considering where to begin, there was a blur in front of me and a crash—a big crash. The next thing I knew, our food was gone, replaced by one of the bikers, flat on his back on our table. Ribs, barbecue sauce, and Michelob were everywhere.

I found out later that the biker who had tried to dance with Penny tried it again. He grabbed her, in the process causing her to lose what was on her tray. Enraged, she took the tray and using it as a ram, shoved the biker, in the chest, away from her. She had some leverage on him and propelled him backward in the direction of our booth. He was too inebriated to keep his balance and wound up falling backward onto our table.

After looking around, he turned his head toward me with a puzzled look. Then he looked over at Hanlen.

"What happened?" he asked.

"God bless America," Hanlen exclaimed. "That's enough!"

I don't think it was the answer the guy was looking for.

Hanlen rose quickly, shoving the table into my stomach in the process.

"Hey!" I yelled. He didn't notice.

I guessed the man who flopped on our table weighed about 180 pounds plus, but Hanlen lifted him by his jacket front as easily as if he weighed a third of that. Hanlen then turned and extended his arms so that the guy's legs were dangling about two and a half feet above the ground. The bar got quiet, as everyone looked over at us. A few people in the dining room peered in with curious looks, all wondering what happened and what was going to happen.

It didn't take long to find out. Hanlen walked slowly, holding the biker in the air, the ten steps or so to where his fellows were sitting at the high-top table. They looked up at their friend, who now had a very concerned look on his face, but nobody moved.

"Was this your table?" Hanlen said, looking up at him.

At that, Hanlen heaved his human cargo toward the high-top. He landed flat on the tabletop, again on his back, but with enough force that he bounced off the table and then fell onto the floor. Most of what was on the table went with him. The guy with the biceps, reacting quickly, managed to get out of the way. The guy sitting on the other side wasn't so lucky and it looked like a lot of the beer and appetizers wound up on him.

After the initial loud bang and subsequent noise of glass and silverware hitting the floor, there was a last lonely noise of one small plate spinning on the ground, then silence, except for a couple pained noises from the guy who Hanlen had dumped. Then the woman behind the bar screamed. It seemed an appropriate thing to do. I pushed the booth table back and got to my feet.

Biceps squared off, in a martial arts stance with arms raised in front of him facing Hanlen.

"It's your turn, you son of a bitch," he said to Hanlen.

His partner on the other side picked up his barstool and raised it in a threatening manner. They looked like they meant business but didn't move directly on Hanlen. Maybe they were expecting him to back off or were intimidated by his size.

When I was a teen, young guys often engaged in hypothetical tough man contests. Who would win a fight, say, between Muhammad Ali and the wrestler Bruno Sammartino, or Smokin' Joe Frazier vs. Bruce Lee. It was fun to think of speed and agility beating brawn, but in the fights I had witnessed, the bigger guy usually won. Hanlen was a lot bigger than the two guys he was squaring off with, plus he had served in combat, so I doubt if they had anything on him in toughness. The only thing these guys had on him was they were younger and there were two of them. I didn't think that would be enough. I was right.

Biceps made the first move. He faked a punch, then launched a high kick with his right leg, aimed at Hanlen's head. Hanlen saw it coming and stepped back, at the same time raising his right arm, with which he blocked the kick. He then quickly stepped forward, reversed his arm and grabbed onto Biceps' leg, causing him to fall back with only his left arm keeping him from hitting the ground. He was bent over, awkwardly in Hanlen's grip.

"You've had some training," Hanlen observed, "but you could use some more lessons." With that he moved forward and drove his knee sharply into Bicep's groin, which was wide open for the blow. I cringed at the impact and the noise Biceps made. Hanlen then let the leg go and the man he had been holding drew himself with a grunt into a ball on the floor. It all happened in less than ten seconds.

"First lesson is, don't mess with someone you don't know," Hanlen said. He turned toward the guy holding the bar stool, who appeared to be reevaluating his situation. If using the stool was still an option, Hanlen immediately took it away, literally. He quickly moved forward, grabbed the stool and slammed it hard into the holder's chest. The guy recoiled backwards a few feet from the blow. He might have regained his footing if Hanlen hadn't then given the stool a powerful push toward the guys legs. It him right in the knees, and down he went.

I glanced over at the other guys at the bar. They got off their stools, looked at each other for a moment, then apparently decided that discretion was the better part of valor. They made their way slowly toward the door, eyes on Hanlen. It occurred to me then that the guys at the bar and the others might not be together.

Hanlen turned to face them and said, "Put the money back on the bar. For the damages." They hesitated, but he stared them down and the money went back on the bar.

Hanlen added, "now you can leave. But don't even think about coming back."

"You haven't heard the last of this, old man," one said. "You can't treat people like this. I'm a lawyer."

Probably not a wise thing to say to Hanlen.

"Did you just call me an old man?" Hanlen asked angrily, moving a couple steps in their direction. The lawyer backed quickly toward the door.

"I'm gonna talk to your sheriff!" he exclaimed, just before exiting.

"Please do," Hanlen replied to the door. "Ed's a friend of mine. Tell him Bill said hello."

The excitement wasn't quite over. Something caught my eye. A rotund bearded man wearing a black AC DC t-shirt looked around the corner from the pool room, cue in hand. He evidently had heard the commotion. I guessed he was a friend of biceps, because when he saw him on the floor, he swore and entered the bar area. I stepped in his path.

"Let it go," I said, keenly hoping he would.

He didn't.

"Out of the way," he said, raising the pool cue.

"I would prefer not," I replied. I was hoping he was a Herman Melville fan, that being a line from my favorite Melville short story, *Bartleby the Scrivener*. It was my response of choice in a wide variety of situations.

"Fuck you!" he said, obviously not a fan of American Renaissance literature. Then he swung the pool cue at me. I was ready for it, ducked and went forward at the same time. The cue missed my head, but I got a pretty good shot on my left shoulder. I felt a burning numbness that went all the way to my hand.

My intent had been to avoid the pool cue, but I took advantage of my forward momentum to headbutt him squarely and forcefully in the jaw. It hurt my head, but it hurt him a lot more. He dropped the pool cue, staggered back a few steps, then dropped to his knees. Blood was coming from his mouth. I picked up the pool cue and raised it to hit him, but he put he put his right hand up indicating he had enough.

I looked over at Hanlen and he nodded at me.

Mitch Bryce came back into the room, with two big young guys behind him. Bryce wasn't using the walker and was carrying a baseball bat. Although he still moved slowly, he had a purpose in his shuffle. And he looked mad.

"What the hell is going on here?" he barked angrily.

"Nothing much, Mitch," Hanlen said, calmly. "Just a little disagreement about the choice of songs on the jukebox."

"So, you decided to bust the place up?"

"No, I just suggested these fellows settle up and leave."

"And the guys on the floor?"

"They must have slipped on their way out. You just get the floors waxed?" Mitch motioned to the two big young guys.

"Get those assholes out of here," he said, motioning to the floor. "If they can't get up, drag them out. Don't be nice about it. And then get this place cleaned up. And for crissakes, turn that music off."

He turned to the people in the dining room.

"Excitement's over folks. Sorry for the commotion. I'm picking up everyone's tabs." He looked at me and Hanlen. "You two, back in my office."

chapter 16

WE WERE SEATED FOR A COUPLE MINUTES in Mitch's office before he said anything.

"What about letting it go?" he said to Hanlen, who shrugged his shoulders in response.

"I hope they don't sue me. Penny said one of them was a lawyer," Mitch groused.

"He said that. Doesn't mean it's so. Anyhow, they're not going to sue you," Hanlen replied.

"By the time they're done with the story," Mitch continued, "you two guys will have put everyone in the place in wheelchairs, and I'll be out of business."

The image of the patrons of the Red Cedar wheeling into a courtroom to bear witness against us caused me to stifle a laugh. Hanlen glanced over at me.

"You're getting too old to work anyhow," Hanlen said. Then he repeated, "besides, nobody is going to sue you."

I didn't know about that. The function of law seemed to be evolving from a system of maintaining justice for all to one of re-distribution of wealth. I'd read recently about two carpet layers who apparently didn't heed the dire warning on the can of adhesive they were using, which was something like: 'CONTENTS HIGHLY FLAMMABLE, FUMES COMBUSTIONABLE, FOR OUTSIDE USE ONLY.' When one of them lit his cigarette, there was an explosion. The resulting lawsuit made them multi-millionaires and put the adhesive company out of business.

"Maybe we should give the county sheriff a call and give him our side of the story," I suggested. "Before he gets it from someone else."

"Do what you want," Hanlen said. "I'm not calling anybody."

"If those assholes file a complaint, he'll be arriving soon enough," Mitch said. "You ought to get on out of here. I'll handle the sheriff if he shows up."

"I didn't finish my ribs," Hanlen protested.

"I'll get a to-go box for you," Mitch said tersely. "Thanks for dropping by. Come by in another ten years."

"Let's not forget why we came here," Hanlen said. "We were going to talk about Banks."

"Oh, yeah, I almost forgot about Chief Banks," Mitch said, leaning back in his chair. Somewhat to my surprise he chuckled.

"Something funny?" Hanlen asked.

"There was a joke I heard years ago," Mitch said. "I can't remember any of it except the punchline, which was 'that was the worst case of suicide I ever saw.' Whenever I think of Banks that comes to mind."

"You think he killed himself?" I asked.

"No, but there was some who tried to make out like he did."

"Who was that?" Hanlen asked.

"Keep in mind, I wasn't sheriff back then. Just got on the county board, as a matter of fact. But when we were told about the circumstances of his death, I said to myself, that sounds mighty fishy."

"Why's that?" I asked.

"Here's the chief of police from a neighboring jurisdiction, involved with the ongoing investigation of a high-profile disappearance, and he gets killed in a very peculiar explosion. And I'm told it was an accident."

"In other words, it didn't make a lot of sense," I said.

"That would be putting it mildly. Still one of the most peculiar things I've seen in my twenty-plus years of public service. I don't think any of the sacks of shit on the board believed it either, but nobody wanted to say anything."

"Who did the investigation of the explosion?" I asked.

"Well, the county fire marshal at the time was a good old boy like me, but at least he had the brains to know he needed to bring in someone more qualified than himself. He brought in an arson expert from Chicago."

"And the expert said it was an accident," said Hanlen.

"He did. At least in his preliminary report. He even suggested the possibility Banks may have deliberately set the fire but didn't realize there was a chance of an explosion. An accidental suicide, if you will."

"Why would he do something like that?" I asked.

"Turns out he was over-extended. Way over-extended. A small-town police chief doesn't make a lot of money, and a farm, even a small one, is a big expense. The expert speculated Banks might have set the barn on fire for the insurance and wasn't expecting an explosion."

"I'm curious," I said. "You just mentioned the expert said it might have been an accidental suicide, plus you were suspicious given the circumstances. Did your expert consider Banks was murdered?"

Mitch looked at Hanlen. "This fellow asks some good questions."

"He's smarter than he looks," Hanlen noted.

"Good thing, too," Mitch said. "The expert didn't want to put something like that in writing before he did a more thorough investigation. Additional forensics, lab tests, more background on Banks, that sort of thing."

"But he didn't do the additional investigation," I surmised.

"The board decided against it. Or rather, paying for it. Those investigations can get expensive and take a lot of time. The board was ok with an accident. Wanted it over quick and forgotten about. Not sure mischief, of whatever type, was even mentioned in the final report."

"Interesting," I said. "I understand you were county sheriff here for a number of years, Mitch."

"Yep. Two terms, eight years total," Mitch replied. "That was some time after what we're talking about it."

"Yeah, I figured," I said. "But when you got elected sheriff, were you ever interested in looking into the Banks case?"

"Sure. Let's just say my curiosity was stirred when I heard that the horseman gangster from Chicago may have been involved in the disappearance of the girls from the Dunes."

"That would have been Luther Brame," I said.

"Yeah, I blanked on his name," Mitch replied. "Did you know Banks got blown up shortly after he talked to Brame?"

"It wasn't right after," Hanlen interjected.

"Close enough. Anyhow, I'd been in office about six months when I got around to asking to see the file on Bank's death."

"What was in it?" I asked.

"Not sure what was in it," Mitch said. "On account of there wasn't even a file."

"What happened to it?" I asked.

"The county used to store its old files in a warehouse by the Kankakee River. This was before computers, remember. Anything over five years old got moved there. Everything and without exception. Guy who took care of records was a little obsessed that way. Strange fellow. As I recall, he got arrested sometime later for soliciting a minor for sex."

"Maybe the pressure got to him," I said. "All the papers and all."

'Right," Mitch replied. "Anyhow, there was a bad flood of the Kankakee in the early seventies. The building took a lot of water before they could get records out. I was told the Bank's file was one of the items lost."

"That was convenient," Hanlen said.

"Well, it wasn't like it was the only thing that got destroyed. It was a big flood. You might remember the Kankakee flooded with regularity here and in Indiana. We had a another big one back in '82. I lost a cabin in that one."

"Maybe the flood put your records guy over the edge," I said.

They both gave me quizzical looks.

"Nobody cares about the records guy. Stay focused here, Logan," Hanlen said.

"I'm curious," I said. "Banks was married. His wife wasn't suspicious about his death being called an accident, was she?"

"Not that I remember," Mitch said. "She got some life insurance money. As I recall, a lot of it. Plus, some insurance for the fire. Seems to me if the insurance company thought something illicit happened they may have delayed the claim, and maybe she didn't want that."

"Did you ever hear anything about what happened to her?" I asked.

"No, other than she got the money. Sometime later she sold the farm. Ended up making some money on that too as I recall, even after paying off the mortgage. I got no idea what happened to her after that."

"I understand you know a lot of people around here, Mitch." I said. "Any chance you could ask around, maybe find out what happened to Mrs. Banks?"

"What do you want to do? Send her a condolence card? It's been twenty years."

"There's no statute of limitations on good manners," I said.

"You're a strange one, Logan. I'll ask around, but don't count on anything."

"Never hurts to ask. If you hear something, give the chief here a call."

chapter 17

As we walked out to the car, Hanlen asked, "where did you learn to head butt like that?"

"I told you, I played football. Make a hit like that and somebody will think twice about catching another pass near you."

"I thought that was called spearing and it was illegal. And dangerous."

"Nobody said it was legal or safe. Let's face it, if they called penalties for everything illegal or dangerous, it would take a week to play a football game."

Hanlen and I didn't talk much on the way back to Prairie Stop. Maybe he was thinking of Steven and Ellen's marital issues, because, after a period of silence, he asked why I got divorced.

"I really don't know," I answered. "Sounds corny, but I thought my wife and I were soulmates."

"That's rough," Hanlen said.

"Yeah, unfortunately for me, my wife met her soulmate while she was still married to me."

Hanlen snorted.

"I wonder myself," I continued. "I think I read once that there are three things that couples argue about: kids, money and sex. We didn't have kids. We had enough money between us. Sex was ok. So, we never had any real big arguments about anything, and we liked doing things together. I think she wanted more, though."

"Like what?"

"A big house on a hill. With four or five freckle faced kids running around," I said.

"There's the kids and money," Hanlen said.

"Yeah, I guess so. I was never going to be able to afford the house on what I made, and the idea of being responsible for kids petrified me. Guess I got a fear of commitment."

"You think you're the only one that ever felt that way? You can't let fretting the future keep you from doing stuff."

"You're right," I replied. "Maybe I was suffering at the time from a bout of incipient insanity. But my wife didn't feel like waiting around to see if I was going to get better."

"Ever think about going back to work?" Hanlen asked.

I looked at him. "Maybe you forgot what happened at the end of last year."

"I didn't forget, but just like you can worry about the future, you can't live in the past. You can't do anything about either one of them."

"Sounds like you've been reading Joyce Brothers again, Chief," I said. "Speaking of which, did I ever tell you when I was five years old, she punched me in the nose?"

"Do you sit around all day coming up with corny jokes? You got too much time on your hands. That's why you should go back to work."

"I don't know," I said. "You don't see much of the good in people when you are arresting them."

"And not everybody is a criminal either. You can't get jaded and cynical on account of what you do."

"Interesting that you should say that. Think about the girls at the lake who went missing twenty years ago," I said.

"I've already been doing that," Hanlen said.

"Well, whoever did away with them, if he's still alive, that is, he's gone about his business for the last twenty years acting like nothing happened. Maybe he's even got people thinking what a real swell guy he is. All the while having this dark secret."

"So?"

"That's cold, real cold. I still feel guilty about slugging my brother when we were teenagers and giving him a black eye."

"Anyone who could kill three young girls is a sociopath," Hanlen replied. "They don't know what guilt is."

"Or maybe I'm not cut out for this stuff."

"Look at it this way," Hanlen said. "Maybe that's what makes you a good detective. Your ability to identify with the criminal mind."

"Not sure why, but that doesn't make me feel any better."

We didn't talk for a while after that, and I drifted off. When I came to it was dark and we were in my neighborhood.

"You ever hear anything from Beth"? he asked, as we pulled into my driveway. He was referring to Beth Wildrick, the wife of our late friend.

"She's still living with her folks in Florida. She sent me a letter a few months after Buzz died. Said she was sorry about what happened and that she and the girls were doing about as well as expected. Didn't say if she would be coming back. She has lawyers handling stuff regarding the estate. She said I could keep her car."

Buzz had let me use Beth's Volvo station wagon after I wrecked my Mazda last year.

"She was a classy lady," Hanlen said. "She didn't deserve what happened."

I tried to come up with a glib response to that, but the only thought I had was that very few people deserved what happened to them. I decided to keep that revelation to myself.

chapter 18

W HEN I GOT INSIDE, THERE WAS A NOTE FROM KATHY on the kitchen table. It read 'I came by around 6 . . . thought you'd be home . . . hoped to have a quickie . . . sorry I missed you.' The 'quickie' had a heart drawn around it.

Not as sorry as me. I called her, and told her about my day trip with Hanlen, and what we found out. I left out the part where we got in a fight in the roadhouse. She apologized again for missing me but said she couldn't come over. She did invite me over to her house for Memorial Day.

The only thing I'd had to eat since breakfast was an apple. My dinner had been squashed at the Red Cedar, and Hanlen didn't offer me any of what Mitch had given him. The only thing of substance in the refrigerator was some leftover fried rice from a few nights ago. Regrettably, one of the shortcomings of Prairie Stop was the dearth of good Chinese restaurants. I was keyed up from the day's events and thought going out for food would help me wind down.

Most of the eating establishments in Prairie Stop closed early on Sunday, and I figured even fewer would be open the night before a holiday. There was a family restaurant, Paulsen's, about a mile and a half from my house. I had not been in Paulsen's for years but recalled there was a bar in the back that stayed open longer than the restaurant. I thought even if the restaurant was closed, maybe the bar would be open, and I could get a burger. If not, Foodchopper, the town's largest grocery store, was on the way there. It was now open 24/7, new hours begun five or so years ago to attract the shift workers from the steel mills and county hospital, as well as hungry BHU students. Having a 24 hour store was a novelty in town back then, and Ivan Rich, now county sheriff, but then in uniform, convinced the store management to hire him as security for the weekend late shifts. He only lasted a few weekends. I asked him later why he quit the lucrative gig, and he confided that the boredom was so overwhelming that he used to dip his balls in the lobster tank just to stay awake.

One of the Paulsen kids, Victor, was in my class in grade school, or the first few years, anyhow. He was held back for second grade. A large rotund kid with a perpetually puzzled look on his face, he wasn't that bright. I didn't hold that against him. In fact, most in the class were impressed that his family owned a restaurant. Unfortunately for Vic, not being bright, at least in the unenlightened educational system back then, could have unpleasant consequences. Corporal punishment was still an accepted approach for correcting behavior, and possibly even for increasing one's IQ. I don't recall any flagrant incident of misbehavior on his part, but he did act out on occasion, probably due to his frustration with the learning process. One morning, the principal showed up, Vic was summarily removed to the hallway and received a paddling. Our class and probably several others could plainly hear the punishment being meted out in the hall. If it was a morality play meant to get us to pay closer attention to the intricacies of vowels and consonants, it worked for me. It may have been even more traumatic for me than Vic. Years later, we played football together one year in high school. I mentioned the incident once after practice. He laughed and said, "I should have told that bastard my grandmother could hit harder than him."

I decided to walk to Paulsen's. It was getting chilly, so I donned my Portage High sweatshirt. Portage was a city ten miles from Prairie Stop, and their school athletic teams were known as the Indians. My dad had a co-worker who served as a part-time football coach for the school and as a small joke, once gave my dad a couple used Portage sweatshirts, which featured an Indian chief on the front. Not sure if my father thought it was funny, but he really liked the stuff, and asked the guy for more. He had a ton of the Portage gear when he died, and I took most of it.

There were more cars than I expected as I cut through the parking lot at Foodchopper, shoppers undoubtedly loading up on supplies for Memorial Day cookouts. On the other hand, when I got behind Paulsen's there were just a couple cars and the place looked closed. One of the cars was a late model BMW sedan with Illinois tags. You didn't see many of those in Prairie Stop. The steel mill executives living in town who could afford such a vehicle wouldn't buy a foreign brand. Neither would most of the business owners or professionals who catered to them.

I was debating whether to just head back to Foodchopper, when an elderly man with a full head of tousled white hair came out of the bar, cigar in hand. He slammed the door, then stumbled and almost fell coming down the three steps to the parking lot. He nodded and raised his cigar in salute as he went by me. I nodded in return and watched him stagger around the corner. I hoped he lived close. As I entered the bar, I saw a large jug of bleach and a mop by the door, so I surmised closing time cleanup was near, another sign I should turn back to Foodchopper. But having come this far, I went in.

Unlike the Red Cedar, where the smell of tobacco was noticeable but not overpowering, Paulsen's bar reeked of smoke, and I let out an involuntary cough as I entered. When I started my first job in law enforcement in South Bend, I started smoking to relieve the alternating down time and periods of extreme tension that come with that line of work. My wife, a nurse and fellow smoker, got me to quit at the same time she did. She put us both in a clinical trial for a nicotine patch. I was not too keen about the idea, but later that was one thing I was grateful to her for. But now even the faint smell of cigarette smoke could make me gasp.

Paulsen's bar looked much the same as I'd remembered it. The lighting was dim, so even though I had been walking in the dark it took my eyes a couple seconds to adjust to the dark interior. The bar was oval, situated in the middle of the room. A couple small tables were tucked in the room's corners, and a passageway on the other side of the room led to the restaurant. There were pictures of local and professional sports teams and players on the wall. The team that won the state high school football title in the seventies was prominently featured.

The bartender was a florid-faced, stocky fellow who looked to be in his sixties. He wore a wrinkled white oxford shirt, black pants, and had a bar rag draped over one shoulder. Three guys sitting next to each other on the other side of the bar were the only other people in the place. They seemed about my age and looked familiar. Having grown up in Prairie Stop, pretty much everyone looked familiar to me, but the one in the middle I was sure I knew from somewhere. The three took a glance at me, then quickly went back to their talking and laughing. I guessed they had been there a while. The bartender didn't look happy to see me plop down on a bar stool.

"We're closing soon, pal," he said, and began wiping the bar with the rag.

"Figures. I just walked ten miles to get here," I said.

He gave me a bemused look. "How are things up in Portage?"

"Not good. I was looking for sand dunes, but couldn't find any," I replied.

Portage was home of The Port of Indiana, one of the largest ports on Lake Michigan. It had been constructed back in the sixties when Bethlehem Steel was building its huge Burns Harbor Works, the last fully integrated steel mill built in the United States. They took out part of the Dunes to make way for the port. The location of the port was controversial and protested by conservationists, but the steel interests got their way. As part of the deal, the Indiana National Lakeshore was created to preserve the rest of the dunes.

That got a laugh from the bartender. .

"You're about thirty years too late. They needed to bulldoze over part of the dunes to make way for the port."

"That's progress, I guess. Suppose I can't get anything to eat," I replied.

"Been a slow night. Cook left a couple hours ago. Want the beer?"

"No, that's ok, I'll be on my way," I said, getting off the stool.

"Does Vic still work here?" I asked, before turning to go. Last I heard anything about Vic Paulsen, he was working in the family business. But that was likely over twenty years ago.

"You know Vic?" he asked, a slight note of suspicion in his voice, and he stopped wiping the bar. Maybe he thought I was a skip-tracer working the night shift.

"We were in the same class in grade school for a couple years," I replied. "And we played football together one year in high school. He was a pretty good defensive tackle."

The bartender's demeanor relaxed.

"Yeah, I remember. He should have stuck with it. He had the size for it. No, he doesn't work here anymore. We may call him in if someone is sick, but that's about it. His folks had hopes that he would run the place, but he doesn't have a real head for business, if you know what I mean. Vic's got a job as a security guard over in Crown Point."

"He's doing ok then?"

"For the most part, yeah. He's been divorced a couple times, and late on the alimony occasionally, but that could happen to anybody, right?"

Hence the earlier suspicion.

"Don't I know it," I said. In fact, I didn't know. My wife married an orthopedic surgeon three months after our divorce was finalized. They now lived in a big house in Evanston near Northwestern University. The word alimony never even came up in our divorce proceedings, which were, all things considered, quite amicable. In fact, my wife even said to me at one point, 'you're pathetic, Logan. You can't even get mad at me for leaving you.'

"He still living in town?"

"You just said you knew him."

Again, the suspicion. I wondered if maybe Vic was in more trouble than just late alimony. I regretted mentioning him.

"I do but was out of town for a while. Working. Been back for years, but never bumped into him," I said, smiling. "I'm not looking to cause trouble for Vic. Just wondering how he is."

He relaxed again.

"Sorry. You seem like an ok guy. I'm Vic's Uncle Dave. He's kind of at loose ends right now. I got a cottage up at Lake Eliza. I've been letting him stay there."

I nodded to him and turned to leave.

"Hey, hang on," Uncle Dave said. "I can toss on a burger and fries on the grill if you're ok with that. It'll just take a few minutes."

He lowered his voice and looked over his shoulder.

"I got to wait until these jokers leave, anyhow," he added.

"I don't want to put you to any trouble," I said. I had already made up my mind to go back and brave the crowd at Foodchopper.

"Not at all. Like I said, it will be a few minutes. Let me get you a beer while you wait. On the house, since you're a friend of Vic's."

I had enough booze for the day, and didn't want to sit in the smoky bar, but I thought to refuse an offer of kindness would be bad karma, plus, it sounded like he wanted some company.

"All right, Dave. Thanks."

He came back with a draft beer and a shot glass filled to the brim with a brown liquid.

"You look like a shot and a beer guy," he said, placing the drinks in front of me.

"Not sure if that's a compliment or insult," I said.

He smiled. "You're doing me a favor. I've been trying to kill a bottle of Bushmills since St. Pat's Day."

"Erin Go Bragh," I said, draining the shot of Bushmills in one gulp, followed by a quick sip on the beer. Then I gasped.

"Smooth," I said, after I got my breath back. "Just like momma used to make."

Dave laughed.

"Hey, you said you had a cottage on Lake Eliza. You got a boat?" I asked.

"Yeah, I got a boat," he replied. "Just my opinion, but not much point to having a place on a lake in Indiana without a boat. The lakes aren't all that exciting just to look at."

"How about Lake Michigan?"

"Not much of that one in Indiana. Plus, you need to know what you're doing to take a boat out on the Great Lakes. It's not like taking a boat out on Eliza."

"I bet," I said.

"Course, I hardly use mine anymore," Dave continued. "My kids are grown, and the wife and I don't go to the lake as much as we used to. Probably ought to sell the boat."

"I've been thinking about getting a boat," I said, taking another sip off the beer. "You need insurance for it, right?"

Uncle Dave shrugged his shoulders.

"I don't know that having insurance for a boat is legal requirement in Indiana, or Illinois. If you kept it at a public marina, the state or city who owned it would want you to have it. Guessing the owner of a private marina would too. For liability reasons."

"That makes sense," I said.

"Plus, if you borrow money from the bank to buy it, they're going to want it covered." And why wouldn't you insure something valuable, like a boat?"

"I see your point. Just seems like you don't hear much about boating accidents. Why pay for something you don't need?"

"They're more common than you might think," he said. "Usually, it's some asshole who's had too many beers and thinks he's Admiral Halsey, and plows into something. What people don't realize is the boating equivalent of a fender bender can be fatal out on the water."

"Yeah, guess I didn't think of that," I said. "Hey, like you said, let's say I had too many beers and rammed my yacht into something and it sinks. I call my insurance company and tell them I need a new boat. What are they going to say?"

Dave thought about that a second.

"I'm guessing the Coast Guard would be checking into something like that. Pretty sure it's against the law to operate a boat while you're intoxicated. That might squirrel the insurance. But if it was a small pleasure or fishing boat, not sure anyone is going to care."

"The insurance company wouldn't ask any questions?"

"Accidents do happen," he replied. "They'd probably just pay the claim."

"I understand a collision, a storm, something like that. What else is there?

"Well, there's a bunch of stuff that can go wrong. You're out on the water, there's gas and a propellor involved. A lot more dangerous than a car, if you think about it."

"Sure. Can you give me an example?"

He thought about it.

"Ok, let's say you aren't careful fueling it and get some fumes in the bilge. A boat can catch fire, maybe explode. Rare, but possible. I've seen it happen. That's why they tell you to always run the bilge blower for at least five minutes before you start an inboard engine. Again, a guy is drinking or otherwise not paying attention, and doesn't do that, and he could blow himself up. Outboards are self-venting, obviously."

"Obviously. What's a bilge?"

He smiled. "It's the part of the hull that's under water. I'll be right back."

chapter 19

As I sipped my beer, I mulled over what Vic's uncle had said. He obviously knew something about boats. There was nothing to suggest that the disappearance of the Dunes Girls was caused by a boat accident. By all accounts, the weather that day was perfect. Thousands of people were at the beaches, dozens of boats in the water nearby, and numerous others further out in the lake. A boat in trouble, possibly on fire, let alone exploding, would certainly have been noticed. Yet, after hearing Dave describe how inattention could cause an explosion, I wasn't so sure. Perhaps the mystery man in the blue boat had taken the girls far out in the lake. Maybe he had his reasons for wanting to be out of sight. Preoccupied, maybe he made a careless mistake, causing an explosion. Whatever debris left could have been dispersed by the tide.

I also thought about what he said about insurance. If there was no insurance on the boat there would obviously be no record of a claim if the boat was destroyed. I also thought that someone who kidnapped three young girls wouldn't be too concerned about a propriety like having insurance. While I considered that, I also took a few quick glances at the three other guys at the bar. I thought I was glancing over surreptitiously but got a sudden rude surprise.

"You lookin' at somethin'?" the one in middle said loudly, glaring right at me.

It was not so much his voice, but the hostile tone and look that made me finally realize who it was. He was an unpleasant guy by the name of Ed Ballard Jr., who had been a year behind me in school. He'd put on weight, his chin now had its own chin, his hairline had receded considerably, but the surly vibe gave him away.

Ed Jr's father, Ed Sr., or Big Ed, owned a large real estate agency in town. Smart, self-assured, and ambitious, Big Ed had cashed in big time on the real estate boom going on in Prairie Stop in the sixties. To bolster his business profile, he volunteered for many of the town's civic organizations, and boards and commissions. In Ed Jr.'s case, the apple had rolled far from the tree. Other than having a well-known, successful dad, he didn't have much going for him. A large kid with a pear-shaped body, he was not good-looking, athletic, or particularly smart, and thus by the narrow standards of high school, not popular. Yet, because of his dad's status, he had an inflated idea of his own importance. The internal conflict thus generated caused his metamorphosis from insipid bore to annoying bully and troublemaker. The thought was that only Big Ed being on the school board kept him from being expelled for his miscreant acts.

Ballard and I had generally avoided each other. He had gone out for football his freshman year. I think it was his dad's idea, since Big Ed had been a sports star at Prairie High. Ed Jr. lasted the first few days of summer training camp, then abruptly quit. He blamed the coach for his failure. His whining about the coach did not endear him to any of the football players and he steered clear of them.

Our paths crossed memorably in the spring of my senior year. In early April, a late winter storm had blown in off Lake Michigan, and the temperature dropped like a stone during the day. Cold rain turned into heavy snow a couple hours before school was over. As kids poured out of the school to board the buses home, Ballard and some of his lackeys took the opportunity to bombard them with heavy wet snowballs.

I was sitting in study hall, by the window, finishing some homework before track practice, and had a good view of the mayhem. Kids dodged and scurried to avoid being hit, either jamming onto the buses or going back into the school. They were soon caught in a crossfire, as some guys in letter jackets on the other side of the drive began returning fire on Ballard's cadre. It would have all been good fun, I suppose, but since it had markedly cooled during the day, and many kids were wearing only light jackets in the snowy, cold temperatures, some slipped and fell on the slick pavement. Adding to the confusion, the bus drivers were reluctant to pull out with the commotion going on. Nobody looked like they were having fun, except for the guys heaving snow. Some brave faculty came out of the building to put an end to the chaos and were immediately targeted. They regrouped and advanced. Ballard and company retreated.

I went back to my homework, figuring the excitement was over. It was a couple minutes later when I heard a noise behind me and felt something cold and wet on my neck. Ballard had pushed the window open and was trying to shove a snowball down the back of my shirt. I guess it was his parting shot. I didn't care for the idea. I jumped out of my seat, turned, grabbed his wrist, and yanked it upwards and back. Then I hopped up on the HVAC unit by the window and, using my knee, pushed the window shut on his arm. Ballard's upper torso slammed into the glass with a thump. I added pressure on his arm, twisting at the same time, then gave an extra yank. There was a popping noise and he let out a yell. I dropped his arm and pulled the window back open. Released, Ballard fell in a heap in the snowy grass, moaning.

The next day he wasn't in school. There was a rumor that he been suspended for instigating the previous afternoon's fracas. I thought it more likely I had injured him enough that he had to miss school. That Saturday, it was sunny, and in the mid-sixties. Buzz and I were tossing a football in the yard, when I noticed three figures walking up the street. As they approached, I saw it was Ballard and two of his cronies. Ballard's arm was in a sling. They stopped when they got in talking distance.

"This doesn't concern you, Wildrick," Ballard said, right away.

"Sure, Eddie," Buzz replied, with a disingenuous grin. "Whatever you say."

"You messed up my shoulder pretty good, Wells," said Ballard, giving me his best menacing glare. "But when it's better, I'll be back to kick your ass. Count on it."

"I guess I shouldn't wish you a speedy recovery then," I said.

"Maybe you want to get your ass kicked right now," said one of his companions.

Buzz suddenly drew back and threw the football hard at the guy who just spoke. All three ducked, and the ball went inches over the head of the one who offered me the ass kicking.

"Fuck!" the target said.

"Sorry," Buzz replied. "It slipped."

"Say, Eddie," Buzz continued. "I got a couple questions for you. If this is just between you and Logan, how come you brought these two idiots along?"

There was no response from Ballard.

"Second question," Buzz said, the grin becoming a menacing smile. "How do you figure you're getting back down the street?"

"Now wait a second, Wildrick," Ballard said, when he understood the implication.

It was then that Buzz's dad, Ben Wildrick, came out of the house. I think he had been watching from inside and had an idea of what was going on.

"Hey, Buster," he said, calling his son by his given first name. "How are you, Logan? "

"Fine, Mr. Wildrick. How are you?" I replied. I liked Buzz's dad a lot.

"Good, thanks. Tell your folks I said hello," he said. He looked over at Ballard.

"I see you have some friends over, son. Would anyone care for something to drink? A soda maybe. Got warm fast, didn't it? Hard to believe it was snowing just a couple days ago."

"No, dad, thanks," Buzz answered said, in a subdued tone. "These guys were just leaving."

Somewhat to my surprise, Ballard respectfully said, "no thank you, sir, we'll be on our way."

chapter 20

"**I**'M TALKIN' TO YOU," BALLARD SAID, jarring me out of my reverie.

"Maybe he needs to get his ass kicked before he says anything," said the guy to his right.

I smiled and shook my head. It was like we were back in high school.

"What's so funny?" said the guy to Ballard's left.

"Nothing," I said. "You know, I hardly ever go out to bars anymore, but I've been in two today, and in both, someone wanted to kick my ass. Quite the coincidence, don't you think?"

"Maybe you'll get lucky and be three for three," the guy on the right said.

"I know you from someplace," Ballard said. "Where?"

"Not sure," I said. "Ever do any jail time?"

"You're a real comedian," Ballard said. "Maybe you won't be so funny out in the parking lot, picking up your teeth."

I decided to end the suspense.

"How's the shoulder doing, Eddie?" I asked.

He looked at me for a few seconds.

"Now I remember. Logan Wells. The snowball fight . . . you tore up my shoulder."

"Guilty, Edward," I said. "I hope you aren't still holding a grudge."

"It was dislocated so bad I needed an operation to fix it. It hurt like hell. It still bothers me sometimes," Ballard said. "Reminds me that I owe you an ass-kicking."

"Consider it paid. Can't change the past Eddie, right? Been finding that out today."

"Speaking of the past, I heard your guardian angel got himself killed last year," Ballard said. "You had something to do with that, didn't you?"

"Let's leave him out of this," I replied.

"Quite the scandal, I heard. From All-American hero to All-American zero."

"Technically, I think Buzz was only a second team All-American," I said. "As for being a zero, I guess it takes one to know one."

I reached back to grade school for that last chestnut.

"Fuck you, Wells. I made over a hundred grand last year and drive a new BMW."

The guy on his right leaned over and said something to Ballard.

"My friend tells me you're still living in a shack on Norwich," Ballard said.

"Lucky my dad isn't around to hear you call it a shack," I said. "He built it. Hey, on the subject of dads, did Big Ed ever get clear of that Pioneer fiasco?"

Pioneer Savings & Loan was a medium sized S&L in Northwest Indiana. It had gone bankrupt a few years earlier, during the ongoing S&L crisis. Some people lost money, there was s scandal, and ultimately an investigation. Ed. Sr. was chairman of the Pioneer Board, on which Buzz also served. The investigation was initiated by federal and state authorities, but I got tangentially involved on the local level when one of the senior officers of Pioneer mysteriously disappeared. His body was found a few weeks later by some hikers in the Dunes, a presumed suicide. According to Buzz, at the next board meeting, they were discussing his death, when Ed Sr. asked, 'can we blame any of this mess on the dead guy?'

"That's it, Wells. You're getting your ass kicked. Here or on Norwich."

"I don't want to fight you, Eddie," I said. "In either place. Or both."

Just then Vic's uncle walked back into the room, a Styrofoam box in his hand.

"What's going on in here?" he barked.

We all looked at him.

"I've been listening to this bullshit back in the kitchen," he said, looking at Ballard. "Why is it when some guys have a couple beers they start acting like twelve-year-olds? Who cares what he did to you in high school? And nobody is fighting in here. Not that I think you got the balls to actually throw a punch."

"Watch it, old man," Ballard said.

Uncle Dave nodded, as if to say, 'I'll fix you.' Then he walked over to me and put the box down on the bar in front of me.

"Here's your food. It's on the house. If you don't mind, I'd like you to clear out now. I'll tell Vic you stopped by."

He walked deliberately to the other side of the bar.

"No, my friend, you watch it. You three sit here until that man has been gone for fifteen minutes. Anybody moves except him, I'm calling the cops. I have them on speed dial. They'll be here in two minutes, and they won't give a gnat's nuts about who anyone's dad is. Finish your drinks and pay your tab. Then get out of here."

I walked out of the bar, picking up the container of bleach in the vestibule on my way. It was almost full. When I got to the BMW, I rested my Styrofoam box on the trunk, opened the gas cap of the car and poured the bleach into the tank. I shook the bottle a bit at the end to make sure I got all of it, then tossed the empty bottle in a nearby dumpster I picked up my food and headed home.

chapter 21

I DECIDED TO WALK BACK VIA SIDE STREETS instead of the more direct way I had come. I wasn't quite paranoid enough to think that Ballard would try for payback by running me over. For one thing, I didn't think he would want to put a dent in his new expensive car. On the other hand, if a drunk Ballard veered at me in the parking lot at Foodchopper, I envisioned a fall and maybe another torn-up knee. He'd of course claim he didn't see me. I also figured with his dad's connections, instead of vehicular assault, Ed Jr. would get off with a ticket for a loud muffler. The burger got cold and the fries soggy on my walk, so I tossed most of it into the trash. I wished I had declined Uncle Dave's offer, the heck with karma.

It took me a while to fall asleep. When I did, I had a couple unsettling dreams. In the first one, Buzz and I were playing football in the small park near our houses, as we had done countless times growing up, except in the dream we were adults. There were some other kids from the neighborhood playing, also grown-up. One was a guy who had lived a few houses down from us. He had died, suddenly, a few years ago. He had been living out of town and we never found out what happened to him. It was kind of spooky since Buzz was now dead and I hadn't thought of the other guy in years. Our football game ended abruptly when Ballard and about ten guys showed up and started heaving snowballs at us.

In the second dream, I was up at the Dunes. It was stormy and large waves crashed against the beach. I was alone, but as I looked out into lake,

I saw a motorboat a couple hundred yards from shore. It looked to be in trouble, as the engine sounded like it was cutting in and out. There appeared to be four people in the boat: a man at the wheel and three women in the back of the boat. I tried to get their attention to see if they needed help. They didn't hear my yells or see me waving my arms. Thinking I needed to get closer so they would see me, I waded into the turbulent surf, the waves knocking me back. I was just about to call to the boat again, when a wave, much larger than the others, struck me. This time I went under the water. I was a competent swimmer, but as much as I tried, I couldn't manage to get back to the surface. I flailed as the undertow dragged me further out into the lake.

I bolted upright in the bed, sweating, and breathing hard. Shaken, I got up and found a bottle of some herbal pills Kathy had given me when I complained to her about having trouble sleeping. I also took a couple aspirin, hoping they would augment the effect of the natural stuff. I fell asleep quickly and thankfully had no more dreams.

chapter 22

MEMORIAL DAY STARTED OUT SUNNY, BUT I THOUGHT it unlikely we'd
have three nice days in a row, at least until mid-June. Sure enough,
in the afternoon, the skies began to cloud up and the temperature dropped.
When I got over to Kathy's around four, the temperature was hovering at
50 degrees. There were dark clouds in the northwest sky, with a gusty cold
wind. Rain appeared imminent.

Kathy's sister and brother were there, with spouses and kids. Her
siblings both lived in the west Chicago suburbs. Their dad's neighbor, a
spritely widow in her sixties named Josephine, or Jo for short, was also
there. She had lived next to the Plemons family for a long time. Kathy was
sure Jo and her dad had had an affair during the period after her mom
passed away a few years earlier. Kathy didn't hold it against her. In fact,
they had become very close since Kathy had been back. They held wine
happy hours a couple evenings a week, to which I was sometimes invited.
On the other hand, her brother and sister seemed to resent the woman.
They were also cool to Kathy at times. Maybe they felt some guilt since
Kathy had come all the way from California to be the main caregiver for
their father. They only a lived couple hours away, but their trips to Prairie
Stop were few and far between. I didn't see them that much, but when I
did, the three siblings always seemed to get into arguments about petty
stuff, a clue that there were ill feelings over deeper issues.

We huddled in the garage, the garage door open, the grill just outside:

a Northwest Indiana picnic. Kathy and her sister argued about the best way to cook the chicken. It turned out to be moot, since it started to rain, and the rain and the breeze made it impossible to get the charcoal going. I gave up trying after a few minutes. Kathy's brother, the engineer, was more persistent and kept at for another ten until he singed all the hair off the back of his hands by using too much lighter fluid. I stifled a laugh when that happened. At that point, the kids got restless and clamored for a pizza, so one was ordered. Kathy and I drove to pick it up. She didn't say much to me on the short drive, but I could tell she didn't care for how the holiday was going. Her siblings were apparently of the same mind and departed soon after the pizza was consumed.

I hung around after they left, and we watched a World War II movie on TV. It was the last half of *Wake Island*, with William Bendix, Robert Preston, and Brian Donlevy. I was trying to remember the name of another film with Donlevy and Preston, in which Donlevy ran around like a maniac in most of the scenes he was in. It was a pretty good action film about the French Foreign Legion, but Donlevy's antics had me laughing whenever he appeared. Kathy's dad said the movie I was thinking of was *Beau Geste*, and that he thought Donlevy had been nominated for an Academy Award. He gave me a funny look when I said, "you're kidding!" He looked tired so we decided to call it a night.

Kathy asked me to walk Jo home.

"It's only fifty feet," I said. "You think she'll get mugged?"

"The streetlight's out again. It's dark and rainy. Just do it," Kathy said.

"What if she comes on to me? I'm a lonely man, a long way from home."

Kathy laughed. "Tell her you're already involved, with the hottest woman on the street."

I gave her a quizzical look. "Oh yeah? What's her name?"

She shoved me out the door.

chapter 23

WHEN WE GOT TO JO'S HOUSE, SHE ASKED ME if I wanted to come in. It had been a long couple days, and I wanted to get home, but I said, "sure, for a minute." Jo offered me a glass of wine. She had consumed a lot earlier and seemed a little tipsy. I'd also had too many beers, but I also said 'sure' to the wine. After all, Memorial Day only comes once a year. Jo told me to sit in the living room while she went to the kitchen to get the wine.

Her house was a multi-level, like many on the street. The kitchen and living room were on the main level and the family room downstairs and the bedrooms upstairs. The couple times I had been in Jo's house with Kathy, we sat in the family room and watched a Cubs game on WGN. I assumed maybe since Kathy wasn't with me, I was more of 'company' which was why I was directed to the living room.

The living room smelled musty. The furniture and decor were right out of the sixties: a burnt orange upholstered sofa with wood and chrome legs, a few mustard yellow accent chairs, a couple light ash end tables. The only thing out of place was a brown leather recliner in the corner which sat facing a stereo console with a TV on top of it. It all made me melancholy. I knew Jo's husband had died when he was in his late fifties. He had been a professor at BHU. I figured he had life insurance and a pension, so I guess Jo had money, but their kids had moved away after college, and didn't seem like they visited much. I wondered why Jo didn't downsize, or move closer to one of her kids, but maybe there were too many memories in her home.

I thought of the John Prine song about old people, *Hello in There*, and about my own mother. She lived in Florida, in a condo complex where the residents were mostly retired people. Although not by nature an outgoing person, she had made many friends since she moved in, and whenever I heard from her, she was always doing something with one of them. She could look out at the ocean and walk the beach most days. It didn't seem like a bad life.

Jo came into the room with two big wine glasses, filled almost to the brim. Some sloshed out when she handed the glass to me.

"Whoops," she said, then, "cheers."

We clinked glasses and then she went over to the stereo console, flicked a switch and Stan Getz was playing bossa nova music. Talk about being back in the sixties. Jo sat in one of the accent chairs.

"My husband loved the samba," Jo said with a wistful expression on her face.

I was now feeling awkward in addition to being melancholy.

"Hard to believe Getz was a drug fiend," I said, instantly wondering why I said it.

"Stan Getz used drugs?" Jo said.

"Oh, yeah. I think he even got arrested once for trying to rob a pharmacy. You'd think a famous guy like him wouldn't have any trouble finding a doctor to write scripts for him."

"That's sad. He must have had his demons to turn to drugs. Addiction is dreadful."

A couple quiet minutes went by. I thought maybe Jo had drifted off.

"I've told you I used to play bridge with your mother. Years ago," she said. "She moved to Florida, right?"

"She's got a place near Jacksonville," I said.

"Vic and I tried to go to Florida each winter. It was so nice to get out of the Midwest winter, even if it was just for a week or two. Do you ever visit her there?"

"No, but usually my brother or sister will go see her in the winter."

"Not you?"

"Kind of far to drive, and flying is expensive," I said.

"Does she ever get back here?"

"Rarely," I answered. "I think she's moved on from the past, both physically and emotionally, if that makes any sense. Specifically, from my father's death and Prairie Stop."

The Girl from Ipanema came on, and Jo's head was nodding down and her eyes closing. It was easy to drift off to Astrid Gilberto's voice. I put my glass down and made to get up.

Jo's head came up, and I eased back down on the sofa.

"Good for your mom. It can be hard sometimes to move on from the past."

"I'm with you on that," I said.

"Speaking of which, Kathy tells me you and our former sheriff are looking into the case of the missing girls. The ones who vanished from the Dunes back in the sixties."

"Nothing formal," I said. "Chief Hanlen has some time on his hands now. He asked me to go with him yesterday and talk to a couple people about the girls."

"Did you learn anything?"

I felt like saying, 'yeah, don't drive around the Illinois backroads with Bill Hanlen.'

Instead, I said, "A few things. Nothing to crack the case though."

I said 'crack the case' for Jo's benefit. I found the term amusing and anachronistic, and never used it when I worked as a detective.

"My husband volunteered for one of the search parties," Jo said.

In the weeks after the girls went missing, numerous search efforts for them were made. The Dunes were combed by search parties, divers went into the lake, and there were air searches.

"Oh, yeah? What did he have to say about it?"

"How tragic it all was," she replied.

"It was, for sure. Did he have much to say about the actual search?"

"As I recall, he was surprised at how rugged the area was behind the dunes."

"Yeah, most people just go to the beaches, or hike up the dunes. Between the highway and the dunes, there's a whole lot of wetlands and woods, most of it unspoiled."

Since it had been made a National Lakeshore, the Dunes was off limits to developers. The federal government had bought a lot of land there and a had an ongoing land purchase program. Affluent Chicagoans who desired vacation properties by Lake Michigan would look to buy in the small towns east of the Dunes in Indiana and Southwest Michigan—places like Long Beach, New Buffalo and, further up in Michigan, South Haven and Grand Haven.

"I imagine it would be easy to get lost there," Jo said.

"Not really," I answered. "If you have a compass and always head north, you're going to wind up in the lake sooner or later. But there are a lot of places where someone could hide a body. And if you do find it, usually animals will have gotten there first."

I immediately regretted adding that last part.

"I think that's what Vic thought," she said. "But he didn't put it quite like that."

"Sorry, that was my years as a cop talking."

We sat in silence for another couple minutes.

"I didn't know your mother that well, but I sensed she seemed unhappy," Jo said, changing the subject back to my mother.

"Now it's my turn to be sorry. That was personal," she added.

"It's ok. I think your perception is accurate," I said. "As for the reason, I'm not sure. For one, I don't think she had a happy childhood. Plus, being married to my dad probably wasn't a day at the beach. He spent a lot of time working. Sometimes he drank a lot."

"Vic worked a lot as well, but he loved his job. Plus, he made a point of never drinking when he was in a sour or sad mood. I wish I could emulate him."

"What did he do when he was in a bad mood?" I asked.

"He would play golf or do some other physical activity."

"My dad played golf. If he had a bad game, he would come home madder than when he left. Then he would have a few beers and chase us around the yard with a chain saw."

"That sounds fun. The neighbors must have loved it," she said.

"I'm kidding. I never saw him out of control drunk. It wasn't like him to be out of control of anything. He was part Native American. It's a stereotype that they are a stoic people and not given to emotion. Like most stereotypes, I don't think it's true, but it was for him."

"Maybe the lack of emotion was why your mother was unhappy," Jo said. "Most women enjoy a little spontaneity and an occasional show of emotion. I know I did. I'm so glad Vic wasn't ashamed to show emotion. He'd cry if he heard a sad song."

"The only time I saw my dad cry was when my brother wrecked the car," I said.

"I had the idea that Native Americans were a mystical, spiritual people. That almost implies some emotional sensitivity."

"I'm inclined to agree with you," I said. "Not that me having some Indian blood makes me an expert. But their version of spirituality was different than the white man's."

"In what way?"

"I think in Native American culture, there was a duality, not a separation, between the spiritual, supernatural, world, if you will, and the material, real world. The spiritual was seen in all aspects of the material world. There were various rituals and customs that were adhered to, to ensure the harmony between the two. Some even had visions where they were supposedly able to enter the supernatural world." I stopped talking when I realized I sounded like I was lecturing.

"The visions," Jo said. "That's why I thought Native Americans were a spiritual people. Did your father ever have visions?"

"At least one for sure. When his own father was dying, he woke from a solid sleep at three AM, jumped in the car and drove non-stop to upstate New York. He didn't say where he was going. He arrived just as his father was breathing his last. My mother thought he had to go into work and didn't tell her. She was therefore surprised when his boss called the next day and asked if he was ok. He never offered any explanation to us for what he did. Our mom told us that 'sometimes your father sees things that other people can't.'

"That sounds like a vision," Jo said. "Were there other ones?"

"Nothing quite as dramatic as that. A couple times he thought he dreamed up winning numbers for the lottery, but that didn't work out. He did get five numbers right on the lotto once and won $800." I smiled. "The dream must have ended right before he got to the sixth number."

"That's a shame. Since I'm getting personal, when Kathy's father goes on to the next life, are you going to just let her go back to California?"

The question took me aback.

"Not sure I got a whole lot of choice in the matter. I don't like the idea, but I can't imagine her staying here," I said.

"Why not?"

"Oh, for one, her job. The cold and snow in the winter. The heat and bugs in the summer. And, as you might have observed, she doesn't seem close with the rest of her family."

"On the other hand, it's her childhood home," Jo said. "It's not bad for a small town. Admittedly, the winter can be daunting, but May to October isn't bad. More importantly, I've known Kathy a long time. I can see that she is very happy when she is with you. You belong together. Don't let her go."

chapter 24

I WALKED BACK OVER TO KATHY'S FOR MY CAR. As I drove home, I thought of my father. He was in his early sixties when he found out he had lung cancer and died shortly after he turned sixty-five. He smoked heavily and worked in a steel mill. When he was young, he had also worked in a shipyard and likely was exposed to asbestos. When I was recovering after my first accident with a car, I had trouble sleeping, and watched a lot of late-night TV. I viewed with cynical humor those commercials for legal firms that pitched taking legal action 'if you or a loved one has mesothelioma or died from it.' I figured whoever added 'or a loved one' was snickering when he did that. One night I called one of the toll-free numbers that were thoughtfully provided. The 'operator standing by' who picked up became animated when I told her about my father dying of lung cancer and working in a shipyard. Her enthusiasm waned rapidly when I said he was also a heavy smoker and last worked in the shipyard thirty years ago. The clincher was when I told her he had been dead for over five years. She said she'd get back to me. I told her I'd be waiting by the phone. She never called.

In his final months, my dad shunted back and forth between the hospital and a skilled nursing facility, with brief stints at home. During one stay at home, my mother convinced him to visit the steel mill to say goodbye to his co-workers. I was going to drive him, but when we got on the highway, he told me he didn't want his fellow workers to see him. He asked instead

to be taken to the Dunes, just a few minutes from the mill. It was a beautiful fall day, and we sat and stared at Lake Michigan for an hour. I could
have stayed there all day, but my dad was getting a chill. Before we left, he
told me the area used to be a hunting ground for the Pottawattamie tribe,
who lived in Northwest Indiana. He said he could sense the spirits of the
warriors. I attributed this comment to the large quantities of pain medica-
tion he was taking.

That night I had another dream. It was about the trip my father and I
took to the lake that day many years ago. In the dream, the weather started
out the same, nice, but then quickly changed for the worse. Dark menacing clouds rolled in. It got stormy, with strong winds, which kicked up
large waves, much as in my dream the previous night. I wanted to leave,
but my dad wanted to go on the beach. I tried to talk him out of it, but he
wouldn't listen. I went to get his jacket from the car. When I returned, he
wasn't there. I frantically looked about, then saw him on the beach. He had
removed his clothes and was wading into the rough surf. His body was no
longer the frail one that had been ravaged by disease, but the strong, wiry,
one of a man who could pound a nail through a 2 x 4 with one blow of a
hammer. I saw him dive under a large wave and then come up on the other
side, shaking the water off his head.

"Come on in, son! It's great!" he called, pausing, and looking back
at me.

"Dad! Get back here! It's too rough!" I shouted.

My father had a vexing proclivity to turn even minor challenges into
trials of manhood. Maybe it was a generational thing, or a reflection of his
own hardscrabble childhood, I don't know. In such moments, he would
scoff, derisively, 'be a man!' I quit playing football my senior year in high
school, and I would tell people the reason was to focus on my grades. It
wasn't grades; it was my dad's frequent criticism of my play, that I wasn't
aggressive enough. Consequently, I missed out on being on the team
that won the state championship, which was a big deal in a small town in
Indiana. My dad didn't speak to me for a couple months after that.

He yelled from the lake, "don't be chicken."

I guess that was better than 'be a man!'

chapter 25

I T WAS 4:30 A.M. WHEN I AWOKE, ABRUPTLY, from the unsettling dream. I knew I wasn't getting back to sleep. I went down to the curb in the dark to get the paper, but it wasn't there. I saw the delivery guy's vehicle down the street and waited. He had a used postal vehicle, driver's seat on the right, to facilitate placing the paper in a tube under the mailbox. Keeping the paper dry was a nice small-town touch, but I had recently received a form letter notifying me that the box service would be phased out. I imagine it was easier and cheaper to just toss the paper in the yard.

"You're up early!" the driver said cheerfully, as he handed me the paper. Then, "how's your mom doing?"

The same guy had been bringing the paper for at least the last ten years, yet I blanked on his name and felt bad. I was thinking it was 'Steve.' My mom would always give him a $10 bill at Christmas. I wondered if the logical next step in the newspaper's cost reduction would be Steve losing his job.

"She's good. Thanks for asking," I said.

"Tell her Rick said hi!"

"Will do, Rick. Have a good day." Boy, he sure looked like a Steve.

"Aw, now you put all the pressure on me! I will if it doesn't rain!" Rick said, laughing as he pulled away. You had to admire a fellow who was upbeat that early in the morning.

There was a cool breeze, but it had decreased in strength from the prior evening. I had a cup of coffee while I glanced at the paper. When I was young, a lead story might have been, 'Mr. and Mrs. Smith celebrated their 40th wedding anniversary with a trip to Mackinac Island.' Now the big story was about an armed robbery at a convenience store near the interstate. The store clerk did not resist but got shot anyway. The good news was that it appeared he would live, and that the police had apprehended the would-be robbers, two cousins from Gary in their twenties. Their getaway car had apparently run out of gas. The authorities blamed the cousin's drug use for their crime. Could be, I suppose. When I was in uniform in South Bend, I had a partner who said, in such instances, 'maybe it was drugs, or maybe they were just real assholes.'

I backed the Volvo out of the driveway. Traffic was light as I made my way over to Indiana 49 but picked up once I got on the highway. There were always people heading to work at the numerous plants, factories, and steel mills lining the south shore of Lake Michigan. Even with the sharp decline in domestic steel production in the mid-eighties, and the resulting cutbacks and layoffs, Indiana still led the nation in steel production and number of steel workers.

Most people heading to the Indiana Dunes, from east or west, would likely take the interstate or toll road to State Highway 49, then head north to the entrance gate of Indiana Dunes State Park. It was about a mile from the gate to the main parking lot and Lake Michigan. The lot was where the Dunes's girls abandoned car was found. Between the beach and the lot was the large bathhouse, built in the 1920s when the state park was established. The iconic art-deco bathhouse was frequently featured in pictures of the park, although the last time I was in it, the building was showing its age. Plans for renovating it were constantly being written about in the paper, but the state park service could never seem to get the funding.

The sand dunes rose nearly 250 feet above the lake. Although they were impressive, they were not, by a large margin, the highest dunes on Lake Michigan. That distinction belonged to the dunes at Sleeping Bear National Lakeshore, almost three hundred miles north, in Michigan. When I was still married, my wife and I made the 'circle tour' of Lake Michigan and stopped at Sleeping Bear Dunes. My wife, as she was wont to do, began chatting it up with a park ranger. When he found out we were from Indiana, he pointedly told us that the dunes at Sleeping Bear were almost twice the height of the ones in Indiana. I gave him a look of feigned disbelief, and said, 'them's fighting words.' He didn't crack a smile, but my wife laughed. I'll admit that the Sleeping Bear Dunes were more scenic. The time we were there, the lake was a beautiful turquoise color, unlike the grayish blue by the Indiana Dunes. I assumed the vibrant color was due to less pollution in the lake up north. My wife had once been on a Greek Islands cruise with her family and said the lake color up north reminded her of the Mediterranean Sea.

I didn't go to the state park, although I was still in the national lakeshore. The state park was contained within and surrounded by the national lakeshore. I exited 49 at Indiana 12 and headed east in the direction of Beverly Shores. I cut over on one of the access roads to Lakeshore Drive, a narrow road which ran parallel to the lake. There were a couple small parking lots off Lakeshore. On a nice summer day, the chances of getting one of the spots was nil. At 5 a.m. on a chilly, grey morning after a holiday, I had the place to myself. I got out of the car and walked the short distance from the parking lot to the beach. The wind was kicking up some decent sized waves, and they were breaking fast.

I wasn't sure what I was going to do when I got on the beach. I didn't presume that the dreams from the last two nights were visions. My miniscule Native American heritage certainly did not qualify me to experience visions; but the dreams certainly were vivid and disquieting, and I knew now I was going to go in the lake. I had the strange, obsessive, thought that if I went into the water, I would gain some insight into what happened to the missing girls. It didn't make sense, but logic wasn't forefront in my thinking.

My father was very involved with teaching me and my siblings how to swim. He was a good swimmer himself and knew that to be like him we had to be comfortable in the water. During the winter, we took swimming lessons at the Y or up at the university. During the summer, he took us to the small swimming lake on the outskirts of town and to Lake Michigan. He even made the somewhat odd decision to join the local country club so we could use the pool there. It was odd, since our family wasn't exactly country club material, even for a small town in Indiana.

He also told us emphatically we couldn't panic in the water. He said plenty of good swimmers had drowned because they panicked. This made sense, but also seemed problematic. Telling somebody not to panic was like telling them not to think of the Empire State Building. What else would you think about after someone says that? His most important, often repeated advice was never swim alone.

As I looked out at the turbulent lake, I already knew I wasn't going to be comfortable in the cold, rough surf. I also had the gnawing thought I might panic once I got in the water, and if I got in trouble there was no one around to help. The main beach at the state park had lifeguards from Memorial Day until Labor Day. If you even dipped a toe into the lake when the guards weren't on duty, one of the park rangers, who always seemed to be present, would brusquely tell you to get out of the water. If you kept at it, they would ask you to leave the park. There were no lifeguard stations where I was, and no rangers or anybody else in sight. I had the funny, inane thought that the one thing I had going for me was there were no sharks in the Great Lakes. I figured whatever plane of existence my father was in, he'd be angry if he could see me, but at least he couldn't accuse me of being chicken.

I got out of my clothes before I changed my mind. I thought about leaving my boxer shorts on but didn't want to ride back to town in soggy underwear, especially since the Volvo had leather seats. If someone showed up on a morning like this, they deserved to see me naked. I gasped when the first cold wave hit me but kept heading out into the surf. I expected a strong undertow, but it wasn't overpowering. I noted the current was pulling me west as well as north. I kept a nervous eye out for anything that looked to be a rip current. I knew that neither an undertow nor a rip current would drag me under the water; they would only move me quickly out into the lake, past where the waves were breaking. At that point, I also knew the force of the current would dissipate, and hopefully then I could swim away from the current and back to shore. My dad had drilled into me that the worst thing you could do if caught in a rip would be to try and swim against it.

In the many times I have swum in Lake Michigan there were one or more sandbars, offshore. I wondered if the rough surf had moved them further out or eradicated them altogether. I was less than 30 yards out when I could no longer touch bottom. I dove into a wave and started swimming.

I swam out another 20 yards, the surf pummeling me, then turned and went parallel to shore. As I expected, the cold water rapidly sapped my strength, but at least I was no longer swimming directly into the waves. But whatever epiphany I was hoping for by entering the lake wasn't coming to me. The only thing I felt was how cold the water was and how out of shape I was, at least for swimming. I decided I had had enough and turned back to shore. I didn't look at the beach right away because I didn't want to see how far out I was. When I did look, I thought I saw something moving on shore near where I had left my clothes. I was well west of where I had entered the water, and the waves were now breaking on me, so I didn't have a clear view. When I was able to touch bottom again, I stood and saw there were three large dogs right by my clothes.

chapter 26

I WADED BACK TO THE BEACH, BUT IT WASN'T EASY. The incoming waves were hitting me hard and fast from behind, but the real problem was the undertow. Either it got stronger the closer I got to shore, or I got weaker, or both. Between the waves and the undertow, I almost went down a few times. Eventually I staggered out of the lake, a good fifty yards west of where I had gone in. Maybe that was fortuitous, since the dogs were still rooting through my clothes, and I was far enough away they didn't notice me right away. I rubbed my limbs, trying to regain some feeling in them, while I looked at the dogs.

They appeared to be some type of German Shephard mix, except their coats were blacker and grayer than brown. They were also larger than any German Shephard I had ever seen. They looked more like wolves, which was impossible, since the closest wild wolves were the few living hundreds of miles north in Michigan's Upper Peninsula. But I knew there were people who kept canine-wolf hybrids as pets.

Speaking of people, I didn't see any around. My luck, some rich person from Ogden Dunes was out walking his dogs, or wolf-dogs, on the beach, figured nobody was out on a morning like this, and decided to let them off leash. As I was considering that, the dogs saw me. They stared intently a me for twenty seconds, then looked at each other, then back at me. Their canine double-take would have been comical had I not been naked and freezing with three big dogs eyeing me as if breakfast was being served.

What followed was even more peculiar. Each of the dogs raised their muzzle and let out a loud, long howl.

The howls were ominously familiar. There is a wolf sanctuary located in Battleground, Indiana, near Lafayette, that I had visited once on their 'wolf howl" nights. You got to sit in the dark while the wolves let loose with their long and mournful howls. The sanctuary's location was fitting, as there had been a large Native American settlement near Battleground in the early 1800s, and many Indian tribes regarded the wolf as the most sacred of animals. The settlement, known as Prophetstown, was founded by the Shawnee war chief Tecumseh, and his brother, a spiritual leader known as the Prophet. Their coalition of tribes, which they hoped would preserve Indian lands from white encroachment, was defeated at the Battle of Tippecanoe in 1811, and the town destroyed. The wolves were still there, so that was something.

I didn't have to wait long to figure out what the animals were going to do. As soon as they stopped howling, they started in my direction. I was surprised they did not charge at me like angry dogs would. Instead, they separated and advanced on me at a lope from different angles. One of the animals was practically in the lake, while the others had moved further in on the beach. It seemed to me a very calculated and wolflike manner of attack.

I knew I couldn't outrun them but had the idea that if I went back in the lake maybe they wouldn't follow me. Maybe in a swimming race, I would be on somewhat even terms with the dogs. Even dogs who were bred to be at home in the water were not particularly fast swimmers. But I wasn't sure if I could get out in the lake quick enough.

I chose a third option, which was to stand my ground. There was a decent size piece of driftwood washed up by the rough surf a couple feet from where I stood. I grabbed it and assumed what I hoped was a menacing posture, crouching forward and holding the driftwood like a spear. I figured if I could hit or jab one of the dogs with it, they might make them think twice about attacking.

When the dogs were about ten yards from me, suddenly there was a peculiar trilling noise. It was like the low-pitched, pulsing hum from a piece of electronic equipment, and vaguely familiar to me. I could hear it clearly over the waves breaking, yet I couldn't tell where it was coming from. The dogs heard it to and instantly responded to it. They turned and ran back the way they came. They didn't stop where my clothes were but kept going down the beach, and then turned toward the dunes.

"What the hell?" I muttered, very relieved, yet very puzzled. The noise stopped.

I ran to where my clothes were. It wasn't a fast run, as I was still recovering from my exertion in the water. The dogs had vanished. I was reaching down for my shorts, when I heard a voice.

"The Large Water must be cold," the voice said. This followed by a loud cackling laugh. It was grating and creepy.

The voice and laugh came from a very old, very round, woman who was standing on the berm in front of the parking lot, twenty feet or so from me. I would have sworn nobody was there a second ago. She was pointing at my cold-shrunk private parts. I pulled on my shorts.

From police work, I had become reasonably accurate in deducing a person's age. Maybe not to the specific age, but within five years or so. This woman defied my age guessing skills. I would have said between 85 and 100. Her face was the color of weathered bronze and was deeply creased, her eyes dark slits within the creases. Tufts of grayish white hair emerged from under the dull red and black scarf around her head. She was short, and just about as round as she was tall, very large busted. She wore a plain, dark, ankle length cloth skirt and a dark shawl, which looked as if they could have been as old as she was. The only thing that looked incongruous on her was the pair of bright turquoise and gold earrings which dangled a couple inches below her ears. From her appearance and the way she referred to the lake by the Ojibway definition of 'Michigan,' I figured she was Native American.

"Where'd your dogs go?" I shouted. More of an attempt at a shout as I was still breathing hard.

No scary cackle this time, but a snort.

"They are not mine. They are as they were before. They are like you."

"What do you mean?"

"They live in two worlds."

"How's that?"

She didn't reply.

"Lady, you can get in serious trouble for letting animals like that run loose. And what was that noise?"

"You look, but you don't see," she said.

She turned and pointed at the berm toward a tree with a small cavity. Just as I looked at it, a screech owl poked its head out. That was why the noise sounded familiar to me. Screech owls don't screech; they make a peculiar trilling noise. It resembles a pulsating electronic hum, and it can be loud on a dark, quiet night. But screech owls aren't much bigger than starlings. It would have been impossible for a bird that size to make a noise like I heard earlier—also, they were strictly nocturnal animals.

"No way that owl could have made that noise," I said.

"Did you not hear it?' she countered.

I didn't say anything.

"The ones you look for are not in the Large Water," she said.

"And who am I looking for?" I asked.

"You know why you are here."

"I just felt like going for a swim."

"If you listen, I will help you find what you are looking for. The spirits of those you seek have been lost long enough."

"I don't believe in spirits," I replied.

The cackling laugh again. "Yet you are here. But you will need to travel further to find what you are looking."

"Further where?"

"South, where it is warm in winter. But there will be danger."

The cryptic remarks were irritating me.

"You mean Florida?," I said. "And if we're talking about my mom, I already know where she is. In Jacksonville. And it's reasonably safe there."

That got her mad.

"You are foolish, but now you will listen!" she said. She stomped her foot angrily on the ground.

The noise from before was back. It was all around me, louder, and quickly escalating to where it was piercing and painful. I dropped to my knees with my hands over my ears and then went completely to the ground. Suddenly it stopped.

chapter 27

I GOT UP, RUBBING MY EARS. I COULD STILL HEAR the waves, so it didn't seem there was any permanent damage. I looked over where the old woman had been, but she had vanished. I put my jeans on, grabbed my other stuff and ran up to the parking lot. I figured that was the only place she could have gone.

"Sunvabitch," I exclaimed, as I got to the parking lot but didn't see her. There was a pickup truck at the end of the lot, by the pavilion, where a man in a dark green uniform was putting a garbage bag in a trashcan. I put the rest of my clothes on and jogged over to him. His jacket had a National Park Service emblem on it. He was a little taller than me, thin, and looked to be in his sixties, white hair, with a scraggly white beard. He stopped what he was doing when he saw me approach.

He had startled a bit at my sudden appearance, but then gave me a bemused look.

"Nice morning for a swim," he said, noticing my wet hair and disheveled appearance.

I tried to catch my breath.

"You ok? Need some help?" he said.

I finally was able to get out, "where did the old woman go?"

"What woman?" he replied.

"There was an old woman down on the beach. I was talking to her and then she just disappeared."

He finished putting the bag in the can and put the lid back on.

"You're the only one I've seen this morning," he replied. "Boy, you could have given me a heart attack, running up on me like that, this time of day."

"Sorry," I said. "About the old woman. She was ancient. Could have been Indian. The American kind. There were three big animals down there too. Looked like wolves."

"There haven't been wolves in these parts for almost a century. You must have seen coyotes."

"I know what a coyote looks like," I replied. "And they are solitary, not like wolves. And how about the loud noise? You had to have heard it."

He gave me a slightly apprehensive look.

"I didn't see any old Indian woman," he said. "You probably saw coyotes. And what kind of noise? The only thing I've heard is the wind and the waves."

"It was like a shriek owl on steroids. You couldn't have missed it."

He shook his head. "You sure you're ok?"

This wasn't going anywhere.

"I need to find her," I said and turned to leave.

He reached out and grabbed my arm.

"Wait a second," he said. "What you need to do is collect yourself. Let's go sit down."

He gestured to the benches in the pavilion.

He was right. I had to calm down. I doubted if I was going to find the old woman. We went up to the pavilion and sat down. He took a small bottle of water out of his jacket pocket and held it out to me.

"I got more in the truck," he said, when I tried to refuse it.

"Name's George Hiatt."

"Logan Wells," I replied. He offered a hand, and I shook it.

"You know, you shouldn't be swimming by yourself, especially on a day like today. The lake can be dangerous. Doesn't matter how good a swimmer you think you are."

"My dad used to tell me never to swim alone," I said.

"He's a wise man. You should listen to him." he said.

He gave me a stern look.

"You weren't trying to do yourself in, were you, Logan?"

"No, just felt like going for a swim. I'll own up now to it wasn't such a good idea."

"I think I heard that drowning isn't a bad way to go," George said. "But how would anyone really know?"

"You got a point there," I replied.

"You been doing this a while, George?" I asked. I had a feeling unless the old woman was a figment of my imagination, I wasn't the first person to ever see her.

"You could say that. Started with the state park service, part-time when I was still in high school. That was before the war. World War Two, I mean. Then I went in the Army."

"What part?"

"I was in the Signals Corp. Trained at Fort Monmouth in New Jersey."

"Near the ocean," I said.

"Yep, first time I ever saw it. Then I got sent to Europe after D-Day."

"See any combat?" I asked.

"I wound up in Belgium, a place called the Ardennes Forest, in winter, 1944. Thought I was lucky because it was supposed to be a quiet sector. Turned out not to be."

"The Battle of the Bulge," I said, realizing what he was talking about.

"Yeah. Hitler figured if he could hit the U.S. and British hard, they'd give up. Then he could beat the Russians. If he wasn't already nuts, he was when he came up with that one."

"I imagine he was always crazy," I said. "He also took some poison gas in the first world war. That couldn't have helped."

"Anyhow, the Panzers broke through our lines. I ended up getting captured by the SS. Me and 25,000 others. I thought for a while they were going to shoot me. They did shoot about a hundred other GIs who had surrendered, near a place called Malmedy. Machine-gunned them down. Any ones still moving, they shot them in the head. Poor bastards."

He shook his head. "Anyhow, I wasn't quite the same man after I got back."

"How so?"

"Not much for being around people."

"Understandable. Then this kind of work must be to your liking."

George nodded in agreement.

"I work outside, usually by myself. I start early. Pick up the trash. Make sure the facilities and restrooms are ok. If we get a storm, I'll pick up branches and debris, and let the rangers know of any beach erosion. Stuff like that. The state retired me a while back, but then I got on with the National Park Service."

"Were you working here back in the summer of 1966?" I asked.

"Sure. Summer is the busiest time here. You probably would have guessed that."

"That was when the three girls from near Chicago went missing from the beach," I said.

"The July 4th weekend, 1966," he replied. "Over twenty years ago. I thought nobody remembered them. You almost look too young to know anything about it."

"I'm older than I look. What do you remember?"

"Well, like I said, I get to work early, before the park is even open. I did notice the girls' car in the lot early the next day, Sunday. 'Course I didn't know it was their car at the time."

"Guess it wasn't that unusual for cars to be left in the lot," I said.

"You weren't supposed to leave vehicles in the lot overnight, but it wasn't like it never happened," George said.

"I can see that," I said. "Maybe you're some young people having a good time on the beach with your friends, or folks you just met. You leave to get something to eat. Stop at bar, have a few beers, then crash at somebody's house, figuring you can get the car the next day. Who knows? Maybe that's what the girls did. Then something went wrong."

"If you're asking me," George said. "I don't think they left the beach in a car."

"Why?"

"I read a lot about those girls in the paper. They didn't seem like the type to go running off with a stranger in a car. If they were leaving the beach, I think they would have taken their own car. Plus, they left all their stuff behind. I can't see any woman doing that."

"I agree," I said. "There's some say they got on a boat."

"I can't see that either," he replied. "At least with a stranger."

George paused. "You know something about this. You law?"

"Used to be."

He thought about that for a second.

"Logan, sure, now I remember. I read about you in the paper. That was some strange story. The professor and his wife. And the football star. That was your friend, right?

"Yeah. Buzz Wildrick," I replied.

"I remember him when he was in high school. I'm not one for crowds, like I said, but I used to go to the football games to watch him play. His last year he led Prairie to the state title."

"Yes, he did. It was a big deal."

"Only thing bigger might have been if Prairie won the state basketball tourney. He was something else. Not many like him."

"He was that."

"So now you're trying to figure out what happened to those three girls."

I nodded my head.

"Well, I wish you luck," George said. "Seems like after all this time, you're going to need a lot of it."

chapter 28

WE SAT AND LOOKED OUT AT THE LAKE. The wind was starting to die down and the water wasn't quite as choppy as earlier.

"I better let you get back to work, George," I said. "I've taken up enough of your time."

"Say, about this old woman you saw," he said, a look of rumination on his face.

"You saw her too?" I said, my voice rising.

"Not me," he said, shaking his head. "Somebody might think I was off my rocker if I said I saw her. And me, an old vet, with battle fatigue."

"This is just between you and me," I said. "To be honest, I might think twice about telling anyone else what I just saw. I told you and you think I'm crazy."

"No, I don't think that. You say she was older than dirt, round as she was tall?"

"That was her," I said.

"You say there were some big dogs around when you saw her?"

"Not right when I saw her," I replied. "They were on the beach when I got out of the lake. Three of them. They looked like wolves and came at me like I think wolves would. Then there was this strange noise, and they took off. That's when I saw the old woman."

"I'm guessing you have at least heard of people who've seen her," I said, hoping to prompt him to talk.

"Well, like I said, I started working here before the war. It was different back then."

"How so?"

"More peaceful and quiet. No big interstate highways along the lake. The Gary Works was the only steel mill near the Dunes. And there was just the state park; the feds didn't own a lot of the land like they do now. A few folks even had cabins back among the dunes. It became different after the war. More industry along the lake. More cars. More people. Heck, the Army even built a missile base in the Dunes back in the fifties."

"I remember my dad telling me about that," I said. "Supposedly it was to protect the steel mills from Russian bombers. That was his excuse for not coming home sometimes. Said he felt safer at work. I don't think my mom bought it."

"That's a good one," George said, chuckling. "But back then, it was more natural up here, I guess you might say. Not near as many people around, including rangers."

George had a wistful look as he recounted days gone by.

"Different isn't always better, I guess," he added.

"I don't know," I said. "More natural sounds good."

"Yeah, it does," George ageed. "Anyway, when I started here, I remember there were stories about an old Pottawattamie squaw who had a cabin back off the dunes."

"What kind of stories?"

"Did you know there's still some Pottawattamie living in the area?" George asked. "Ones that managed to not get removed west when most of the other Indians were."

"I did know that. I understand it's the Pokagon Band of the tribe," I replied. "There's some living in Laporte and Knox Counties. More of the tribe live up in Michigan."

"My brother's oldest boy married a girl who has some Pottawattamie blood," George said. "She's real proud of it. Knows a lot about their history and customs and such."

"I got a little Indian blood myself," I said.

"Oh yeah? What tribe?"

"My dad's family were Iroquois," I replied.

"They lived in upstate New York, right?"

"A lot still do. Some are in Canada. What about the old woman?"

"In the descriptions I heard of her, she looked like you said. Round and old. Real old. She was described as ancient, even back then."

"What kind of stories were there?"

"Some hikers complained they'd been chased by a large dog or dogs she had."

"Those dogs I saw, if they were dogs, weren't fifty years old," I said.

"I wouldn't think so," George agreed, but I had the idea from the way he said it, maybe he didn't believe I had seen any dogs.

"And a few campers also said she looked like a witch, and that she held strange rituals in the middle of the night," he said.

"What kind of rituals?" I asked. "Bonfires and people dancing naked?"

"Maybe just the bonfires and her dancing and yelling. 'Course it would be easy to imagine things on a dark night out in the woods. I've spent more time than most in this place, but not sure I'd care to be wandering around out here in the middle of the night."

"Me neither," I said. "Anything happen with the complaints?"

"The guy who was in charge back then wasn't one to fly off the handle. I think he would have liked to leave the woman alone. I'm not real sure he even believed she existed."

"I guess because of the complaints, doing nothing wasn't an option," I said.

"Yeah. He decided to go up to have a talk with her."

"How'd that go?"

"Fine, except he couldn't find her," George said. "He hiked up in the woods, and found a derelict cabin, in the area where people claimed they saw her, but he said it looked like it hadn't been lived in for years. No woman or dog. There were remnants of a campfire, but that was all."

"The fire could have been built by anyone," I said. "And that was the end of it?"

"It should have been, but there was another fella working here who wasn't like the boss."

"How so?"

"He was a bit of trouble-maker. Maybe he was bucking for the boss's job, who knows?" George paused. "He was also the type who doesn't care for folks different than him, if you know what I mean."

I thought about that.

"He didn't like the idea of an old Indian woman scaring the white folks," I said.

"I guess that was it. You would have thought we'd done enough to those people. Kicking them off their land and giving them all kinds of diseases, ones they never had before."

"Don't forget about the whiskey," I said. 'What did this fellow do?"

"He decides to stake out the cabin at night and surprise the old woman. Maybe he thought he would be a hero if could scare her away. He hikes up there as it's getting dark."

"And he never comes back," I said.

"Oh, he came back, alright," George said. "But he quit the next day. Not only did he quit, but he also lit out for parts unknown."

"Anybody ever hear from him again?"

"Nope. Odd he did that, seeing how jobs weren't real easy to come by back then. I heard he was white as a sheet when he came out of the woods. One fellow who saw him said he looked like he had seen a ghost."

I thought about that for a second.

"You're saying I saw a ghost, George?"

"Well, Logan, I got to be honest with you, I don't think you saw a 150 year old Pottawatomi woman and some wolves."

"Any stories about people seeing the woman after that?"

He paused before he answered.

"Not that I'm familiar with, but I didn't start right back after the war. Took a little time off. As I said, things seemed different before and after the war. More hustle and bustle and people around. Seems to me, if she was still around someone would have seen her."

"Yeah. I guess this woman was a figment of my imagination, then. Or a ghost. Maybe I just dreamed her up."

"Didn't and wouldn't say that," George said, shaking his head. "You got a dog, Logan?"

"Not at present. Had many of them growing up."

"Well, I got a dog. My dog can hear things I can't hear, and smell things I can't smell. When it's dark, he can see things I can't see. Does me not being able to see, smell and hear the things my dog does mean they don't exist?"

"I guess not," I said. "But I'm not sure what you mean."

"Well, this may sound strange, but maybe you were the only one meant to see this old Indian woman," he said. "And maybe there's a reason for that."

George asked me several times if I was alright before he let me go. He wrote his name and phone number on a small piece of paper, and I gave him mine. He told me to call him if I wanted to talk more.

chapter 29

I SLEPT LATE THE NEXT DAY. I WAS GLAD I DIDN'T HAVE any more bizarre dreams, although I briefly wondered if my trip to the Dunes yesterday was a dream. Then I was emptying my pants pocket and found the piece of paper on which George Hiatt had written his name and number. Not sure why exactly, but I stuck it in my wallet.

After I got up, I went for a long run, to sort through the strange experiences of yesterday. The only plausible explanation I could come up with was that maybe they were related to the concussions I'd had in the two car accidents I'd been in the last eighteen months. The first concussion was severe, the second one not so much, but I understood the effect of head injuries could be cumulative. Maybe throw in another one or two from my football playing days. Perhaps my addled brain couldn't process all the odd activity of the last few days. Twenty-year old mysteries, bar fights, and run-ins with high school antagonists weren't in my normal routine. It was disturbing to think I was hallucinating but wasn't sure I could rule it out.

On Thursday, Kathy and I spent a couple hours together. I told her I'd gone up to the Dunes but didn't tell her about my quest into Lake Michigan. She would have thought I had taken leave of my senses if I told her about my swim in the turbulent lake. And if I said anything about the old Pottawattamie woman I saw, or thought I saw, she would have called for the men in the white coats. I wouldn't have blamed her. Aside from that, she had her own problems. One of her clients in California was pressuring her to return there for a big project. She didn't want to go but didn't want to lose the business and was trying to figure out an acceptable compromise. The thought of Kathy leaving added to my level of agitation, and further convinced me I might be taking leave of my senses.

Hanlen called early Friday afternoon, the first day of June. The temperature was near 80 with no clouds in the sky, just white contrails from jets heading to or from Chicago. I took the weather as a good omen for the rest of the summer.

Hanlen didn't identify himself when I picked up, just said, "you play golf?"

"Used to," I replied.

"Not now?"

"The PGA confiscated my clubs. Said I was a menace to the golf community."

"Figures. I was thinking we could meet me at Deer Creek and talk while we played. I'm in the clubhouse now."

"I don't play," I said. "And we are talking."

"Yep, but I'd like to do it in person," he said. "And it's too nice a day to waste."

"That's on one of my running routes," I said. "I can be there in half an hour."

"It takes you half an hour to get over here from where you live?" Hanlen said, skeptically. "I think I could walk the distance in that time."

"I want to get my running for today in case you decide to throw me in the car and drive off to parts unknown. Plus, I need to work off some stress."

There was a pause, then, "suit yourself. I'll be on the practice green."

Considering it wasn't that big of a town, Prairie Stop had not one, but two, municipal golf courses. The first, Deer Creek, opened in the 1930s as a private nine-hole club, only a mile from downtown. The family who owned the club donated it to the city after World War II, along with some adjacent land where nine more holes and a clubhouse were built. As the town's population grew, desirable neighborhoods sprang up around the golf course, and there was speculation that the city would sell the land to a developer. It wasn't commonly known, but the family donating the land stipulated in the deed that it could be sold only if the city opened a comparable course elsewhere. Five or so years ago, Big Ed Ballard built a nine-hole, par three course, on a tract of land he owned not far from the town's sewage treatment plant. He called it Stony Creek, but it soon and aptly became known as Smelly Creek. Big Ed waited a decent interval, then pitched a proposal to the city council to swap Smelly Creek for Deer Creek. The editor of the town paper wrote a scathing denunciation of the deal, comparing it to Peter Minuit's purchase of Manhattan from the Indians in 1626 for $24 in trinkets. That was a good one. The resulting public outcry killed the deal. The city kept Deer Creek. Big Ed, with no further use for a golf course, sold Stony Creek to the city for one dollar. The big loser was the newspaper editor, who lost his job, as Ballard threatened to pull his considerable advertising business from the paper unless he was let go. So much for freedom of the press.

I put on my running shorts and Portage Indian t-shirt and was on my way. School was out for the summer, so I cut through the massive and modern Prairie High School complex, part of which bordered the golf course. The school districts in Northwest Indiana seemed to have no issues with funding. The Prairie Stop High School was big when it was built and had been added on to a couple times. It was much larger than the local junior college, and the football stadium was much more impressive than that of the town's college, Benjamin Harrison University.

The gate was open to the stadium, so I ran a few laps around the all-weather, ten lane track. As I did, I admired the massive scoreboard on the north end of the field. It was new and expensive. It was also a bit of a scandal, purchased and installed without prior approval of the school board. The football coach and athletic director later apologized to the board for the oversight. I thought one of them might be fired. They weren't, proving the adage that it's easier to ask for forgiveness than permission. I exited the stadium to the third hole of the golf course. Considering it was a beautiful day, I was surprised there weren't more golfers out. Hanlen was alone on the practice green, by the clubhouse. He missed a long putt as I approached and raised his putter in frustration.

"Sorry," I said. "I messed up your concentration."

"I've been missing them all day," he replied.

"I thought you were just going out."

"I already got 18 in. I was thinking of playing another nine, if you played."

"I could caddy for you, I guess," I said.

"I don't need a caddy."

"Hey," I said, "you ever see that guy on ESPN who speed golfs? Runs between shots. He can play 18 holes in under an hour."

"Why would someone do something like that?"

"Maybe he likes golf so much, he wants to pack in as much as he can," I said.

"How many clubs does he carry?" Hanlen asked, curious about the running golfer

"The time I saw him, he had a three wood, a five iron, and a putter." I don't watch much golf, but it was entertaining watching somebody run around a golf course.

Hanlen thought about that.

"That's what I would carry if I was doing something crazy like that," he said.

"Speaking of liking golf, where is everybody?" I asked. "The place should be jammed on a day like today."

"Temporary lull. The men's over 50 league played this morning. Under 50 starts at 4."

We walked over to his car. Hanlen put his clubs in, then got out a small cooler.

"How about a beer?" he said, pulling out a six pack of Hamm's.

"I still got to run home," I replied.

"You'll be ok. Just don't blow through any stop signs and signal all your turns."

He handed me a can. There were a couple benches between the clubhouse and the first tee, and we went over and sat down. Right after we did, a large man of about Hanlen's age ambled down the path from the clubhouse. He had a cigar in his mouth, and in addition to a pull-cart, he had a big shaggy dog on a leash. It looked like a St. Bernard mix. I had seen the man and the dog on the course before when I was out running. Unless there was an event going on, or the course was crowded, the parks department wasn't too strict about keeping non-golfers, of the two and four-legged variety, off the property. Not sure what they could have done anyway about the large number of geese and deer that made the place their home. Perhaps they figured allowing communal, natural use was one way to keep the course out of a developer's hands.

I figured Hanlen would know the guy with the dog. I was right.

"Going out again, Deke?" Hanlen addressed the man. When he said Deke, I knew it had to be Donald 'Deke" McKnight, the long-time chief administrator of the county hospital. The clincher was his golf cap, which had 'County Hospital' on it. When I got out of the hospital after my first car accident, I had received a form letter from him. It was regarding the considerable balance due, after insurance, for my lengthy stay in his facility. I was also warned of disagreeable consequences if I didn't pay. It was all very perplexing to me, since I had been employed by the county when I'd been hit by the car, plus I thought I had good health insurance, also through the county. I guess it wasn't that good.

"Yeah, but not 'cause I want to. I'm still in mourning from the way you kicked my ass this morning," Deke said.

Then he looked down at his dog. "But Barney needs his exercise. Right, boy?"

Barney did look like he could stand to lose a few pounds, but his disposition indicated that he would prefer to take a nap.

"If I had sunk a few more puts, I would have been ok," Deke added.

"Drive for show, putt for dough," Hanlen observed.

"I had a feeling somebody was going to say that," I said.

Hanlen and Deke looked at me.

"Your friend looks familiar, but I don't recall his name," Deke said.

"This here's Logan Wells. He used to work for the county prosecutor."

Dekes's wrinkled brow wrinkled further. Maybe he was remembering the hospital bill.

"Sure," he said, after a few seconds. "You got some ink in the paper last year."

I ignored his last comment but rose and extended my hand.

"Nice to meet you, sir. I've seen you out with your dog on occasion."

He gave me a closer inspection. "Sure, I've seen you out on the course."

"Sometimes I see what Barney leaves behind, even if I don't see you," I added.

Deke laughed.

"You should know, maybe better than most, Logan, that you got to watch where you step," he said. "You fellows have a good afternoon."

chapter 30

W E WATCHED MCKNIGHT CONTINUE DOWN THE PATH to the first tee. He badly hooked his drive. It went on the fly into the yard of one of the big homes which backed to the course, and I heard the ball clank loudly against the second-floor siding. For McKnight's sake, I hoped the owners weren't home. In a similar instance a few years ago, the enraged homeowner chased the golfer with a rake, then took the guy's clubs, only surrendering them when the police were called.

Deke let out a loud, 'Jesus in a dump truck!'

Hanlen and I looked at each other and grinned. Barney barked, either in reaction to his owner's errant shot or blasphemy. McKnight hit another drive, this one again hooking, but it went into a tree, hit a branch, and took a very fortunate bounce back into the fairway.

"He needs to ease up on his grip," Hanlen observed.

"It's a dogleg. Maybe he should have let the dog hit it."

Hanlen finished off one can of beer and popped another.

"Oh, yeah," he said. "You were right."

"Thanks. I figured I was. About what?"

"Ellen's insurance friend from Chicago called me."

"No kidding," I said. "That was quick. I thought it would be weeks before she found out anything. If she found anything at all, that is."

"Ever the optimist," Hanlen said. "It was your idea to try and find the boat, remember?"

"When did she call?"

"She called me the day after our talk with Ellen. Then again yesterday."

"If it was twice," I said, thinking about it, "how come you're just telling me now?"

"I needed to check some of the information I got," Hanlen replied. "I would have done it right away if I was still sheriff. Thought I needed to be careful since I'm not."

"That implies that you needed to pull someone's sheet."

Criminal records are public records, and anybody can access to them. Maybe not quickly, as there was a procedure to follow, and since there was a procedure, a paper trail was created. But I thought Hanlen, being who he was, could have called just about anybody in the sheriff's office for information and they would have provided it, right away, no questions asked. That he thought he needed to be covert surprised me.

"That and a little more," he said. "I didn't want to get the new sheriff curious."

"Curious about what?"

"I'll get to that. You know much about insurance, Logan?"

"Only that I apparently got the pretty crappy kind, health-wise," I said.

"Blame the county procurement department for that," Hanlen said. "They always go with the low bid."

"Remember when they ordered bars of soap for the courthouse?"

"That was someone pulling a hoax," Hanlen scoffed.

And I knew who it was. Years ago, for reasons unknown, the men's rooms in the courthouse were frequently out of soap. This went on annoyingly for a couple months, despite the many complaints. Buzz and I placed cakes of soap in a few of the metal, empty liquid soap dispensers. A judge opened one of the ones thus rigged. He wrote a scathing memo to the county purchasing director, inquiring if the cakes were low bid.

"Now I remember," I said.

"Sounds like a prank Buzz would have pulled," Hanlen said.

"Yeah. Not many like him," I said, repeating what George Hiatt said. "What did the insurance woman have to say?"

"A lot. Her name is June, by the way."

"How about that," I remarked. "It's the first day of June and the woman you talked to was June. Coincidence or something more?"

"It's a coincidence. I'm not superstitious. I didn't know you were, Logan."

"Big time. I even believe in ghosts," I said. "What did June say?"

"She wanted to let me know what we were up against, in terms of locating a 20 year old insurance claim on a boat. June said it's a longshot, at best."

"I would have guessed as much." I replied. "But what were her reasons?"

"She tells me that insurance companies provide their claims information to a couple firms that compile the data. The firms provide the information, for a fee, to interested parties."

"Like who?"

"Other insurance companies, mainly. A driver that's been in a lot of accidents isn't a good insurance risk," Hanlen said. "Or a bank will use them. If they see there's been a lot of claims on a house, flood, theft, whatever, that could mean there is a problem with the house or the neighborhood. A bank would like to know that before writing a mortgage."

"Makes sense. But I have a feeling they don't keep records forever."

"Yeah," Hanlen replied. "June tells me the bad news is that the services only keep them for about seven years, or maybe in a few cases, ten years."

"That makes sense too," I said.

"How's that?" Hanlen asked.

"Well, now you got computers, but think of the effort and expense involved in maintaining records indefinitely, especially if they were paper. Storage space, clerical staff, etc. Why bother? I got to think there is a statute of limitations on insurance claims like everything else. Seven years sounds like what it ought to be. How about the insurance company itself? Maybe they got their own record policies on top of what they furnish the service."

"I thought to ask June that," Hanlen said. "She said, sure, each company had its own records system, and some keep stuff a long time. But the insurance business is like any other. Companies merge, people come and go, records get lost. Things change over twenty years."

"That's the bad news," I said, "yet you started this conversation by saying I was right. That implies there is good news."

"June tells me there are a lot fewer boats than houses and cars. Consequently, a lot fewer insurance claims on boats. Plus, not everybody who has a boat buys insurance for it. It's not a legal requirement everywhere."

"I've heard that. So even less claims," I said.

"Right. As you said, if this guy with the boat destroyed it to cover his tracks, and if he had insurance, and filed a claim like it was an accident, June thinks there is a chance she can track it down. Even if it was 20 years ago."

"That's a lot of ifs, but still good news," I said.

"Yep, but there's more. June is friends with an agent who wrote a lot of policies on boats. He's with a big company in Chicago. Guess he owned boats himself and saw a niche. June says he's got memory like a hawk."

"It's an elephant," I said, "as in a memory like one. Hawks are known more for their eyesight. Eyes like a hawk."

"How do you know hawks don't have good memories? Anyhow, when June calls me back yesterday, she's got her friend on speaker with her. Italian fella, name is Vince Moretti. Vince checked some things, made some phone calls, but says he's got nothing on any paid claims for a boat of our description, sometime in summer 1966."

I gave Hanlen a frustrated look.

"You build me up, buttercup, just to let me down," I said. "Remember that one, by The Foundations?"

"No, but if you call me buttercup again, I'll put your head in the ball washer."

"That might help clear my mind, which is swimming right now," I said. "I think it's doing the backstroke."

"If you reach my age, Logan, hopefully you'll develop a little patience. Vince does not find or recall any *paid* claims for a boat like we are looking for, but he does remember an odd situation with an *unpaid* claim from that summer. Well, not even a claim really. More of a possible claim. But for a boat matching our description. A fifteen or twenty foot runabout with a blue hull and white interior."

"Huh. Was it a fire? Explosion?"

"None of the above. The owner said the boat was stolen."

I thought about that.

"I wouldn't know," I said, "but stealing a boat might be difficult. I doubt if you can waltz in a marina, hook the boat up to a trailer and traipse off without anyone noticing."

"Vince would agree with you. Did I mention he's owned boats himself? He tells me boat theft wouldn't be easy at any of the marinas in Chicago.

There are always people around. And if you steal a boat, what are you going to do with it? Take it out on the lake, have someone see it and say, hey, look, there goes the guy who stole Joe's boat?"

"Did this guy have his insurance policy with Vince?"

"No. It was an agent who worked at the same company. That's how he heard about it."

"Where did this boat theft happen?" I said.

"You know where Lake Murphy is?" Hanlen asked.

"I think we drove near it on Sunday," I said, recalling a road sign I'd seen.

"Good memory. It's a medium sized, man-made lake in Newton County, near Morocco."

"Near where the Spilotro brothers met their demise," I recalled. "Guess if it's good place to make people disappear, it's a good place to make a boat disappear."

"Yeah, out in the middle of nowhere. The owner claimed he took it from the Chicago marina where he kept it, to a buddy's hunting camp near Murphy Lake. They did some fishing. He didn't feel like hauling the boat back to Chicago and left it there. When they came back a couple weeks later the boat was gone."

"Does the boat owner have a name?"

"I'll get to that," Hanlen said.

I figured he had a reason for deferring on the name.

"When did Mr. X notice his boat gone, and when did he call the agent about it?" I asked.

"End of June, sometime, for missing it. After the Fourth of July for calling his agent."

I thought about that.

"That's even better," I said.

"How so?"

"If you remember, my original idea was this guy destroys the boat which links him to the girls, and files a claim with his insurance saying it was destroyed before the girls disappeared. But that only works if nobody on the beach that day can positively ID him or the boat."

"Which is what happened," Hanlen said.

"Right, but how does he know that's what will happen? He's got a better alibi if he says the boat was stolen before the girls disappeared, and therefore whoever was in it when the girls vanished wasn't him. Even if it looks like him. Did Vince know what the agent told the owner?"

"He asked him something like, 'didn't we just sign you up for a policy,'" Hanlen said.

"What does that mean?" I said.

"That's an insurance joke, Vince says. New customer calls up with a big claim, which insurance companies hate. The agent says we didn't get your check, so the policy isn't valid."

"What if the customer then shows up with a copy of a cancelled check?"

"You tell him we got it, but hey, sent it to the wrong place, so we still can't cover your claim. If that doesn't work, you go on to the next excuse."

"Sounds like my health insurance."

"Yeah," Hanlen said. "The agent remembers remarking to the guy how he never had a customer whose boat was stolen. Says the company will need a police report on the theft. And a notarized affidavit signed by the owner attesting he doesn't know what happened to the boat."

"I assume since you said there was no claim filed, the guy had a change of heart when he was told that."

"He said he'd call the agent back," Hanlen said. "And he never did. Vince remembers that because it was peculiar."

"I'll say. Guy claims his boat was stolen, wants to file a claim then doesn't follow up. Was that the end of it? At least as far as the agent went?"

"Well, of course, the agent doesn't want to seem like he's not helpful, so he tries calling the guy back, but never hears from him. He eventually puts a note in his pending file and forgets about it."

"You said you had the boat owner's name," I said.

"You think I'd tell you that story if he didn't? The boat owners name was Gerald 'Jerry' Needham."

chapter 31

"Needham," I said. "Doesn't ring a bell with any name I recall from the case file. How about with you?"

"No, but I checked him out. He used to be a cop. A detective."

"Where?"

"Eldon, Illinois. Next town over from Glenwood."

"Where Mason Banks was chief," I said. "That's a coincidence. Guess they probably knew each other."

"I would guess so," said Hanlen. "There's more, though. He also was pals with Luther Brame."

"How do you know that?"

"You probably know that Brame went to prison in the early seventies for the murder of his partner. They owned a couple stables and a bunch of horses together. The partner also happened to be his cousin."

"I did know that," I said. "Not all the details, but that's the reason Brame went to prison."

"Brame didn't pull the trigger on the partner himself," Hanlen said, then added, "not that he didn't like getting his hands dirty. He paid a couple guys to do it for him. They did the job, but got caught, rolled on Brame, and they all went to jail."

"How is Needham connected?" I asked.

"He wasn't, with that murder, at least. What you may not know was that wasn't Brame's first attempt to get rid of his cousin. He knew Needham, and previously asked him if he knew anyone who might be interested in the job."

"How did he know him?"

"Brame had a lot of police and political contacts. Got to think he wouldn't be able to get away with all the stuff he pulled unless he did. Needham apparently did some security work for him, and they became pals."

"Who better to ask for a reference for a contract killing than a cop?" I said.

"That's not as silly as it sounds," Hanlen said. "Corruption and Chicago go together like cookies and milk."

"They say Al Capone and Mayor Bill Thompson were on the same volleyball team together, back in the Roaring Twenties," I said.

Hanlen snorted.

"Anyhow, Needham lines someone up, an ex-con he knows, who meets with Brame. They agree on a price. Needham furnishes the prospective hit man with a gun."

"I take it something went wrong," I said.

"Right. The wannabe hit man gets stopped for running a red light. He panics, being a felon with a gun. He turns on Needham and Brame. Everybody gets charged with conspiracy."

"Nothing happened to Brame, I take it," I said. "At least that time."

"Correct. Brame's expensive lawyer gets him off, on a couple technicalities. One Brame never gave his real name to the would-be killer, and two, he never tells him specifically he wanted his partner to be killed. It's all done in a roundabout, vague manner."

"As in, I got a 200-pound problem I was hoping you might help me with," I said.

"Or he may have left it to Needham to name the target. Which leaves Needham and the hit man ex-con on the hook. The latter takes a plea and goes back to prison for a year, then probation. A good deal, all things considered. Part of which is testifying against Needham."

"The prosecutor's thinking being if the con rolls on Needham, maybe Needham will do the same for Brame," I said.

"Correct again. Needham isn't particularly bright, but he is astute enough to realize that if he fingers Brame, he's a dead man. Especially if he winds up in prison."

"He was a cop. He would have been put in protective custody," I said.

"I'm not sure how 'protective,' protective custody is," Hanlen said. "To paraphrase Joe Louis, in prison you can run, but you can't hide."

"What did Needham do?"

"He does the standup, and probably smart thing to do, and pleads to solicitation of a crime and furnishing a weapon to a criminal," Hanlen said.

I did a quick calculation based on my experience in the prosecuting attorney's office.

"What did he get for that? Ten years?"

"He should have," Hanlen said. "But nobody got killed, or even close. Brame surely isn't going to testify against Needham, plus no one ever likes the testimony of an ex-con. Judge still gives him five years since the judge wants to set an example. He's out in under two."

"Guess Needham figured two years in prison was preferable to testifying against Brame and end up buried in a cornfield. Or mysteriously succumbing to athlete's foot in prison."

"Yeah," Hanlen agreed.

"What did he do after he got out? He can't go back to being a cop,"

"I tracked him down," Hanlen replied. "He likes boats, apparently. He had a fishing charter in Michigan City for a short time. Then he relocated to Florida, and runs a charter out of Clearwater, Florida."

"Guess he got tired of the cold weather," I said.

"Who doesn't? Plus you can run a charter all year round in Florida. He's still at it. Know where Clearwater is?"

"Sure, it's south of Tampa. My ex's parents had a place near Clearwater," I said.

"I would have hung on to the wife, if only for the condo," Hanlen said.

"I told you, breaking up wasn't my idea," I said. "And I liked her folks. We'd go to see them in the winter. Although as I recall, you could get some cool days in Clearwater in January or February. People there treat sixty degrees like people act when it's twenty degrees here."

"I grew up in Wisconsin. 20-degrees is T-shirt weather."

I thought of something.

"By the way, how does an ex-con afford a big, expensive, charter fishing boat? And relocating to and living in Florida?"

"Maybe his old friend Luther Brame helped him get started," Hanlen replied.

"I could see that," I said. "Perhaps Luther didn't like the idea of Needham hanging around the area. Who knows? And maybe a business like that you take in a lot of cash. Could be he laundered some money for Luther if the need arose."

"Maybe, I guess."

"Makes you I wonder if Needham tried to help Brame out with other problems over the years," I said. "Like maybe back in 1966."

"I thought you didn't like Brame for the girls," Hanlen said.

"I didn't. But I've always been one to reevaluate my thinking based on new information. "I know, that's not the norm in the law enforcement profession."

"That's a little harsh," Hanlen replied, "and I hope you didn't mean me. Although I admit I've seen some stick with a theory, even if the facts don't support it. Anyhow, not sure I would call this new information, just previously overlooked. My question is what we do with it."

"That's easy," I said. "At this point, there is nothing to do except go to Ivan with it. I just hope he isn't mad when he finds out what we've been doing behind his back."

"I was afraid you were going to say something like that," Hanlen sighed, and shook his head. "Alright, I'll give him a call when I get home."

Hanlen threw his first empty beer can in a high arc toward the trash can behind the first tee, at least fifteen feet away. It clanked on the opening of the can and then dropped to the bottom. He drained what was left of the second one and tossed it at the can with the same result.

"Impressive," I said. "You play basketball and football in school?"

"In high school I played both. I was all-county center, second team all-state. I had a pretty good outside shot, too. I was going to do both in college, but only played football."

"Football coach change your mind?"

"No. There was an accident at Purdue before I got there. Part of the bleachers in the gym collapsed during a game. Three kids were killed. A real tragedy. I took that as an omen."

"I would have too," I said. "But I thought you said you weren't superstitious."

"I did, and I'm not, but that seemed like a sign too obvious to ignore," Hanlen said. "Oh, and one other thing, Mitch called me."

"Don't tell me; he wants to hire you as head bouncer," I said.

"No. He found out what happened to the wife of Chief Banks."

"Really?" I said. "This has been an informative day."

"Mitch tells me after her husband blew himself up, she moved to Nashville, Indiana."

"Brown County? I asked.

Brown County was southeast of Indianapolis and on the perimeter of the Hoosier National Forest. Unlike most of Indiana, which was relatively flat, the south-central part of the state containing the national forest had varied and scenic topography, with rolling and steep hills. Brown County was a popular tourist area, and Nashville was a quaint town in the middle of it. A number of artists made the place their home.

"Yeah. The wife and I've been to Brown County a few times," he said. "They got a nice state park there, with a lodge. And a golf course I like."

"What did Mrs. Banks do in Nashville?"

"Mitch said he heard she opened up a gift shop. They got a ton of them there. He even knew the name of it . . . the Blue Hen. As far as he knows she still has it."

Hanlen got up to leave. "I'll call you after I talk to Ivan."

I tossed my empty beer can toward the trash receptacle. It was well short of the opening, took a big bounce off the side, and landed just off the tee. I'm not sure I could have made a worse attempt to toss if I tried. Hanlen gave me a disdainful look.

"I'm an Indiana native, but I never really cared for basketball," I said, shrugging.

"It shows," he replied. "Don't forget to pick that up. They don't cotton to litter bugs here."

chapter 32

O N SATURDAY, KATHY AND I PLANNED TO GO for an early dinner at a new restaurant in New Buffalo. It had recently opened, with good reviews, and overlooked the harbor. I was looking forward toward going and thought it odd when Kathy changed her mind. She said she wanted to stay in town and eat at one of the 'old' local restaurants. She picked Paulsen's, of all places. We entered via the front entrance, so I didn't get a chance to say hi to Uncle Dave.

After dinner, we drove downtown to walk around the square. We bought some fudge from a candy store a block from the courthouse. We then stopped for a beer at the Lincoln Tavern, directly across from the courthouse. On weekdays, at lunchtime, it was packed, but not early on a Saturday night. On the way back to my place, Kathy said she wanted to buy some wine, so we stopped at a dingy liquor store up near the university. Despite being dingy, it had a decent selection of upper end wine. She picked out two bottles, both on the expensive side, also odd, since she claimed if you knew what you were doing, you could get as good a bottle for ten dollars as twenty. When we got back to my place, we sat on the deck and consumed one of them while the sun went down. I could sense something was going on from the way Kathy was acting, but figured she would tell me when she was ready.

It started to get chilly, so we went inside. We poked at the fudge for a bit, then Kathy excused herself to go to the bathroom. When she came back she had taken off her jeans and had unbuttoned her shirt.

"I need to get back to my dad soon, Logan. And I don't want to put you on the spot, but I'd like you to make love to me now."

"Alright," I said.

Afterwards we didn't talk for a while, but then she said what I had been dreading.

"I've decided to go back to California, Logan," Kathy said. "Too many things I need to do there. I'm on a flight to LA tomorrow afternoon."

I had an idea it was coming, but it still made me numb when she said it.

"For how long?"

"I don't know. At least a couple weeks, maybe longer."

Then she added, "you know, you could go with me if you wanted to. I would like it very much if you did."

"What would I do while you are working?"

"There's plenty of things you could do," Kathy said, becoming enthused. "Paint my condo. Meet my friends. We could run on the beach together. You'd love that."

"I've had it with beaches for a while," I said. "Plus, I'm a lousy painter. And what makes you think your friends are going to like me?"

"Don't sell them short," Kathy said, smiling. "But it's not like you got tons of stuff going on here."

"Thanks for noticing. What about Hanlen and the mystery of the missing girls?"

"You yourself are doubtful about solving that cold case."

"Maybe I'm changing my mind."

"Ok, other than that, there's nothing holding you here."

"Again, thanks for the observation, except it's my home and I sort of like it here. And a big reason I like it here now is because you showed up."

"California is nice," she said. "You would like it there too."

"Maybe for a week, then I think the traffic, smog, and trendy people would get to me. I can only eat so many salmon and avocado frittatas."

"Oh, please," Kathy said.

"What about your dad?" I said, to change the subject.

"I've arranged care for him with a local nursing agency. Someone will be over with him. Plus, my siblings promised they would drop by."

"I can look in on him too. Nursing care sounds expensive."

"It is. That's one reason I need to get back to get some work done. And it's just not possible from Prairie Stop."

"I thought you liked it here," I said, realizing that I sounded like a miffed child.

"I do. But the reality is a big part of my life is still in California. I've been away from it for a while and can't put off going back any longer. It will only be for a few weeks, max. Maybe only a couple, if can get accomplished what I need to do."

I had the feeling it would be longer than a few weeks but didn't say anything.

"Well, at least let me give you a lift to the airport."

"I'm going to take the shuttle, since I don't know exactly when I'm coming back. Plus, I can't stand the idea of saying goodbye to you. Even for just a couple weeks."

I didn't have a response to that.

"You're not mad at me, are you?" Kathy said. "I couldn't bear that."

chapter 33

I WENT OUT FOR ANOTHER LONG RUN SUNDAY MORNING, to take my mind off my evening with Kathy. When I got home, I figured it was a shame to waste a sweaty t-shirt, so I cut the grass. When I went back in the house, around noon, I saw that Hanlen had called.

He answered the phone with, "where you been?"

"Distracting myself from my sorrows," I replied, but not identifying what my sorrows were.

"Doesn't sound like you've been drinking," he said.

"Saving that for later. What's going on?"

"I talked to Ivan," he said. "Filled him in on what we found out."

"What'd he say? Tell you to run out into the street and yell polecat?"

"Why would he do that?"

"Was he pissed?"

"No," Hanlen replied. "He was calm enough."

"That's a start. What now?"

"He called this morning and wants to see us in his office. As soon as possible, today preferably. He said to call him when I got a hold of you, and he'd meet us at the justice center."

"On a Sunday?"

"I was wondering about that too," Hanlen replied. "But that's what he said. I'll tell him an hour if you can be ready by then. Want me to pick you up? Or you going to run over?"

"Already ran. I'll drive. Guess I'll see you there in an hour."

The County Justice Center used to be downtown, behind the court-house. With the rapid growth in the county's population, doubling in twenty years, the justice center and county administrative center, also downtown, had become overcrowded and antiquated. The courthouse was also in dire need of updating. There had been talk of building a new county center, including courthouse, justice, and administrative centers on the northeast edge of town. The proposed move was controversial, with numerous supporters and opponents. Hanlen initially opposed the reloca-tion of his office from downtown, but then came around to the idea, and put his considerable influence behind it. His support tipped the balance in favor of the move, at least as far as the justice center went. In the early eighties, a large and modern new sheriff's office and jail was built a couple miles from downtown. The old justice center was torn down and replaced with a new county administrative building. The courthouse was updated. It was one of those rare public works projects that seemed to please just about everyone.

Hanlen was in the parking lot when I got there. There were a dozen or so cars in the lot, but not nearly the number as on a normal week-day. Although the sheriff's department was a 24/7 operation, many of the ancillary administrative staff had weekends off.

Hanlen nodded hello.

"Strolling down memory lane?" I asked him.

"I haven't been gone long enough to miss it," he replied. "That reminds me of a country song: 'How Can I Miss You if You Won't Go Away?'"

"The greatest hit of Dan Hicks," I said.

"I didn't figure you'd get that one," Hanlen replied.

We walked up the steps to the front entrance.

"What are your thoughts on why Ivan wanted to see us on a Sunday?" Hanlen asked.

"Probably the same as yours," I said.

"Which is?" Hanlen said.

"Fewer people seeing us."

Hanlen laughed. "Yeah, that thought crossed my mind."

He used a plastic card to open the door next to the main front door, which was locked after nine at night and during the weekend.

"Thought you were supposed to turn that in when you retired," I said.

"I musta forgot."

Every time I entered the new justice center, I always had the same thought: this is one sparkling building—sparkling not just in the sense it was clean, which it was. The two-story brick entrance area was bright, open, and spacious. There was a lot of natural light, created by skylights and large windows where the tan brick walls met the ceiling, and the carpet was a neutral gray. It was impressive yet at the same time calming, sort of like walking into a church. I understood Hanlen had been very involved with the design of the center, particularly the entrance area. He wanted people entering the building to be impressed, if not slightly awed, hopefully to encourage respectful behavior toward his staff.

The deputy sitting behind the raised front desk got a big smile on his face when he saw Hanlen. I recognized him but couldn't recall his name. He hopped out of his chair and came around and shook the chief's hand.

"You're a sight for sore eyes, Chief," he said.

"Your eyes must be real sore, then, Tom, but thanks. How you been?"

"Getting by. Wish you were still here."

"Aw, it was time for a change. I was getting crotchety and forgetful. It happens when you get old," Hanlen paused. "Did I just say I was getting crotchety?"

Tom laughed. "You're in better shape than most, age be damned. What's your secret?"

"Clean living, I guess," Hanlen replied.

"And a twelve pack of Hamm's a day," I said.

They both looked at me.

"You know Logan here, right, Tom?" Hanlen said.

"Sure, how's it going, Logan?" he said, extending his hand.

"I'm hanging with the chief. What could be better?" I replied.

We shook hands. He didn't seem surprised I was with Hanlen. I would, had I been him.

"What brings you guys down here on a Sunday afternoon?" Tom asked.

"We got an important meeting with Sheriff Ivan Rich," Hanlen said, lowering his voice. "He claims some office supplies disappeared when I stepped down, and thinks I had something to do with it. I retained Logan here to investigate the matter."

Tom smiled, figuring he was having his leg pulled, and looked at me.

"Yeah," I added. "Not sure why, but white-out is in short supply in Prairie County. Maybe you can sniff it and get a buzz, I don't know. There is even a big black market for it. Ironic, don't you think? A black market for white-out."

"Thanks for the tip," Tom said. "I'll lock mine up when I leave."

"Keep it under your hat that we stopped by, Tom, if you don't mind," Hanlen said.

"Sure, whatever you say, Chief," Tom replied.

"Thanks," Hanlen replied. "Guess Ivan is back in his office."

"Yeah, I saw him head back there a little while ago. Was wondering what he was doing here on a Sunday. You know the way."

chapter 34

THE DOOR TO HANLEN'S COMMODIOUS FORMER OFFICE was open. His successor as sheriff, Ivan Rich, was sitting behind a large oak desk in the middle of the big space, talking on the telephone. A couple high backed chairs were in front of the desk. There were two flag stands behind the desk, one holding the U.S. flag and the other that of the State of Indiana. A leather sofa was on one side of the room, and a table and some office chairs on the other.

Ivan looked small behind the desk. It would be fair to describe him as a fireplug of a man. He was 5'8" and weighed around 200 pounds. He had been the starting center on a couple good Prairie High football teams, a few years before I played. He was also on the wrestling team. I knew a few guys who wrestled, and they always seemed to be in great shape, although anyone I ever knew who wrestled seemed to double in size after giving the sport up. Until recently, Ivan was a lot heavier, but when he decided to run for sheriff, I noticed he had lost weight, perhaps hoping it would enhance his appeal to the electorate. Although in looking at him now, it appeared he had found some of it. Probably the stress of the job. As I listened to his part of the phone conversation, it sounded like he was on the receiving end of a chewing out. I heard a lot of 'yes sirs,' and, 'we're doing our best,' and 'there's only so much we can do.'

I had worked with Ivan numerous times since I had been back in Prairie Stop, starting when he was in uniform. He had been promoted to detective, and later made lieutenant. I liked Ivan but wasn't sure of the merit of the promotions. On one hand, he was a competent police officer. He was thorough and could be tenacious. Yet I thought it took a different mindset to be a decent detective. Deductive reasoning and creative thinking didn't seem to be his strong suit. He did have an outgoing and generally affable personality, and it seemed like he knew or was related to half the people in the county. He was also a relentless self-promoter, so it wasn't a stretch to see how he had been elected sheriff. The phone conversation went on another minute or so before Ivan was able to end it with a 'I'll have to call you back, sir.' He shook his head as he put the phone down, and then looked at Hanlen in frustration.

"Does this shit ever end?" Ivan asked.

"Nope," Hanlen said. "What's going on?"

"That was Ed Ballard. He called last week. Somebody poured bleach in the gas tank of his son's new BMW when he was in town last weekend. The car broke down on 49 when Ed Jr. was going back to Chicago. It's toast. Big Ed said it was lucky Ed Jr. hadn't gotten on the toll road before the engine seized up, otherwise he might have been run over by a semi."

"And he said that was lucky?" I asked.

Ivan gave me a dirty look. "You don't know anything about it, do you?"

"Why would I?"

"Oh, I don't know. I talked to Ed Jr., and he said you and he had words in Paulsen's on Sunday night."

"You got me, Ivan," I said. "Ed Jr. threatened to kick my ass, so I sabotaged his engine. Good thing I always carry a jug of bleach with me."

"You could have done it later," Ivan accused.

"I don't even know where Big Ed lives now," I replied. That was true. I knew at one time the Ballard family lived in a large restored Victorian home near downtown.

"Ed sold his place on Madison to Doc Bailey, the dentist," Hanlen said. "I heard it went for 250 grand. I didn't know dentists did that well. Big Ed lives in a mansion he built by the country club."

"Bailey isn't a regular dentist," Ivan said. "He's a periodontist . . . fixes gums. He did my wife's and it cost a fortune. He might as well own a gold mine."

"Is it pyrite or pyorrhea?" I asked.

"What are you talking about?" Ivan said, annoyed.

"I think one's fool's gold and the other's bleeding gums," I replied.

"Are we playing Jeopardy now?" Ivan said.

"Knock it off, Logan," Hanlen said. "What does Ballard think happened to the car?"

"Big Ed thinks some kids did it when the car was in his driveway," Ivan said. "He's been calling a few times a day to find out if we've caught the culprits. Like I don't have anything better to do than track down some juvenile delinquents."

"It comes with the job, sorry to say," Hanlen said.

"You could be working the wrong angle on this, Ivan," I said. "Maybe it wasn't kids and a prank gone wrong. Maybe it's something bigger. Have you stopped to consider someone was looking to get back at Big Ed?"

"For what?"

"Maybe he sold somebody a house with termites or had mold in the crawl space."

Ivan gave me another dirty look.

"Will you tell him to shut up?" he said to Hanlen.

"Fellas, let's not get off track here," Hanlen said.

"You're right," Ivan said. "I don't want to be here any longer than I have to."

He nodded at the door. "Close that, Logan."

I complied. Ivan leaned back in his chair and put his hands behind his head.

"The chief has filled me in on what you guys have been up to," he said, looking at me. He appeared like he was about to say something else to me but didn't. He put his hands back on the desk and looked at Hanlen.

"First, let me say, chief," Ivan said, "I got the utmost respect for you. And being in this job for a couple months, I got even more respect. But I'm not good with you getting involved in an open case without letting me know about it. And I don't care how cold the case is. Logan has always been a bit flaky, so I would maybe expect that from him. But not you."

"Well, Ivan," Hanlen said, after a pause, "you know me. If I make a mistake, I admit it. And if I owe you an apology, consider it made. But speaking of pranks, this all started out with me trying to figure out if someone was trying to play one on me. Then I asked Logan for help. He may be flaky, but you got to admit he's pretty sharp. And just for the record, he wasn't too gung-ho on helping me. And as soon as we found out something that might be worth checking into, he said we needed to contact you. So here we are."

Ivan glanced at me after Hanlen was done talking.

"What he said," I said, shrugging.

Ivan leaned back in his chair.

"Alright," he said. "First, just so we're on the same page, this is a twenty-year old unsolved case. And to be real clear, when I say unsolved, that means it's been twenty years, and no one's figured out what happened."

"No need to get sarcastic, Ivan," I said.

"That's realistic," he said. "Don't you think, that given the years gone by it's unlikely that anyone is going to solve it?"

"We aren't saying we solved anything," I said. "As you just cynically, yet correctly noted, this is a very cold case. But we did find something that is worth checking out."

"Alright, then, let's look at what you got," Ivan said, sitting forward.

"You got a guy who *may* have owned a boat, which *might* have been involved with the girls' disappearance. There's no proof it was involved, just maybe. Said guy knew a second guy, who *may* have had a connection to the girls, and could have had an, as yet unknown, motive, for harming the girls. Oh, and by the way, the second guy died a few years ago, so even if you link him to the girls' disappearance, he's going to be hard to prosecute, seeing as how he is dead. Judges have a little problem with sending corpses to prison. They're full enough with live bodies."

Ivan leaned back again in his chair.

"Does that sound about right?" he asked. I didn't care for the smarmy tone in his voice, and apparently Hanlen didn't either. He made a growling noise as he cleared his throat. Ivan and I both looked at him. He didn't say anything right away.

"Ivan, I'm going to pass something on to you," Hanlen said. "You can take it or leave it. But when someone comes to you in a serious manner with information about an unsolved crime, you don't disregard them, no matter what you may think."

Ivan sighed. "Ok, your right, I'm sorry. What would you have me do, Chief?"

"That's easy. First, talk with Bob Shannon," Hanlen said. "See what he thinks."

Shannon was the county prosecuting attorney, and my former boss. I knew he would like nothing better than to solve a twenty-year old case, especially this one, yet he was also a realist, and had his hands full keeping up with the growing crime rate in the county. He probably would have the same, unenthusiastic, attitude Ivan had. He would also want to know specifically what Ivan planned to do with the information we gave him. I decided to help him.

"How about this, Ivan," I said. "Like the chief said, talk to Shannon. See if he would consider sending a detective down to Florida to talk to Jerry Needham. If I had to pick the guy to go, it would be Carl Ingram. The chief and I could fill him in on what we found out."

Ingram was a veteran detective who had been with the county for over twenty-five years. I knew him to be intelligent and thorough. Because of his length of service, he was also familiar with the case of the missing Dunes Girls. The only downside to Ingram was he seemed to share my opinion on Ivan, which wouldn't make him Ivan's first choice.

"Carl's a good man," Hanlen agreed.

"You would need to contact the authorities in Clearwater," I said. "Brief them on what's going on. They would need to send a man out with Ingram to talk to Needham, of course."

"Of course," Ivan said. His tone indicated he didn't like being told what to do, especially by me. We sat in silence for a minute while Ivan deliberated.

"Well, Ivan, what do you think?" Hanlen asked.

"With all due respect, Chief, you gave me a lot to consider. I'm gonna need some time to think about it."

"Think about what, exactly?" I asked.

"What you said, genius," Ivan replied. "Everything. Talking to Shannon. Sending Ingram to Florida. Contacting someone down there about this Needham guy."

I was going to say something, but Hanlen touched my arm, indicating I should not.

"That's your call, Ivan. You're sheriff now," Hanlen said. "Can I ask why, and how much time you might need?"

"Ok," Ivan said. "First, if I thought there was even a remote chance we could solve a 20 year old crime, especially this one, believe me, I'd be all over it."

"Then what's the problem?" I said.

Ivan seemed like he made a deliberate effort to not look at Hanlen when he answered.

"No offense, but what you got isn't going to do that."

"But . . ." I began, before Ivan cut me off with a wave of his hand.

"Let's say I give you the benefit of the doubt and say maybe this is worth checking into," he said. "And I when I say maybe, it's in the very generous sense of the word."

"Then what's the issue?" Hanlen asked.

"I'll tell you. As you know, I'm new in this job. Further, it was a close election. Some aren't too happy I won."

"No way," I said. Hanlen hit my upper arm with his open hand. It hurt.

"Thanks, Chief," Ivan said. "If I send someone off to Florida, I believe some folks will say it's a wild goose chase. That will lead to questions about my judgment. I don't need that right now. In due time, I could see maybe following up on this. But it's not going to be now."

"So, preserving your job is a reason for not doing anything?" I said.

"You're one to talk," Ivan shot back. "Last time you got involved in something that wasn't any of your business, some people got killed."

I almost came out of the chair when he said that, but Hanlen put one of his big hands over on my chest and stopped me.

"I'm afraid that's my final word on the subject," Ivan said. "Maybe things will be different in six months or so. Come back and see me then. This mystery has been unsolved for twenty years. I don't see how another few months is going to make much difference."

We all stared at each other for an awkward thirty seconds or so.

Hanlen broke the silence. "Ok, Ivan, I think we got it. We appreciate your time."

We got up and Hanlen shook Ivan's hand. We turned to go.

"Oh, and one other thing," Ivan said. "I want you two to cease and desist on this, immediately. Don't even think about going to Florida. Unless you're going to Disneyworld."

chapter 35

"I GUESS THAT'S IT, THEN," I SAID TO HANLEN, when we got outside.
"It's not over until the fat lady sings," Hanlen replied.

"I thought he just did."

"I'm talking about Bob Shannon," Hanlen said.

"Well, I know you and Shannon are on good terms, but going around Ivan isn't going to be well received by Shannon, or anybody," I said. "You of all people should know that."

"I suppose you're right," Hanlen replied.

"Even if he listened to you, he will defer to Ivan on this. And if you ruffle Ivan's feathers, he may never do anything."

"Yeah, I know."

"Cheer up," I said. "We can come back in December. Maybe sooner if Ivan resigns."

"That's not going to happen."

"Give him some time to get in his own way. Maybe if he doesn't solve the case of the bleached gas tank, Big Ed will have his ass."

"Squeaky wheels do get the grease," Hanlen said. "Changing the subject, you ever been to Disneyworld?"

"Once. It was years ago," I said. "It was ok. Not sure I'd rush back. I'm not one for crowds."

"I've never been, but I heard tell you can't see everything at Disneyworld in one visit."

"That's probably true, but much as I like your company, Chief, I'm not going to Florida with you. For one thing, that's got to be a twenty-hour drive."

"Who said anything about driving? Midway Airlines flies non-stop into Clearwater, out of Midway. None of the hassle of getting in and out of O'Hare," Hanlen said, like he was imitating a commercial for the airline.

"That is convenient. But are you forgetting the last thing Ivan told us?"

"He said something about going to Disneyworld," Hanlen replied. "He didn't say anything about how we get there."

"Speaking of convenient, that's a convenient way of interpreting what he said," I said.

"Sez you. Aw, we just caught him on a bad day. Bet we could talk to him in a couple weeks, and he'd have a change of heart."

"Ok. Let's wait two weeks," I said.

"I don't feel like waiting that long, let alone six months."

"In case my opinion matters," I said, "I don't think what you got in mind, whatever that may be, is a good idea."

"Speaking of what's on my mind, you like fishing?" Hanlen asked.

"I'm not much for fishing. Especially if it involves a boat on a large body of water."

"You get seasick? You can take something for that."

"I've never gotten seasick, but not sure I want to find out what it's like."

"I was thinking we could get in some deep sea fishing while we're in Florida. Maybe take a charter out of Clearwater before we head over to Orlando." Hanlen paused, then added "or maybe just skip Orlando altogether."

""There's one other thing you should know, Chief. I don't have the money to fly to Cleveland, let alone Clearwater."

"You let me worry about that. I'm thinking I can get us a pretty good airfare."

"You're kidding, right?"

"Does it look like I'm kidding? I'm going, with or without you. Don't want to get all mushy on you, but I'd rather have you with me. You're the brains of the operation."

"That in itself is a sad statement," I replied.

"Look at it this way. Maybe you'll keep me from getting in trouble."

"That's more than a one-man job."

"You're probably right but go home and get a bag packed. I'll call you later."

chapter 36

MAYBE IF KATHY HADN'T GONE BACK TO CALIFORNIA, I would have straight out refused to go to Florida with Hanlen, I might have even convinced him it was a bad idea. I had a different perspective as I thought about sitting around an empty house for a couple weeks. Plus, I figured, what was the worst that could happen? We go to Clearwater and talk to Jerry Needham. He would deny any knowledge of the missing girls, and that would be the end of it. I would get some time at the beach and a chance to eat fresh seafood. There could be worse things.

Hanlen called that evening.

"I got us a flight out tomorrow at two pm. We'll be in Clearwater in time for dinner."

"Grilled grouper here we come. What about the return?"

"I left that open-ended. At least a few days. A week at most."

"Ok," I replied.

I couldn't see his reaction, of course, but had the feeling he was surprised I didn't object.

"Oh, I also hired a fishing charter from Needham and lined up for Wednesday morning. Going out early from Clearwater Beach."

"You could get one that quick?" I said.

"It's midweek, plus it's not the real big time of year for charters. That would be snowbird season or maybe starting in a couple weeks. We'll be going out on the 'Lucky Strike,' Skipper Jerry Needham, formerly of

Joliet State Prison, in command."

"Where he was once a fish, and now he catches fish for a living. Life is full of odd coincidences, don't you think, Chief?" 'Fish' was a term used for first-time inmates in prison. A 'fish out of water' was the derivation.

"Whatever you say," Hanlen said.

"You think it's a good idea to be out on a boat in the middle of the ocean with a felon, and possibly a murderer?"

There was a pause.

"Back at Chosin, I had 100,000 Chinese trying to kill me in thirty degree below zero weather," he said. "Hope I don't come off as flip, but it's hard for me to sweat what an ex-felon, sea captain might do to me."

"You don't find the idea of getting tossed overboard and eaten by a shark is a little disturbing?"

"There's that. But look at it this way; it would probably be over quick. Beats rotting to death in a place like that nursing home we were in the other day."

"I don't know. That place might be looking like the Drake Hotel when you're eighty years old. By the way, where will we be staying in Clearwater?"

"I have a buddy who's got a condo on Sand Key. It's just across the bridge, south of Clearwater. He spends part of the winter there. I've visited him so we could play some golf. He says the place is mine if I want it."

"Sand Key was where we used to go when I was married," I said. "My in-laws have a place there. Or used to, last I knew."

"Well then, it will be just like old times. I'll pick you up around 11."

"I'll be ready."

chapter 37

Most of the major airlines operated out of Tampa International Airport. It was about a 25-minute ride from there to the Clearwater Beaches, longer if it was spring break season. A couple times my ex and I flew into the older, smaller St. Pete-Clearwater Airport, which oddly enough, was neither in Clearwater or St. Petersburg, but located across the bay from Tampa. It was used mainly by regional airlines and had limited service. On the other hand, it was easier to get in and out of, and closer to the beaches. I knew Midway Airlines, which had started up in the mid-seventies out of Chicago's Midway Airport, had a couple non-stops a day into Clearwater.

Hanlen handed me a ticket when we got to the gate at Midway. I didn't look at it, but was surprised when, after the gate agent did, she gave me a big smile as she handed it back to me. She also said, 'have a nice flight, Mr. Wells.' I was traipsing down the aisle to my usual spot back in the cattle car section, when Hanlen, behind me, tapped me on the shoulder in the first-class section.

"We're up here," he said.

I had never flown first-class before. When I dropped myself into the large leather seat, I felt like I didn't belong. I quickly decided I could get used to it.

"How does a retired county sheriff afford to fly first class?" I said, turning to Hanlen. "On a last-minute flight, no less."

"I got back problems," Hanlen replied "Playing football for ten years will do that to you. I can't sit for two hours in one of them cramped seats back in coach."

"Ok, makes sense," I said. "But that wasn't what I asked."

"I used some of my campaign funds to buy the tickets," he said.

Hanlen had rarely been seriously challenged after his first couple elections to the sheriff's job, yet I imagined he had a lot of supporters who wanted to make contributions to his campaigns. Stay on the right side of the law, so to speak.

"I thought using campaign funds for personal expenses was against the law," I said.

"No kidding? I should let my wife know that. She's does all the campaign stuff."

"Yeah, maybe she won't be too happy when she finds out she may be going to jail."

"Nobody is going to jail. Who's to say I might not run for office again? And if I do, I got to have a sound body. Campaigning is hard work. Be difficult with a bad back. As far as I'm concerned, saving my back is a legitimate expense."

"How about my ticket?"

He thought about that. "I'll put you on as a consultant."

"For what?"

"You'll pick out what beer we're having once we get up in the air. Pretty sure they won't have Hamm's."

chapter 38

I HADN'T BEEN TO CLEARWATER FOR YEARS. As we were driving from the airport to Sand Key, there were more condos, restaurants, and shops than I recalled. When we crossed the causeway bridge over the bay and turned on Gulf Boulevard, I was sure there were a dozen or more new high rise condos. Hanlen pulled into the entrance to one of the biggest ones that I did remember. It was down and across the street from where my former in-laws place was.

The man in the guard booth at the entrance gate gave us a respectful greeting, which was a little surprising. Normally I was good for a suspicious look, and I thought Hanlen's beard might have gotten a double-take. Hanlen had rented a late model Cadillac, so maybe the guy figured we belonged. Hanlen told him we were staying in Donald McKnight's unit. The guard handed him an envelope and a parking permit and told us where we could park in the garage.

"You public servants do ok in Prairie County," I said, as we pulled away from the booth. "Flying first class, renting Cadillacs, and beachfront condos. Pretty sweet."

"Deke does ok, plus his wife comes from money," Hanlen said. "Her father was president and owner of the McShane ball-bearing plant."

"Whatever happened with that place?" I asked. The plant was located on a ten or so acres half a mile from downtown Prairie Stop. In my youth, it was thriving, the parking lot full every day with employees' cars When

I moved back home, the place was shuttered and weeds were growing in the empty parking lot.

"Most of their customers were in the defense and auto industries," Hanlen said, as we drove into the garage. "Then the Vietnam War ended, and the auto industry fell on hard times, after that first oil embargo. Business took a nosedive. McShane saw the handwriting on the wall and sold the place to some conglomerate out of New York."

"The new realities of the rust belt," I said.

"Yeah. McShane had always treated his employees good, almost like family. When the new outfit took over, they announced they'd be letting a lot of employees go."

"There's family, then there's family," I observed.

"Turns out they didn't intend to make a go of the place at all. Shut it down within a year of buying it. I always wonder why they'd buy a place just to close it."

"There's always reasons, if all you care about is the bottom line," I said. "A loss on the plant could be used to offset profits on another part of the company. Or maybe the pension plan was over-funded, and the new owners could appropriate the surplus. There are always creative ways to get things done, if you aren't too concerned about who gets screwed over."

Hanlen looked over at me with a quizzical look on his face.

"I took a lot of accounting courses in college," I said, shrugging.

"Wouldn't have figured it," Hanlen said, pausing for a reaction. "Get it? You said accounting and I said, 'wouldn't have figured it.'"

I smiled despite myself. "There's hope for you yet, Chief. You're becoming hip."

"Not really sure what hip is," he replied, then added, "but I'm sure you'll tell me."

"Be glad to. A hip person is one who is intelligent, perceptive, and empathetic towards others. Plus, it's real important to have a sense of humor," I said.

"That's a big description for a three-letter word," Hanlen replied.

"It's easy to remember as an acronym: humor, intelligence, and perception. HIP."

"I already forgot it. Anyhow, on a Monday morning, a couple weeks before Christmas, the remaining McShane employees show up for work, but the doors were padlocked. It was noted there were several large trucks coming and going from the plant the prior weekend. They apparently took anything of value that wasn't nailed down."

"Getting laid off for Christmas. The gift that keeps on giving, all year round," I said.

"Yeah. Someone who worked there told me he got a letter from the new owners informing him he that he'd been 'right-sized.'" He said he had been worried that he was going to get laid off. Right-sized didn't sound so bad."

"It's all about the spin you put on it," I noted.

I thought about the closed ball-bearing plant. It was situated in a desirable area of Prairie Stop. Normally developers would salivate over a property in a location like that.

"Why is it still vacant?" I asked. "You could drop a lot of nice homes in there."

"Good question," Hanlen replied. "An industrial place like that requires a lot of cleanup work after you tear it down, and it's expensive. The city asked the conglomerate if they would lend a hand paying for it. They got a one finger response. The city threatened to sue. The conglomerate referred them to their law firm, which immediately said they would sue back."

"For what?"

"Anything and everything they could think of. Their reputation was for winning at all costs. Someone said their business card had skull and crossbones on it."

"You don't want to mess with guys like that," I said.

"That's what the city attorney thought. He was going to go after McShane, but McShane was getting so many dirty looks when he went around town that he decided to move to Arizona."

"Good thinking," I said.

"I wasn't too happy about what happened with the plant, but I hated to see him go. We played golf together. Deke said McShane had a heart attack and died shortly after he moved."

"Was he playing golf when it happened?" I asked.

"Matter of fact he was. Deke said it was a hundred degrees out."

"Karma can be a bitch," I said.

"It does have a way of biting you in the ass. The mayor is trying to get a grant from the EPA to fund the cleanup, but I understand that the city is at the back of a very long line."

"I heard in New Jersey, you can't swing a dead cat over your head without hitting a toxic waste dump," I said.

"Maybe the EPA should consider sawing the state off and letting it float away."

"Guess then at least it would be someone else's problem."

chapter 39

THE PLACE MY FORMER IN-LAWS HAD ON SAND KEY was nice, although it was in a much smaller building than Deke's. Their place was a spacious two bedroom, two bath unit, and it had views of both the Gulf and Clearwater Bay, although their views of the Gulf had been steadily diminished over the years by taller condos built on the other side of the road, such as Deke and his wife's. Their place was even nicer, a large, three bed, three bath corner unit on the 15th floor and had expansive views of both the Gulf and the landward side.

"Deke and his wife got in on the ground floor," Hanlen said, as if reading my mind. "And I don't mean they originally had a first-floor condo. They bought in while U.S. Steel was just thinking about building this place."

My ex-father in-law had told me that U.S. Steel had purchased most of Sand Key Island back in the earlier seventies, with the intent of building vacation properties. I thought that was an odd project for a steel company to undertake, but maybe that was when the big steel companies figured they needed to diversify to survive. Whatever the motivation, the project was a success. There were two dozen or so high-rise condos on Sand Key, and a few resort hotels at the north end of the island, although I don't think the steel company owned any of it anymore.

"In view of how the steel business is going, maybe U.S. Steel should have stuck to vacation property development," I said.

"Yeah, maybe they could convert the Gary Works to beachfront condos."

"Not sure how many people would want to own a condo on Lake Michigan when it's fifteen degrees out."

"Eskimos, maybe," Hanlen said. "Fifteen degrees would look pretty good if you were used to twenty below."

"If cleaning up a small ball bearing plant is expensive, imagine what the cost on a big integrated steel mill is," I said.

"If I were to head south, it might be near Hilton Head," Hanlen said.

"Why?"

"More golf courses. It's not as warm there in the winter, but that might make it a little cheaper. It gets a little buggy in spring and fall, but that's what they make insect repellant for."

"You think you could ever live in a condo?" I asked him. "Not sure I'd care for it."

"What's not to like?" he asked, glancing around the room, raising his up-turned hands.

"Even if I could afford a place like this, I don't think I'd like using an elevator all the time. I want to be able to just open a door and step outside."

"Why, you got a dog?" Hanlen replied. "That's easy. Get a place on the first floor. Although the first floor here is a garage."

"No, I don't have a dog but you don't have a view, plus people above you are making a racket." I said.

"Life is about trade-offs, Logan. That's part of the deal. Sounds to me like you're anti-social. Maybe it isn't so much the elevator, as the people on the elevator."

"There's that then," I said. "Making small talk with strangers all the time. In the lobby, the garage, and the elevator. I'm not a backslapper like you and Deke."

"I'm no backslapper," Hanlen replied. "I leave the small talk to my wife. She's a social butterfly. I just stand there and nod my head while she or someone else goes on. Every once in a while, I'll smile and add, 'that's right,' or 'you don't say.'"

"Then that could be a problem," I said. "As noted, I don't have a wife."

"Can't help you with that, but small talk is easy. Mention the weather or talk about restaurants. Nobody's looking for your life story. Fact is, I doubt if they could care less about you. They just want to feel comfortable with the neighbors. That's so they know you aren't a maniac and won't be heaving a body off the balcony any time soon. That might lower the property values some."

"Plus, they'd have to add a body removal charge to the monthly condo fee," I said. "On the other hand, they could put a positive spin on it. As in, people are dying to live here."

"Like you said, it's all about the spin," Hanlen said. "Stow your stuff away and we'll go get something to eat. There's a crab shack that's close."

chapter 40

WE DROVE SOUTH ABOUT HALF A MILE from of the condo to the crab shack. I recalled it as being a small, unpretentious, yet popular establishment. Sure enough, when we got there, there was a line of about twenty people trailing from the front door down the side of the small concrete building. I suggested we go elsewhere, but Hanlen said the line would move fast. It did, and to make the wait more palatable, or at least less thirsty, the manager brought out a couple pitchers of beer. Hanlen, belying his claim that he didn't care for socializing, or fueled by the beer, struck up a conversation with some people behind us, when he found out they were from Wisconsin. Guess their distinctive Northwoods accent gave them away. They and Hanlen had a friendly argument about whether Wisconsin or Purdue had the better football program. We ended up sitting with them at one of the large communal tables. When we finished, Hanlen picked up the tab for the table. The food wasn't overly expensive, considering we were in a tourist area, but it wasn't cheap either.

On the drive back to the condo, I asked Hanlen about his spontaneous generosity.

"Just felt like doing something nice, is all," he said. "Maybe it was because they were from my home state."

"Doesn't have to do with going out on a boat with Needham in a couple days, does it?"

"Why'd you say that?" Hanlen asked, puzzled.

"Well, it wouldn't hurt to have a little good karma before we go on a long boat ride with a potential killer."

"I told you I'm not superstitious. I also told you I'm not worried about Needham."

"We don't have to go out on the boat," I said. "We could talk to him on the dock. That would save us some time and money, for one thing."

"I got the money and the time," he said. "Plus, I've given this some thought. I figure once we're out in the middle of the ocean, he might feel more inclined to talk. You agree?"

"If he knows something, maybe," I said. "He won't be able to run away or call his lawyer. Plus, we'll have the element of surprise. At least I hope we will."

"That's what I thought," Hanlen said, nodding.

"You should have been a detective," I said. "You weren't thinking about working him over, were you?"

"That's not a bad idea," he said. "Remind me to take a phone book along."

I gave him a questioning look.

"You know me better than that," he said.

"What if he denies anything and everything about the girls?"

"Then I'll apologize to him and just do some fishing," Hanlen replied. "Oh, and by the way, you don't actually hit someone with a phone book. You hold the phone book against the body and hit the book with a night-stick. Supposedly that way there wouldn't be a mark. By the way, I never did that, and if I ever heard of any of my officers doing it, they were gone."

"I thought that's how it worked, but I didn't want to correct you and sound ignorant," I said. "Hey, speaking of Needham, how old you figure he is?"

"Think he was thirty-five when he went to prison, which was in 1970, so that would make him about sixty-five or so. Thirty or so when the girls disappeared."

"And he is still at it with the fishing charter," I remarked.

"So?"

"That can't be a real easy job, physical wise."

"Probably not. Guess you're moving around a lot, plus lifting and load-ing stuff. Trying to land a 300-pound tuna can't be too easy."

"And you're out in the hot sun all day," I said.

"What's your point?" Hanlen asked.

"A lot of guys might find something easier to do."

"Maybe he really likes fishing. Plus, I guess if he had a pension from his law enforcement days, he forfeited that when he went to prison. I understand it's tough to make a go of it on just social security."

"You're probably right."

"Oh yeah, you're going to be on your own tomorrow morning. I'm going golfing."

"Where you going to play?" I asked. "A ritzy country club, I imagine."

"Deke and his wife belong to a club on the other side of the bay," Hanlen replied. "We've played there before. I guess it is exclusive. Deke said they only allowed women to wear shorts on the course a few years ago."

"What are you going to use for clubs?"

"He keeps an extra couple sets down here. Good thing we're about the same height."

chapter 41

THE BED I HAD WAS COMFORTABLE ENOUGH, but since it was an unfamiliar one, or for other reasons, I didn't sleep well. At least I didn't have any dreams. I was up early and put on my running stuff, figuring I'd get a few miles in. When I went into the kitchen, Hanlen was sitting at a small table overlooking the bay. He had a bowl of Wheaties in front of him. There were also a few bananas and a couple doughnuts, and a containers of orange juice and milk on the table.

"The breakfast of champions," I said, looking at the cereal box. Johnny Bench was on the cover. "Here's one for you. Who's the only Native American to be on the Wheaties cover? Let's leave Bench out, even though he was part Choctaw."

Hanlen thought about it. "I'm going with Jim Thorpe."

"Good guess. Nah, it was the guy you mentioned at the run. Billy Mills."

"Semper Fi. Although I got to think Thorpe was the greater all-round athlete."

"I wouldn't argue that," I said. "You get the stuff at the convenience store by the hotels?"

He nodded. "Help yourself. There's a bottle of Gatorade in the frig, too. Thought you might want to go running on the beach. If you do, you should go early. I was listening to the news, and it supposed to get close to ninety today."

"Good idea," I replied.

I got the Gatorade, sat down, and peeled one of the bananas.

"Potassium," I said. "Just the thing for running on a hot, humid day."

"There's some beer in there, too, for when you get back," Hanlen said.

"Bananas, Gatorade, and beer. The official race day diet of Bill Rodger's, I understand. Did I ever tell you I got Bill Rodger's autograph?"

"He won a bunch of marathons, right?

"The big ones in Boston and New York, four times each. I got his autograph when he did the Chicago Marathon some years back."

"Did he win that one?" Hanlen asked.

"No, but he might have been past his prime then."

"It's a bitch getting old," Hanlen said.

"True, but a lot of distance runners don't hit their prime until their late twenties or early thirties. Matter of fact, the guy who won the 1984 Olympic marathon, Carlos Lopez, was 37 years old. Speaking of which, I'm getting old sitting here," I said, and rose to leave.

"I'll be leaving myself soon," Hanlen said. "Be careful running. I don't want you to get hurt before tomorrow."

"Yeah. Let's save everything for tomorrow," I replied.

chapter 42

RUNNING ON THE BEACH ISN'T ALWAYS AS ENJOYABLE as it might seem. That should have been my comeback line to Kathy when she said I'd love running on the beach in California. The firm sand near the waterline provides dependable footing, but the stuff further away from the water is loose and makes for shifty, tedious going. Maybe that was just sour grapes on my part. The only shore in shouting distance at home was Lake Michigan, where it was freezing cold almost six months of the year. The other problem was a lot of the property by the lake was privately owned. Other than the two national lakeshores, one in Indiana, the other in Michigan, and assorted state and municipal parks, almost 80% of the Lake Michigan beachfront was privately owned. While there was a general, court-decreed understanding that everyone had the right to walk on the beach, by the waterline, there were sometimes differences of opinion on what constituted the waterline, and who had the right of access. Once in a while, you read in the paper about the differences of opinion escalating into shouting matches and vandalism.

Nobody told me to get off the beach behind the condo, in fact there weren't many people there. The few out walking were mostly solitary old folks, getting their daily constitutional in before the heat and crowds which would come later. I wondered if they were widowed. It might be depressing if you relocated to Florida, especially to an upscale area like this one, and then your spouse passed away. That would depend on how you felt about your spouse, but it might make you wish you had stayed in Peoria or Oshkosh. The cold and gloomy winters with family and friends might be preferable to the warm and sunny ones without.

I decided to run north toward Sand Key Park, a large county park next to Clearwater Pass, the inlet between Clearwater and Sand Key. It was the first place you came to when you crossed the drawbridge between the two places, and a popular spot for visitors to the area. While there were a few, legally required, beach access points between the condo buildings on Sand Key, they were not easy to find and parking at them was limited. I guessed that was on purpose, to keep the commoners out. I could understand that. If I shelled out two hundred grand for a beachfront condo, I wouldn't want to share the view with a guy wearing an Elvis t-shirt and drinking Meister Brau. The county park had a large parking area, a wide beach, and bathhouses.

The breeze fell off some as I ran through the tree lined road in the park, making the rising heat and humidity more noticeable. By the time I got to the rock-lined channel at the end of the island, I was sweating heavily. I stopped, took off my shirt, and wiped the sweat out of my eyes. I had a moment of dizziness, and instinctively dropped to my knees. This was the traditional remedy for faintness and numerous other conditions, per the coaches at the high school football camps I attended. I figured 'take a knee' was still sound medical advice, but still, I retched up a little Gatorade.

It was then I heard the noise; a loud, cackling, and unsettling laugh. It was coming from behind and above me. I knew where I had heard it before. I closed my eyes a couple times to make sure I wasn't hallucinating. Nothing looked out of the ordinary. When I heard the cackle again, I turned around. To my relief, there was no old woman there, but a very large crow at the top of a 30-foot-high scrub pine tree.

When I was kid, there was a retired widower who lived along our route to school who had rescued an injured crow and nursed it back to health. After the crow's convalescence, it declined to leave, I guess figuring that table scraps and a garage to sleep in were preferable to life in the wild. It even learned some words from his patron. Turns out crows are not only among the smartest birds, but among the smartest animals, and can mimic a lot of sounds. They are also mischievous and not timid, sometimes to the point of being aggressive. The crow would occasionally swoop at us, while cawing 'dammit,' or other obscenity. Some kids found it amusing, but the bird scared me. I was glad when it was hit and killed by a garbage truck. I told my father about it, including my reaction. He chastised me, telling me all animals were sacred but the crow especially so, due to its wisdom.

I thought about that briefly, as I stared at the bird. It again made the same loud cackling, and to my ears, derisive, noise. I took it personally and looked for a rock to throw. I found one and launched it at the bird. My aim was accurate enough that the crow hopped off the branch and flew up about ten feet. It seemingly paused in mid-air, then, to my astonishment, dove straight at me. Shades of grade school days. I hit the deck as the miniature black Stuka whizzed by me. It made an abrupt landing on the ground twenty feet away, and then looked at me with cocked head, as if to say, 'take that.' I got up to my knees while I looked for another rock. But the crow seemed to have lost interest in me. It was pecking at a small white piece of paper on the ground. It appeared to be a food wrapper or napkin. I rose slowly and walked toward the crow. I didn't like being intimidated and the crow seemed to sense now I meant business. With one final angry cackle, it abandoned the paper and took to the air. This time it climbed up in wide circle, then gradually flew out of sight, across the channel toward Clearwater, where I'm sure there were plenty of dumpsters to plunder.

"Watch out for garbage trucks," I muttered.

I went over to where the crow had been and glanced down at the piece of paper. It wasn't a food wrapper, but a piece of paper torn from a small spiral note pad. Curious, I picked it up. On the paper, in red ink, in an almost illegible scrawl, someone had written 'NASENA.' Beside it was drawn a circle with a small arrow pointing at it. I guessed it was the name of a place, maybe a person. I stuck it in the pocket of my running shorts, which was fortuitous since there was a forgotten ten-dollar bill in there. Instead of running back via the beach, I hiked over to the main road to the convenience store. I got a sandwich and a coke. As I was standing in the checkout line, a young, fit looking guy behind me tapped me on the shoulder.

"I had a coach who used to do that," he said, pointing down at the laces of my shoes, to which I had tied the keys to the condo.

"Old running trick," I said. "In my case, real old. But I can't claim I invented it."

I noticed he was wearing a North Central College Athletics t-shirt. North Central is a small-midsized college in Naperville, Illinois, outside of Chicago. Going to Wallace, I was aware the school was a small college athletic powerhouse.

"You guys crank out some pretty good teams," I said, gesturing at his t-shirt. The one year I competed with Wallace in the D3 cross-country championship, the team from North Central won. We didn't do too bad ourselves, finishing in the top fifteen. I think they had some good football and basketball teams as well.

"You've heard of us," he said. "Not to brag, but I was on one of the teams that won the D3 cross-country championship."

"It's not bragging if you can do it," I replied. "Say, I always was curious about something about your school."

"What's that?"

"What do they put in the food there?"

He laughed. I paid for my stuff, wished him well, and walked back to the condo.

chapter 43

I DECIDED TO EAT MY SANDWICH ON THE LARGE BALCONY with a table, chairs and a couple chaise lounges facing west towards the Gulf. Deke had an expensive stereo system near the sliding glass door to the balcony. After a couple minutes, I figured out how to turn the thing on. I noticed 'The Very Best of Johnny Cash' CD was sitting out. I started it and left the balcony door open so I could listen. Instead of the coke, I had a beer. As I was finishing it, Cash was singing one of his biggest hits, Kris Kristofferson's melancholy "Sunday Mornin' Comin' Down." The beer tasted good, so I took the example of the protagonist in the song and had another one. I then moved over to a chaise and drifted off to sleep.

I had another dream. I was again up at the Dunes, but this time I was not on the beach. I was well out in the lake, a couple hundred yards from shore. Like the other dreams I'd had, the weather was stormy, and the grey lake was turbulent. Large cold waves were making it difficult to keep my head above water. I knew I would not be able to swim back to shore, and panic rapidly set in. Then I saw a small motorboat further out in the lake. I yelled for help, as best I could, while fighting the waves. I was elated when I saw the boat turn in my direction and slowly approach my position. When it got within twenty yards of me, I was surprised when the motor revved loudly. The boat immediately sped up and made right for me, the operator not intent on rescuing me, but running me over. I immediately dove under the waves, getting deep as fast as I could, but still felt the wake of the boat rush close over me. I stayed down for as long as I could, then broke through to the surface, gasping. Inexplicably, the boat was no longer in sight; not just that, but I was now within twenty yards of shore and the waves had also dissipated. As I waded out of the water, I looked up toward the beach berm and the old Pottawattamie woman was standing there. At her feet was a large crow, scratching something into the sand with its claw. I started to head toward them but my legs were cold and tight. I stumbled on something and looked down. When I looked back up at the berm, the woman and crow were gone. I walked over to where they had been and scratched on the sand was the word 'nasena,' and an arrow pointing at the water.

chapter 44

I BOLTED UPRIGHT IN THE CHAISE. SEEING THE MASSIVE blue of the Gulf, I thought I was back at Lake Michigan. Then I realized where I was and sank back into the chaise. The dream was more vivid than the previous ones, and since the old Pottawattamie woman was in it, I wondered again if the first time I saw her was also a bizarre dream. Or maybe I was just losing it. And what was nasena supposed to mean? A place? A name? It sounded foreign. I went into the kitchen and rummaged through the cabinets until I found a Clearwater phonebook. There was no one with the last name Nasena. There were a few small black and white area maps within the front pages, but I saw no place or street in the area with that name. Then I had another thought.

It was after 2:00 Eastern time, an hour earlier in Northwest Indiana. I figured if George Hiatt started work real early, he might be home by now. I still had his number in my wallet. He picked up and didn't seem surprised that it was me calling. I asked him about that.

"Oh, I don't know. I just had feeling I'd be hearing from you again."

"I'm flattered," I replied.

"Don't get swell-headed. What's going on?"

"The old Pottawattamie woman we talked about . . ." I started to say, but George interrupted me.

"You didn't see her again, did you?" he said.

"No," I said, pausing. "Well, not really. I had a dream with her in it."

"You mean you had another dream with her in it," he replied.

I could almost see him with a small grin on his face.

"Sorry, go on," he said, after a pause.

"Well, maybe I am losing it. Did I tell you I had a couple concussions recently? Car accidents. Plus, I took a few hard hits to the head when I played football in high school. I could be getting punch drunk."

"You're a little young to be punch drunk," George said. "But if you are having trouble that way, I could understand. Guys I saw in the war with head wounds had a tough go of it. You can fix an arm or leg, I guess. Not sure about the brain."

"Yeah," I said. "George, what I wanted to ask you was, in the stories you heard about the Pottawattamie woman, did she have a name?"

"Not that I recall."

"Does the word nasena mean anything to you?"

"Nasena," he replied, slowly repeating me. "Is that her name?"

"I don't know what it is," I said.

"Yet you think it has something to do with her. Was it in the dream?"

"Yes," I said, deciding to leave the part out about the crow in the park.

"Ok, so maybe it's an Indian word. Be logical to assume it's a Pottawattamie word."

"That occurred to me."

"Is there any way to track down what it means?" he asked.

"There's a little problem with doing that," I said.

"Which is?"

"Well, my understanding, admittedly limited, is that most indigenous languages are no longer widely used. Many are not used at all. Plus, except for a couple tribes, the American Indians were not a literate people. Tribal culture and history were passed down orally or with drawings, or other symbols. In other words, there are no Indian dictionaries to look up words. I just made a bad pun, but you see what I mean."

"I do," George replied.

"You said your nephew's wife was part Pottawattamie," I said. "You think she may know what nasena means?"

"You just said that native languages aren't used anymore," George said.

"I did. But in some tribes, there are young people trying to preserve the tribal culture. That might involve talking to elders in the tribe. Some of the old people still know some of the old ways and words. You said she was proud of her heritage. Could she be a person like that?"

"I don't know, but I could ask her, I guess," George said, not sounding too optimistic.

"Is she hard to reach?"

"What's the hurry?" George asked, but didn't wait for an answer to his question.

"They got a couple young kids. She takes care of them and isn't working right now. I can try and reach her. Should I call you back at the number you gave at the lake?"

"No, I'm in Florida right now. Let me give you the number."

"What the heck are you doing in Florida? Ah, never mind, I'll see what I can find out."

About 45 minutes later the phone rang.

"It's Logan," I said picking up.

"It's George. I talked to Winnie, my niece," he said. "Her folks wanted to call her Winnetka but thought she would get made fun of."

"Good idea," I said. "I believe Winnetka is a Native American word, but I don't think it means 'north Chicago suburb where rich white folks live.'"

"It's Pottawattamie. So is your word, she thinks."

"What does it mean?"

He paused before answering.

"I wrote this down, so as I wouldn't forget. First, she said the syntax of Native American language is different from English. Not sure I know exactly what syntax means, but in English, word, nouns, verbs, etc., are put together in structured form in sentences to convey something."

"I think I remember that from second grade English class," I said.

"You do want to hear this, right?"

"Sorry, go ahead."

"In Indian dialects, she said words tend to be longer, and can be pronounced differently depending on the context it's used in. It's possible for one word to convey slightly different meanings, again depending on context. And one word in Indian could convey the same thing a sentence or two might take in English."

"Interesting. So, what does nasena mean?"

"She said it was a word which, defined in English, might mean a 'warning.' Maybe depending on context, something like 'beware of danger.'"

I thought about that.

"You in any kind of danger, Logan?" George asked.

"I sure hope not," I said.

I thought about the word scratched in the sand, and the arrow pointing to the water. Then I thought of going out on the boat tomorrow.

"Does this have anything to do with the missing girls?" George asked.

"Up until now, I would have said no," I replied. "Now I'm not so sure."

chapter 45

I WAS IN THE KITCHEN WHEN HANLEN GOT BACK, a couple hours after I had talked to George. His nose was sunburned, and his hair was hat-mussed. I also detected a whiff of alcohol.

"Stop at the nineteenth hole?" I asked.

"I played twenty-seven with some fellas, so I guess there was a nineteen in there somewhere. I wanted to play another nine, but they were wore out."

"Twenty-seven holes on a hot day . . . I could see why," I said. "That's a lot of golf."

"We had something to eat afterward, and a few beers," Hanlen said, placing a Styrofoam container on the table.

"Crab cakes were the special in the grill. Hope you don't mind seafood twice in a row. I got the baked potato instead of the fries. Figured the fries would get mushy on the way back."

"That was thoughtful. Thanks," I said.

"You ok?" Hanlen asked. "You had a funny look on your face when I walked in."

"From running in the sun, maybe," I said. "Who'd you go out with?"

"One was a retired judge. Found out he played football at Notre Dame. Just so happened one year was when we beat them. Broke a thirty-nine game unbeaten streak for the Irish."

"Impressive," I said.

"Not really. We won only one other game that year. Notre Dame lost four, their most in fifteen years," Hanlen replied. "The judge also said he played ball one year with John Lattner."

"The Heisman winner. Very impressive. Although I understand he won it by the slimmest margin ever, at the time, anyhow."

"Nobody remembers who finished second," Hanlen observed.

"Nice guys finish last. Winners never quit and quitters never win," I said. "I just called your sports cliché and raised it by two."

"I met Lattner. He was a nice guy who didn't finish last. He wasn't lucky though."

"In what way?"

"He only played one year in the pros, then he went in the Air Force, and ruined his knee in a service game," Hanlen replied. "Bet you'd have to look long and hard nowadays to find a professional athlete who served his country."

"Yeah, during Vietnam, I understand teams pulled strings to get their players assigned to the reserves or National Guard. That way they wouldn't have to go to Vietnam. "

"Guess Rocky Bleier didn't get the word on that," Hanlen said.

"Preferential treatment, in other words. Kind of like a senator from Indiana got."

"I wouldn't pick on Quayle. He wasn't the only one," Hanlen said.

"That's what I mean," I said. "Vietnam was a poor man's war. Or an unlucky one's. Guess if you're poor, by definition, you're unlucky."

"Would you want someone who's making big decisions who wasn't smart enough to get out of going to Vietnam? I sure wouldn't."

"We've been hanging out together too much, Chief," I said. "You are getting awfully cynical. Where'd you meet Lattner?"

"He had a restaurant in Chicago in the sixties. His Heisman Trophy was on display there. Then the place burned down and melted the trophy into a doorstop."

"Buzz had a football signed by him and Paul Hornung in his office," I said. Buzz was once given a game ball for his play in a Notre Dame win. The two Irish Heisman winners from the 1950s were at the game, and signed it. Buzz seemed to think it was worth a lot of money.

"I remember. I wonder which one of his partners took it."

"Like I said, you're getting cynical," I said.

"They're lawyers. They refer to thievery as protection of assets," Harlen replied.

He left the kitchen while I started in on the food he brought me. When he came back he put six hundred dollars on the table, four hundreds and four fifties.

"What's that for," I asked.

"I made the charter in your name. Needham wanted $600 for the two of us, for half a day, and wanted a credit card to hold the boat. I told him I'd pay him $400 cash for three hours, when we showed up. He grumbled a bit, but was ok with it, at least then. The fifties are for in case he pulls a fast one and holds out for more."

"Ok," I said.

"See if you can negotiate fifty at a time."

"I'm not much for bargaining," I said. "By the time I'm done, you'll be paying $600 for a thirty-minute tour of the bay."

"He said to be there at 5:30 a.m., sharp," Hanlen said.

"That's early, even for fishing. Maybe he doesn't want anybody seeing us."

"Maybe. But then again, the early bird catches the worm."

chapter 46

I FIGURED HANLEN WOULD WANT TO LEAVE EARLY, and I was ready when he knocked on my door at 4:30 a.m. I didn't sleep well, again, but at least I didn't have any more dreams. I had a quick bowl of cereal and then we were heading to the garage. The guy manning the gate looked like he was asleep, but the exit gate opened automatically as we approached. I guess they only cared if you were trying to get into the place and not if you were leaving. It was eerie driving through the normally busy streets. I assumed that the few people we saw were workers heading to their early shift jobs at the hotels. At the marina parking lot entrance, there was a sign saying it didn't open until 6 a.m., but Hanlen pushed the red button on the ticket machine, the parking arm raised and in we went.

"Needham said his slip was towards the end of the last dock," he said. He drove down the end of the lot and parked.

We walked a good way down the dock until we saw a large, handwritten sign for the Lucky Strike, illuminated by one of the dock lights. I noted it had a blue hull and remarked on that to Hanlen.

"Maybe he's a sucker for blue boats," he replied. "If you were thinking this was the same one from the Dunes, two decades ago, forget it. That boat was at most half the size of this one."

The engine of the Lucky Strike was idling and there was a light on in the cabin, but no one was in sight. We were very early, and stood there for a couple minutes. Hanlen coughed loudly, but there was no response.

"Ahoy on the boat," Hanlen called out, his voice booming out in the stillness. There was a banging noise from the cabin.

"Ahoy yourself!" came an angry retort. A large man with patchy white hair and a scraggly gray beard poked his head out of the cabin. He was wearing a wife-beater t-shirt and tan painter's pants. Large tattoos decorated his upper arms. His look of anger changed to puzzlement, then comprehension.

"Which one of you is Wells?" he said, striding over to the stern.

"I'm Logan Wells," I replied. "This is my Uncle Bill," I added, nodding at Hanlen.

"I'm Needham. You're early and you owe me $450. Cash."

"I thought we agreed on $400," I said, a mild note of protest in my voice.

"Like I said, you're early. If we go out now, that's more time," He looked at Hanlen appraisingly.

"Plus, your uncle weighs 250 pounds, easy. That's more weight to haul."

I smiled at that, thinking he was kidding.

"I thought he would be good ballast," I said. "In case we hit some rough water."

That got a stone-faced look.

I shrugged, reached for the money, and handed it down to him.

"Here you go," I said to him. Then, to Hanlen, "you need to go on a diet."

"You don't sound like you do on the phone," Needham said to me, as he took the money.

"Probably allergies," I replied. "They're hell this time of year."

That got a grunt in response.

If Jerry Needham was in his sixties, my quick impression was that he had lived a hard life. His face was bronzed and deeply creased, with broken blood vessels on the sides of his large nose. Maybe his worn visage was from spending a lot of time on the water, out in the hot sun and wind. Or maybe his time in prison had something to do with it. He had a massive gut, which along with the nose was suggestive of someone who drank a lot. I could see his big hands, and his biceps were formidable, and from the brief display of his temperament, and the sight of his arms, I figured he wouldn't be the type to run away from a fight.

"Well, what are you waiting for?" he said. "Get on the boat and let's get going. And watch your step. I don't need anybody suing me."

After that cordial introduction, we got on board the *Lucky Strike*.

chapter 47

Needham went back into the cabin, and we heard him rummaging around. He emerged carrying a couple worn vinyl pilot seats, with cylindrical steel posts attached. He affixed the posts to metal brackets in the deck. He moved agilely despite his bulk. As he got close to me, I detected the sweet smell of a drinker's sweat.

"You guys look like sittin' down fisherman," he said, then went back to the cabin.

"Did he just insult us?" I asked Hanlen. "By the way, I think he's a drinker."

"Some guys like to fish standing up, some standing down," he replied. "I think you're right about the drinking. Let's hope he hasn't started already."

The seats of the chairs had what looked to be cushions with some straps attached to it. Hanlen examined one of them with a quizzical look.

"What's wrong?" I asked.

"Odd, these appear to be what you would call a 'bucket harness,'" he said, "but it looks like he's got them glued to the seats."

"So?"

"Usually, the harness is just attached to the seat with belts. The harness holds your fishing rod. You need to be able to stand up with it on."

"Why?" I asked.

"Leverage, for one, if you're fighting a fish to get it to the boat."

"Can fish really fight?" I asked. "Seems to me, once the fish gets hooked it's at a considerable disadvantage."

"Easy for you to say. Try catching a thirty-pound fish on a ten-pound test line. I was just saying the seat was odd, that's all. Not sure I can even squeeze my big carcass into it."

"Maybe he didn't want anyone running off with it when he got back to the dock."

Needham came back out with a couple rods and reels.

"What's that stuff for?" I asked.

That got another dirty look.

"I don't need a comedian," Needham said. "I got some more if those don't suit you. We'll be going after mahi-mahi, out a few miles."

He glanced at Hanlen. "You look like you been on a boat before. Give me a push off the dock. Doesn't need to be hard, so don't get a hernia. When you hear the idle rev up, push."

Hanlen gave a half salute. "Aye, aye," he muttered as Needham turned back to the cabin.

After a couple minutes, the engine growled louder, and Hanlen pushed the boat away from the dock. In short order, we were heading into the harbor. I didn't see much activity among the other boats as we went by. There were some much larger boats, 40-50 feet long, on the other side of where the *Lucky Strike* had been moored.

"Those must be yachts," I said to Hanlen. "They look pricey."

"Yeah," he replied. "But they probably belong to rich people passing through. If you got real money and live here, you got a home on the water and your own dock."

In short order we were in Clearwater Pass. The sun was making more of an appearance now behind us as we approached Sand Key Bridge. The colors created by the rising sun over the blue green water, along with the lights on the drawbridge above us and the buildings over in Clearwater beach, combined to create a colorful tapestry. Hanlen gave a low whistle of appreciation as we passed under the bridge.

"Ever been on the bridge when the lift conks out?" I said. "You'd be in traffic for hours."

"Anyone ever tell you you're a half-full glass type person?" Hanlen replied.

"You're the first. Was just saying about the bridge, that's all."

"I heard about that, but never had the pleasure of experiencing it," he replied. "They'll be replacing it soon enough, what with all the people moving here."

The current in the channel got rougher as we approached the entrance to the Gulf. As we went by Sand Key Park, I looked over at where I had been yesterday. Although it still wasn't entirely light, I saw a big crow at the top of one of the taller trees, in the area where I had been the day before. I jumped up to get a better look, but when I got to my feet, it was gone.

"If you're thinking of jumping off, might want to wait until we get into the ocean," said Hanlen. "The current here would probably pull you all the way back into the bay."

We were going faster, heading out into the Gulf, and the boat was bouncing a bit as we hit the waves. After a few minutes I started to feel sleepy. I attributed it in part to the motion of the boat, but mainly to the couple Dramamine I took before we left. I thought if I drifted off, and we hit some big waves, I'd be out of the seat and onto the deck, so I attached the seat harness with the clip at my waist. It was hard to fasten—kind of like some of the ones you get on the airlines, after a few thousand people of substantially varied waist sizes had handled them.

I did drift off. I'm not sure how long I was asleep, but I woke to Hanlen calling my name. He was sitting on the transom. The first thing I noticed was the boat had stopped. The second thing I noticed was Jerry Needham was standing about eight feet away and pointing a shotgun in our direction.

chapter 48

"AM I DREAMING OR IS HE HOLDING A SHOTGUN ON US?" I asked Hanlen. "God forbid I'm in one of your dreams," he replied.

I deduced in short order that if Needham was going to shoot us, he would have made it quick and a surprise. He evidently had something else in mind, but I didn't think it was to rob me of what remained of the money Hanlen had given me.

I took a closer look at his weapon.

"It looks like a coach gun," I said. Coach gun was the popular term for a double, short-barreled shotgun, derived from the similar weapons carried by stagecoach guards in the Wild West. It was very effective at close range and appealed to some as a weapon for home defense. Me, I'd say outdoor lighting and an alarm system were better options. I knew very few were killed in home invasions, but guns were the weapon of choice for domestic violence . . . or suicide.

"I believe you're right, Logan," Hanlen said. "You got a pirate problem, Jerry?"

"You could say so," Needham said. "Once in a while, I'll get a small shark or barracuda eating on a fish I've hooked. I've had them come all the way to the boat. I give them a little surprise when they get here. This packs a punch for its size."

"I bet it does," Hanlen said, "but I thought shooting fish was illegal."

"You might be right on that. But so is me owning a gun like this, so I'm not going to sweat shooting a fish," Needham replied.

"How about sitting down and attaching your harness, like your nephew," he added. "Never know when we'll hit some rough water."

Hanlen looked at Needham, as if deciding whether to do as he asked, then sat down, the seat barely handling his bulk. He had to adjust the harness belt to get it on.

Needham sat down in the deck chair. There was a small flask in a pocket below the arm of the chair and he picked it up and took a swig. That worried me.

"That's fine," he said. "Now we can talk without being bothered by any sudden movements." He shook his head slightly.

"You shouldn't have come here, Chief," Needham said. "Not after all these years. I had nothing to do with those girls at the Dunes."

Hanlen and I looked at each other. Somewhat surprisingly, he gave a wry smile.

"Well, I didn't say you did," Hanlen replied, after a pause. I thought it wise that he didn't add 'yet' to his reply.

"You know something about it, though," I said.

"Who's he?" Needham asked, gesturing at me with the gun.

"That's Mr. Logan Wells. It was me on the phone the other day," Hanlen said.

"I thought so. He law, too?"

"He's the lead investigator for the Prairie County Prosecuting Attorney."

I looked at Hanlen. The county investigative staff was composed of only five people and there was no 'lead' investigator. There was a senior investigator, but the title was mainly administrative. He coordinated work assignments with the prosecutor.

"I'm on leave right now," I said, adding what I thought was important clarification.

I looked around and noticed there was no land in sight. Since I'd been sleeping, I wasn't sure how many miles out we were. I thought I remembered that the viewable horizon at sea was around three miles, so I assumed we were out at least that far. I didn't see any other boats, maybe because it was still early.

"By the way," I said, "you don't think we'd come out here without somebody knowing where we are, do you?" I hoped I sounded convincing.

"You know," he said. "I thought about that. I heard you retired, Chief. Guess your friend here isn't official either. Seems to me, if this was a legit investigation, you would have met me on the dock with a couple Clearwater detectives. You guys are fishing in more ways than one. My bet is you're doing it on your own time, and nobody knows you're here."

"I wouldn't wager much on that," Hanlen replied. "But you're right, we're not official. We're taking another look into what happened to those three girls. Your name came up."

"How so?"

"We know that the girls left the beach in your boat," I said.

"Huh. And which one of my boats was that?"

"A fifteen foot or so runabout with a blue hull and white interior," Hanlen said.

"Guess mine was the only one like it on the lake that day," Needham said.

"Probably not," I said. "But witnesses said the girls were seen getting on one like that."

"Even if that's so, how do you know it was me in the boat?"

"Witnesses on the beach described a man who looked like you," I said. That was an exaggeration. He was in the right age bracket, but the descriptions varied.

"Plus, we found out you were at the lake with the girls the weekend before," I added. That wasn't even an exaggeration, it was a supposition based on what Debbie Musick's grandmother told us back at the nursing home.

Needham gave a short laugh, and looked at Hanlen.

"He reminds me of me, in my detective days," he said. "Throw a lot of shit at the wall and hope some of it sticks. Guess now I'm supposed to start blubbering and confess. If there was any proof of what you say, somebody would have come looking for me long before now."

"Nobody linked you to the boat before," I said. "To be precise, not sure anyone tried."

"But you were able to."

"You talked to your insurance company about filing a claim on the boat," Hanlen replied. "To report it stolen. You never actually filed a claim, so there is no record of one."

Needham's brow scrunched up.

"My boat got stolen. Funny, I should remember something like that," he said. "Ok, if there was no claim, then what are you doing here?"

"We got lucky and found someone who knew the agent you talked to," I said. "I assume you intended to cover your tracks by filing a claim, then changed your mind. It was your boat at the Dunes that day, Jerry. Maybe you didn't kill the girls, but you did take them off the beach."

"That was real lucky, for you, after twenty years," Needham said. "And it was dumb, if it was me who did it. Since we're making stuff up here, what's my motive for taking them?"

"A favor for a friend," I said.

"I don't have any friends."

"Everybody has friends," Hanlen said. "Or at least you had one twenty years ago."

"Oh, yeah? And who was that?"

"Remember Luther Brame?" Hanlen asked. "Speaking of prison, he helped put you there. You got caught helping him arrange a murder for hire back in the early seventies. He must have been a real friend if you did time for him. I hear life is rough for a cop in jail. And who knows, maybe it wasn't the first time you helped him."

"Funny that you mentioned Luther, Chief," Needham said. "Why don't you go talk to him about the girls? He's the one who knows what happened to them." He shook his head.

"Oh, yeah, I remember why. Old Luther died of cancer a while back. Now I guess you figure it's my turn in the barrel. I didn't kill those girls and I'm not going back to prison."

"Who said anything about prison?" I asked. "We're trying to find out what happened to the girls. I'm guessing you didn't do anything other than take them off the beach and deliver them to Brame. You didn't know what he was going to do. From what I hear, he was an unpredictable man with a bad temper."

"You must think I'm an idiot," Needham said. "There's no statute of limitations on murder. Or kidnapping. Or being an accessory to either one."

"Like I said, maybe you didn't know what he was going to do with the girls," I said. "But I bet you knew what the girls had on him. Must have been something big enough for him to want to get rid of them, permanently.

And technically, it's kidnapping for ransom, not just kidnapping, that the statute of limitations doesn't apply to."

I thought the latter point would be moot to most prosecuting attorneys, including Bob Shannon. He'd just figure out another charge.

As if reading my mind, Needham said, "I doubt some hard-ass district attorney is going to care about that detail. I'll be back in prison before the ink's dry on the indictment."

"If you helped solve a twenty-year old mystery, they'd go light on you," I said.

"He's kidding, right?" Needham said, looking at Hanlen.

"Not to change the subject, Jerry," Hanlen said, "but I got to ask How did you know we'd be paying you a visit?"

Needham took a few seconds to answer.

"Let's just say I got a guardian angel," he said. "He told me someone might be looking into the disappearance of the girls, and it could be you."

"Does your guardian angel happen to work in law enforcement?" Hanlen asked. It was a good question. As far as I knew, only Ivar Rich knew we were thinking about going to Florida.

Needham didn't answer.

"I almost forgot about it until you showed up," he said, instead. "I knew you when I was a cop. A big guy like you is hard to forget. The beard's different, but I recognized you."

"Was your friend involved in the case years ago?" I asked.

"Listen to you," Needham said. "Playing twenty questions with someone holding a shotgun. Let's just say he really is an angel. He even lives in a monastery. Since we're changing the subject, Chief, I got to ask, did you ever kill anybody?"

Hanlen didn't say anything right away. When he did, his voice was subdued.

"In the Korean War, I did. I was with the Marines at Chosin."

"How many?" Needham asked.

"Not sure, but more than a few. Know anything about Chosin?"

Jerry shook his head slightly.

"We had the North Koreans whipped," Hanlen said, "but the Chinese had other ideas. They sent six divisions against us, near the Chosin Reservoir, in the dead of winter. They came at us in mass attacks, at night.

The reporters referred to them as the 'Chinese hordes.' The idea was the mass of bodies would overwhelm our firepower. Imagine the body count you could pile up if you could get off thirty rounds a minute. That was easy to do with a M-1 rifle."

Needham gave a low whistle. "How about when you were sheriff?"

"I didn't carry a weapon when I was sheriff. I had enough of killing in the war. I also figured if someone was going to kill me, it would have happened over in Korea."

"Sheriff Taylor of Prairie County," Needham said.

"Something like that," Hanlen replied.

"I never even shot anyone, while I was on the job," Needham said "I did kick a lot of ass when I was a cop. I took bribes. I did other bad stuff, Chief. Even wound up in the pen. But I never killed anybody. I can say that. You can't."

"That was in the service of his country," I protested.

Needham ignored me, "yet you come here, like the Lone Ranger, wanting to pin some old unsolved murders on me. Seems mighty two-faced to me."

"What the chief did wasn't murder," I said. I was about to add something about self-defense, but Hanlen interrupted me.

"No, Logan. I'm not going to justify what I did by saying it was for my country."

I was at a loss for words when he dropped that one.

"I've thought about it," Hanlen said, "and decided that killing stands out among all the awful stuff humans can do to each other. It's wrong, no matter what for."

"Did you tell your deputies that?" I asked. "Imagine they found that confusing."

"I'm not that naïve. Sometimes it's a necessary evil, but that doesn't make it right."

"Ok, Chief," I said. "I appreciate your declaration of ethics, odd timing notwithstanding. But Jerry here doesn't have any superiority over you. If he didn't kill those girls, he knows what happened to them. They deserve more than rotting at the bottom of Lake Michigan."

Hanlen looked at me but didn't say anything. Then he addressed Needham.

"Logan just put things in perspective, Jerry. You said you never killed anybody, and I don't think you're going to start with us. Why don't you just tell us what happened?"

"I was wondering when you would get back to me," Needham said. "Way I look at it, nothing I say will change what happened to those girls. But maybe somebody will get the idea they got enough to charge me as an accessory, and I wind up back in prison."

We stared at each other for thirty seconds or so.

"Couple points to consider, Jerry," I said. "One, I don't think you did away with the girls. No motive that I see. You barely knew them. If you were doing a favor for Brame, how could you know what he was going to do? And three, as far as we go, there are some people who know what we know. If you get rid of us, you'll still be looking over your shoulder."

chapter 49

"JUDAS PRIEST," NEEDHAM SAID.

He lowered the shotgun, but it was still pointed in our general direction. I was hoping he would put the safety on. He didn't.

"I knew this day would come, but thought when it would, I'd be long gone," he said.

"You mean like dead?" I asked. "Or like in Mexico?"

"Either one," Needham replied. "Man, I could never catch a break. I take that back. I got plenty of breaks. All bad. Like you two being here. Nothing goes right for me."

I'd heard that outlook expressed many times in my law enforcement career from people looking at doing time. Blaming fate, or others, and not accepting the consequences of their actions was endemic among the criminal set. I once knew an erudite detective who would sometimes cite Shakespeare in response to this reasoning.

"Maybe the fault lies not in our stars, but in ourselves," I said, before thinking about it.

"What the hell he is talking about?" Needham asked Hanlen.

"No idea," Hanlen replied. "Logan went to an egghead liberal arts college. But maybe he's saying that people get what they deserve."

"Maybe that's true, but I'll still say go screw yourself," Needham said.

"Ok," I said. "But those girls didn't catch a break either."

"You can make it right and tell us what happened," Hanlen added.

Needham sighed.

chapter 50

"IT WAS LUTHER BRAME," HE SAID. "He liked women, especially the young kind. I always thought it strange, since they didn't have to be real good looking, just as long as they were young."

"There are a lot of guys like that," Hanlen said. "You start getting old, you want something that makes you feel young."

"Yeah. I always wondered why parents let their daughters ride at his stables. 'Course he was smart enough to stay away from the real young ones. Doubt if he wanted to go back to prison for statutory rape."

"Any girl's parents ever have a problem with him?" I asked.

"Once in a while, some suspicious dad would come in and have words with Luther. Luther would laugh and imply maybe the guy's daughter had been passed around among the stable hands, and it would be embarrassing if word got out."

"Nice," I said. "So, he had something going on with one of the three girls?

"Maybe even more than one of them," Needham said. "It wasn't like he had to worry about statutory rape."

"Just regular rape," I said. "So Luther was a ladies' man."

"A real Romeo," Needham said. "The problem was he knocked one of them up."

"Which one?"

"Not the married one," Needham replied.

"Janet Blair was the one who was married," Hanlen said. "That would leave either Betsy Collins or Deborah Musick. They both kept horses at the Twilight Stable."

"Not sure which of those two it was. I want to say it was the Musick girl," Needham said.

"I'm assuming that Luther Brame wasn't looking forward to father-hood," I said.

"No, he wasn't." Needham replied. "He told her she needed to take care of it. When she said no, he got mad. Threatened her, maybe even roughed her up a little."

"How did you get involved?" I asked.

"I told you. I did security for Brame."

"Why did a tough guy like Luther need security?" Hanlen asked.

"Luther wasn't easy to get along with," Needham said. "He could be smooth if it suited him, but God help you if you crossed him. He had a bad temper, plus he was on the paranoid side. He didn't trust the people that worked at his stables. That's where I came in. I did background on the people he hired. He fired and hired a lot of people."

"Is that all you did for him?" I asked.

"I showed up at the stables a couple days a week if Luther wasn't there. To make sure the help knew someone was keeping an eye on things in his absence," he said, then paused. "If Luther or one of his men got into some minor jam, I'd try and help him out."

"What did you consider a minor jam?" I asked.

"Traffic stuff, misdemeanors, like that. If I got wind of some other cops investigating him, I would try and let him know."

"Ok," Hanlen said. "What about the girls?"

"Luther thought the pregnant girl was going to make trouble for him. Maybe even claim he assaulted her. He said the other girls would support her story and he'd be in deep shit."

"How did he think you could help him?" Hanlen asked.

"I knew two of the girls from seeing them at the stable. Not well, but we'd say hi. They knew I was law. Luther seemed to think 'cause of that they would trust me. I was supposed to make friends with them, see if I could find out what they were planning to do and let him know."

Hanlen raised an eyebrow.

"Yeah, I know what you're thinking," Needham said. "I'm a fat old guy with a bad attitude. But back then, I wasn't old, mean and fat."

"What happened?" Hanlen asked.

"I found out that the girls liked to swim. I told them I had a boat and asked if they wanted to go out on it some time. They were skittish at first, guess since they didn't know me that well, but then said ok. We agreed to meet at the Indiana Dunes. I figured they'd feel comfortable in a place like that, with a lot of people around."

"That was the weekend before the girls disappeared," I said.

"Yeah."

"What happened then?"

"I picked them up at the beach and we went out into the lake. Two of the girls got in for a swim. I had brought some beer and had the Cubs game on the radio. It was a sunny afternoon, and we were having a good time. So good, I almost forgot why I was there," Needham said.

He shook his head slightly, then continued. "When we're all back in the boat, I said I wanted to talk serious with them. I said I knew there was a problem between them and Brame, and I thought I could help get it resolved."

"Which wasn't exactly true," I observed.

Needham shook his head.

"Like I said, I didn't know them that well. All I knew was what Luther told me. I guess the girls trusted me because they knew I was law. Or maybe it was the beer."

"And they confided in you," I said.

"Yeah, after a bit of hemming and hawing, the one said she was pregnant, and it was by Luther. The next thing she says causes me to almost fall out of the boat."

"What was that?" Hanlen asked.

"She said she was going to have the kid. She adds that if she had some money she would go away and start a new life with the baby, somewhere else."

"How much money?" Hanlen asked.

"At least twenty-five grand. She implied more would be better," Needham said. "Twenty-five grand may not be much now, but it was a lot of money back in 1966."

Hanlen and I looked at each other.

"I'm guessing she wanted Luther Brame to give her the money," I said.

"Good guess. Luther may have had it, but I didn't think he would be giving it to her."

"I assume you didn't tell her that," I said.

"No. I just said it was a lot of money."

"How did she take that?" I asked

"She says if she doesn't get it, maybe she'll say what happened between Luther and her wasn't a mutual idea. And that he roughed her up. She said maybe she'd go to the police. She said her friends would back her story up."

"What did you tell her then?" Hanlen asked.

"I said that wasn't a good idea. I told her before she did that, I could talk to Luther for her, and convince him to do the right thing. That he would be reasonable."

"Which also wasn't true," I said. "As noted, Brame had a temper. He had a prior for rape and multiple charges for assault. His record for being reasonable wasn't so good."

"The girls were ok with letting you talk to him," Hanlen said.

"I think she was too scared to talk to him herself. I would have been too."

"What was Luther's reaction when you told him what the girl said?" I asked.

"He didn't go nuts, which surprised me. He said he would talk to them and get things straightened out. Told me to invite them to the Dunes again the next weekend. He knew someone that had a cabin cruiser. He was going to borrow it and meet us off the beach."

"You were supposed to bring the girls out to him?" I asked.

"That was the idea."

"It didn't occur to you that he had something else, other than just talk-ing with them, in mind?" Hanlen asked.

"I sure didn't think he was going to kill them, if that's what you mean," Needham replied. "I assumed he was going to try and get the girl to agree to a smaller amount. I remember thinking, if he gave her enough money, maybe all three of them might have left town.

"Why?" I asked.

"From the way they talked, I don't think the one who was married was that happy with her husband. And the other two had boring jobs and no boyfriends."

"Maybe it would have been better if they forgot about Brame and left town on their own," I said. "Tell us what happened the next weekend, when they disappeared,"

chapter 51

"THE PLAN WAS BRAME WOULD MEET ME, MID-MORNING," Needham said. "Off the main beach. Then I would bring the girls out in my boat."

"He must have had someone with him," I said, figuring among Brame's talents, operating a boat was probably not one of them. "Who was it?"

"I didn't see who was in the cabin," Needham answered, hesitating slightly.

"But there was somebody else," I said. "Who?"

Needham looked at Hanlen.

"You get many perverts there in Prairie County, Chief?" he asked.

"How do you mean?" Hanlen asked.

"Creeps who hang around public restrooms, bus stops, like that."

Hanlen paused before answering.

"Not many when I started. As the county grew, we got some. Maybe the more people you get, the more aberrant behavior you get. Why?"

"We had a guy once who got brought in for trying to pick up a fifteen-year old girl at a school bus stop," Needham said. "She screamed and ran off, but a patrol car was nearby and picked him up. He got put in a holding cell with some bikers. Not sure how, but they found out why he was there. The next morning, they needed a squeegee to remove him from the cell."

"So much for due process," I said

"What does this have to do with Brame?" Hanlen asked

"He had a few unsavory pals. Real deviants. I wondered why he kept them around. Like I said, he had a temper, and if you got him mad, he'd hurt you, but he wasn't bent that way."

"From what you're saying, Jerry, I guess that you saw one of Brame's unsavory associates on the boat," I said. "Who was he?"

"Guy by the name of Vesco. Martin Vesco. I'd seen him around the stable."

"I assume you checked him out," Hanlen said.

"His sheet was as long as a donkey's dingus. Starting with assault and attempted rape."

"And those were just the 'A's, I bet," I said.

"Yeah," Needham replied. "He got looked at hard in the disappearance of an 18 year old girl from Oak Park back in the early sixties. Her father was some big shot at DePaul University."

"Why wasn't he in jail?" I asked.

"They couldn't make a case in that one, but he did time for other stuff. A lot of stuff. First stint in his late teens. But he was lucky, like Luther, in that regard."

"In what way?" Hanlen asked.

"Well, it seems in a lot of his arrests, the witnesses either refused to testify or suddenly came down with amnesia. Plus, he had good lawyers. Crime pays, I guess."

"What did you think when you saw him on the boat?" I asked.

"I figured he was there to intimidate the girl, in case she didn't accept whatever Luther decided to offer her," Needham said. "Plus, he also knew something about boats."

"Brame himself wasn't enough to intimidate her?" I asked.

"At some level, Luther had scruples. I don't think Vesco did."

"But you didn't say anything when you saw him?" Hanlen asked.

"How was I supposed to know what was going to happen? Luther told me he would get them back to the beach. I got out of there."

"How about when you found out they had disappeared?" I asked.

"What do you think? I got a sick feeling."

"Feeling too sick to tell anyone what you knew?" I asked.

"I was on the hook as an accomplice."

"Did you ask Luther what happened with the girls?" Hanlen asked.

"When I got the nerve up to. He told me they weren't going to be a problem anymore, and I didn't need to be concerned about them. That was it. I wasn't about to ask him twice."

"What do you think happened, out on the boat that day, Jerry?" Hanlen asked.

"I think Luther had a talk with the girl," Needham said, "but maybe it didn't go well. Then he turned Vesco loose on them. Or maybe he skipped the talk and just let Vesco at them."

"Then it became a matter of getting rid of the evidence," I said.

Needham shrugged. "Yeah."

"How about Vesco?" I asked. "What happened with him?"

"I saw him a few times after that," Needham replied. "Then he disappeared too."

"When?" Hanlen asked.

"A month, maybe six weeks, after the girls did."

Something clicked when Needham said that.

"You remember Mason Banks, Jerry?" I asked.

I thought I could see a reaction to the name, but if there was one, he quickly disguised it.

"Banks? Doesn't ring a bell," Needham replied. "Should it?"

"I would think so. He was the police chief in Glenbrook, near your town."

"A couple of the girls were from there," I added. "Banks did some of the background stuff on them when they went missing. I'm surprised you don't remember him."

"Oh, yeah, sure, Banks," he said. "It's been a while since I heard the name. Something happened to him. A weird farm accident, wasn't it?"

"You could say that," Hanlen said. "Not every day a guy blows himself up in his barn."

"Farming must be more dangerous than it looks," Needham said.

"You ever talk to Banks about what he was working on?" I asked.

"No, why would I?"

"You said before you would let Brame know if he was being investigated," I replied. "Seems to me you would try and find out what Banks knew so you could let Brame know."

"I didn't talk to Banks about any investigation."

"What would you say if I told you Banks found out that the girls were at the Dunes the weekend before they disappeared?" I asked.

"Big deal. That's no secret," Needham answered.

"You're right, "I said. "It wasn't widely known, but it wasn't a secret. But what if Banks found out that it was you they were there with? And maybe Banks then made some assumptions about what happened to the girls, figuring if you were involved maybe Luther was."

The shotgun, which Needham had pointed down, ominously rose.

"What are you trying to say?" he asked.

"I'm thinking Brame has three people to worry about, as far as linking him to the disappearance of the girls. You and Vesco, of course. But you and Vesco are accomplices, so if Luther goes down, you two go with him. Heck, Luther blames Vesco for the girls and that just leaves you and Banks."

"Banks supposedly interviewed Brame," Hanlen said. "But if he did no one ever knew what was said, 'cause shortly after Banks blew himself to kingdom come."

"And now you say Vesco disappeared the same time as Banks," I said. "That's a coincidence, don't you think? A good one for Brame. Maybe not so much for the other two, especially Banks. Makes you wonder if Brame and\or Vesco had something to do with it."

"Maybe Vesco just decided to leave town," Needham said. "Maybe Luther gave him some money and told him to take a vacation."

"Sure. I can see that," I said. "And on his way out of town, he decides to visit Banks and blow up his barn. Unfortunately for Banks, he's in it at the time."

"You might be on to something there, Logan," said Hanlen. "Be mighty convenient for Brame if Banks wasn't around asking questions. Vesco disappearing is icing on the cake."

"What I'm wondering about, Chief," I said, "is if Jerry here had any idea what Brame and Vesco had planned for Banks. Jerry being Luther's chief security guy and all."

"Good question," Hanlen said. "Imagine a prosecutor would take a dim view of someone withholding information on the murder of police chief."

"You're getting irritating," Needham said. "Real irritating. Now I'm responsible for the three girls plus a police chief." He got up, slowly, the shotgun now pointed directly at us.

"Don't do anything you'll regret, Jerry," Hanlen said. I noticed he was surreptitiously fiddling with his harness.

Stock, if very sound advice, I thought, but I wasn't sure how receptive Jerry Needham would be to it. Perhaps I'd been right when I said to Hanlen maybe it wasn't a good idea to be on a boat alone with him in the middle of the ocean.

chapter 52

I SAW IT OUT OF THE CORNER OF MY EYE. It was a crow, as big or bigger than the one I saw yesterday. It appeared out of nowhere, flying purposely and fast, directly at the boat, twenty feet or so above the water.

Needham saw it before I did, bewilderment showing on his face. Hanlen didn't see it at all, since he was facing Needham and had his back to the crow.

"What the hell . . ." Needham muttered.

The next few moments were surreal. When the crow got within ten feet from the stern, it suddenly stopped, flew straight up, then, flapping its wings in midair, with its hackles raised, let out a startling angry screech.

"I'll get you anyway!" Needham growled and raised the gun skyward.

Hanlen broke out of the harness and lunged forward. He was a second too late. Needham got the shotgun back down just as Hanlen ran into him. There was a tremendous explosion. Hanlen bellowed in pain but grabbed the barrel of shotgun. The two struggled for the weapon. Hanlen got the better of it and pushed the gun upwards towards Needham's head. There was another deafening explosion.

I made the mistake once of going running late at night on July 4. Some lowlifes driving by, the type who seem to find me like flies do shit, tossed a M-80 out of their car. I heard their laughter before the booming explosion. That was the only thing I had to compare to two shotgun blasts so close to my head within seconds. The auditory overload put me into a momentary state of painful suspended animation.

When I came out of it, in seconds, but it seemed longer, I felt something warm and wet on my forehead, and a stinging pain down around my ankles. I reached up to my forehead. It was blood, but since there was not much of it and no pain, I realized it had to have come from either Hanlen or Needham, each sprawled on the deck a few feet from me. Needham appeared to have taken most of the second blast to his head and neck. He had twisted slightly as he went down, so I couldn't see all his face. If I hadn't been dazed, I think I would have thrown up looking at what I could see. Hanlen's trouser legs were covered in blood from the knee down, the right leg with much more than the left. I looked up to see what happened with the crow, but it was gone.

I got out of the harness and looked down at my ankles. There was some blood. I assumed a few pellets from the shotgun had bounced off the deck and hit me. I got to Hanlen, and pulled him over to the side of the boat and propped him against the gunwale.

"That's the same leg I got hit in Korea," he stated, nonchalantly. His voice sounded to my dazed ears like he was speaking from the bottom of a metal trash can.

"It's not that bad," he added, "but we should get a tourniquet on it. Look in the cabin. He's must have a first aid kit. And locate the radio. We need to call the Coast Guard."

"You ok?" he asked me. "You got some blood on your face."

"Must be Needham's, or yours. I'm ok."

"Needham dead?"

I looked over at his motionless, blood covered, body.

"I don't think he's just taking a nap," I said.

"Peculiar he was just asking me if I ever killed anybody."

"He sure picked an odd time to ask that question," I agreed.

I got up and went in the cabin. On one side of the small space there was a built-in cushioned seating area, which looked like Needham used for a bed, although it would have been tight for him. There were some storage drawers in the base, which I got down and took a quick look through. They were packed with various stuff, mainly clothes and fishing tackle. When I stood, I saw a red, medium size bag hanging on a hook on the back of the door to the head. It had a white cross on it, so I grabbed it and got quickly back out on the deck.

Hanlen's face had lost some color. We each had brought jackets and he was pressing his against his leg. He looked at the bag.

"I've seen that brand before," he said. "There'll be a tourniquet kit in there."

I almost said, 'quit being so damn cool and business-like, there's a man dead,' but I didn't. I found the tourniquet kit.

"We need to get this on and elevate your leg," I said. "Then I'll radio the Coast Guard."

"Right. But we need to get our stories straight before you get on the radio."

"What story? Needham tried to kill you and got his head blown off." As I said that, I had the disquieting thought that maybe that wasn't entirely true. Needham was pissed off and drunk and startled by the strange appearance of the crow. He was going to shoot something, but it might have just been the bird.

"They'll want to know why he tried to shoot us," Hanlen said. "That could put us in an awkward spot."

Hanlen was right. Ivan Rich had ordered us not to get involved in an ongoing, though ancient, investigation. It wouldn't be a stretch for the authorities to say we had no authority to accost Needham. Maybe even threatened him into confessing and thus made us legally culpable in some way for what just happened.

'If someone thinks to call Ivan, we're in deep shit anyhow," I said.

"Not necessarily," Hanlen replied. "He may not want to be associated with us."

The Ivan I knew would toss someone under a bus just because he could, but in this case, I could see him disavowing all knowledge of us. I don't think he would care for people to know that we had ignored him.

"We just need something halfway plausible," Hanlen added.

"Alright, let's go with this," I said, thinking on the fly. "We decided to come to Florida for some fishing. You talked with someone who knew Needham back from when he chartered on Lake Michigan and gave him a call. When we showed up, there was an argument about the price, which continued when we got to sea. Needham started drinking heavily. He told us he was turning back unless he got more money. The argument escalated. He came out of the cabin with a gun, waving it around. You wrestled with him and the gun went off."

"That's not bad," Hanlen said. "Not exactly true, but in the ballpark. Let's add, it happened so fast we're not real sure how it happened."

"The less detail, the better," I said. "I've had some concussions and you're old and senile. We can sell not remembering everything. Oh, one other thing. I think we should keep quiet about the crow."

"What crow?" Hanlen asked.

I gave him a look. I wasn't sure if he was putting me on or if he didn't see or hear the bird. I decided not to say anything else about it.

"Go see if you can get the Coast Guard on the radio," Hanlen said. "Before I pass out."

"Sure, how?"

"You never used a two-way radio before?"

"Not that. How do I let the Coast Guard know where we are?"

"If you got a boat, you're supposed to keep the radio tuned to the distress channel. Just hit the send button, and say 'Mayday, Coast Guard, this is the *Lucky Strike* about three miles due west of Clearwater. We have a medical emergency. Need immediate assistance.' Say it a couple times, a few minutes between each one. They'll find us."

chapter 53

FROM MY PRIOR TRIPS TO THE TAMPA AREA, I KNEW there was a large Coast Guard airbase next to the Clearwater\St. Pete Airport, where their helicopters were stationed. They also had a couple small patrol boats stationed on Sand Key Island. I knew it wouldn't be long before they showed up, but it seemed long as I sat with Hanlen. I tried to avert my eyes from Needham's body, and the blood pooling on the deck.

Hanlen's head nodded down a couple of times, and each time I shook him to keep him awake. I hoped he wasn't going into shock. We heard the radio squawk.

"You should stay by the radio," said Hanlen, when I didn't move.

"Like you said, they'll find us," I replied. "Probably be just a few more minutes. I don't want to tell them we got a dead body here. That might complicate things."

"Ok, but maybe you ought to take a look around the cabin."

"What for?"

"Needham said he had a guardian angel. Might be interesting to know who that is. Maybe he's got an address book or something around with numbers in it."

"And you said you weren't a detective," I told him.

I looked more thoroughly in the drawers under the bed. When I tried to shove one back in, I felt it rub against something. I took the drawer out again and turned it over. Taped to the bottom was a plastic bag, inside of which was a passport, a couple credit cards, ten hundred dollar bills, and a small, worn, spiral notepad—kind of like one a TV detective from one of the cop shows in the sixties might have. A lot of the pages were torn out, but the rest had names and numbers written on them, some crossed out. I took five of the hundreds to give back to Hanlen. I put the other stuff back where it was and stuck the notebook in my pocket.

chapter 54

A HELICOPTER APPEARED FIRST, FOLLOWED BY A quick-moving patrol boat. The helicopter hovered overhead while the boat slowed and came alongside ours. A stocky young man wearing a dark blue uniform and carrying a large medical bag jumped onto the *Lucky Strike*. Two other guys in uniforms on the boat watched intently as he came over. One was wearing a sidearm.

The guy who came on the boat looked from Needham's body, to the shotgun, to Hanlen and me. He took a couple steps toward the body and kneeled down to get a closer look. I heard him say under his breath, 'whew.' Then he walked back over to me.

"I'm petty officer Sanchez," he said. "That man's dead. What happened?"

"It was an accident," I replied. I pointed at Hanlen. "This man here is hurt. That's the medical emergency I called in."

"He get shot too?"

"Yes," I said, "same accident. Some fishing trip, huh?"

"What's your name?"

"Wells. Logan Wells."

"You think this is funny, Wells?"

"Not in the slightest. It's been a bad morning."

"I'd say so," Sanchez said. He was looking at my ankles. "I guess you got shot too."

"It's nothing, a few pellets in the leg. My friend is going to need some medical attention, pronto. I think he may be going into shock."

"He'll get it," Sanchez said. "Are there any other weapons on board besides the shotgun?"

"As far as I know, no," I said.

"Are there any illegal drugs aboard this vessel?"

"Not that I am aware of," I said.

He walked over to his boat quickly and said something to the two men, then came back.

"Ok, I'm going to examine your friend. I would appreciate it if you had a seat while I do so. Do not move unless I ask you to. One of my men is going to board and look around while I examine your friend. You got a problem with that?"

"No, but it's not my boat . . . it belongs to him," I said, pointing at Needham.

"I don't think he'll mind," Sanchez said.

He opened the medical bag and began getting Hanlen's vitals. When he was done, he walked back to the boat and spoke with the two men on board. I heard, 'this guy's lost a lot of blood, we got to get him to the hospital asap,' Then he lowered his voice and I couldn't hear the rest of what he said. When he got back on the Lucky Strike, one of the other men came with him.

Sanchez walked over to me, and gestured down at Hanlen.

"Your friend is going into shock. We need to get him to the hospital. We could maybe lift him out of here in the chopper, but that would take a while. I recommend we take him back to base on the boat. We can have an ambulance and paramedics standing by, and it would take them only about ten minutes to get him to the hospital."

I nodded my head in agreement with his plan and Hanlen did too when Sanchez kneeled down and asked if he was ok with it.

"What about the boat?" I asked.

"I thought it wasn't your boat," Sanchez said.

"It's not, but it's a crime scene. You aren't going to just leave it, are you?"

"One, I know what my duty is. Two, are you law?"

"Used to be. Him too," I said, pointing at Hanlen.

"Either one of you got a badge or id?"

"Only my driver's license," I replied. "He's retired."

"What jurisdiction are you from?"

"County sheriff's department, Prairie County, Northwest Indiana," I said. "He was the sheriff. I was a detective for the County Prosecutor."

"I don't know how things are done in Northwest Indiana," Sanchez said, "but here we don't like people shooting up a fishing boat, including the owner."

"If it makes any difference, he started it," I said.

That got a grunt.

"We radioed the Clearwater Police. My man will stay on the boat until they can get here. Since you're hurt, you'll come with us. Me, just from this brief exchange here, I hope when the CPD catches up with you, they toast your ass. I don't like wise guys."

"I truly am sorry, Petty Officer Sanchez. I did not mean to offend you. You seem like a decent guy. Let me just say that that man had it coming." I pointed at Needham.

I got a small nod from Sanchez.

"We're going to transfer your friend now," he said. He started back to his boat, then stopped and turned toward me.

"Oh, yeah, Wells," he said. "Don't try any funny stuff between here and shore. We don't want any more accidents."

chapter 55

The there was a welcoming reception at Sand Key, consisting of two police cars, an ambulance, and a fire department emergency vehicle, a big SUV, the type I'd heard described as a 'tactical vehicle.' I found the adjective 'tactical' amusing, for describing a fire-fighting vehicle. It implied that you could outwit a fire. As in, 'this is a pretty smart fire,' better get the tactical vehicle.' Odd things always come to me when I'm under stress.

The reception seemed to be overdoing it, but I guessed they didn't get many fatal shootings in Clearwater, especially ones at sea. While the EMTs were checking Hanlen, I noticed some discussion going on between Sanchez and the police officers. It looked like there might have been a difference of opinion about something. At one point, Sanchez turned and pointed directly at me. Eventually one of the police officers nodded. Sanchez came over to me and told me I could ride in the ambulance with Hanlen.

A pleasant nurse practitioner in the ER named Jason cleaned up and bandaged my ankles and gave me a tetanus shot. He even gave me a new pair of socks. I asked him about Hanlen, and Jason said he didn't know but would try and find out. He also told me that there were a couple of Clearwater detectives in the waiting room who wanted to speak with me. I got a smile from him when I responded by asking where the back door was.

A uniformed officer was standing in the waiting room, talking to two middle-aged white men, who I took for detectives. They introduced themselves as Higgins and Lorenz. The uniformed officer didn't introduce himself, but after the detectives did, he nodded to them and turned to leave. Guessing he must have been there in case I decided to make a break for it. The detectives asked if I would like to step outside for some privacy. Once outside, Detective Higgins pulled out a pack of cigarettes, and offered me one before he lit up. I declined.

Before the two asked me about the events on the boat, they started with the basic stuff, names, where we were from, what we did. When I told them Hanlen was a long-time former county sheriff and I used to be a detective, the tone of the conversation changed noticeably. My experience was that most who worked in law enforcement had what you would call an 'us against them' mentality.' 'Us' being the police, and 'them' everyone who wasn't. Since in police work, on a routine, if not daily basis, you dealt with criminals and victims, you were, to put it charitably, not seeing people at their best. Also, there was always the slim, but very real, possibility, that someone might take umbrage to your presence and try and harm you. In other words, respect and trust could often be in short supply in the day of a police officer. Since they are also two important components of most successful relationships, that sometimes made problematic interactions between police and others.

Higgins and Lorenz had a number of questions while I recounted the shooting on the *Lucky Strike*. Most were ones I would have asked had I been them. Otherwise, the detectives seemed noncommittal about my version of what happened. I took that as a good sign. They asked where I could be reached, and if I could come to the police station the next morning, I presumed after they got a chance to talk to Hanlen. They then were nice enough to take me back to the dock so I could get the car. When I thanked them, they said they would be in touch.

chapter 56

I TRIED TO CALL HANLEN LATER BUT COULDN'T get through. I was told by his nurse that he was having some tests done. I thought briefly about trying to call Hanlen's wife, or one of his sons, to let them know what happened, but thought it would be better to wait.

I walked to the crab shack where we had dined our first night in Florida. While I ate, I glanced through Needham's notebook. I assumed most of the names in it were customers. I was interested to see there were some phone numbers with the southern Indiana 812 area code.

Detective Lorenz called me at 10 a.m. the next morning. He said they'd like to talk to me again at police headquarters. Just standard procedure, he assured me. He said they would send a car for me, and told me to be ready in an hour. Well done, I thought, as I hung up. He was making sure I would show up at the appointed time, giving me short notice, as well as letting me know, subtly, that I wasn't free to come and go as I please. If I was a suspect, which I hoped I wasn't, making me feel a little uneasy was a tried-and-true pre-interview technique.

Lorenz sent an unmarked car to get me, for which I was grateful, not wanting to alarm the residents of Deke's condo. The Clearwater police station was on the other side of the bay. I had a pleasant conversation on the way over with the young officer who was driving, as he had some relatives up in the Chicago area. When we got to the station, I was ushered into an interrogation room and given a cup of stale coffee. The room had a mirror in it, with a speaker grill below it, which allowed someone outside to watch and listen to the proceedings within.

Having been on the other side myself, I knew what the routine would be. I'd be asked to repeat my story, the detectives noting any inconsistencies in the details I previously gave. Initially the conversations would be serious, yet cordial, but if there were inconsistencies, things would quickly become less cordial. As far as the actual shooting went, my story would be factual. Where I might get tripped up was if they focused on what led up to the fatal dispute, or if Hanlen's version of events differed from mine.

I waited for about 20 minutes, another way of making me nervous. Lorenz and Higgins eventually came in. Higgins apologized for keeping me waiting.

"No problem," I said. "My fishing trip charter this morning got unexpectedly cancelled."

"Anybody ever tell you, Wells, you got an odd sense of humor?" Higgins asked.

"First time. How's Hanlen doing?"

They glanced at each other, but didn't say anything right away.

Lorenz eventually spoke.

"Did your boss ever mention any health issues he was having?"

"Just for the record, I didn't report to Hanlen," I replied. "I worked for the Prairie County Prosecutor, guy by the name of Bob Shannon. But no, he never mentioned any health issues."

"So, I'm curious," Lorenz said, "if you didn't work together, how did you get to be fishing buddies?"

I smiled. "I didn't say we didn't work together. I just didn't report to him. We got to know each other a little better since we're not on the job anymore. We both like fishing. Like I told you yesterday, Hanlen's retired; I'm on disability. What kind of health issues?"

Higgins and Lorenz looked at each other.

"Your chief should tell you," Lorenz said, eventually.

They had me go over again what happened on the boat and asked some of the same questions from the previous day. They seemed to be half-hearted about doing so, and the interview didn't take long. There was a tap coming from the mirror.

"Our boss would like to talk to you," Lorenz said, abruptly, and they both got up and left.

A large black man wearing a suit came into the room about ten minutes later. I guessed he was about fifty, as there were flecks of gray in his hair. He had a file folder in his hand.

"I'm deputy chief Alonzo T. Jefferson the second. My friends call me Al. You can call me Chief Alonzo T. Jefferson."

I guess he had used that one before and looked for a reaction, but I didn't give him one.

"Most call me AJ," he said, sitting down gingerly.

"Damn sciatica is acting up," he said. "Ten years of playing football coming back to haunt me. Your chief played ball, right?"

"He was all Big Ten at Purdue," I replied.

"I was second team Big Ten, one year. Played guard for Michigan State."

I thought about that for a second.

"Did you play in the 'Tie One for the Gipper' game?" I asked him. I was referring to the 1966 "Game of the Century" when #1 ranked Notre Dame ran the clock out at the end of the game to preserve a 10-10 tie with #2 Michigan State. Ara Parseghian, the Irish coach caught flak later for not going for the win.

"Matter of fact I did. I can't blame Ara for not going for the win. Both his starting quarterback and halfback were out with injuries."

"You sound like a reasonable man," I said.

That got a small grin from AJ.

"Is that wishful thinking?" he asked, as he opened the file folder.

"First, I got to tell you," he said, "in case you hadn't guessed, that we don't get much in the way of violent crime here. Most of what we get is petty stuff, burglary, theft, some disorderly conduct when spring break is going on. Like that. Over where you are, on Sand Key, most of the places got their own security, so not even much of that over there."

"My former in-laws had a place on Sand Key," I said.

"So you know what I'm talking about. We get maybe one or two homicides a year. Me, I spent twenty years with Detroit Metro before relocating here. If we didn't get a murder or shooting a day, we locked the door and had a parade through the office."

"I understand," I said. "Does it make a difference if this one happened out at sea?"

AJ nodded. "I like the way you think. I tried to foist this off on the

Coast Guard. They told me it didn't happen far enough out in the ocean. Imagine that."

"Wait until the tide goes out," I said.

"There's that," he said. "But here's the thing. Many of our residents are older people, retirees. They get upset when they hear about violent crime. So, while, I don't think anyone is going to miss Mr. Needham, a shooting death is a big deal. But we don't want it to be a big deal, if you catch my drift."

"You want this cleaned up quickly with as little press as possible," I said.

"I couldn't have said it better myself."

"I made all conference at left drift in high school," I said.

"Thing is, I listened to your story and something about it doesn't jive."

"How so?"

"If you handed me a homicide to solve quickly, I'd say, give me a former county sheriff with a spotless reputation. Have him shoot, accidentally, and in self-defense, a drunk, ex-con, who was threatening said sheriff for money. And he's got a witness too. I'd say, 'thank you, that's too good to be true."

"So why look a gift horse in the mouth?" I asked.

"Good question. But earlier this morning, I gave your former boss a call. Nice fellow by the name of Bob Shannon. I wanted to hear what he had to say about your chief and you."

"What did Shannon have to say?" I asked, starting to get a sinking feeling in my gut, wondering if Ivan had spoken to Shannon about us.

"Well, he couldn't sing Hanlen's praises loud enough. Made him out to be the second coming of Wyatt Earp and Elliot Ness, all rolled into one. Said that if Hanlen said something happened, then that's what happened."

"How about me? I guess he trashed it up pretty good."

"No, not at all," said AJ, "matter of fact, quite the opposite. Said you were one of the best investigators he had. He did mention you were a bit of a lone wolf."

"I prefer to think of myself as an autonomous canis lupus."

"He also said you were a wise guy. But here's the thing. Shannon seemed mystified that you two would be going on a fishing trip together. Or any kind of trip, for that matter."

"Not sure why he would say that," I replied.

"He told me you and Hanlen were involved in something at the end of last year that ended with a few people dead. Said the sheriff wound up with egg on his face."

"One of the few people was a close friend of mine," I said.

"Sorry to hear that," he replied, "Shannon told me Hanlen eventually resigned. Wouldn't think he was too happy about that. So how do you wind up in Florida together?"

"We flew," I said. That got a stone-faced look.

"We patched things up. Neither one of us are grudge holders." That wasn't true. I couldn't speak for Hanlen, but I was a grudge holder of long standing.

"Ok, you two come to Florida for a second honeymoon. Maybe you were planning on going to Disneyworld later. But then there is the matter of Jerry Needham."

"What about him?"

"Seems peculiar is all. Of all the places to fish in Florida, and all the charters to pick from, you wind up here, on a boat with an ex-cop felon from your backyard."

"You sound like Rick from Casablanca," I said.

"I never saw that movie."

"Really? It's a classic. Rick was played by Humphrey Bogart."

"I'll have the wife pick it up from the video store."

"If you put it like that, maybe it is peculiar," I said. "But I understand Clearwater is a good spot for fishing, and Hanlen had heard of Needham. In hindsight, using him wasn't such a good idea, but, as the saying goes, hindsight is 20/20."

"Sure, but somebody might think it was more than just a bad idea."

"Like you? What's your theory?"

"Let's say the sheriff and Needham's paths crossed in the past. Maybe something they both worked on. I found out Needham was a detective in a town called Eldon, near Chicago, in the sixties, before he went bad. I looked at a map. It's not that far from Prairie County."

"It's not as close as you might think," I said. "Traffic is a bitch. Anyway, I'm pretty sure Hanlen was busy enough in his own county without going over to Illinois looking for trouble."

"Sure," AJ said, "but bear with me. The thought occurs to me, perhaps Hanlen retires, but he has some unfinished business with Needham. He finds Needham is in Florida and enlists you to help him. You're a bright guy and, like Hanlen, got some time on your hands."

"We just met, AJ," I said, "but my quick opinion is you got an overactive imagination."

"We used to have a detective here who was like you, a smart guy, but a wiseass. He's like me too . . . a refugee from the rust belt. Except he was from Chicago, not Detroit. He worked for the Chicago PD for over twenty years before he came here. He retired a while back. I gave him a call this morning, too."

"Why'd you call him?" I asked. "Don't tell me he knew Needham."

Alonzo laughed. "Nah, that would be too good to be true, wouldn't it? Mainly I was taking a longshot thinking he'd have an idea of what connection there might be between Hanlen and Needham. Turns out he had heard of Hanlen."

"That's not a surprise," I said. "Hanlen was sheriff for a long time and well known."

"Right," Alonzo replied, nodding.

"So you didn't get anything from him," I said.

"Not initially. But something must have rung a bell when I told him Needham worked in Eldon in the sixties. He calls me back ten minutes later and says he recalls the police chief of the town over from Eldon died mysteriously, while he was investigating the disappearance of three young women from the beach at Lake Michigan, in 1966. Said beach being located in Prairie County. I checked and Hanlen was sheriff of Prairie County in 1966."

He paused. "Three young girls disappear one day and are never seen again. That's something you wouldn't forget, especially if you were one of the ones investigating."

"If I'm following you," I said, "which I'm not sure is possible, you're saying there is a connection between the missing girls, Needham, and this police chief who died. And Hanlen had an idea what it was and came down here to talk to Needham about it."

"Something like that. And don't forget the part of bringing you along. Of course, I can't prove any of it, at least right now. Needham is dead, so I can't ask him. For what it's worth. I don't think Hanlen meant to kill him, but nonetheless, I think there is more to the story than you're letting on.

By reason of me saying that, I spoke with the Coast Guard guy who talked with you on the boat. According to him, you said Needham 'had it coming.' What do you figure I should make of that?"

"He was drunk and he had a shotgun," I said.

"I didn't think you were going to tell me. Guess you don't want to reconsider that?"

I didn't say anything, and we stared at each other for thirty seconds.

"I guess this is where you tell me not to leave town," I said.

"I thought about that," he replied. "But then I thought it would be better if you left, as soon as possible. Less chance of you talking to any nosy reporters. In fact, I'll have one of my men drive you to the airport this afternoon. There is a 3:45 flight to Chicago. I understand you got an open-ended ticket, so that shouldn't be a problem. Imagine you can get a shuttle from Chicago to home. Or call a friend to get you."

"Sounds like you thought of everything," I said.

"I like to be thorough."

"What about Hanlen?"

"He's going to need to hang around another couple days."

"So you can charge him?"

AJ sat back in his chair.

"Why would I do that? I just told you. I can't prove anything. Hanlen has got some health issue they want to check before he gets out. I'm going to call his wife after we're done here."

"Health issues? Like what?"

"I guess I can tell you. You're his friend. They did some blood tests, kind of routine. He's got leukemia.

"That's crazy. He's healthy as an ox."

"Hanlen said he knew about it. One of the reasons he stepped down. Guess he didn't say anything to you about it."

"Not a word," I said.

"Me, I was thinking if a guy figures his days are numbered, maybe that's another reason to revisit something unsettled from out of the past."

chapter 57

I STILL HAD $500 IN MY POCKET, SO I COULD HAVE called a cab when I arrived at Midway, or at least figured out the shuttle to Prairie Stop. Instead, I took a cab into downtown and got on the South Shore Line. It was gray and rainy in Northwest Indiana, and consequently the train journey through the impoverished industrial area that was East Chicago, Hammond and Gary was more depressing than usual. Fortunately, the stewardess in first class on the half-empty flight from Florida took a liking to me, and as I was getting off the plane she gave me a couple extra small bottles of wine, which I drank covertly on the train. It made the time go by quicker. Then, when I was making a trip to the bathroom, on the equally half-empty train, I recognized a guy who had been on the football team with me in high school. I don't recall us being that close in high school, but he was glad to see me. Maybe it was seeing a familiar face with all the depressing scenery outside. He said he'd been attending a seminar in Chicago. Of like mind to me, he had a couple beers in his rucksack, and we had a pleasant interaction on the remainder of the journey to the Dunes station, laughing and carrying on as we told stories about times and teammates past. He even gave me a ride home, saving me cab fare.

The first thing I did the next morning was call the hospital in Clearwater. When Hanlen picked up, I said, "leukemia, really? And you couldn't tell me?"

"I don't got leukemia," he said, puzzled. "Who told you that?"

"The black deputy chief in Clearwater," I replied.

"Alonzo? He heard it wrong. I have what you call a smoldering lymphoma."

"Smoldering lymphoma?"

"Yeah. Almost makes it sound like you could douse me with a bucket of water and I'd be better. My doctor says it's treatable, but I'm not even doing that. Just watching and waiting."

"Ok, but maybe you need to get a second opinion. Find a specialist in Chicago."

"He'll just tell me the same thing with bigger words," Hanlen replied. "What did you tell the Clearwater detectives?"

"Got some bad news for you. I panicked when they got out the rubber hoses and told them everything. Including some stuff I made up. What do you think? I gave them the story we came up with."

"Did they buy it?"

"They seemed to. Not sure about Alonzo. You talked to him? He was the pain-in-the ass suspicious type."

"He stopped by yesterday for a bit. Mainly we talked about Big Ten football."

"Brothers in pigskin," I said. "Hope your bond is strong enough that he doesn't start making more calls and asking questions."

I told Hanlen about my talk with the deputy chief.

"Nothing we can do about that," Hanlen said. "I'm thinking he's going to just let it go."

"We can hope," I said.

"What are you going to do now?" Hanlen asked.

"I was thinking of making some calls to a couple of the numbers in Needham's book. Not sure how productive that's going to be."

"Won't know till you try. Let me know what happens. I should be back in a day or two."

chapter 58

AFTER I HUNG UP WITH HANLEN, I CALLED one of the numbers in Needham's notepad with the Southern Indiana area code. The woman's voice answering said, "Blue Hen Gifts. How may I help you?"

I was surprised, if not stunned, when she said that. It was the name of the establishment Mitch Bryce had given Hanlen, as to where Mason Bank's wife was. Why would Needham have her number in his book?

"Hello?" the woman said, confused.

"I'm sorry," I said. "I just dropped my pen. Have I got the Blue Hen Gifts in Nashville Indiana?"

"Yes. Can I help you?"

"Yes, please. The wife and I are thinking of making a trip to Brown County, and I just wanted to check your hours. A friend recommended your establishment."

"We just started our summer hours. We are open 9:30 a.m. to 8 p.m. daily."

"Great. It will be the first time for us in Brown County. We're looking forward to our visit, including your store."

"You'll like it here. Where are you staying?"

"We were thinking of the lodge at the state park," I said.

"There are some nice places in town, too. I can give you some names if you like. The lodge is frequently booked solid this time of year, especially on weekends."

"I may take a rain check on that. We aren't sure exactly of our plans. Say, our friend was very complimentary about the woman who owned the Blue Hen. Would I happen to be speaking with her?"

"Why, yes you are. My name is Betty. Betty Banks."

"Thanks for your time, Betty. Hope to see you in person soon."

I called the second number with the same area code.

"Monastery Caskets, John speaking," was the answer.

That one took me aback too. Needham had said on the boat that his guardian angel lived in a monastery.

"Anybody there?" John asked.

"Sorry," I said. "I just dropped my notepad."

"No problem," was the reply. "A lot of our customers are at a loss for words." I figured John had used that one before.

"How can I help you?" he asked.

"It's my dad," I said. "He's in a bad way. We don't think he's got much time left. A friend recommended your company."

"Sorry to hear that," he said, his voice more subdued. "We have a variety of caskets available, at reasonable prices. We would be pleased to help you out when the time comes."

"Thanks. You are located in southern Indiana, correct?"

"That's right. St. Anselm. Know where that is?"

"Heard of it. I got to say, first off, I'm not real familiar with your business."

"Most aren't, until the time comes. Let me tell you a little bit about us."

John told me that Monastery Caskets was an enterprise run by the brothers of St. Anselm Monastery in St. Anselm, Indiana. He said the caskets they made were initially like the plain pine ones made for the monks who passed on, but now they made a variety of more elaborate ones, using all types of wood. Some of the monks worked in the shop, he said, but there were lay people, such as himself, who also worked in the business. He said all the caskets were hand-crafted. He said, with pride, that they were a much better value than the ones people purchased from the funeral home, implying that funeral homes took advantage of people in dire emotional straits by overcharging for caskets. Based on my experience with my father's passing, that sounded right.

"Thanks, John," I said, when he was done. "That was educational."

"No problem."

"Say, I was curious about the lay people you mentioned," I said. "Guess to get on there you would need some wood-working experience."

"You looking for a job?' he asked.

"No, just curious is all."

"Wood working experience is a definite plus," he said. "But we can likely teach you that. It's more important that the person fits in, I guess you would say. We're part of a religious organization, so somebody who drinks and swears a lot, cheats on their spouse, or beats their kids, well, probably isn't going to be a good match here."

"Sinners need not apply," I observed.

"Everybody sins," he replied. "it's recognizing it and trying not to do it again that's important. Reflection and repentance, as the monks might say."

"Judging from watching the news on TV and reading the paper," I said, "neither a lot of the former or latter is going on."

"I hear you. Speaking of lay people, we have a fellow here who used to be a policeman. He doesn't talk much about his former life, but I asked him once, what's with the crime and violence going on in this country, especially in the big cities. He said that somewhere along the line, people had confused doing what they wanted to do with doing what was right."

"Huh. Sounds like a wise man. I'd like to meet him. Did he used to work in a big city?"

"Not sure. Like I said, he doesn't talk about it much, but I think it was near Chicago," John said, 'He's got that kind of Chicago accent to his voice."

"Hey," I said. "if I wanted to come down there and look at your product, would that be ok?

"Absolutely. We welcome visitors," he said. "When would you be arriving?"

"I got some stuff going on tomorrow. How about later this week?"

chapter 59

I KNEW FROM MY YEARS INVESTIGATING CRIMES of all kinds, that you could sometimes spend hours, making dozens or more phone calls, doing personal interviews, trying to get information, and not learn anything more than when you started. That's just the way it worked. I'd made two calls and found out some very interesting information. I was lucky, for sure, but the question was what to do with it.

I thought, for a few reasons, waiting for Hanlen's return would be the smart thing to do. The main reason being this was his case, and he deserved to be there at the conclusion, if there was one. On the other hand, I wasn't sure the assumption I made from the phone calls was correct. In the end, I left it up to the weather. The rain and clouds from yesterday were gone and it was a good day for a drive.

I took out my mother's old typewriter, that she left for me when she moved to Florida. I spent about thirty minutes composing the note I typed:

NEED TO SEE YOU TODAY ASAP. SOMETHINGS COME UP.
HAS TO BE HERE. NOT SAFE ELSEWHERE. DO NOT CALL.
CALL FROM PAYPHONE WHEN YOU ARRIVE. MEET AT CHURCH.

Although I had never been to St. Anselm, I had seen pictures of the monastery before, including the large, Gothic-style church. I stuck the note in an envelope, packed a bag and was on my way.

chapter 60

I WASN'T IN A RUSH, SO I DECIDED TO FOREGO the interstate and Indianapolis traffic, and instead took Highway 41 south to Terre Haute. I cut over east on Highway 46 to Bloomington. I always liked driving through Bloomington. It seemed like a nice community, and I enjoyed seeing part of Indiana University. I sometimes wondered how I would have fared had I gone to a large state university like IU instead of a small private liberal arts college. I wasn't much for crowds, so probably would have done a Larry Bird and headed for home after a few weeks. He wound up a millionaire, all-star pro basketball player. I would have wound up hauling trash out to the dumpster at Paulsen's.

I drove on to Brown County. When I was a cop in South Bend, I once attended a conference at the lodge in Brown County State Park, so I was somewhat familiar with the area. I got a room at a motel on the edge of Nashville and had a pizza for dinner.

I was up before daylight. I put on my running gear and ran up the main drag until I saw the Blue Hen. I shoved the envelope through the mail slot in the front door. I went back to the motel, showered, dressed and checked out before 8:30. It looked to be another nice day.

There was a café on a side street from where I could see the Blue Hen, so I had a leisurely breakfast while waiting for someone, hopefully Betty Banks, to show up. Around 9:15 a stout woman who appeared to be sixty showed up, unlocked the front door, and turned around the 'CLOSED,

PLEASE CALL AGAIN' sign. About ten minutes later, she was hurriedly reversing the sign, and heading for her vehicle, a dark blue Subaru wagon.

I figured it was about a hundred miles from Nashville to St. Anselm, via local roads, longer, but much quicker, if you went via the interstate. I assumed you could make it just as quickly on the local roads, if you drove fast on the many curvy roads through the Hoosier National Forest, but I wasn't that good of a driver. I spent part of the time driving behind Betty, but thought I knew where she was going, so didn't want to give myself away with an obvious tail. The roads were not that busy, and I thought she would notice the same car behind her. I figured we would eventually arrive at the same place. If not, I would just turn around and head back to Prairie Stop. It was a nice day for a drive out in the country.

chapter 61

THE MONASTERY CAMPUS, AND BUILDINGS, OF ST. ANSELM were much more impressive in person than the pictures I'd seen, the large church especially. It was situated on a hill above the campus and built of large light colored stone blocks, which I assumed were Indiana sandstone. The church had two steeples at the entrance nearest the road, and two larger ones on the other end of the structure. I'm not good with measurements, but I guessed the two larger steeples were easily 40 feet higher than the roof peak of the church, which itself was probably 60 feet tall. There was lots of green space and gardens throughout the campus, providing an overall feeling which was peaceful and tranquil. It wouldn't be a stretch, from standing in the middle of the campus, to imagine you were in a bucolic valley in Germany, where I understand the monks had originally come from over a hundred years ago.

I parked in a lot below the church. There were only a couple cars in the parking lot and neither was a blue Subaru. I walked up the hill to the church, and stood outside the entrance for a few minutes, admiring the building close up. Then I sat on the wall to the brick stairway which led up to the church and waited. No one else was in sight, but after fifteen minutes, I noticed a heavy-set, older man walking slowly toward the parking lot. He stopped when he got to the parking lot, and looked up to where I was. No one else was around, and I thought about giving him a friendly wave, but decided against it.

Another ten minutes went by, and the Subaru appeared on the entrance road. It slowly made its way over to the lot where my car was. When Betty Banks parked, the man standing in the lot walked over to the car. She didn't get out, but lowered the window and they had a conversation, the man leaning down. The woman handed him something. After he looked at it, he straightened up and turned to stare up at me. This time I did wave to him. He turned back to the car, said something to the woman, then turned and started slowly up the hill toward me.

He was breathing hard when he got up to where I was. He plopped his large backside down heavily on the brick wall near me. I saw that my note was in his hand, but let him collect himself before I said anything.

"You ok?" I asked.

"Give me a minute," he said. "Got the emphysema. Two packs a day for almost fifty years. You smoke?"

"Used to, off and on, when I was young. Thought it was cool, I guess. Gave it up for good about fifteen years ago."

"Wish I had quit years ago. I'm a dumbass." He said, "Guess you're law."

"Used to be an investigator with Prairie County, Indiana," I said. "My name's Logan Wells. You must be Chief Mason Banks."

That got a non-committal look.

"Were you aware you're supposed to be dead?" I asked.

"Like the guy said, reports of my death are greatly exaggerated," he said, then, scratching his head. "But I'm not sure who the guy was."

"I believe it was Mark Twain," I said. "And I think he was misquoted. You are Chief Mason Banks, right?"

"Well, I haven't been police chief for over twenty years," he said. "And I don't go by that name anymore. You work with Bill Hanlen?"

I nodded.

He held up the note. "How did you find us?" he asked. "And how did you know I wasn't dead?"

"A little deductive reasoning, and a whole lot of luck," I replied.

He nodded. "That's usually the way it works. Say, would you be ok if my wife went back to Nashville? She's got a business to run. This is my story, not hers. She wouldn't be able to testify against me anyhow, on account of we are still married."

I shrugged. Banks waved to his wife, and we watched her drive away.

"I guess you got some questions for me," Banks said.

"Why did you set this in motion, after all this time?" I asked. "You mailed the locket to Hanlen, right? By the way, that locket didn't really belong to one of the girls, did it?"

"Nah, my wife got it for me," he said. "Guess you know she runs a gift shop."

I nodded.

"As for why, I wanted to clear my conscience, I suppose, about what happened to those three girls. I figure I don't have much time left. My lungs are shot, and now I have heart problems. Getting old is a bitch. Plus, making caskets all day tends to remind you that your days are numbered."

"I imagine it would do that," I said. "When did you decide you needed a clear conscience?"

"I heard Hanlen was stepping down and decided to send him something, maybe to spark his interest in the case again. I figured there was a slim chance he would go for it. If he did, there was an even slimmer chance, after all these years, he would find out anything. Plus, by the time he did, I'd be long gone."

He shook his head after he said that.

"Since you are here, it appears I was wrong on all three counts. Like I said, I'm a dumbass."

"Why didn't you just go to the authorities yourself?" I asked.

"I wasn't going to spend my final days in a prison cell. Last I heard, there's no statute of limitations on murder."

"You killed Marty Vesco, right?"

"I did. It was him in my barn. The way I looked at it, I didn't have a choice, but not sure a jury would see it as self-defense."

"Tell me what happened, then," I said.

"Guessing you know I was acquainted with a detective named Needham. He worked in the town over from mine. I knew he had a boat, what it looked like, and that he used it on Lake Michigan. I was doing some background on the girls after they vanished, and found out they had been at the Dunes the week before, and knew they had done some boating then. Then it came out later that the girls had left the beach that day in a boat like Needham's. And I knew Needham did security work for Luther Brame. You know about him, right?"

"Yeah. How did you know Needham worked for him?"

"Needham liked to brag, and he told me how much money Brame was paying him. Later on, I found out the girls knew Brame from his stable. I connected the dots and figured Brame and Needham had something to do with the girls disappearing."

"But you didn't know why Brame wanted the girls gone?"

"I did not. But I knew if Brame was involved, it couldn't be good. He had a pretty bad reputation."

"What did you do then?"

"I had a conversation with Needham and told him what I knew."

"What happened then?"

"He denied everything, at first. Then he got scared. Said if I fingered him and Brame for the girls, a shitstorm would fall on both of our heads. I told him he better get an umbrella."

"What did he say to that? I asked.

"He said there might be another way out."

"Which was?"

"He would talk to Brame, see if he would pay me to keep what I knew to myself."

"A bribe, in other words. Did you agree to it?"

"I said I might be interested. I told myself I was just stalling for time. I'd agree to take the money, while I figured out exactly what Brame did with the girls. When I did, I'd be a hero. I met up with Needham a couple days later. He said Brame would give me $20 grand to come down with a case of amnesia. That was more than I made in a year."

"I guess at that point finding out what happened to the girls and being the hero went out the window," I said.

"Yes, to the hero part. I did find out what happened to the girls. Brame had them killed. If you believed Needham, that is."

"He told you that?"

"In a matter of speaking, he did. I arranged, through Needham, to have Brame get the money to me at our farm down in Kankakee County. I wanted Brame to bring it himself."

"I'm guessing Brame didn't go for that," I said.

"No. He wasn't about to be caught bribing a police chief. Needham tells me a guy named Vesco would be bringing the money. Then something peculiar happened."

"What?"

"A couple hours before Vesco is supposed to show up, Needham is calling me again. He's been drinking. He tells me to watch out for Vesco. He says something like 'he did for those girls and he's going to do the same for you.' Then he hangs up."

"He was warning you," I said.

"Yeah. Maybe he was feeling guilty. Either that, or he didn't want to get into any deeper than he was."

"Then what?"

"I figured Brame needed to get me out of the picture, and if this Vesco had already killed three people, one more wasn't going to be a problem for him."

"You killed Vesco and made it look like you died in the barn explosion," I said.

Banks nodded. 'I was with the engineers in Korea and knew some about explosives. Plus, I killed men in combat who were trying to kill me. Killing Vesco didn't seem much different to me. Damn thing was, Vesco had the 20 grand on him."

"I'm guessing that was his fee from Brame for getting rid of you, and then disappearing." I said. "What then?"

"I got lost for a while. The twenty grand made it easy. My wife eventually used my insurance to buy the place in Brown County," he said. "I got on here a while back. It's not a bad place to work. The wife and I got a place out in the middle of nowhere between here and Nashville. No neighbors."

"Jerry Needham's dead," I told him.

"No kidding? How?"

"Guess you would call it a boating accident."

"Boating accident, huh? Were you and Hanlen there?"

I nodded.

"Were you the one who warned him we might be coming?" I asked.

"I felt like I owed him for telling me about Vesco. After I sent the locket and note to Hanlen, I called Needham and told him there was a slim chance someone might be looking into the girls' disappearance, and to be on guard."

"I bet he was happy to hear that," I said.

"He was pissed. He asked me who it would be. I told him I wasn't sure, just heard someone involved in the original investigation might be taking another look at it. I told Jerry he should consider retiring to Mexico. He said he'd think about it."

We sat in silence for a minute.

"What are you going to do?" Banks asked.

"If you mean about what you just told me, not sure there is anything to do," I said. "Doubt if I can substantiate any of it. The girls are dead. The ones responsible are all dead: Brame, Vesco, Needham. And by the time I prove you aren't dead, you'll probably be dead."

"What about Hanlen?' Banks asked.

"I've gotta talk to him, but I have a feeling he'll be of the same mind as me. In fact, I'm almost sure of it. He's not one for opening a can of worms when no good will come of it."

"By the way, where is Hanlen?"

"He decided to stay in Florida for another few days," I said. "For his health."

Banks thought about that.

"He get hurt in the same accident that got Needham?"

I nodded. "Yeah. There was a shotgun involved. Hanlen took a barrel to the leg. And, to paraphrase our former president, Jerry forgot to duck."

"As for right now," I said, looking up at the church steeple, "I was thinking of maybe going to church."

Banks pondered that.

"I know we just met, Logan," he said. "But you don't exactly strike me as the church going type. No offense."

"None taken. I might have said the same thing myself. My mother is a devout Catholic. She used to drag us to church every Sunday when we were growing up. Can't say I miss it much, but on occasion I do."

Banks laboriously got up. For a second, I thought he was going to go down, and jumped up to brace him. Thankfully, he didn't fall.

"Can I give you a lift back?" I asked him. "I could bring the car up here."

"Nah, it's downhill," he said. "If you can hang around a while, I think the monks do a noon prayer. It's open to all, including them that's fallen off the wagon. If you go, say a prayer for me. And maybe a couple for them girls."

chapter 62

I TOOK MY TIME GETTING BACK HOME. I DECIDED TO STOP for the night at the French Lick Resort in French Lick, Indiana. It wasn't too far from Brown County. My ex and I spent a night there about ten years ago. The resort looked to have seen its better days then, and the ten years didn't do much to improve the place. It had prospered in the twenty years prior to the Great Depression, with visitors coming from all over the Midwest, by train, to take in the mineral waters in the area, but then the place went into a long, gradual decline. The property had changed hands many times over the year, each new owner trying to find a way to revive the place, but with minimal success. The final death knells were the interstate highway system and jet air travel. Who'd want to hang out in the middle of rural Indiana when you could easily get to more exotic locations?

There were two large hotels at the resort, the one in French Lick and the other one just up the street in the town of West Baden. When it was built in 1902, the West Baden Inn was advertised as the 'Eighth Wonder of the World' for its large, free-standing dome, supposedly at the time the biggest in the world. I knew the inn had closed, but was hoping to take a tour of the unique domed building. Yet when I checked in at French Lick, I was told that tours of the other hotel had been terminated due to the deterioration of the structure.

The French Lick Hotel wasn't in great shape either. The room I was in needed a coat of paint, the carpet was worn, and the bathroom fixtures appeared to date from pre–World War II. I had a mediocre dinner in a half-empty dining room. On the plus side, I walked down the 'wall of fame' hallway, where there were hundreds of pictures of the well-known people who had stayed at the resort, as well as the famous entertainers who had performed there. I saw pictures of everyone from George Ace, the writer whose house we stopped at in Newton County, to Zeppo Marx. I wondered if anyone got removed from the wall if they committed a scandalous or embarrassing act, or if someone in charge decided that person wasn't famous enough anymore.

I kept going out the door and walked down the street to the closed West Baden Inn. Even though it was closed, and I could see visible signs of damage to the roof and exterior, it was an impressive structure. Four teens were drinking beer and talking and laughing by one of the outbuildings. As I went by, they clammed up. I nodded hello, anyway, getting some sullen looks in return. I heard a clink behind me, then laughter, and realized one of them had tossed an empty beer can in my direction. I thought briefly of wheeling about and charging at them like a madman, but decided it wasn't worth the trouble. Although it probably would have given them a good story for later.

After a fitful night's sleep, I headed back to Prairie Stop. When I arrived home, there was a message on my machine from Kathy. She said she was wrapping up a project but hoped to be back in town within a week. I took that as a good omen after the events of the last few days, and immediately began to clean the house up.

It was few days later when Hanlen called and said he was back in town. He asked me to meet him at Paulsen's around 4. I was sure putting a lot of time in there lately. I should ask about a courtesy card.

We sat in the restaurant of Paulsen's, which was almost empty at that time of the day, the late lunchers gone and early birds for dinner not having arrived. After Hanlen inquired as to the choice of beers, and was told Hamm's was not on draft, he ordered a pitcher of Old Style. After the beer arrived, he asked me if I had ever been to Lacrosse, Wisconsin, where he said Old Style was brewed. I said I had not.

"They got some big metal tanks there, by the brewery. They hold like 20,000 gallons of beer and are painted to look like Old Style cans. The brewer claim it's the world's largest six pack. If you ever get up that way, you should check it out."

"I can hardly wait. Will I need a reservation?"

"Nah, just get there early in the day. If you take the tour of brewery later, they'll even give you a free beer."

I told Hanlen about my trip to southern Indiana and my conversation with Mason Banks. I tried to make it concise, yet didn't want to leave out any details, so it took a while. Hanlen sat in silence for a minute after I was done.

"Who'd a figured Mason Banks was still alive?" he said, then added, "I said you were a smart guy."

"WE got lucky," I corrected him. "But maybe not all that lucky. since you almost got killed. The bigger question is what are we going to do now? Not sure telling Ivan is a good idea, if that's what you had in mind."

"He's already found out from Shannon about our trip to Florida," Hanlen replied. "When Ivan heard I was back, he called to give me hell."

"How'd that go?"

"I let him go on for a while, then told him next time I saw him, he'd better run."

"And I bet that lardass runs slower than you," I said. "That leaves the question as what to do? Everybody who was involved in the girl's disappearance is dead. All we have is Bank's story. He looked like he had one foot in the grave and the other on a banana peel."

"Can you think of any reason Banks would lie?"

"No," I said, "not sure what reason he would have. But do you think Ellen Musick is going to get any satisfaction knowing how her sister died? It's probably going to be traumatic for her. Then again, maybe she can handle it, being a psychologist and all."

"There's that, I guess," he said.

"And maybe you're right, about not telling her what we found out. Not sure what good it's going to do. Can't bring back the dead. Yet I'm of the mind that we need to tell her."

"If you feel like that, I'll leave the how and when up to you."

"I'll give it a couple days, then call her," he said.

We each took another swig of beer.

"Hey, wanted to tell you something else," he said. "I'm thinking about going into business for myself."

"What kind of business?"

"A security and investigative service. Times are changing and not in a good way. Crime is going up in Prairie County. I figure there's a demand for one."

"You're probably right," I said. "By the time Ivan Rich's reign is over, Prairie County will be like Dodge City in the Wild West."

"Don't be too hard on Ivan. He's just in over his head," Hanlen said.

"Or he's got his head up his ass."

"Yeah. Assuming I get this thing going, I could use a man like you, Logan."

That took me aback.

"Exactly what for?" I asked, with no doubt a puzzled look on my face.

"You're a damn good detective for one thing. "For another, you apparently got some business sense," he said. "I could use some help running the office. Would only be part-time at first, and I couldn't pay much, but if we do good there'd be more money in it for you. Don't say yeah or nay right away. Think about it."

I did. "Will I get my name on the door?"

Hanlen laughed. "Let's not overreach here, Logan. Why don't you order another pitcher while I hit the can. As someone once said, you can't buy beer, you can only rent it."

chapter 63

HANLEN CALLED ME A FEW DAYS later.

"What do you think of 'Chief Security and Investigations'?" he asked.

"As a company name, I assume," I replied.

"Right."

"I like it, but how about Big Chief Security and Investigations?" I asked.

"'Cause I'm a big guy?"

"That, plus we could hand out Big Chief Pads to potential customers. You know, like a promotional thing."

"What's a Big Chief Pad?"

"Your kids never used Big Chief Pads in school? It's a spiral notebook with lined paper inside, and a picture of an Indian chief on the cover. Hence, Big Chief Pad."

"I was working a lot when my kids were in school. My wife helped with the homework."

"Forget it, they probably don't make them anymore," I said.

"That's ok. I was only kidding about using chief," he said.

"Why not?"

"I'm not comfortable with it. For one, it makes it sound like I'm trying to cash in on my years as sheriff."

"What's wrong with that?"

"I just don't like doing it, is all."

"There's no place in this world for an honorable man," I observed.

"I was thinking of H&W Security and Investigations. For Hanlen and Wells."

"I thought I wasn't going to get my name on the door," I said.

"We'll start with the initial and go from there," he replied. "Plus it's shorter and easier to remember."

"You're thinking like a businessman, already," I said, nodding approvingly,

"Oh yeah, I talked to Ellen. Told her I had some news, " Hanlen said. "She's in Chicago tomorrow. She asked if we could meet up somewhere tomorrow evening before she heads back."

"You have a place in mind?"

Hanlen didn't answer right away.

"I thought by the lake," he said.

"Where exactly?" I asked,.

"I was thinking of that one pavilion right at Beverly Shores there. You know where I'm talking about?"

He was referring to where I met George Hiatt. I grunted a yes.

"I'll pick you up around 5:30."

chapter 64

THERE IS A SMALL FLORIST SHOP DOWN THE STREET from Paulsen's. It had changed names a few times over the years, and was now known as Lester's. I didn't have much occasion to buy flowers, but when I did, I bought them from Lester's. A girl who had been in grade school with me worked there. She had been held back for third grade, which at the time I found confusing and disturbing. I asked my mom about it, and she tried to explain by saying, "Vicki is just slow." I thought there was a more technical term now for it in educational system jargon.

I went into Lester's the next afternoon and was disappointed when my former classmate wasn't there. I asked about her, and the older woman waiting on me didn't offer any explanation for her absence, except to tell me curtly it wasn't Vicki's day to work. I irrationally inferred there was more to it than that, but just told the woman to say hi to her for me.

Hanlen picked me up at 5:15.

"You shouldn't have," he said, when he saw the flowers.

"They're not for you," I replied.

He thought about that.

"I'll give you this, Logan, You're a considerate sunuva gun."

The day had started out in the seventies with sunshine, but as frequently happens, a quick moving front had come in off Lake Michigan, and by the time we got to the Dunes, there were billowing gray clouds on the horizon and the temperature had dropped at least five degrees. There was only a couple cars in the parking lot of the pavilion. Ellen Musick was standing near the pavilion, looking out over the gray lake, her hair whipping up in the strengthening breeze. She was wearing black jeans and a black top.

"If it's ok, I'll do the talking," Hanlen said.

"Ok. I was hoping you would say that," I replied.

I noticed a bottle of wine sitting at the end of the picnic table where we sat down.

"I thought I might need a drink after I heard what you had to say," Ellen said. She looked quizzically at the flowers I was holding but didn't say anything about them.

Hanlen meticulously went through the events of the last couple weeks. It was meticulous, but he didn't overdo the detail, which I have a tendency to do, so I was glad he chose to do the talking. I could see how he would have been an effective force at all the meetings and events he certainly had attended over the years.

When he was done, we sat in silence for a minute, then Ellen handed the wine bottle to me, along with a corkscrew, and asked me to open it. It was red wine. Kathy would sometimes spend $30 or more for a bottle of wine which, from my uncultured perspective, seemed like a lot. I noticed the price tag on this one was twice that. I poured each of us some in the plastic cups Kathy had brought. I gave myself an extra generous pour.

"So it was as I thought. Brame had my sister murdered," Ellen said, "Because he got her pregnant."

"We believe so, Ellen," Hanlen said. "but there is no one left alive to say exactly what happened."

"And no one to hold accountable," I added.

"This was never about retribution, Logan," Ellen said. "I just wanted to know what happened, although to be honest, it hasn't brought me the solace I thought it would."

"Maybe after some time goes by, it will," Hanlen said.

We looked out again over Lake Michigan. The gray surf had picked up and although I knew the water was still warm, it looked cold.

"I hate to think of her out there," Ellen said.

She sighed and stood up and reached for the flowers I brought.

"If it's ok with you Logan, I'd like to put these in the lake." She got up and walked toward the water.

Hanlen and I watched her walk down to the water.

"Maybe this was a rock we shouldn't have turned over," Hanlen said.

"Once you get something like this started, it's hard to put the brakes on," I said, the words sounding fatuous even as I said them.

"Yeah, I guess." He nodded toward Ellen and stood up. She was tossing the flowers one by one into the water as we walked down to join her.

Aᴛᴛᴇʀ ᴀ ʟᴏɴɢ ᴄᴀʀᴇᴇʀ ɪɴ ᴘᴜʙʟɪᴄ ꜰɪɴᴀɴᴄᴇ, Mark took early retirement to pursue his dream of performing Barber's Adagio for Strings at Carnegie Hall. Mark soon realized that since he didn't play violin, indeed, had never taken a lesson, achieving this dream wasn't likely. Not one to be discouraged, Mark turned to his second dream, writing a novel, which was the first Logan Wells' mystery, *The Sword of Tecumseh* (pub. 2019). He recently finished a second book in the series: *The Last Dunes Girl*.

Mark grew up in Valparaiso, Indiana and Pittsburgh, Pennsylvania. He attended Franklin & Marshall College in Lancaster, Pennsylvania, where he was a Dean's List student, and a member of the cross-country and track teams. (He set a couple of school records in track.) Mark now lives in St. Louis, Missouri with his wife Carol (yes, Carol Carroll) and dog Lucy. He still runs an occasional road race. Speaking of running and dreams denied and fulfilled, Mark recently won his age group in the Popcorn Panic Run, a popular 5-mile race held each September in Valparaiso.

www.ingramcontent.com/pod-product-compliance
Lightning Source LLC
Chambersburg PA
CBHW010735130726
47899CB00015B/3270